VERDICT DENIED

LEONARD RUHL

Published by **B**ig **C**orner **P**ublishing

Cover art and author photo by Samson Ledesma

AUTHOR'S NOTE

Anyone familiar with South-Central Kansas and South-Eastern Oklahoma will realize that I have taken several liberties in naming the roads and cities and in describing the geographical and topographical details of the countryside surrounding them. While the cities and the areas exist, I've altered them according to the demands of the story and my whims, therefore they should be regarded as totally fictitious. Further, any similarities between the characters and events in this novel and real persons, living or dead, is entirely coincidental.

ACKNOWLEDGMENTS

Many thanks to Rob Leininger for his advice, generosity, tough love, and tireless support. Thanks to Joslyn Pine for the title, help with the early drafts, and everything else. Thanks to John, Zach, Cassity, and Elizabeth for their help with the early drafts. Thanks to the folks at Big Corner Creative, especially DeeAnna Stout, Ian Roseberry and Clay Schmidtberger. Thanks to Salty Media House, especially Samson Ledesma. Special thanks to David Heim, Task Force Agent (Ret), for his help with the trafficking and GPS passages and other aspects of the book. Special thanks to ATF SSA Neal D. Tierney for his help keeping the firearm and ammunition passages accurate. Thanks to LuAnn Rivera for her translations. Thanks to Brent "Moose" Washburn for his technical advice regarding locks. Any mistakes in the text are mine, not those who I've leaned on for help. Special thanks to Marilyn Targos, whose help with finicky programs kept me from smashing hardware to bits.

This book is for

Amy, Will and Caroline.

Without justice being freely, fully, and impartially administered . . . society fails of all its value; and men may as well return to a state of savage and barbarous independence.

– Justice Joseph Story

State of Kansas v. Vaughn Rummell
Three Counts of Capital Murder
First Day of Evidence
May 28, 2019

The Honorable Benjamin Joel

WHEN I ENTERED *the People's courtroom on Tuesday morning, they stood, not for me, but out of respect for the rule of law and the Constitution. They stood against the tyranny of men, with respect in their eyes, not knowing I'd crossed the line. I felt their reverence—now more than ever—for the American flag, the law, fellow citizens deceased and living. Looking out across them, I knew this proceeding was an obscenity—an obscenity that was eating me in secret from within.*

Like some of the cons and killers I've sent to prison, I tell myself it's not my fault. I had to break the law. I had to agree to this sham trial and I had to commit . . . murder is such an ugly word. It doesn't capture the essence of what went down. I can't properly tell this story without going way back. It doesn't start with me.

It's complicated. What would you expect from a lawyer?

1

Jorge (aka Chicken George)

THE LAST TIME Jorge Mendez-Rodriguez killed a man was the Fourth of July in 1989, northwest of Laredo behind a bar with a tin roof and a hardpan floor. He unloaded three rounds of buckshot into the man before tearing out of the parking lot in the man's pickup with a pregnant St. Bernard named Suzy in the cab and five kilos of cocaine in the fuel tank.

Ten minutes later he was fifteen miles north of the bar doing ninety when he spotted the flashers of a patrol car approaching on the empty highway stretched out before him. He slowed to sixty. When he recognized Deputy Harold Reynolds' face, Jorge lifted a hand to acknowledge him as the two blew past each other.

Reynolds was the first cop Jorge had bought north of the border, a masterstroke owing to the fact that the drug mule he'd just gutted with a shotgun had been balling the deputy's wife every Wednesday night for a month. Cutting the guy down just sealed the deal. Life was good.

He beamed at Suzy. Stomped on the accelerator. "Welcome to Texas, girl."

* * *

Fourteen Months Prior to Rummell's Capital Murder Trial
March 26, 2018

Jorge watched the sun slip behind the foothills of the Kiamichi Mountains thinking he knew who'd stolen his twenty pounds of crystal meth in Kansas last month.

Harold "Buster" Reynolds stood at the fire pit with Jorge. Between them was a St. Bernard six generations removed from

Suzy. The spring air was cool and crisp and smelled of the pine trees around them.

Buster spoke through a cigarette between his lips. "I had a sit-down with Miguel and Juan like you asked. Separately, of course. I won't hazard a guess at what you should do about them two."

Jorge clenched his teeth. "If they weren't my sons, I'd have them killed right along with Dandurand and Carter." He glanced up the hill at the cabin and saw his wife, Luciana, through the big bay window closing the shades.

Buster pulled the cigarette from his lips as smoke drifted out of his nostrils. For a moment Jorge studied Buster's profile— long on nose, short on chin—looking for a reaction to what he'd just said. He and Buster had met at a Mexican cockfight twenty- nine years ago—before Buster had a nickname, before Jorge had managed to compromise the then-deputy and put him in his pocket, not that Buster hadn't benefitted financially by their arrangement. That night years ago when Jorge approached Harold on the bleachers surrounding the cockpit, he didn't know Harold's name, but he already knew the man was a deputy across the border in Webb County, Texas. He even knew the deputy lived with a woman in a double-wide trailer five miles west of Highway 83. He'd tracked the rival's drug runner to the double-wide the week before and watched through binoculars as the man parked his truck and went inside, reappearing in the doorway twenty minutes later kissing a pantless woman in a long shirt. Jorge followed him north before passing tracking duties on to his brother and returning to the double-wide where, at dusk, he watched the deputy arrive with a pizza as the woman in the long shirt greeted him in the doorway.

After Jorge gave Harold a beer and told him about the drug runner and his woman, Harold sat stone-faced and watched roosters hack each other to death while listening to his proposal. Jorge would kill the son of a bitch who was fucking Harold's woman. In exchange for this service, Harold would divert deputies from certain drug routes on certain days and even get paid to do so. Jorge would also tip Harold about when rival vehicles carrying loads of cocaine would be coming through

Webb County—your basic win-win. Harold was, of course, free to bust them. And he did. A lot.

The plentiful busts earned Harold the nickname *Buster,* and eventually, a job as a detective with the Laredo Police Department, making him even more valuable to Jorge. The two of them worked both ends of the legal system for twenty-seven years until Buster retired from law enforcement two years ago. But he never retired from the drug trade. He still had law enforcement connections, a detective's instincts, and a penchant for rode-hard hookers.

Jorge poked at the fire with a stick. "You think either of my boys were in on the theft? Or was Juan just loose with information about the location of the dead drop around Dandurand and Carter like he told me over the phone?"

Buster looked Jorge in the eye and said, "Miguel's tellin' the truth but Juan's in it up to his ears. He lied to you over the phone and he lied right to my face."

Jorge winced at the certainty in the ex-deputy's voice.

Buster pulled at the neck of his wool-lined hoodie and cut his eyes to the fire. "You of a mind to let me have a word with Maria's boy?"

Maria Rummell was Jorge's adult daughter with a woman he knew prior to marrying Luciana. Maria's 'boy', Vaughn Rummell, was her son, early twenties—her only child and Jorge's only grandson.

Jorge knelt and scratched the St. Bernard behind her ears. He knew what Buster meant by having a 'word' with Vaughn and he wasn't ready to answer that. Not yet. This was complicated. Finally he said, "Vaughn's addicted. It's hard to imagine him resisting the temptation if he got his hands on that meth."

"Self-discipline ain't his strong suit, I'll grant you that."

Glancing at the cigarette in Buster's hand, Jorge noted the irony but was unable to enjoy it. "Bring my boys to me tomorrow."

"Only Miguel and Juan, right? Not Vaughn?"

"Let's leave Vaughn out of it for now. I don't know where his head's at. I'll talk to Maria." Jorge saw his first love's eyes in his "illegitimate" daughter—Maria. Just the thought of Maria made him long for the past in a way he could never share with Luciana. He tried not to favor his daughter over his sons, but he knew he did.

He tossed a pebble into the fire, his thoughts turning to Rabbit, the mid-level gringo crystal dealer who'd told them Dandurand was a snitch. He looked up at Buster. "What the hell'd you do with Rabbit, anyway?" Rabbit's real name was Randy Harris. The dumb shit had a warrant out for his arrest for jumping bail in Kansas. Another complication Jorge didn't need. He needed Randy.

"Got him holed up in Kansas City 'til this blows over."

"Holed up where?"

"He's floppin' at his cousin's pad, payin' the guy's rent for him and smoking up half the weed in Kansas City. That shit-bag cousin of his probably thinks he hit the jackpot."

"Couple of the local biker gangs Randy sells to won't buy crystal from us at the moment. They want to know what we did with him. Say they trust him, if you can believe that." Jorge's eyes wandered to Buster and locked on. "How 'bout you? You trust him?"

Buster appeared to think on it. "I do. We wouldn't't've known Dandurand might be a snitch if it wasn't for Randy. He came to us straight out, right after he bonded—told us how the detective came at him and tried to turn him on us. That says something, don't it? And look, Jorge, Randy's only lookin' at fifteen months on a state beef for givin' a dime bag to his ex-old-lady in Kansas. Just got unlucky as hell with the bitch going undercover on him, and that's got nothin' to do with us. Fifteen months isn't enough time to make him think about crossin' us."

Jorge snapped the stick he was holding and dropped it in the fire. "In all my years, Buster, I've never had a dead man cross me."

"Killin' Randy sends the wrong message and I'm not seein' the purpose in it. This is a case of a small-time detective trying to make a name for hisself on a case that doesn't have enough heft in it to leverage anything useful out of anybody. Far as what Randy says . . . about that detective telling him durin' the interrogation that Dandurand's snitching on you and Miguel—now that does ring true to me. Dandurand damn well knows we're on to him for boostin' the crystal and my guess is he wakes up each mornin' and shits hisself three times before lunch. I've seen this before—a greenhorn gets caught with a shit-pot full of drugs and panics, starts askin' cops for protection. Sees it as his only way out. When things start breaking that way a smart cop knows he's within spittin' distance of a tell-all if he plays his cards right. If Dandurand was facing a lot of prison time, and was scared enough—which, how the hell could he not be?—I could see him telling that detective where he stole $360,000 worth of crystal and from who."

"I'm having a hard time imagining any cop tossing Dandurand's name out there like Randy says he did. I don't see a cop throwing a snitch under the bus like that."

Buster scratched the stubble on his cheek. "Yeah, well, cop coulda got word of the theft in a lot of ways. So he may've been bluffing Randy. Maybe so. Huh. But I believe Randy."

"Either way, it's strange—a cop putting a target on Dandurand's back like that."

"How's that? Dandurand and Carter was dead the moment they stole your crystal. Cop would know that. Some cops are happy turnin' up the heat on everyone. May've thought he could drive Eddie Dandurand right into his waiting arms. May've worked too."

Buster took a drag, watching Jorge. When he finally released the smoke, he said, "What're you thinkin', far as a time frame for getting rid of Carter and Dandurand?"

"I'm not concerning you with that."

"No?"

"Miguel's almost thirty. I've taken care of things for him too long now. It's made it hard for him to shed all the stupid."

"So," Buster said, "you don't want me to help him with this?"

"Miguel can arrange it himself."

"He might see fit to send Juan on the killin'. You okay with that?"

Jorge stood the way old men do when they've been in one position too long. "Juan's a man now. Still young, but I can't protect him anymore. Maybe he gets culled from the herd. Maybe he becomes useful."

Buster dropped the cigarette to the dirt, stepped a boot on it and twisted. "To be honest with you, it's not his age that concerns me. Anyone willin' to take a chainsaw to a man for laughin' at a goddamn haircut—"

Jorge's gaze shifted to Buster, eyes narrowed.

"—I know, I know, we're not to talk 'bout that, but Son-a-Man, that little devil on a killin' mission like this, if Miguel uses him. I expect there's a fair chance he'll set a certain tone you won't necessarily agree with. I mean, you should hear him— oh, I didn't tell you 'bout this. Juan raps. You know what rappin' is?"

"Uh-huh."

"He and Vaughn both do some rappin' with Dandurand and the Carter kid and I've been unfortunate enough to of been there when they was doin' it. Saw 'em at Miguel's bar in Wichita when I went through there few weeks ago. They call it death-metal rap and the name of their group is Chainsaw, of all things. And, to be honest, the sound they make does sound an awful lot like a chainsaw, and I reckon we're among the few to know the secret behind the name. Anyway, they run 'round on Miguel's stage there at The Porte like headless chickens. And they grab their own cranks for some reason. Seems to be their signature move. And the singing—well you can't call it that. They're screechin' the whole time like stuck hogs and the crowd sort of writhes, like the devil's dick was up in their asses. I can't understand much of it is the only good thing, but the general tenor of the whole show seems to be nailin' pussy and wackin' punk-ass bitches with their gats."

Jorge looked at his Rolex, then at Buster, who threw his arms out and shrugged.

"My point is this, Jorge. You don't want this lookin' like goddamn Mexico up here in Oklahoma. In Kansas I mean to say—where all this mess'll land, I guess. Goddamn kid's got a lot of Mexican-style cartel violence he wants to show the world he's up for and this ain't the job for it and it ain't the place either."

Jorge's brother, Alejandro—a cartel boss in Mexico known as "the South Pole"—was at the center of the kind of violence Buster spoke of. Jorge was known as "the North Pole"—the de facto stateside boss and overall second in command in Alejandro's cartel. Forty-nine members of the cartel were found decapitated last week on unpaved backroads winding among farms and ranches near the tiny town of San Juan, seventy-five miles south of the U.S. border town of Roma, Texas. As the war with Trevino's cartel escalated, Alejandro, his family, and his men escaped to the Tarahumara mountain range to re-group and plan their next move. Jorge and Alejandro knew what to do— step up the bribes and increase the violence. But they were on their heels now. And the Trevino Cartel's presence was increasing in Oklahoma City. This was no time to show weakness. Maybe now was the time for a psychopath like Juan to make a niche for himself. If so, Jorge wasn't going to stop it.

Buster pulled the pack of cigarettes from the kangaroo pocket of his hoodie, looked at them, and put them back. "There's somethin' else you need to know. 'Bout Miguel."

"What's that?"

"He thinks we need to kill Vaughn."

Jorge stared into the firelight. "My son wants my grandson dead. He's told me that before."

Buster looked toward the path leading down the hill through the pines to his Suburban. There was enough light for him to see the John Deere Gator and the man standing next to it with an AK-47 strapped on his back. His ride awaited. "Well, I got the feelin' Vaughn'll cull hisself from the herd soon enough anyway."

"Seems to be playing out that way," said Jorge, glancing at the cabin. He smelled Luciana's chicken-fried steak. "I better get going."

Buster put another cigarette between his lips. "Say hi to Luciana for me."

Jorge took a deep breath and admired his cabin. It looked warm and there was a beautiful woman who'd loved Jorge for forty-five years inside of it.

2

Caroline

KBI AGENT CAROLINE Gordon stood in the front room of the house, flashlight illuminating a dead man skewered like a hog on a makeshift spit. At twenty-seven, she was the youngest agent with the Kansas Bureau of Investigation, and it was only her fourth month on the job. When Caroline was assigned to rural South-Central Kansas, she figured the pace would be slow—a steady stream of drug sale cases and the occasional violent crime. She shook her head at the abomination before her, thinking maybe she should've stayed home in Kansas City, where she spent the first three years of her law enforcement career in a police uniform refereeing everyday violence of the street—beatings, stabbings, gangland drive-by shootings. Nothing freaky or satanic or whatever the hell this was.

The room's south window was ajar and a strong wind blew the curtain inward so that it hovered over the bloody floor near the man's head where his mouth gaped to take the rebar.

Someone had run a ten-foot length of pointed rebar through the man's torso, entering the mouth and exiting from that place designed specifically for exits. He looked like a lifeless nude jockey on an invisible racehorse, mounted as he was on the rebar, which sat atop a mahogany roll-top desk at one end and the back of a couch at the other. His arms and legs dangled, his knees bent, feet resting on the floor.

Two men in olive-drab BDU's carrying AR-15's ambled down the staircase of the farmhouse and one of them said to Caroline, "You got two more DB's upstairs."

Caroline nodded, not taking her eyes off the dead body before her. She'd never seen a Blood or a Crip get this creative. A light came on in the room and someone came up beside her. She turned and saw Detective Raymond Mallory taking in the spectacle.

"Burglary gone wrong?" he said, grinning.

"Horribly." Caroline looked around the room. "They didn't even get the TV."

"I wonder if you know who that is?"

"You're the local. You tell me."

"I will, but I wanna see your process. How's the city mouse roll here?"

"I ask the country mouse to tell me who the hell that is, that's how I roll. Stop wasting time." Caroline knew fourteen-year-old Haley Dandurand had somehow escaped from an upstairs window while the murderers were still in the house. A neighbor found her running down a dirt road half a mile away. An investigator was meeting with her now, trying to get a line on the killers, and time was of the essence. The early word from Haley was there had been two killers here.

Mallory rolled his eyes and said, "This here is Eddie Dandurand. Remember me telling you about him?"

She vaguely remembered Mallory connecting a local guy to a major drug dealer named Miguel Mendez-Mendoza that no one in law enforcement had been able to touch. Miguel was a big enough blip on the local DEA's radar that they dropped his last name from their regular discussions about him and the rest of law enforcement followed suit. To a cop in this part of the country the name "Miguel" referred to only one man. Whatever connection Mallory thought this kid could have to Miguel last month seemed a little trumped-up to Caroline at the time so she let it go in one ear and out the other. But now, with this, everything had changed. "He's the kid you were going to pump for information about Miguel's operation, right?"

"Bingo. Except I *did* talk to him."

"Judging by your lack of concern, I'm guessing he told you to kick rocks?"

"Yep, told me to fuck off nine days ago. Now I'm wondering if he made the mistake of telling someone that I pulled him in for questioning."

Caroline wondered what Detective Mallory still wasn't telling her. Her predecessor had warned her about Mallory. Said he was passionate about chasing both criminals and skirts and was prone to break rules in pursuit of either one.

"Okay," Caroline said. "Now tell me the whole story."

"What whole story?"

"The one that explains how this farm kid could've known anything useful about Miguel." She frowned at the corpse. "What is he, early twenties?"

"You think guys in their twenties, teens even, don't know stuff? Of course I went after him. I'd question him now, but it don't look like he's up for it."

"What'd you think he knew? I want to see the video of your interview with him."

"There's no video. And you need to climb down out of my ass. Maybe I don't need the KBI's help on this one."

"You asked for the KBI's assistance, so here I am. If we're uninvited, this shit-show's all yours, Bucky."

She got as far as the front door before Mallory said, "Hold up—I'll tell you everything I know."

Caroline stopped and turned back to Mallory. To the horror-show on the spit behind him.

Mallory held his hands up in mock surrender. He gestured toward the corpse. "Eddie here was in some kind of rap-metal circle-jerk music group with Miguel's younger brother, Juan. They called themselves Chainsaw. There's some urban legend going 'round Wichita about the origin of that name. Tell you about it later if you're interested. Anyway, Eddie was the drummer and they played a regular gig at Miguel's bar in Wichita on Friday nights."

He put a piece of gum in his mouth, then looked at her.

Caroline waited.

Mallory chewed, turned and stared at what was left of Eddie, smiling distantly.

"Okay, for Christ's sake," said Caroline. "What else?"

Mallory faced her. "What I thought, seein's where Eddie was working, people he was around all the time, odds are he'd seen some shit. Knew stuff."

"That's it?"

He smiled. "Well, there might be a little more. Nothing I can confirm, just hearsay, but my CI told me the word is that Eddie D here, and the lead guitarist, Kramer Carter, stole twenty pounds of cartel crystal."

"From who?"

He shrugged. "Old guy by the name of Jorge Mendez-Rodriguez, a.k.a. Chicken Jorge."

"Chicken Jorge?"

"He's into cockfighting."

A smile creased Caroline's face.

Mallory grinned. "Made ya' smile."

Caroline looked at Eddie. "Well, the punishment does seem to fit the crime, I'll give you that. In a drug dealer's world, that is. "

"I promised my CI I'd never use his name in an official report. Told him I wouldn't use his information without saying it came from an independent source. That was the deal with this guy. I can't budge on that I'm afraid."

"I get it." Caroline knew confidential informants like this were priceless, and like Mallory said, all he had to go on was hearsay. Mallory didn't have an eyewitness on his hands. It was the cops' job to find independent ways to verify, and then prove what the informant told them. While this practice limited the utility of the information, it kept the bad guy's attorneys from identifying the rat, the rat from being killed, and the information coming.

The phone in Mallory's pocket trilled.

Caroline watched as he put the phone to his ear and listened. Immediately he was making eye contact with her and smiling.

"I'll be right there," he said into the phone, before ending the call.

"What is it?" said Caroline.

"They've got Vaughn Rummell in custody up the road."

"Great. Who's Vaughn Rummell?"

"A local meth-head. Also . . . the lead singer of Chainsaw."

Caroline looked at Eddie's corpse and back to Mallory. "I don't suppose this here is over creative differences?"

Mallory laughed. "Could be there's another piece of rebar out there with Vaughn Rummell's name on it. Twenty bucks says Rummell gets me into Miguel's farmhouse up on Eden Road."

"A search warrant? Wait, Miguel has a house in *this* county?"

"Not according to the register of deeds, but when I sit off the place, Miguel's the only one ever stays overnight. Twenty bucks says Vaughn Rummell gets us inside."

"Do you even have twenty bucks? Thought your exes took all your money."

Mallory pulled a twenty from his pocket and held it up. "I hid this from them."

"You're on. But do me a favor and record the interview this time."

"Of course." Mallory turned to leave, then paused, thinking. "Can you get the search warrant affidavit for the Dandurand premises together for me? And call Judge Joel. Give him a heads up. He'll be up most the night with us, looks like."

They were already in the Dandurand house legally without a warrant due to the exigent circumstances, but now that the place was secure it was time to get the search warrant to gather all the evidence.

"Sure," said Caroline. She'd gotten search warrants from Judge Benjamin Joel before. He didn't fit the mold of other judges she'd known—aged men and women with soft bodies and stern faces that hinted at some internal struggle, maybe constipation. Benjamin Joel was different—a tall man in his mid-thirties who was built like a wide receiver or a centerfielder. They'd talked guns and watched each other shoot on the sheriff's range two weeks earlier. A chance meeting. Casual. He was intense, but friendly, approachable. She'd seen one other man shoot like the judge. Her father.

She went outside and pulled out her cell phone. She stroked her neck, thinking about her choice of words. And then Judge Joel answered.

3

Ben

AS CHIEF JUDGE of a five-county judicial district in south-central Kansas, I sign search warrants on almost a daily basis. Most of them are legitimate, like the one I signed for the Dandurand premises at two in the morning, and the one I signed for Vaughn Rummell's Ford Mustang later around three. But this affidavit—the one requesting a search warrant for Miguel Mendez-Mendoza's abandoned farmhouse—lacked probable cause. Wasn't even close.

I flung it across my desk toward Detective Mallory and it came apart on its initial landing before skidding off the edge to the floor. I didn't mean to be curt, but I'd had my fill of Mallory and the prosecutor—a young man with the bearing of a boy scared of his drunk uncle.

I'd turned thirty-six in January, and Mallory was about my age. He leaned back in his chair, intertwined his fingers behind his head, and tried to make eye contact with the prosecutor sitting next to him. He then turned his gaze on the elderly sheriff perched on a courthouse window ledge chewing on an unlit cigar wedged in the corner of his mouth. Caroline Gordon seemed detached from the moment, standing behind Mallory, faced away, looking at photos of my late wife, Natalie, and our two young children on the bookcase.

"Is there a problem?" asked Mallory.

I felt my eyebrows jump toward the ceiling. "My God, Mallory, that warrant application was a piece of . . . I mean, seriously, aren't you embarrassed? You lose a bet or something?"

A burst of laughter escaped from Caroline, which drew the sheriff's glare. He was a man who dabbled in law enforcement and relished his authority. But he meant well. He'd been the sheriff in this county since I was a kid. I gave him a chore to keep him from doing something authoritative.

"Sheriff, you mind cracking a window?"

The sheriff stood with a groan from his makeshift seat and opened the window behind him. Spring air chased his smoky funk around the room and I heard the traffic on Main Street which would pick up in twenty minutes once the morning rush hit, such as it was.

"How's that not enough for a search warrant?" said Mallory at last.

I opened my mouth to answer—

"Benny, we got a killer loose on the streets."

An example of how the sheriff dabbled in law enforcement, stating the obvious and calling me Benny. Lots of folks in Worthington called me Ben or Benny—if they knew me as I was growing up. Outside of the courtroom or my chambers, I liked it from some, tolerated it from others. It kept relationships real—not so stuffy. Here in chambers, however, it was inappropriate. But I didn't want to quibble with the sheriff.

I kept my eyes on Mallory, until I noticed Caroline standing right behind him, watching. Her smile from a moment ago was gone.

"First off," I said, "this isn't going to be a debate. But, you want to talk. So, let's talk. I'll tell you what I took from that affidavit of yours, boiled down, and I'll give you a chance to tell me what I missed."

Dammit. I forgot to include the boy wonder of a prosecutor. "Tommy, chime in anytime."

"It's a close call," said Tommy.

Mallory rolled his eyes. "Attaboy kid, way to take a stand."

Red splotches appeared on Tommy's neck. I winked at him to loosen him up but he didn't see. Tommy wasn't big on eye contact.

"The girl," I said, snapping my fingers while the name came to me, "the teenage girl, Haley, wakes to the sound of gunfire in her parents' bedroom upstairs. Two men in black ski masks come into her room, turn on the lights, and pull her out from under her bed. The skinny Hispanic one shoots her in the head, but Haley's hair clip deflects the bullet and Haley lies there on the floor in a haze. But she's with it enough to know to play dead."

I stopped and looked around the room. "So far, so good?"

Sensing agreement in the silence, I continued.

"Within earshot of Haley, the two men discuss something that apparently has to do with Eddie. When they finally go downstairs, Haley escapes through the upstairs window and runs . . . just runs, she says. Dr. Hawks finds her running down a dirt road and picks her up. He takes Haley to his house and calls 911.

"Deputies responding to the scene run across a Mustang flipped over in a ditch a mile north of the Dandurand house. Lo and behold, look who's trapped there, arm pinned beneath the Mustang. It's our friendly neighborhood meth head, Vaughn Rummell. And a pistol that may be one of the murder weapons is found in the Mustang."

I pointed at Detective Mallory. "Here's where you come in. You interview Rummell, who appears to be one strung-out son of a bitch, judging from the video Caroline played for us on her laptop a while ago. Surprise!—he confesses. Except he says he acted alone. And Rummell won't budge from his story, ridiculous as it is, given Haley's account. Not to mention how unlikely it is for one man to get a length of rebar through all those innards by himself."

"Only take one man," Mallory said. "Pointed rebar, stick it in his mouth, keep pounding till it comes out his ass. No problem."

"Je-sus." Caroline shook her head.

I nodded at her then looked at Mallory. "Sure, one man could do it, but without somebody holding the body down, it'd be sliding all over the place. That could take a while."

"But it probably didn't because there were two of them, I agree. I'm just sayin', one guy could do it if he had to."

I shook my head at the turn this discussion had taken. "My point is this, when you finally straight-up ask Rummell about Miguel, he admits nothing more than having heard of him. But anyone involved in the drug culture 'round here has heard of this guy, wouldn't you say?"

I spread my arms and shot looks around the room. "Okay, then. What am I missing?"

Mallory retrieved the clip that had held his affidavit together. He gathered up the sheets, found a photo, and held it up. "This is a photo of Miguel standing in front of his bar. The Porte. Vaughn Rummell and his band played here Friday nights of late, so he must know him. I got this photo from a member of the DEA task force, and they believe Miguel has big-time cartel connections. I put all that in the affidavit."

"I got all that. So what?"

"So what?" said Mallory. He rifled through his affidavit and pulled out the photo of Eddie D on the rebar and slapped it down on my desk. "If *that's* not cartel violence, I don't know what is?"

"Maybe so," I said, "but nothing you put in that affidavit supports a reasonable belief that Miguel is involved or that there might be evidence in his farmhouse. I suspect you know more than you're letting on because you'd have never jumped to the conclusion that there was evidence of murder in his farmhouse from what's in your affidavit."

I could see I might be on to something, judging by the way Caroline's lips were pursed. Mallory adjusted himself in his seat, shaking his head and staring at the ceiling as if he were asking a higher power to intercede. I kept on, like a rock rolling downhill. "I'm starting to think you've already walked through Miguel's farmhouse."

"Pardon?" Mallory jerked in his chair, eyes now glaring into mine. The look on his face was pure *I'll kick your fuckin' ass.*

"Your Honor," said Caroline, "Detective Mallory's been with me or interviewing Vaughn Rummell all night . . . or here with you. He couldn't have—"

Mallory leaned forward. "You accuse me of somethin', you better be able to back it up."

"You'll know when I accuse you of something. We're just talking here. I've seen a lot of drug cases as a prosecutor with the feds and with the D.A.'s office in Kansas City. Talked to a lot of detectives and put a lot of these kinds of warrants together in the middle of the night. I can tell when a cop leaves out big pieces of the puzzle. I may not know exactly what piece got left out or why, but I can sense its absence. Maybe you didn't rifle through Miguel's farmhouse tonight to see if all this effort was gonna be worth your time. I see the way you're bristling at the whole idea of it. And your righteous indignation seems real genuine. But maybe you've been able to peek under the covers some other way. Maybe you have an informant you don't want to burn or get killed—"

Caroline's bright eyes opened wider behind Mallory.

"Maybe that's it?" I said, looking back and forth between Mallory and Tommy.

Mallory looked down. Tommy tucked his hands behind his elbows. I tried to make eye contact with Tommy but my face must've been as bright as the sun because he wouldn't look directly at me. That's the kind of thing that pisses me off and I was about to tell Tommy to grow a sack, but that wasn't proper, so I swallowed the frustration in the name of judicial decorum.

Caroline laid a hand on Mallory's shoulder. "Time to go. We've got loose ends to tie up and Vaughn Rummell's still upstairs in jail."

I didn't like her touching him for some reason—something hard-wired deep inside me—a base instinct. She was the kind of girl that was hard not to like. A tough blonde with an infectious laugh and a Glock holstered on her hip. A Glock is a fine pistol and she was great with it—I'd seen her shoot. But, aesthetically speaking, it didn't go with that hip. Too blocky and utilitarian. I had to force myself not to stare at her—deny my programming. She seemed too put-together for Mallory and his baggage—a trio of ex-wives all of whom hated him. If he hadn't tried to get in her pants yet, he would. The man was a tomcat. One day, if he didn't wise up, that would cost him his badge.

I looked at the four people in my chambers. "You all can take the last of the coffee in Nancy's office on your way out if you need it. It's been a long night for all of us." It was a dismissal and they knew it.

They filed out of my chambers, lingering in the connecting room—my administrative assistant's office. Through my doorway, I watched them hover around the coffee maker with Styrofoam cups, passing around the carafe. I heard Mallory say something about going upstairs to the jail to make another run at Rummell. He was going to rattle his cage to see if he couldn't shake loose the identity of the other gunman. That accomplice was in a tough spot, his destiny riding on the fractured mind of the meth addict in custody.

When they finally left the outer office, I felt that first pinch of exhaustion from having been up most of the night reviewing warrants. I looked at the clock on the wall and saw it was 7:48 a.m. I hadn't seen my kids since yesterday morning when I dropped them off for school. Leo was in second grade, Lindy, first grade.

I'd been hammering out a long overdue opinion at the courthouse late last evening and when I finally got to Pops' house, the kids were sacked out. Pops was my grandfather. I was hoping to have time to slip over there to see them before school—experience a lighter rhythm before that morning's criminal docket. But, it wasn't to be. School started at eight and Pops would be walking them down the alley to school. St. Anthony's Catholic Academy was practically in Pops' backyard.

At least I had time to tackle other matters that needed my attention before the 9 a.m. criminal docket call. Next to a stack of briefs on my desk about a sentencing I had later in the morning, I noticed the photo of poor Eddie Dandurand. Mallory must have missed it when he gathered his affidavit in retreat. I flipped the photo face down on the desk and drew in a deep breath. Most judges go their entire career without ever handling a death penalty case, and here I had one after only fifteen months on the bench. I knew from my experience as a prosecutor in Kansas City that cases like this never really go away. They forever linger in the courts and on the news and in a lawyer's dreams.

4

Ben

THREE MONTHS BEFORE that meeting in my chambers I passed Keri Chalmers in the public area between the courtroom and restrooms. She was at one of those fold-up tables you see at potluck dinners.

"Don't take this the wrong way," said Keri. "I've enjoyed these daily flybys of yours . . . maybe more than you. But, are you ever gonna stop and drink a cup of coffee with me?"

Adrenaline trickled into my veins.

She'd been haunting this spot the last six months because an Oklahoma oil company got the idea we were all sitting on a massive underground reservoir of oil in this county, so it was trying to lease as much property as it could for the right to drill. Keri had a binder containing a long list of properties and owners the oil company land man told her might sign contracts. She was a paralegal, working under the supervision of the oil company's attorneys. It was her job to read every deed, divorce decree, probate, and civil file affecting the properties in order to compile a list of every human on the planet who had any rights to the black gold underneath. If I'd wanted to avoid this prisoner of tedium I could have taken the back hall, but she was a girl who'd been noticing me, which I found quite charming.

"Excuse me?" I said. I would have liked to say something cute, but she'd caught me off guard.

"Uh-oh. He stopped. Now I'm embarrassed."

She licked her lips and smiled. "Okay. Maybe I'm not."

"Flybys, huh? Is that what you call 'em?"

She shrugged. "You leave vapor trails. You never stop and say hi."

"Well, then. Hi."

"Hi," she said brightly. "Guess what? Today's my birthday."

Escaping a bored person isn't easy, not that I wanted to right then. She had long tan legs and the body of a college volleyball player. And—I had been alone for over two years. Escaping wasn't my first priority. She sat there waiting for a response. She was a brunette, in the grip of the kind of boredom that only reams of legalese could cause. Perhaps I didn't need to say anything cute.

"Happy birthday. Twenty-one at last, right?" Okay, maybe a little cute.

She laughed. "A little more than that. I was going to have a little party tonight but my friends can't make it so it's just me, filet mignon, and a bottle of Chateau Musar Red."

"A party of one. If you tell jokes, who laughs?"

"Oh! Now that was just mean."

"Chateau Musar Red? Don't know much about wine, but that sounds awful sophisticated for a twenty-one-year-old."

She pursed her lips. "It's not customary to deliberately underestimate a woman's age until she's at least thirty."

Right. I felt a witty comeback coming on but suddenly my throat had gone dry. Hallway repartee with a beautiful girl? I felt out of practice.

She said, "I'm old enough to drink if you're old enough to be a judge."

"So, thirty-six? Thirty-seven?"

"Oh, wow! You get *seriously* mean under pressure. Good to know. Well, if you need a number, I'm twenty-six." She winked at me and added, "Old enough to keep a secret."

Her comment took me by surprise and her eyes were all over my face, reading me. Then our eyes met directly, almost intimately, and she smiled at me in such a way that I felt something seductive had slipped into the conversation. "I'm discreet," she said quietly, "in case you think other people won't think it's been long enough."

Long enough for what, I didn't ask, but her comment flooded me with warmth. This had gone quickly from hi to . . . to something else. I knew what she meant by *long enough*, but the reality was that Natalie had been gone too long. Two years was too long to go without my wife. I still had dreams about her, and when I woke from them, I felt the bitter pain of loss all over again. She was killed by a drunk driver two years ago, when we both still lived and worked in Kansas City. Sometimes it felt like yesterday.

Keri's eyes stayed on me. She wasn't pussyfooting around and I liked that. When it came to matters of the heart, Natalie hadn't minced words either. I was into forward women who were into me. Like I said, I found it charming.

"You in?" she said.

"In? In what?"

"You know what."

* * *

That was three months ago and this morning Keri was again at that table in the public area, now listening to Detective Mallory. He still had the coffee he'd gotten in my chambers. Probably cold by now, but Mallory would drink pig urine if he thought it had caffeine in it.

Keri's twenty-sixth birthday was actually yesterday, not three months ago. She doesn't feel particularly tethered to the truth sometimes. I'm still trying to decide if I find that beguiling or annoying. I was at her rental in the country last evening when the cell phone call for the search warrants came. I left her naked in her bathroom leaning over a sink, peeling contact lenses out of her eyes. I still smelled like her lotion now—like rain. I'd never felt this way about an odor before. When I finally peeled Keri's top off for the first time two weeks ago I thought about silver linings. I dove into my new world, into the warmth of her skin, the smell of her lotion, the touch of her long fingers on my back—the soothing sensations of another world.

Now here she was at her table talking with Mallory. When I walked by with my empty coffee carafe her smile interrupted whatever Mallory was saying to her. It sounds naïve to think no one knew about us, but it probably wasn't common knowledge. We were keeping the relationship low profile. Our little secret. I had warm domestic fantasies about sitting across a kitchen table from her when she looked like this—studious and thoughtful.

Mallory and I exchanged half-hearted nods and he went back to drinking the last of my coffee. I didn't like him talking to her. When I stepped into the clerk's office I looked back and Mallory was still with her. He should have been upstairs in the county jail interview room with Vaughn Rummell for round two, trying to get the name of the other murderer.

Rummell was under arrest for capital murder. The state's death penalty advisory committee had developed a protocol for such occasions. It was recommended that judges bring death penalty suspects into the courtroom for the appointment of the death penalty defense unit, even before formal charges were brought by the prosecutor. I was the only prosecutor on the original committee that helped develop the protocol so it would've been strange to overlook the recommendation. I could've warned Mallory about what was about to happen but I didn't. That was his problem.

*   *   *

Deputies had Vaughn Rummell by his arms and were stopped by Mallory at the courtroom's double doors. From the bench, I watched the action through the windows in the doors. Mallory was pointing the deputies back to the elevator. A crook of my finger caught the deputies' attention and they marched Rummell right through Mallory's last stand. He turned and looked after them, then at me through the glass. He looked like he wanted to say something, but didn't know where to begin.

The deputies walked their charge through the doors to the podium where I was waiting for him, robed up, ready to give him a legal spiel. Even with two deputies on his arms, which were cuffed in front at his wrists, he was still trying to grasp his genitals through his orange jumpsuit with his right hand. He copped a hard look on his face—striking a pose. He's got ninety-nine problems and his dick ain't one.

Rummell walked fine, despite the ankle clasps, despite the cuffs, despite his grip on his junk—and he had no visible injuries. All of this was remarkable considering that eight or nine hours ago when he was leaving the Dandurand farm, he had swerved to miss a deer and flipped his Mustang. At least that was Rummell's version of the truth. The deputies found him in the ditch, his arm pinned to the ground by the Mustang's roof. There wasn't a scratch on him, but he looked like an accident—a chaotic jumble of mannerisms.

On the books, Vaughn Rummell was only twenty-one years old. The bright institutional shine of the fluorescent lighting exposed how hard those twenty-one years had been. He had a collection of demented clown tattoos on his right arm. His gaunt, cadaverous frame and bloodless pallor would mark him to all but the least informed or naïve souls as an addict. He was an experiment gone wrong. If he were a mouse, PETA would protest.

Detective Mallory had crept in behind the convoy of deputies and sat in the back. Keri followed, taking in the sights of the oak-paneled courtroom—the ragged carpet and the off-white water-stained walls—a living mold-spore monument to the overflow from inmates on the third-floor jail plugging up their toilets with sheets in the spring of '85.

I was about to begin when I noticed a woman peering through the glass of the double doors. I waved her in. This was Maria Rummell, Vaughn's mother. It's a small town and I'd seen her around and knew her name, but couldn't remember how or how long I'd known it, though I knew in a general sense from growing up in Worthington that the Rummells had had brushes with the law before. Maria had her son's shiny black hair, almost a blue hue. Her skin was much darker than her son's, but they had the same straight eyebrows, hovering over chocolate brown eyes set deep in their sockets.

Maria's face was awash in a mother's anguish. The sun began setting on her son's hard, devil-may-care vibe. He unclasped his genitals. It's hard to hang on to some things with your mother hovering. Perhaps the mood wasn't right anymore.

"You've been arrested on allegations of capital murder, Mr. Rummell," I said. He looked at me like a cow looking through the air holes on a cattle truck. "Three counts of premeditated murder and one count of attempted premeditated murder."

His mother could hardly sit still.

Rummell looked down. His jaws clenched. His left arm twitched and he shook his head as if a fly had landed on his nose. But there was no fly, only spasmodic contractions in his face—the tics of a meth addict. His eyes were set so far back in their sockets that they resembled two empty chasms. His head was a skull with skin stretched over it, like the rest of us, but when you looked at Rummell you couldn't forget it. Finally, he raised his head, winced at another invisible fly, and took his rights from me like a brow-beaten dog.

Do you understand you have a right to hire an attorney of your own choosing? Yes. If you cannot afford an attorney I will appoint a team of attorneys called the death penalty defender unit at no cost to you. Nod. Just fill out this financial affidavit if you want me to appoint the death penalty defender unit. Nod.

Rummell's father, Baltozar, entered the courtroom and stood by Maria. They both spoke out of turn like parents do, asking for bond to be set. I declined, noting that this could be a death penalty case which caused Maria to slump into Baltozar, who said they would be hiring an attorney for their son. Rummell perked up enough to agree. Baltozar said he didn't want attorneys appointed, even temporarily. Rummell nodded.

Mallory licked his lips and nodded too, as Baltozar chimed in again. He was hiring a *real* attorney for his son, he said. Not one whose check came from the government. The government cheese won't do—and it never did for the Rummells. They always hired their own attorneys and did pretty well with that. But damn few can afford a death penalty defense. You can't tell people they can't afford an attorney. They usually learn that the hard way.

Before the hearing ended, Mallory slipped out of the courtroom. I saw him heading toward the elevator. Probably heading upstairs to wait for Rummell in the interview room. If Mallory could get him to give up the identity of his accomplice, he would lose the leverage to save his own life. The state might then make the case against the accomplice without the distasteful prospect of giving Rummell a plea deal in exchange for his trial testimony. Instead, the state would have at its disposal evidence gained from all the things flowing from his un-counseled disclosure, like the fruit of any search warrants of the accomplice's house: firearms evidence, DNA, another murder weapon, etc. Both killers would get the needle. Fine. We all live with regret and the consequences of our stupidity until we die. Why should Vaughn Rummell be any different?

*   *   *

Aside from some local reporters I recognized from the Wichita TV stations stalking the hallway outside the courtroom, it was business as usual—the standard fifty-case docket—bonds were lowered and raised, probations were revoked and reinstated, defendants were given prison and probation. There was never enough quiet after this overdose of stimulation, even when I wasn't running on two hours of sleep.

Keri watched through the windows from the hallway as I adjourned court at 11:56 a.m. I left the courthouse and climbed into my black four-wheel-drive extended-cab Ford F-350 with dried mud caked on the sides. I lived way out in the country in a low-lying area amongst the wheat fields where the roads washed out during heavy rains. Tornado sirens began wailing like they did once a month at noon on spring days without a cloud in the sky. It was only a test. I put the windows down and drove south two blocks in the alley past a funeral home and a bank shaped like a triangular slab of cake. I was picking up Keri at our meeting spot in the alley behind the Downtown Thrift Shop. The many dumpsters and neglected back sides of stores and bars and rundown empty buildings gave the view down the alleys of this five-block stretch of downtown an urban feel.

Keri climbed in and said, "I locked my keys in the car this morning."

I took my foot off the brake and crept forward in the alley several yards to Eighth Street. I was wearing leather cordovan wing tips, charcoal-colored suit pants, and a sweat dampened off-white shirt, the top button undone and the knot in the burgundy tie loosened. I normally would've taken a right to Highway 81 and headed south to Keri's house in the country where I planned to take it all off and relax the best way I knew how on a bed with a smooth-skinned girl next to an overworked A/C window unit. But I turned left, and the view down the alley and the urban flavor that came with it vanished. Worthington was a town of about ten thousand people.

"Where you goin'?"

"We . . . are goin' to my grandfather's house. He has a set of . . . rods, for lack of a better word. These rods can get us into any vehicle made."

"Yeah, that doesn't sound illegal at all."

She was smiling and I couldn't help but smile back. I felt the stress of the day loosen its grip on me.

"The rods are illegal only if you intend to commit a burglary while in possession of one. But, don't let a cop see you with these things. It's kind of like carrying ten thousand dollars in cash. That's not illegal either but it won't matter when a cop takes you down to the station to ask questions."

"So why's your grandfather have these rods anyway?"

"Pops used to own the glass shop in town. He was who you'd call when you locked your keys in the car. We've got a lot of old tools."

I turned right into the alley running behind Pops' house which was only a block and a half east of Main Street. I parked under the big cottonwood tree on the left side of the alley behind his detached garage. To the right of the alley was a large, treeless playground with baseball backstops on either end.

"Here we are," I said.

"So this is where you grew up?"

"Starting when I was about eight anyway. Me and Ashley." Ashley was my younger sister.

I pointed at a school building down the alley on the right at the far end of the block. St. Anthony's Catholic Academy. The playground ended where the school began.

"Ashley and I walked down this alley to school every day. I played ball here almost every day when I was in elementary school. Looks like my kids are on the playground right now."

"Oh, where are they?"

"See the kickball game?"

Keri nodded.

"Leo's on first base and it looks like Lindy's next in line to kick."

We watched for a moment.

"Who's the blonde?" said Keri, breaking the silence.

"What? The blonde?" My daughter Lindy was blonde, but she wasn't *a blonde*, she was a child, and the only teacher I saw on the playground was decidedly brunette.

"The blonde in the KBI windbreaker . . . she was at the courthouse this morning."

Over four hours ago—ancient history. Now I think I knew where this was going. "Oh. Agent Gordon. Caroline Gordon. Why?"

"Never saw her before today."

I shrugged and said, "She's new."

"She any good?"

I smiled.

"Why are you smiling?"

"You want to know if I think she's . . ." I was in trouble. Hadn't thought this through.

"Finish your thought, Benny."

"It's your thought. You want to know if I think she's hot."

"No I don't. But apparently you think she is."

"Okay then. Guess I'll answer the question you asked, but don't want the answer to. She's competent, so far as I can tell. And she's handy with a pistol."

"You've seen her shoot?"

"Yeah, at the sheriff's range."

"She a better shot than me?"

I knew Keri wasn't serious so I laughed. I'd shot with Keri in the woods behind my house in the country half a dozen times. She was learning. "Maybe a little," I said.

"She a better shot than you?"

I smirked and immediately wished I hadn't.

"Oh, like, how could that even be possible?" said Keri in a playful tone.

"She can't shoot like me and you're definitely prettier than her so let's leave the poor girl alone now, I'm starting to feel sorry for her."

Keri punched me in the arm. "Do any of the cops around here shoot like you?"

"They all hold the gun with the muzzle pointed away from them, yeah."

That got me another punch in the arm.

"None of the cops 'round here grew up with Pops. He taught me how to use and control what he calls the deadliest weapon on Earth." I pointed to Keri's head, then my own, and said, "The human mind. He also made sure I could take care of myself with about any other weapon out there."

Keri knew what I meant. I'd shown her Pops' arsenal. He was a Marine in the Vietnam War, an intense man who owned over fifty firearms. All kinds. None of them were illegal, yet. I was proficient with all of them. More than proficient. Through most of my teenage years I'd planned on a military career. Follow in Pops' footsteps. I applied for the Naval Academy and got accepted, but in the end I went to college at Oklahoma State on a baseball scholarship. I think Pops was relieved. And it had worked out for the best. I met Natalie at Oklahoma State and she gave me two beautiful children. We'd been married eight years when she died.

I shut off the truck before stepping to the garage so I didn't have to take Pops' garage key off the ring. When I came back with the tools Keri was watching the children play. I climbed in and shut the door and watched with her, breathing in the spring air, listening to the spirited voices of the children playing.

"Keri, I need you to know . . . that I'd be fine with people knowing about us . . ."

"But before you bring me into your children's lives, you need to be sure we will last."

"Yes."

"Of course."

I started the truck, backed down the alley to Eighth Street, and headed for Highway 81. When I glanced at Keri, she was looking out at a house on the corner where my fourth-grade teacher once lived. The old Victorian style home with the wraparound porch shimmered in the sun and I felt a familiar feeling coming on—the kind that settles deep and comes out years later coated in nostalgic gloss. It might be new love or the love of a child and when you're older you have a deeper appreciation for these flashes in time, now bittersweet, because you know the world will turn again and never be the same. A vision of Natalie in the seat next to me took over—her strawberry-blonde hair, her cut-off jeans, the little scar above her left eye and the freckles the sun brought out each summer. I tried to remember what it felt like with her in the seat next to me. I tried to recall the sound of her laugh but the replay didn't do it justice.

"What's wrong," said Keri. She was facing me now. I'd been idling at the stop sign on the corner too long with no traffic in sight.

"Nothing," I said. "Nothing at all."

She slid her hand into mine and smiled. "I can't tell if you look happy or sad."

I lifted my foot off the brake. "That sounds about right."

5

Fourteen Months Later
Four Days Before Presentation of Evidence in
State v. Rummell
Friday, May 24, 2019

Ben

FROM THE KITCHEN window above the sink I watched my sister Ashley's Lincoln Navigator roll away, down my long gravel driveway to the road in the rain-soaked darkness after eleven p.m. I told her she should stay the night, especially since her Navigator didn't have four-wheel drive. I thought she might get stuck on Seventieth Avenue, the dirt road in front of my home in the country. But she wanted to get back to Pops' house and out of my hair, as she put it. She was down from Omaha for the Memorial Day weekend, but Pops and I both figured her solo visit had more to do with her abusive husband. We'd told her before, and I knew I'd tell her again, g*et out of the marriage before you have kids with this guy. While you're young.* She'd been fired from three different waitressing jobs and couldn't be counted on to show up for work. Somehow she'd got on as a secretary at a middle school and that seemed to go okay for a while, but judging from comments she'd made earlier that night, things were going south again and it was anyone's fault but hers. I'd grown weary of worrying about all her bad choices.

"She stuck yet?" said Keri. She walked through the kitchen, put her arm around my waist and looked out the window with me. We saw the beams from the Navigator's headlights floating east above Seventieth. Keri had yet to spend the night at my house, but it looked like Mother Nature had decided tonight was the night. Keri's Honda Civic didn't stand a chance on Seventieth in this downpour.

"So far, so good," I said. "Kids finally give it up?"

"Just peeked in on them. They're sound asleep. Last day of school wore them out."

I dunked plates into the sudsy water in the sink and kissed my fiancée on the lips. We'd been engaged a month and were thinking of getting married the last Saturday in June but balked on finalizing the date because Vaughn Rummell's jury trial was an unpredictable albatross that loomed over the whole summer. We wanted the case in the rearview mirror so we could better enjoy the occasion. She nuzzled her head into my neck.

Things were going well, despite the fact that I'd spent the last three weeks officiating the laborious process of picking a jury in Rummell's capital case. But even that was going about as good as it could so far. Twelve jurors and five alternates had been selected and sworn in yesterday—Thursday. This morning, the attorneys gave opening statements. Judging from the jurors' faces and the evidence the prosecutor said she would present, it wasn't looking good for Rummell.

As bad as it looked for him, he never ratted on anyone, despite the state offering to take the death penalty off the table in exchange for his testimony against any accomplices. Criminal types might've liked to give the guy points for that but Rummell probably didn't have a choice. If a cartel was indeed involved like Detective Mallory thought, Rummell's folks were in danger of ending up on the rebar if he squealed.

The opening statements concluded around noon and I adjourned the case early for the holiday weekend at the request of both parties. The state would call its first witness on Tuesday morning.

"Aaaaand, she's stuck," Keri announced.

The lights had stopped moving east.

"Yep." I put on my waterproof hiking boots and grabbed a rain slicker off the rack on the way out the door to the attached garage. I threw a towrope into the bed of my pickup, climbed in, and hit the garage door opener on the visor.

After turning left out of my driveway, I stopped and put the truck in reverse, realizing I'd forgotten my cell phone. I wasn't going far and probably wouldn't need it anyway, so I backed down Seventieth toward my sister's Navigator as sheets of rain pelted my truck. Grit from the road tumbled and clanged in the wheel wells. She'd gone less than a quarter mile.

When I got close enough for the towrope to reach, I put the truck in park and stepped into the mud. The rain sounded like thunder on the slicker's hood. I reached for the rope in the truck bed. Something hit me so hard in the back of the head the lights blew out and I didn't feel a thing.

*　*　*

I woke belly down on a rumbling floor, tasting mud. My eyes opened to slits. Looked like the back of a cargo van from what I saw. No windows or seats in sight—a rolling metal box that smelled of grease and gasoline. My right cheek vibrated against the cool steel floor. Mud and muck churned in the wheel wells and a pulse kicked like a mule inside my skull. After a few seconds I could make out a man in a dark ski mask sitting on the floor, leaning back against the wall of the van opposite me in the darkness. A pistol hung loosely in his hand, his wrist draped over his knee. He was looking toward the driver.

My kids. Keri. Ashley. Where were they? Were they alive? Panic flickered through me. Beads of sweat popped on my head. I let my eyes open further. I scanned the van as best I could without moving my head. It was just me with the ski mask in the back. Good. Maybe they just wanted to kill me. Leave my family out of it. If that was the case, Keri would eventually walk the quarter mile down Seventieth in the rain when I didn't return and find . . . what? Not me. Could be that'd already happened— I didn't know how long I'd been knocked out. Perhaps Keri was standing next to my truck right now, dialing 911. I hoped. The ski mask grabbed at his crotch like he was adjusting his balls. Maybe I was looking at a mad husband from one of my divorce cases. But that didn't compute.

My left hand was right in front of my face. Shit, my hands were free. I wiggled my fingers, watching the ski mask as I did. A man's voice from the front of the van said something. In Spanish. The ski mask caught something thrown from the front of the van. More Spanish. The image of Eddie D on the spit flashed through me. That didn't make any sense either.

The ski mask went to his knees and slipped his pistol into the drop-leg holster on his thigh. He inched closer and held zip ties in front of his face as if to see what he was working with in what light there was. That pistol was right in front of my face. The hammer was cocked. Looked like it might be a 1911. Pops carried a 1911 in Vietnam. All the Marines did. Pops still owned four of them.

When he reached down for my left wrist, I thrust up from the floor, twisting through the space I'd made underneath me, swinging with my right arm. Right uppercut—kind of. Everything I had in one motion. Pounded his Adam's Apple.

He grabbed his throat and dropped face first to the floor and balled up, while I scrambled for the pistol. I slipped it from the holster and flicked the thumb safety down as gunfire erupted from the front. I dropped prone where I was behind the ski mask, squeezing off rounds blindly over him toward the front of the van which then lurched right, hurling me onto my back and toward the left wall.

The van stopped with a jolt and I skidded on my back toward the driver, the pistol still in my hand pointing haphazardly toward the front.

I trained the pistol on a man in a ski mask facing me from the front of the van. He was braced between the passenger seat and the dashboard, bent over, one knee wedged into the backrest, his other leg planted on the floorboard. He was clutching his stomach with both hands and the crown of his head was pressed against the roof. No gun. The driver was still seated, facing the windshield before him, breath coming in a

liquid death rattle. A bullet must've passed through his seat. I'd
hit both of them. Blind luck.

The man I'd punched in the throat was to my right, face
planted on the floor, making a gurgling noise in his throat. I
rolled to my stomach and stood to a crouch, keeping the gun
trained on the man on the passenger side clutching his gut. The
floor of the van was tilted to the right and slightly to the front.
Behind the man clutching his gut and the web of fractured glass
behind him, beams from the van's headlights illuminated a
water-filled ditch and part of the road that descended directly
into it. The water looked no more than knee-deep.

I was three or four feet from the two men in front. My head
and hands felt heavy. The tip of the pistol started shaking. The
man with the gut wound reached for something. I snapped off
two rounds. Blood spattered the glass behind him and he
crumpled between the seat and the dashboard, head dangling to
one side, blood gurgling into the cup holder. I'd hit him in the
head. Probably the second round. Terrific shooting. I'd been
aiming for his chest.

I looked down at the guy in the ski mask I'd punched in the
throat and noticed red streaks of blood on my yellow slicker. I
took a quick inventory. I wasn't hit. The guy had been shot by
his own man. My lucky night. Not his. I fired a round into his
head. I didn't need any surprises while I chatted with the driver.

Through all of this the driver struggled to breathe, still
staring out the windshield. I moved closer. He wasn't wearing
a ski mask. He was a Mexican with ancient acne scars on a face
glistening with sweat. His thick head and shoulders bobbed up
and down to the frenetic pace of his gasps.

"Who *are* you?" I yelled.

Brake lights flared like a pair of red eyes in the distant gloom
beyond the driver's side window. I pointed. "They with you?
They have my sister?"

A phone jingled. It seemed to be coming from the man
slumped between the passenger seat and the dashboard but it
was hard to tell for sure. I pulled the mask off the dead man
whose brains were still dripping into the cup holder. I didn't
recognize either of these men.

Up the road in the distance, beams from a vehicle's headlights swept across a field. Whoever was up there was turning around.

"Who's in that fuckin' van?" I yelled.

I didn't think the question registered. His chest heaved faster. I put the pistol to his temple. As I'd thought, it was a 1911. It would hold eight rounds, which meant I had to be about out of ammo. I wasn't sure how many rounds I'd fired, but the slide wasn't locked back, so I knew I had a round chambered. He turned his head to me as best he could, but his eyes looked as if they were taking in some horrifying scene visible only to him. I pulled the pistol from his temple. The breathing stopped, then he bucked one last time before he went limp, ending the racket.

The headlights were coming toward me now.

I frisked the driver for a gun. Nothing on him. Not even a wallet. There was a pistol at my feet. Another 1911. I stuffed it into one of the pockets of my slicker. Then I saw the AK-47 on the floor of the van. I stashed the 1911 I was holding into my other pocket.

When I picked up the AK, my fingers felt thick and clumsy and I was light headed, but I managed to hit the magazine release. Good. Full thirty-round magazine. I jammed it back in and flipped the firing switch from safe to semi-automatic. This wasn't the scenario for full auto, and thirty rounds would be gone in less than two, maybe three, seconds of holding down the trigger anyway. No good. I wanted to find the phone I heard earlier, but the lights were coming. I went out the back door of the van, waded through the ditch, and slipped into a muddy field full of waist-high green wheat. The rain had stopped.

Using the wheat as cover, I ran toward the oncoming vehicle. I figured it would stop with its headlights illuminating the van in the ditch and when it did, I wanted a clear view of the driver. One way or the other, this vehicle wasn't getting away. It could have my sister in it. Hell, for all I knew, it had my whole family in it. Probably did. A savvy kidnapper would do anything to squelch a timely 911 call and the flood of cops in the area that would result from it.

The vehicle headed my way was a black or navy blue cargo van similar to what I now saw was a GMC van in the ditch. The back left tire of the wrecked van was practically in the roadway, its headlights pointing thirty degrees right of the road. As the van coming toward me inched closer, it hedged to my side of the road, casting light on the van in the ditch as I'd expected. I now had a side view of the van in the road. Its only windows were up front. I scurried through the wheat until I had a sight line to the rear doors too. Brake lights kicked on and I heard the driver shove the gearshift into park. I lay prone in the wheat at the field's edge, in position to see both the barn-style rear doors of the van and the driver. I took aim at the driver. Dammit. I was still in my yellow slicker which didn't blend into green wheat. Light from the wrecked van washed over the top of me and into the field behind me. I forced myself back, further into the wheat, so that only my muzzle poked out. This was where I had to be. I was about twenty-five yards from the van in the road. Easy range with a rifle, but I was breathing loud and heavy. I took in a long deep breath. Held it. Slow exhale. I did it again.

6

Jorge

JORGE AND BUSTER watched as the driver killed the headlights and eased the Tahoe into the middle bay of a machine-storage building the size of a basketball court. They were sitting on a couch against the back wall facing the bays. Two floor lamps flanked the couch, providing the only light in the place. There were new lines on Jorge's face and he carried the fifty pounds he'd gained over the last year in his belly which stretched his dirty Carhartt jacket to its limit.

Jorge rubbed the nape of his neck. It had been forty-eight days since Trevino's men had gunned down his brother Alejandro in front of the Hotel Palacio Del Sol in Chihuahua City. Alejandro—the South Pole—was gone, and the world wasn't turning on its axis so well anymore. For the first time in three decades the money spigot had run dry. Jorge still had more money than a person should ever need, but his problems were more profound than money. The walls were closing in on him. The men he'd ordered to Kansas from Mexico for this kidnapping, an operation previously forbidden by Alejandro, were second tier. Not as reliable, not as smart, not as well trained as the many men they'd lost to death and defection.

As the garage door to the middle bay rattled down to the concrete with a bump, the Tahoe stopped several feet short of a long empty workbench that ran along the back wall near where Jorge and Buster sat. Except for two Chevy Suburbans and the Tahoe, the building was free of the kind of heavy equipment that used to be stored there. Three metal folding chairs faced Jorge and Buster across a card table. A voice-changing device and a single typewritten page of notes were on the table.

Buster lit the cigarette stuck between his lips, one eye staring at the driver exiting the Tahoe. Jorge stuck his right hand into the pocket of his jacket and clutched the grip of a pistol. Like his fighting roosters, he wasn't going to die without a fight, whenever it came.

Jorge knew his mystique wasn't the same. He saw it in the way his men responded to him. There was still fear in their eyes, but it wasn't the kind of fear he'd relied on for decades. This was the kind of fear that came with change. A mutant strain that swung both ways. Jorge imagined he'd see fear like this in a man's eyes right before a bullet passed through his own brain. If it was coming, he wanted to see it so he could take a chunk out of the son of a bitch who was taking him out.

Everyone in Jorge's world had felt the paradigm shift, even the meth head on trial for his life. Miguel had been right about Vaughn Rummell. Jorge would gut Rummell with a buck knife now if he could. But the time for killing his only grandson had passed. Rummell was in isolation—untouchable to the cartel, but otherwise still desperate, and, in a way, emboldened. He told the lawyers—lawyers Jorge had paid for, and wasn't that a *bitch*—that he was seriously considering rolling on the whole lot of them to save his own skin. Jorge had made sure the cockroach knew who'd paid for the lawyers, so he probably understood who the lawyers reported to—may have counted on it. When shown a motion to set a bond—a motion the attorneys planned to file after the requisite judicial leverage was in place—Rummell said he didn't want the motion filed, nor would he sign an appearance bond or accept any money put down by a third party. Said he knew he was a dead man if he was released prior to trial. He seemed to understand that he'd be tethered by travel restrictions and pretrial release monitors, a sitting duck for the cartel. He told the attorneys he wanted nothing less than a not guilty verdict or an outright dismissal of the charges so he could be on the run from the Mendez-Rodriguez Cartel without having the government after him too.

Fucking cockroach was taunting Jorge from the safety of an isolated jail cell, enjoying the only ounce of pathetic control he'd ever had in his whole miserable life.

For a dumb son of a bitch, Rummell understood the situation perfectly. He seemed to know Jorge wouldn't kill his own beloved daughter, Maria Rummell, mother of the cockroach. Jorge toyed with the idea of threatening to kill Baltozar, Vaughn's father, but knew he would never follow through and actually do it. Baltozar had been loyal to Maria. Loyal to Jorge. He didn't want to widow Maria, and he didn't want the cockroach calling his bluff.

"Donde quieres a la chica?" said the driver. He wanted to know where to put the girl. The driver stood before Jorge and Buster, his face drooping with paralysis. Beads of sweat rolled from his bald brown head, which hung permanently over his left shoulder like his neck had been thrown out in some way.

Jorge waved toward a door with a wreath hanging on it—the living quarters of this building that no one had ever lived in. The driver nodded, walking to the rear of the Tahoe.

"So," Buster said, "Whisperin' Jim told you this could work?" Whispering Jim Daniels was Jorge's long-time lawyer from Albuquerque. Both men called the cartel's lawyer "Jay Dee" to his face.

"No. He told me it *has* worked."

"Come again?"

They watched as the driver at the rear of the Tahoe fended off kicks from the shoes of a woman. Muddy shoes.

Jorge laughed. "Look at that girl go." He turned to the ex-deputy. "In the past, Buster. It's worked in the past."

"Here in America?"

Jorge smiled as the struggle continued at the back of the Tahoe. Bitch was a wildcat. "Something similar."

"I call this a Hail Mary, at best."

Hail Mary—a term co-opted from the religion of Jorge's youth. He smiled at Buster's reference to American football's last-second desperation pass. "Whispering Jim called it that too. I told him that's kind of where we're at right now."

Buster stroked an eyebrow. "Are we sure Miguel's men got the family out of the house without a 911 call?"

"Miguel hit the house same time as my crew hit the judge. What do you think?"

"I think yes, but I'd like some confirmation, that's all."

Jorge was rolling his eyes when the phone in his pocket rang. He pulled it out, saw Miguel's number, and took the call.

"If you've got a Plan B, I need to hear it right fuckin' now!"

Jorge sat bolt upright on the edge of the couch. Miguel was panicked. Jorge heard children crying in the background.

Gunshot. Jorge heard a gunshot. Glass breaking. Yelling . . .

7

Ben

THE SECOND VAN had stopped ten feet in front of the van in which I had killed three men. For a while nothing happened. All I heard was the sound of its idling engine. Whoever was in the van wasn't playing it smart. The more of them I neutralized, the better the odds for me. I had my cheek firmly on the stock of the AK. I inhaled, then exhaled through my mouth, sighted on the driver of the van and put increasing pressure on the trigger until the AK fired. The driver's head snapped, recoiled. Blood and bits of brain blew through the front of the van and slap-spattered the windshield. The driver slumped where he sat, held up by a seatbelt.

I heard men yelling, at least two. And screams—children—*my* children? Screams like that shouldn't be recognizable and they weren't, but who else's children would be in that van? I didn't see anyone so I jumped up and charged. I got as far as the knee-deep water of the ditch before the van's rear door swung open. A man in a ski mask appeared in the doorway, forearm under Lindy's chin, holding a pistol to her head. Lindy's hands were tied behind her back.

"Not another step closer," the guy said. "Drop the AK or we'll kill the girl, your boy, your fiancée. All of 'em."

For an instant I was paralyzed. Drop the gun and get killed? Get Lindy killed? Keep it and get them killed anyway? I'd never been in a situation anything like this before. I didn't know what to do, but I didn't drop the gun. "What do you want?" I yelled.

"*Hold on a minute*, motherfucker. And drop that gun."

"Not happening. The girl who was in the Navigator. Is she alright?"

"Your sister? She's fine. Shit, man, we weren't planning on hurting *any* of you. You completely fucked this up."

He spoke English with an accent from south of the border. What the hell was this? He hadn't planned on hurting anyone? Maybe. He'd had all the opportunity in the world and hadn't. Yet. It didn't look as if he was about to kill anyone right away, so I yelled, "What did I fuck up?"

"I said give me a minute here. Let me think."

Standoff. For now. But it gave me time to think too. These guys could've killed all of us and been in Oklahoma by now, so this was . . . what? A kidnapping? I gave that some thought, couldn't come up with anything else. But I'd killed four of them and that hadn't been in their game plan, so now what?

"What do you want?" I said loudly. "Let's get this figured out."

The guy kept his gun on Lindy's head. "I'm still holding the cards here, bitch. Drop the AK in the water."

"I told you that's not happenin', and it isn't. What do you want?"

"Ahhh, this fucker's crazy!" the guy said, apparently to someone behind him in the van.

Four dead, at least two alive in this second van. The guy was right, he was holding all the cards—except one. I wasn't about to drop the gun. I said, "Turn everyone loose and have them walk toward me. We'll go into the field, out of range. You drive away. You don't end up dead, neither does anyone else. How's that work for you?"

"Hold on goddammit," the guy yelled, distracted by something or someone in the van.

The door closed, not all the way. I could still see Lindy and the guy behind her. It looked as if someone in the van was giving him an earful and he was trying to take it in, nodding, while keeping one eye on me. I glanced at the dead man in the driver's seat. Four dead and these guys were still negotiating. At least they weren't tossing dead bodies out the door. The van's engine was still running. They might be trying to figure out how to drive it out of here without one of them getting a head blown off. Maybe they would put Keri in the driver's seat. If they did that, I'd take out their tires. Maybe they'd thought of that, too.

"Okay, motherfucker," the guy said, still using Lindy as a shield. "Do what I say and we all walk out of here. First, I'm gonna cut the zip ties off this little girl and send her your way."

He paused and listened to someone behind him, then said, "A gesture of good will so that you understand our intentions. No one was supposed to die here tonight, man. All we wanted to do was talk. Now we've got this fucking mess."

Another pause, as if he was being told what to say next.

Then he was back. "You aim that gun our way or move out of that ditch, we kill your boy and your fiancée. You got our word on that. You got that?"

"I got it."

A hand appeared behind Lindy and cut the zip ties with a knife. The guy in the ski mask released her and she ran to me with bare feet as the guy ducked back inside the van. When Lindy got to me she half-jumped, half-climbed up on me. I caught her and held her with one arm, holding the AK away from my body with the other.

I kept both eyes on the van as I said, "Were Leo and Keri in the van with you, Lindy?"

She nodded against my neck. "Yes."

"Were they alright?"

"Yes." Her voice shook.

"Was Auntie Ashley in the van with you?"

"N-No."

"Okay, okay. I need you to be strong now Lindy. Wade through the water and get in the wheat field behind me. If anything bad happens, anything at all, I want you to run and hide in the wheat. Duck down and be very, very quiet. No matter what happens. Do you understand?"

"I don't want to go."

"I have to get Leo and Keri back from these bad men now. You don't have to go very far into the field unless something bad happens. I need you to be strong right now, all grown up, okay?"

"Okay."

I looked into her face and saw one of Natalie's expressions—determination. My girl was seven years old and already tough as a railroad spike. I lowered her into the water and gave her a nudge toward the field, keeping my eyes on the van. "Into the wheat and duck down, Lindy. I'll come for you soon. Listen to what happens here, baby. If you hear gunshots, run far and hide."

The guy in the ski mask appeared in the doorway again, this time with Leo. Leo's face was blank. Wide-eyed and blank. Disturbing. His hands weren't tied.

"Let him go," I said.

"Shut the fu—"

The guy looked back in mid-sentence, listening. A moment later he said, "The boy stays right where he is. Time to talk business, Judge."

Judge. This was about me being a judge and these guys were Mexican, which meant this was about Rummell.

"Let's hear it," I said. I lowered the AK another few degrees in his direction.

"If you want your sister back, alive, here's the deal. You're the judge in Rummell's trial. You cut him free."

"That's a job for the jury."

"What?" The ski mask was listening to someone behind him again.

I yelled so they both could hear. "That's a call for the jury." That was the truth, but not the whole truth. After the state presented all its evidence and rested its case, the power to cut Rummell free—*permanently free*—would be squarely before me, like it was in every other case that went to trial. It's called a motion for judgment of acquittal—a standard defense motion made after the state's case-in-chief which should only be granted when no reasonable person might fairly conclude guilt beyond a reasonable doubt from the evidence presented. When granted, a judgment of acquittal takes the case from the jury. Here's the thing. I could grant Rummell's motion and be wrong as hell. Wrong, wrong, wrong, and it wouldn't matter. The prosecutor would have no recourse. No appeal. Nothing. Trial over. Rummell would walk. It's a nuance in the law I didn't expect these assholes to know about without a dirty lawyer in the mix.

The ski mask's attention was on me again. "Stop playing dumb with us, motherfucker. You can grant a judgment . . . a judgment of acqui—, acqu—" He looked back into the van for help.

"Judgment of acquittal," I said.

"Yeah, motherfucker. That. You in? Or do we have a problem here?"

"I'm in if you set Leo and Keri free now." And my career would most likely be over, but right now that wasn't my concern.

The ski mask nodded, apparently satisfied.

I waited ten seconds, fifteen. Leo's eyes were wet with tears now. "Okay," I said. "You've got a deal. Turn them loose."

But there was more in the script it seemed. "In a minute. Now listen up, motherfucker. We'll know if you tell the cops or the prosecutor, anyone, because you'll be taken off the case. Do that, your sister dies. And your whole family, amigo. You talk, we don't stop coming after you. If you're taken off the case for any reason, same thing. Understand?"

I did, and didn't need to be told, either. This might be the clearest example of a conflict of interest in the history of the world. If word of this got out, I'd be off the case in a heartbeat.

"I understand," I said. "Now let 'em go."

"One last thing. Rummell's a patsy in all of this. I know he looks guilty as shit, but he didn't kill the Dandurands. I know because I know who did, but if I tell you that, it'll confuse things. Just know, it wasn't Rummell. Might make it easier for you when you cut him free, knowin' you'll be doin' the right thing."

"I feel better already." You son of a bitch.

The guy laughed. "There's a truck a mile up the road with our guys in it. Sort of a clean-up crew. They already put your sister's Navigator in your garage next to your truck, in case you were wondering about that. Pretty soon they'll clean up this fuckin' mess you made like it never happened. I'll turn your family loose in a minute, but remember I've got an AK on your sister. Any problems and she's gone and you can fry Rummell and eat him for all I care. You're on your own, far as getting home."

"Cut 'em loose," I said. "No problems, unless you come for us."

The guy laughed. Probably because these guys could come after me and my family any time they wanted, but not before Rummell went free.

The guy turned loose of Leo and he ran over to me in bare feet. I saw movement in my peripheral vision somewhere around the driver's seat. The dead man was gone.

"Now Keri," I yelled. I caught Leo and spoke quickly to him. "Go into the wheat, Leo. Find your sister. She's in there. Be quiet until I call for you."

He said "okay," waded through the water and ran. Good kids.

The guy in the ski mask showed me his AK. "Nothing stupid, Judge."

"No shooting you mean."

The ski mask stared at me for a long moment. I nodded and said, "Nothing stupid."

"If it was up to me," said the guy, "I'd kill all you motherfuckers."

I held my tongue because I believed he'd like to try. Wanted an excuse to do so, even now. He glared at me for another long moment, then snapped out of whatever trance he was in and disappeared from the doorway. Keri appeared, crouched in the doorway on her bare feet. She jumped and hit the ground running as the van spun out in the gravelly mud and took off.

Keri ran up and stood beside me. We watched the guy in the ski mask slam the van door shut as the van disappeared into the night. Whether he realized it or not, he had just told me what to expect when the trial was over. This wasn't over yet. It was just on hold.

8

Ben

THE FOUR OF us slogged through the soft, wet loam of the wheat field as fast as we could manage, away from the road. I stopped and looked back. The clouds had cleared and there was a half-moon lighting the field. I didn't see any signs we were being followed and there weren't any headlights in the roadway. I gauged we were two or three hundred yards away from the road. If a clean-up crew was back there in the darkness, they were working without the aid of any light I could see.

"Hold on a second," I said. I dropped to my knees and bent over, sticking the butt of the AK in the mud and holding it perpendicular to the ground while I threw up. When that ended, I felt better. But I was still breathing heavy from the retching. I managed to look up enough to see the mud-caked knees of Keri and Lindy. When I caught my breath I sat up straight on both knees and saw their mud-streaked faces staring back at me in the moonlight. Keri's lips parted like she was about to say something, but she didn't. Leo was looking toward the road, wiping his hands on his Spider-Man pajama bottoms with the terror of a nightmare on his face.

"You okay, Daddy?" said Lindy. Her chin trembled and the Rapunzel nighty was wet and sticking to her little body, but she wasn't clutching her arms to her sides like she was cold, even though I knew she had to be.

"Yeah, I'm fine baby. Must've been something I ate." No one laughed. I knew I had a concussion from the blow to my head. The last time it felt this bad, a Texas Longhorn pitcher had bounced a ninety-two-mile-per-hour cutter off my cheek. I threw up then too.

Lindy gritted her teeth to stop her jaw from trembling.

I looked my little girl in the eye. "You want my slicker? Don't know how warm it is—"

"I'm not cold, Dad. Besides, I won't be able to walk in that thing."

I nodded and looked to Leo who was still watching for kidnappers. "Hey, Leo," I said. "See anyone coming?"

Leo shook his head without diverting his eyes from watchdog duty.

"Then I think we're alright, Buddy."

"Maybe we should all get down," said Leo. "Just in case they're back there."

Keri nodded and tapped Lindy on the shoulder and they all got on their knees so that we formed a little circle.

Keri leaned in to me, and in a steady voice said, "Do you know where we are?"

"No," I said. "I haven't seen any landmarks I recognize, but I've been a little distracted. Spent the last five minutes trying not to pass out." I didn't know if it was from the blow to the head or the huge adrenaline dump. Probably both. I put my hand on Leo's shoulder. "You think it'd be alright if I stood real quick to take a look. I don't think they're coming after us right now. But you're right to be careful."

Leo nodded. "You can look."

I stood and looked around. Listened. Wheat rippled and swayed in the wind all around us, giving me the sensation we were adrift in an undulating ocean, and the sound of wind through wheat—the murmur of a million tiny rattles—was not unlike surf in its undertone.

"Well, the good news is, we're still in Kansas," I said.

"What's the bad news?" said Leo.

"Bad news. The bad news is, I'm not sure which way to go, you know. I'm not seeing any yellow brick roads."

Leo chuckled, but Lindy frowned.

"You okay, Lindy?" Keri said.

"We shouldn't be joking, or laughing," said Lindy. "What are we going to do about Aunt Ashley?"

"We're going to get her back," I said. "You have to believe we will get her back. I joke to stay loose. It keeps me calm."

My daughter furrowed her brow. She probably didn't think staying loose served any useful purpose, and wouldn't find my joke funny in the best of times anyway. She was a grinder like her mother. Task driven. Jokes were a distraction at crunch time. "What's the one thing we can do to help Aunt Ashley right now?"

"Find a way home without the cops finding out," said Lindy.

Keri's mouth fell open and she looked at me and added a little smile. I was impressed too. I cupped the back of Lindy's head, leaned over, and gave her a little kiss on her forehead. My little girl had it right, except for one thing. She wasn't going home any time soon. She and Leo were going into hiding. I already had something in mind.

"Smart girl," I said.

I looked to the sky and found Polaris—the North Star—at the tip of the Little Dipper's handle. "For what it's worth, that way is north."

"Let's keep heading east, away from the road," said Keri.

"Yep," I nodded and looked west. I wasn't expecting them to come for us now, but I couldn't've stopped myself from checking if I'd wanted to. Looking over my shoulder seemed like something I'd have to get used to. I pointed east. "Let's walk. Keep your eyes and ears open."

We'd trudged through the muck for an hour and were standing on abandoned railroad tracks that split the field when I saw a glow on the horizon. Only thing around here that lit up the sky like that was the chemical plant. An old high school buddy of mine owned a bar and grill a mile north of the plant on Ridge Road. I'd been there a few times and I told Keri where we were and how I knew. We were in Sedgwick County now, near the outskirts of Wichita. The tracks went right across Ridge Road and then between the plant and a grain elevator. My little girl groaned when I said we could follow the tracks like Dorothy followed the yellow-brick road.

After about an hour of walking at a good pace up the tracks, we came to a paved road and got our first glimpse of the brilliantly lit chemical plant, with its massive vessels, distillation towers, and storage tanks all interconnected by piping of various sizes. Its glow illuminated the fields for half a mile around.

I pointed to the wheat field to our right. "Hunker down over there. I'll run up ahead to Dugan's Place and call Pops. We'll pick you up here at the crossing."

Keri and the kids didn't like my plan, but the bar closed at two in the morning and I needed to cover a lot of ground in a hurry. I started walking toward the field. "Follow me."

I walked into the field and they followed. We got on our knees in a little circle and I set the AK on the ground behind me. I pulled the pistols out of my slicker and released the magazines and counted the rounds, then slid the magazines back in place. I tucked one pistol, cocked and locked, with one round in the chamber, into the waistband of my jeans at the small of my back. I held up the other pistol for Keri to see.

"Okay Keri, you have three rounds in this pistol. One in the chamber, and two in the magazine. You've actually fired this kind of pistol behind my house. What position is this firearm in?"

"Cocked and locked," she said.

I handed it to Keri. "Yep. And how do you fire it?"

She held the grip of it as if she were going to shoot it. This pressed the grip safety of the 1911 down with the web of skin between her thumb and index finger. She then slid the thumb safety down with—what else?—her thumb.

"Good," I said.

Keri re-engaged the thumb safety.

"This AK behind me is a fully automatic weapon and will get you a stint in federal prison if—"

"Just go. I'm not touching that thing," said Keri. "And take off that slicker. I can still see blood on it."

I took it off. I was relatively dry from the waist up.

Keri inched closer to me and used the inside of my dry shirt to wipe mud off of my cheek. She kissed me on the forehead and said, "Hurry. I won't let anyone touch 'em."

I hugged my children, and ran out of the wheat and across the paved road into the field on the other side.

* * *

Dugan's Place was at the intersection of Ridge and West MacArthur Road. Both roads were paved at this juncture, but it was still out in the middle of nowhere. When I walked in, late 60's Elvis was singing karaoke in front of the fireplace and ten or fifteen women were cheering him on. This was how the night always ended on karaoke night, with Elvis, singing on his own karaoke machine. And this guy not only sounded good, he looked the part. He was a professional Elvis impersonator, winning awards for his work in Vegas, and tonight, for me, he was also the perfect distraction. Nobody even saw me walk in, mud on my jeans up past my knees. I spotted Dugan behind the bar and went straight to him. Most of the patrons were in the eating area at tables in front of the fireplace with Elvis. There were a few farmers in the back near the bathrooms playing pool. When I stepped to the bar, Dugan finally saw me, feigned shock, and smiled.

"A little late aren't ya', Ben?"

I laughed, sounding fake I'm sure. "Having car trouble and my cell phone stopped taking a charge sometime yesterday. Need to use your phone."

He pointed to his office door behind him—behind the bar. "Come on around. Phone's on my desk. Left my cell in the car."

I walked behind the bar and into the office, then shut the door behind me and sat at Dugan's desk. I picked up the phone and dialed Pops' number. I leaned back in Dugan's chair and tried to put together a phrase or two for when Pops picked up the phone. But instead, I found myself in a staring contest with the stuffed head of a ten-point buck mounted on the wall before me. Through the wall, I heard late 60's Elvis on the sound system, thanking his fans and reminding them that every Friday was Karaoke night at Dugan's Place. I shook off what felt like the absurdity of a dream, the horror of a nightmare. I pictured my baby sister's face and swallowed the pain. Then Pops answered his phone.

* * *

We'd been driving due west a little less than four hours.

When I parked Pops' van next to the gas pump at the Conoco station off I-70 in Goodland, Kansas, it was eight in the morning and the sun had been up for almost two hours. I shut off the engine and looked at Pops, laid all the way back in a reclining passenger seat, mouth agape. His eyes fluttered open and he stared at the roof with startling intensity. I wouldn't want to tangle with the old warhorse, even now. Even at seventy-three. I would always see the warrior in those blood-flecked eyes. He was balding, and the hair he had was buzzed tight to his head, silver and white. The thin skin on his face turned red at the tips of his nose and ears. Leo and Lindy were zonked-out in the rear seats.

Keri parked Pops' Silverado at the pump behind me. I got out of the van and waved at her and watched as she waved back. If this night hadn't scared her away, nothing would.

I walked into the Conoco with one of Pops' Glocks holstered under my brand new jacket. We'd been to a twenty-four-hour Walmart in Wichita three and a half hours earlier for supplies: thirty-dollar prepaid burner phones to keep our calls and whereabouts a secret; food; water; and clothes. We didn't want to risk being followed, so we never went to my house for supplies or a change of clothes, just to Pops' house to get a second vehicle and then to the ATM. In the Conoco, I prepaid for the gas with cash. Everything we bought was with cash. Everything Pops would buy this summer would be with cash. We weren't going to make it easy for anyone to track my kids' route to the Sawtooth Mountains of Idaho. From my days as a federal and state prosecutor, I knew how detectives found people that didn't want to be found. Cell phones, tracking devices, credit card purchases, phone bills, and loose lips.

Tomorrow, I'd call my friend at the post office and get him to hold Pops' mail until Pops could get the formal request in as a precaution against anyone snagging it and getting information that might be used to find the children. The folks I knew who tracked people for a living (U.S. Marshalls, detectives, private investigators) were creative people. The less a tracker knew, the better.

Pops' Marine buddy from Idaho—whose life he'd saved—was dead now, but he had a reclusive son who lived in the Sawtooth Mountains off the grid. The "Kid," as Pops called him, had stayed in touch—honoring a deathbed request of his father to help Pops in whatever way he would ever need. The Kid had been calling Pops on a monthly basis for many years. Pops said he asked the Kid one day why his number changed every few months. The Kid told him he used prepaid cell phones because he didn't think anyone needed to know his business. Somewhere between Wichita and Goodland before Pops fell asleep, he commented that we could all live off the grid with the Kid, if it came to that. Pops gritted his teeth and added, "And we'd be ready for Armageddon, too." The Kid liked to talk about guns, God, and war. Pops didn't.

Keri and Pops went into the Conoco as I pumped gas into both vehicles. When they came back, Pops climbed into the driver's seat of the van and buckled up with the door still open as I put the handle back on the pump and screwed on the van's gas cap.

"No one followed us," I said.

Two hours earlier, I'd pulled over on the side of the road at daybreak a few hundred yards from an exit on I-70. Keri pulled in behind us, both of us with flashers on. We let cars pass for a good ten minutes, taking note of the vehicles and their passengers—folks with young children, college age kids, tractor trailers. Not one of the thirteen vehicles we saw stopped or took the exit ramp. Once ten minutes passed, we took the exit ramp and traveled west on dirt roads for fifteen miles before getting back on I-70. I never saw any of those cars that passed us on I-70 again.

Pops nodded and said, "I'll call when I get there."

I opened the sliding door to the van, climbed in, and kissed my kids on their sleeping heads, feeling soft and vulnerable as I did. They were my soft underbelly. I had a lot to lose. I stepped back onto the pavement and shut the door.

Pops shut his door, started the van, and rolled down the window. "I'm coming back to help you, Ben. The Kid's wife is a nice woman. She can look after Leo and Lindy for us. You can't do this alone."

"Pops, I'm sure they're nice enough people, but you can't leave Leo and Lindy alone with strangers."

"Goddammit, Ben, those bastards have my granddaughter. My only granddaughter—"

"Send the Kid here, if he'll come. Nobody knows him here. The anonymity will help. But you have to stay with Lindy and Leo. Protect them. I'll get Ashley back, one way or another. But I can't do what I need to do if these sons of bitches get their hands on my children again."

Pops nodded and I walked away.

I'd only taken a couple steps when Pops said, "What're you going to tell Rod when he calls."

Rod was Ashley's husband and the manager of an auto parts store in Omaha.

I stopped. Turned to Pops. "I think I'll tell him that I don't know where she's at."

Pops nodded. "Fair 'nough."

"Fair 'nough then."

I walked away and climbed into the passenger seat of the Silverado.

Keri took a deep breath and put the truck in gear. "Lay back and get some sleep."

I needed it. I watched the van turn west onto I-70. Pops had a lot of driving ahead of him, especially for a seventy-three-year-old man. But he was in great shape and sharp as ever. If anyone could protect my kids, it was my grandfather.

We went east on I-70—four hours back to Worthington. I was asleep immediately.

9

Caroline

CAROLINE STOOD IN the prairie, holding binoculars to her eyes as the mid-afternoon sun blazed high in the cloudless sky. Detective Mallory stood beside her, squinting, hands on his hips, looking out across the scene before him. They were at the crest of a gently sloping hill looking down at Miguel's white stucco two-story farmhouse with a collapsed front porch and tinfoil on the windows. A dirt road ran in front of the farmhouse. A shelterbelt—a swath of trees protecting fields from wind and erosion—lined the far side of the road to the south of the premises for as far as they could see. Up the road sixty yards to the north of the house was a railroad crossing. A field of waist-high green wheat flanked the farmhouse and its small yard on all sides but the front.

A pickup truck kicking up dust came into view in Caroline's binoculars. She pulled them from her eyes and looked at the ground, then at Mallory. It had rained hard last night in Wichita at her apartment. "Man, it really didn't rain here at all did it?"

Mallory nodded. They were in the far west end of Sumner County just west of Miguel's house on Eden Road, about twenty-five minutes west of Worthington. "I guess not. It came down in buckets in Worthington."

Caroline looked at the farmhouse again through her binoculars. "That dump of a house really spoils the view." She dropped the binoculars from her eyes again and looked at Mallory. "What's it look like on the inside?"

Mallory's mouth fell open. Then he smiled.

Caroline said, "Fourteen months of surveillance and nothing to show for it. You must be frustrated."

Mallory shrugged. "All I did was plant a surveillance camera in the weeds across from the property and check it every seven or eight days."

Earlier in the day at the sheriff's office, he'd shown Caroline and Gwendolyn Sweeney, the state attorney general's lead prosecutor, a video taken thirty-three days earlier at night. It showed a man Mallory believed was Miguel parking in the driveway and carrying a box into a side door at the back end of the house in the eerie green glow of the camera's night vision. He left, sans box, thirty minutes later. According to Mallory, this was the only time the video had caught anyone entering the house the entire fourteen months since the murders.

Caroline turned and walked down the gentle slope away from the farmhouse and toward Mallory's Impala sitting in the prairie fifty yards away. "Come on, let's get this camera back in the ground and get outta here. My parents will be at my apartment in a couple hours. I'm making dinner."

Back at his car, Mallory opened the trunk and grabbed a fluorescent orange vest off the rows of police reports in accordion folders and threw it on over his shirt. Caroline plucked a hard hat that the railroad had loaned Mallory from between a couple of folders and turned it over in her hands, thinking about the meeting they'd had with Sweeney.

"When we met with the prosecutor today," Caroline said, "after you stepped out, she asked me if I thought it was suspicious that Rummell was found pinned in the ditch by his Mustang the way he was."

Mallory straightened the vest, took the hard hat from Caroline, and said, "What'd you say?"

"I told her it'd always sort of bothered me."

"Bothered you? How so?"

"It didn't strike you as convenient?"

"Certainly . . . it was convenient. For us. But I don't think he was set up if that's what you mean. And listen, four or five years ago when I was still on patrol, I worked a DUI rollover accident. Some drunk father rolled his SUV. The five-year-old girl, not in a seatbelt of course, ends up outside in the ditch, arm pinned to the ground by the SUV and not a scratch on her. It happens."

Mallory put the hard hat on his head, "How do I look?"

"You look like a real railroader, Bucky. You think the disguise is necessary?"

Mallory shrugged. "Cut me some slack, would ya'?" He grabbed a shovel out of the back of the Suburban. "Is Ms. Sweeney starting to think Rummell was set up now?"

"No no. I think she's worried how this all plays to a jury. Pinning your accomplice in a ditch next to a murder weapon and crossing your fingers that he won't rat you out is a bad setup, even for the dimmest of criminals. I'm sure she gets that. Like us, she's more concerned about who's paying for the defense attorneys. Thinks it has everything to do with why Rummell won't take the plea offer."

It was an offer that—theoretically speaking—kept a needle full of state-funded Jesus juice out of his arm, but it required Rummell to testify against his accomplices and that wasn't happening. The state hadn't executed anyone in fifty-four years. His accomplices rarely went fifty-four days without executing someone. Bad deal. The incentives weren't right.

"I can't believe there's nothing she can do about that."

"She did do something," said Caroline, wishing immediately that she'd kept her mouth shut.

Ms. Sweeney had opened an inquisition into the Mendez-Rodriguez Cartel for the stated purpose of investigating violations of the state's drug laws. As part of her investigation, she'd subpoenaed financial records without the court's approval. When she first asked Caroline to serve the subpoenas and gather the evidence, she shared her concerns with Caroline. Ms. Sweeney explained that as an assistant attorney general, she was expressly authorized by law to subpoena information without court approval for the purpose of investigating drug-trafficking crimes. But Ms. Sweeney knew, realistically, that the information she was seeking had more to do with the Rummell murder case than any drug-distribution conspiracy. The problem was, inquisitions and subpoenas for matters involving murder required judicial approval and she didn't think a judge would approve subpoenaing the financial records of the two criminal-defense attorneys representing Vaughn Rummell in his capital murder case. Ms. Sweeney knew her move was controversial, and had asked Caroline to keep the subpoenas she'd served on the down-low as best she could. If Sweeney found anything she could use to prove that Rummell's two attorneys were hired by cartel-connected murder suspects, she could show a conflict of interest and get the attorneys bounced off the case, while shedding light on the nature of the ongoing drug-trafficking conspiracy. She figured this might go a long way in justifying her investigation into violations of the state's drug crimes and the use of inquisition subpoenas without judicial approval.

"I must've missed it," quipped Mallory. "What'd she do?"

"I'm not supposed to talk about it, but trust me, Sweeney's got grit—"

"Spit it out, why's she keeping secrets from me anyway, I'm the lead—"

"It's not a secret from you, per se. She's just trying to keep a lid on some things the legal eagles generally frown upon."

Mallory's glare demanded more.

Caroline took in the look. He chased bad guys for a living and worked for peanuts. Based on that alone, he probably deserved better. Caroline saw that the secret offended him. Hurt him even. She felt her walls coming down. "Sweeney ran some rather controversial subpoenas through me to get served. Her idea was to keep all the locals out of the loop. It's been her experience, and mine, that you guys like to talk. It's nothing personal."

She cringed. Clearly, it was personal.

Mallory pointed the shovel he was holding at Caroline. "I'm quite capable of slapping salve on my own ass thank you very much, can you just tell me—"

"She opened up an inquisition and subpoenaed bank records—the records of the defense attorneys. She also subpoenaed the Rummells' records—Vaughn, Maria, and Baltozar."

"Did you two find anything interesting?"

"Found no record of any payment from the Rummells to the attorneys at all."

Mallory tilted his head. "That jives with what McMaster told the press—that he and Thompson were taking on the case for free—some do-gooders-against-the-death-penalty shtick."

"Yeah, well Sweeney's not convinced and neither am I."

"You sure you've located all their financial records?"

"I'm almost sure we haven't. We've run into a wall on this, but you can't say Sweeney's not trying to figure this out. As you know, she made sure the plea offer got communicated to their client by announcing it at pretrial in open court in front of Judge Joel with Rummell sitting right there. Rummell told the judge himself he knew about the offer and wasn't interested. We have no way of showing that the defense attorneys were hired by the cartel, or an accomplice to the Dandurand murders. So what's Sweeney supposed to do?"

Mallory's face softened. "I get tired of folks telling me there's no solution to a problem, that's all. If the system can't cope with a problem, time to work outside the system."

Caroline looked up the slope in the direction of Miguel's farmhouse and thought about Mallory's words. Curiosity was getting the best of her. She wanted to know if Mallory knew more. "What's inside that farmhouse, Raymond?"

Mallory took a deep breath, picked up the surveillance camera, and looked Caroline in the eyes. "There ain't shit in that farmhouse." He turned away and walked toward the railroad tracks. After a few strides, he stopped and looked back. "Nuestra Señora de la Santa Muerte."

"No comprende, Bucky. What's in that house?"

"Our Lady of Holy Death." Mallory bobbed his head, like he was working out how to explain that. "It's a shrine . . . to a . . . female Mexican deity. It's a fucked-up shrine. Mexican drug dealers' religion."

"What makes you think this place is worth monitoring now?"

"You saw on the news that Alejandro was murdered, probably by Trevino's cartel, right?"

Caroline nodded. She knew the boss of the Mendez-Rodriguez Cartel had been murdered. She also knew that Alejandro and Chicken Jorge were brothers.

"Alejandro's photo is part of the shrine inside that house. It sits next to a mounted rooster. Between the war with the Trevino Cartel and the power vacuum caused by Alejandro's death, things will get hot. And when things get hot, people tend to go to holy places and hiding places. This farmhouse could be both in a pinch."

"Mounted rooster?"

"Stuffed. You know, taxidermy."

Caroline furrowed her brow.

"Remember me telling you about how Jorge Mendez-Rodriguez got the nickname Chicken Jorge?"

"You said he raises gamecocks. Gambles on 'em."

"You got it. The rooster's right there next to Alejandro's photo at the feet of the shrine."

"Foot," said Caroline. "You mean foot of the shrine."

"I mean feet. She has two of them."

"She?"

Mallory squinted. "Our Lady of Holy Death. The Santa Muerta."

"Which is a . . ."

"Skeleton," said Mallory. "It's a skeleton dressed in flowing robes. She's in there right now, hanging on the wall, marijuana cigarette crammed in her fuckin' mouth. Guess you never ran across anything like that in Kansas City?"

"No. The gangbangers I dealt with didn't bother trying to justify their lifestyle with any religion." Caroline had never realized how refreshing that was. Then another thought struck her. Kramer Carter, the lead guitarist of Chainsaw, had been missing since the night of the murders. She cleared her throat. "That skeleton—it wasn't a real one was it?"

"I don't know." Mallory smiled. "It kind of looked like the real thing to me."

Mallory turned and walked toward the tracks. Caroline couldn't tell if he was joking or not. She already wished she hadn't pressed him into disclosing that he'd broken into the house for a look-see. Now she knew he had committed a crime in the line of duty on a case she was working on. She didn't like knowing his secret, and she didn't like that he trusted her with it. It made her feel conspiratorial and somehow closer to Mallory. She looked at her cell phone and saw it was 2:47 p.m. She needed to get back to Wichita to spend time with her folks.

10

Ben

OVER A YEAR ago I'd denied Detective Mallory a warrant to search Miguel's farmhouse, and here I was at three in the afternoon at a spot where the edge of the wheat, the farmhouse yard, and the end of the shelterbelt met, primed to break in and search it myself. Since the law couldn't save Ashley, I couldn't think of a good reason not to break it—thick irony for a judge sworn to uphold the law.

Our first attempt at finding my sister had failed earlier in the day. During the ride back from Goodland, Keri woke me up as she exited the highway near Wichita. She drove the backroads until we located the deep ruts where the van had been stuck in the ditch. We followed the tracks we found, but the trail went cold when the dirt road met with a paved one.

After that we continued on to Pops' house in Worthington to pick up Diablo, a champagne-colored pit bull with a red nose. Diablo needed a place to stay and I needed a guard dog. Whether I wanted him to or not, he'd run through the waist-high wheat surrounding my house until he was exhausted as was his wont since he was a pup.

At my house, Keri and I found the Ford F-350 and Ashley's Navigator parked in the garage like the kidnappers had said they would be. I cut Diablo loose and walked through the yard to the edge of the wheat field and threw a stick into it for him. If anyone was hunkered down out there, Diablo wouldn't like it.

I checked all the vehicles for GPS trackers and the house for listening devices and video surveillance. I checked every place I knew to check and found nothing. Once I was reasonably sure I wasn't being monitored from inside my house, I showered and changed into olive-green cargo pants and slipped my hunting knife into its sheath and strapped it across my chest. I put on my lightweight long-sleeve camo pullover over my holstered Glock and filled my backpack with bottled water, protein bars, binoculars, a burner phone, a small flashlight, a ski mask, Mechanix gloves, a digital camera, a second Glock and five extra magazines.

When we walked outside, Diablo looked up from a water bowl Keri had set out, panting, water dripping from his jowls. Keri put him in the kitchen with his food and water and we left in Pops' truck. Keri drove while I studied Google Maps on the burner phone, trying to figure out the best way to approach Miguel's farmhouse. We decided I'd approach from the east on foot through a creek until I came to the wheat field that backed up to the property.

That was the easy part. Now here I was on a warm day drinking warm water getting cold feet. The place looked dead and I got the feeling I was wasting my time.

I'd barely settled into my spot when I was shocked to see Detective Mallory walking up the far side of the road from the direction of the railroad crossing. He was wearing a fluorescent orange vest and a hard hat—a railroad man going for a walk down a back country road on a nice day. That Mallory was a real master of disguise. With a shovel, he dug a small hole near the top of a ditch directly across from the house. I wondered what Mallory thought this would look like to a paranoid drug dealer passing by. *Nothing to see here—a railroader planting tulips probably.*

What Mallory did plant amongst some high weeds was a video surveillance camera. As a young prosecutor, I owed one of my earliest guilty verdicts to footage that showed the defendant tending to his marijuana crops.

Caroline Gordon appeared on the hill with binos to her eyes. I slipped a little further back into the wheat, watching her watch

Mallory until he finished and walked up the road toward the tracks and they both disappeared.

All I could do was watch and wait. I took it as a good sign that Mallory hadn't given up on this place. Must've still been important. I wondered if it was important enough for them to stick around on the other side of that hill. I kept tabs on the crest of the hill for another half hour and never saw them.

I pulled out the burner phone and called Keri. The plan was for her to wait at the Chikaskia River with a fishing pole in the water until I called. The pickup spot was fluid, depending on the situation, which now involved the presence of two cops. When she answered the phone I gave her the news and she said, "Holy shit! So, you're headed my way, right?"

"No, I'm gonna stay, see if there's something brewing."

"Are they still there?"

"Don't know for sure. I watched Detective Mallory plant a surveillance camera across the road. I'm inclined to think that means they're not sticking around to watch the place in person, but who knows. I'm here until dark, then I'll let you know what I'm doing."

"You're not still thinking about going in are you?"

"If I went through the second-story window in the back, the video wouldn't catch it."

"Benny, no!"

"Why not?"

"You're crazy. It's way too risky now."

Maybe, maybe not. Time to change the subject. "Have you heard from Pops?"

"Yeah, no problems. They're in between Denver and Cheyenne."

"Good. I'll call you at dusk, if not before. Stay tuned."

"Be careful, and hurry. It's not good to leave a girl alone, fishing in the dark."

I laughed and said, "Fishing in the dark should be a two-person sport, I agree. Keep your eyes open."

* * *

Dusk came. No one had arrived and I hadn't seen Detective Mallory or Agent Gordon. In five hours, only four trucks and a combine had passed by on Eden Road. I called Keri and told her I was going in. She didn't try to talk me out of it this time. Instead, she told me Pops and the children had almost made it to Idaho before we told each other to be careful again.

I put on my gloves, slipped further back into the ocean of wheat behind me, and crawled to a position that put the house between me and the surveillance camera. Then I ran past a junked truck on cinderblocks toward the house and took cover behind a toolshed packed with assorted items. I listened for voices or approaching vehicles and once I was satisfied there were none, I made my way to the back of the house.

The only door near the back was on the side of the house next to a gravel driveway. I wanted to jiggle the door knob to see if it was unlocked, but I wanted to avoid Mallory's camera more. Unfortunately, there wasn't a window on the lower level of the back side of this house, so I dragged an old ladder from the toolshed and climbed to the roof, then scaled its slope to get to the second-story window. I slipped my knife from the sheath and cut the screen, then broke out a small piece of glass with the butt of the knife. I popped through a sheet of foil and released the lock, catching a whiff of something nasty as I did.

I heard an engine in the distance, growing louder, so I climbed to the peak and looked over the apex of the roof to see a combine lumbering down the road in dusk's final light. The farmers would be cutting wheat in two or three weeks if it didn't rain. I watched as it passed by, then worked on the window which had been painted shut, probably years ago. When I got it open, the odor of death and decay wafted out and damn near buckled my knees. I turned away from the window, gripping the ledge so I didn't fall down the slope. When I recovered, I pointed my flashlight into the room. There was a yellowing mattress and dirty sheets on the floor. A rat inched along a wall lined with traps that had been tripped on the necks of other rats. When the rat scampered away I forgot the smell and realized how on edge I was. I turned away again and leaned back as far as I could, hanging on to the ledge with one hand. I took a deep breath—of not entirely fresh air—and climbed through. Once in, I shut the window and replaced the foil as best I could.

The smell—rotten fruit mixed with spoiled meat and feces—took me back to when I found my mother dead in a trailer home. I was eleven years old at the time. She'd been dead a week, and I hadn't seen her in three years. It had been Ashley's idea to bike across town to see her. I recognized it was Mom on that couch before she did but it hit her as I got her out of there. I remember how it took all my strength to pull Ashley out of there and then hold her back while I locked the door to keep her from going back in. I remember leaving her behind and her screaming as I rode away. Now, I had the sensation I was floating, like the way I floated across town on my bike, back to our home with Pops where I told him about his daughter rotting on a couch.

I covered my mouth and held my breath, trying to shake the stench and the memory. I went into the other upstairs bedroom with my flashlight.

What the hell was I seeing?

My ears were hot and I felt blood pulsing through them. It took a moment to take in the scene—a skeleton hung by its clavicles on railroad spikes nailed into the wall, a white robe with wings draped over its head and shoulders. At the dangling bone-white feet lay what was left of several maggot-ridden roosters with razor blades strapped to their legs, a jawless human skull, a framed photo of a Mexican man, a mounted rooster, and assorted porcelain figurines holding globes and scythes with a mess of candles and crosses encircling the whole show.

Breathing in short controlled puffs through the sleeve of my pullover, I snatched up the framed photo of the Mexican man, scrambled down the stairs, bent over, and filled my lungs full of air. But there was no escaping that unholy smell.

Eyes watering, I fought back the impulse to puke. After reaching an uneasy truce with my gag reflex, I set the photo on the floor, slipped out of the backpack, and pulled out the digital camera. I shot the beam of my flashlight around the house. Kitchen to my right. Living room and front door to my left. I was probably standing in what was meant to be a half-ass dining room—a long, wide hall of a room that connected the living room to the kitchen. There was a desk against the wall in front of me and a window covered with foil above it.

I lit up the photo of the man—all head and shoulders—a brick wall behind him. His big meaty head filled most of the frame and he was shaved bald, his eyes squinted to slits like a gunfighter facing the sun. His collar was up around the back of his sunburnt neck and his shirt was unbuttoned—a sinister man of leisure. This was Alejandro Mendez-Rodriguez—the Mexican drug kingpin reported to have been recently murdered by the Trevino Cartel. I'd seen his picture on the news, like everyone else. My stomach did a flip.

"Ah shit, Ashley, should I just call the cops," I whispered. I was in way over my head, but I already knew that. I closed my eyes. Well, I wasn't calling them from here.

After snapping a digital shot of the Alejandro photo, I noticed there were disturbances in the dust on the desk in front of me. I'd come back and check the drawers in a minute. I needed to give the rest of the house a quick going-over first.

I went right, to the kitchen. There was a case of Miller High Life in the refrigerator, which was running, so I knew the electricity was on. Still, best to stick with the flashlight, even though I saw the windows were covered with foil. There were canned goods in the cabinets. In a room adjacent to the kitchen, there was a bed, but nothing else. Crushed cigarette butts lay in ashtrays here and there. There were tracks in the dust on the hardwood floors. The bathroom between the stairs and the downstairs bedroom had a bar of soap and a six-pack of toilet paper in it and that was it.

I crossed back through the dining room into the living room, which had an old television with rabbit ears in the far-right corner. To my left, the living room extended another fifteen feet to a wall with a foil-covered window, making the room as wide as the house and forming an L with the dining room. There was a dusty couch along the wall facing the front door.

When I got back to the dining room at the foot of the stairs, I whipped open the desk drawers and found dozens of photos. I needed time to study them. Lots of faces in lots of places. Some of the photos had writing on the back. I rifled through them, giving them a glance before splaying them out on the desk so I could photograph them. I started snapping shots of the front, and when necessary, the writing on the backs of these photos. I'd taken twelve, maybe fifteen, photos when the hum of an engine in the driveway disrupted the silence and adrenaline rushed through me. The engine passed, trailing off in the direction of the back yard. I clicked off the flashlight and swallowed hard against my constricting windpipe.

I reached over the desk, peeled back the foil on the dining room window, and looked out at the driveway. Nothing. What the hell? I snatched up the backpack, set it on the desk, and traded out the camera and the flashlight for the ski mask which I slipped over my head. I peeled back the foil again and peered through the window, repositioning myself to see out at any angle I could, trying to catch a glimpse of who might be coming through the door. I couldn't see a car or a person anywhere.

"Son of a . . ." I whispered, grabbing the backpack and slipping to the living room where I threw my back against the wall with the couch that faced the front door.

I unholstered my Glock and looked at the door. Despite the prospect of being captured on Mallory's camera, heading out that door seemed like my best option now.

I took a step, but the kitchen door rattled open behind me, stopping me cold. I slipped back to my spot against the wall in slow motion.

Light from the kitchen clicked on, spilling through the dining room and into the living room. I glanced at the front door—maybe three big strides away. This old house creaked with every step, and I'd be fumbling with an unfamiliar lock.

I heard the refrigerator door open, a cardboard box being ripped, and the unmistakable sound of someone opening an aluminum can.

The Miller High Life.

Welcome to the High Life, asshole. I doubted this was Mallory now. Everything about this break-in was a gamble—high risk, and maybe, high reward. I figured the odds had turned in my favor. The floors creaked—someone walking from the refrigerator. Time to get the drop on whoever this was and do what was necessary to get the location of my sister.

I whipped around the corner and sighted the Glock on a skinny Mexican man, early twenties, frozen in the kitchen doorway looking back at me. He had a beer to his lips and a serious gun in his other hand, dangling by his thigh.

Muscles flared on his neck.

I knew.

This had gone to shit.

His gun hand zipped up and I dove behind the wall, landing on the couch. Bullets pummeled the front wall and shredded its window into shards.

I dropped to the floor behind the couch.

He fired a short burst through the walls between us. Plaster dust drifted down in a soft flurry around me. The way rounds flowed out of that weapon like liquid death, he could run out of ammo in a hurry firing through that wall, guessing at where I was. I wasn't feeling lucky—I wondered if he was.

But what else could he do? If he came around that corner, I'd get a bead on him before he could get one on me. Still, if he wanted, he had the gun for it—a short automatic weapon that looked like a MAC-10 machine pistol.

He fired a couple more rounds through the walls. Single rounds—like he was conserving ammo. I winced each time he shot and saw the last round tear through the arm of the couch.

"Let's talk," he said.

I recognized the voice from the night before—the man in the ski mask from the van with his arm around Lindy's throat. Second night in a row I find myself in a standoff with this guy, except this time I'm the one in the ski mask. Now that I'd seen his face I knew this wasn't Miguel. I'd seen photos of Miguel in Mallory's search warrant affidavit and other case materials and knew he was pushing thirty.

"This is your lucky night," he said. "I can get you a million dollars in cash. All you gotta do is give me Trevino."

I kept mum. I wasn't about to disabuse him of his assumption that I was . . . what? A hitman sent by Trevino?

I glanced at the television set angled in the corner. On the TV's old glass screen I saw the man's reflection, backlit from the kitchen light, creeping forward, toward the corner.

I took it that his offer had been withdrawn.

The floor creaked under his foot, which seemed to freeze him. He took another step forward. I raised up over the couch and fired six rounds into the wall as fast as I could, hoping to catch him with one on the other side.

A short burst of gunfire erupted again.

I dropped to the floor, training the gun on the corner in case he had the guts to come around it, wincing in anticipation of catching a bullet. The shooting was almost over before I hit the floor. I eye-balled the TV screen and saw him check his gun, slow-walk backwards, and disappear into the kitchen. Maybe he was out of ammo.

I heard the kitchen door rattle open, then shut. I swopped the magazine in my Glock for a fully loaded one, slipped the straps of the backpack over my shoulders, and moved to the kitchen.

Standing to the side of the kitchen door, I tore the tinfoil off the window and it exploded in another burst of gunfire. I dropped to the floor, scrambled out of the kitchen, and ran to the front door. I unlocked the door, swung it open and zipped across the porch into the grass, taking center stage in Mallory's movie—a masked man of the night.

There was no sign of Mallory and Gordon. Nothing. I considered running into the wheat—live to fight another day. A sensible choice, considering my foe's superior firepower. But I couldn't imagine getting a better opportunity to save Ashley. I had to take the risk.

I ran to the front end of the house on the driveway side and looked around the corner toward the backyard. Didn't see him.

From there, I ran to the back end of the house by the kitchen door, now peppered with bullet holes, and peeked around the corner into the backyard. The toolshed sat fifteen yards away, halfway between me and the truck on cinderblocks and left of my sight line to it. There was enough moonlight to see the outline of a car beside the truck. A light jerked about underneath the truck. When I honed in on the movement I saw glimpses of someone working franticly in the flickering light. What was this shit? Maybe that truck was a dead drop for drugs or money and the cops somehow knew about it. If that was the case, they'd be right behind me shortly. I looked back. No one was coming, so I ran to the shed and stopped behind it, using it as cover. I leaned around the shed in time to see the light underneath the truck go out. He'd seen me or he was simply done with whatever he was doing.

The dome light to the car kicked on and I saw a man open the driver's side door. He was holding a duffel bag and if he had a gun on him I couldn't see it, but I was only getting glimpses. His back was to me now so I made my move. He bent over and reached across the front seat to the passenger side as I shuffled in behind him. He threw the bag in the back seat.

I was ten yards away, drawn down on the man, stepping closer.

"Don't move or you're a dead man," I said.

He twisted within the confines of that doorway like a rodeo bull in a chute.

I snapped off three rounds into the man and his gun spewed bullets into the bucket seat as he slumped belly first on top of it. His knees hovered above the base of the door opening and the tops of his shoes slid back and forth in the grass like he was sluggishly trying to climb imaginary stairs. My ears sang from all the shooting and the guttural noises coming from the man danced on the edge of a throbbing silence.

I holstered my pistol and reached into the car and pulled the man's gun out from under him and dropped it in the back seat. Then I dragged him into the grass by his ankles. His shirt was soaked in blood on the right side below his armpit. I flipped the man face up, straddled him with my knees on the ground by his waist, and pulled off my mask. I leaned over and got nose to nose with him so he could see me and know what I wanted. His eyes rolled back in his head—I may as well have been invisible. I wasn't even close to his biggest problem anymore. I plugged the bleeding holes in his side with my gloved palm.

"Tell me where my sister is and I'll get you to a doctor."

He kicked at the dark, writhed against my weight, his moans interrupted by gasps. As I fought to maintain control of him, I felt a vibration on my leg. By the time I pulled the man's vibrating cell phone from his front pocket, the caller, "E.C.", had ended the call. I clicked through the call log and saw that the man I'd shot had called "E.C." five minutes earlier. I was sure he'd made the call sometime after his first encounter with me in the house. I stuffed his phone in my pocket and looked to my left across the wheat field toward the railroad crossing.

The dull glow of headlights emerged on the northern horizon—could be his crew coming to help him in the fight against the Trevino Cartel, or it could be the cops. Even if this was a farmer, it was definitely time to get the hell out of here.

I grabbed the man underneath his shoulders and hauled him up. He was light and small boned. He mumbled something semi-coherent, so I slammed him on his back, straddled him, and got in his face again. His flashlight was somehow on the ground next to his head so I grabbed it and flicked it on and illuminated my face.

"Remember me, motherfucker?"

Recognition registered in his eyes. I looked back toward the road. Headlights closing in—now so close I saw the beams of two vehicles.

"Tell me where my sister is right now! Do that—I'll get you to a hospital."

The man struggled to speak but he couldn't. His eyes closed. I shook him but he was gone again.

"Boy, we're goin' for a ride."

I picked him up and heaved him head first across the bucket seats of his tricked-up Cutlass Supreme. He landed face down on the front passenger floorboard and I crammed the rest of him into the passenger half of the car and jumped into the driver's seat.

When I started the car his legs went into motion—not so much of a kicking action as it was a sluggish upside-down run. The lights from the vehicles on Eden Road were within a hundred yards of the driveway. I'd be driving without headlights. I brushed off his legs as best I could as I pinned the accelerator, shooting the car into the waist-high wheat. Wheat swooshed all over the car as the engine struggled in the field. I kept the accelerator floored—figuring to drive this heap till it dropped.

The man caught me in the jaw with a kick which seemed too precise and powerful to be accidental. He had some fight left in him, it seemed, which wasn't all bad. I didn't want him to die, I wanted to get information out of him. But dammit—I was running out of time, caught between creating space between me and the vehicles behind me and interrogating this man while I still had the chance.

I emerged from the wheat into a patch of prairie none too soon, since I'd almost slowed to a dead halt in the fine dirt of the field. Once I hit this low-cut prairie, I caught more traction and accelerated—when the car went nose down, weightless, right over a drop-off.

The engine screamed.

We slammed to the ground and I was face-first into an airbag.

I shook off the jolt, pushed back the bag, and pulled the man out of the Cutlass by his legs. He was limp when I dropped him on the ground. I pulled a wallet out of his back pocket and stuffed it in my pack. His phone vibrated—in my pocket this time. I pulled it out and looked at it. "E.C." was calling again.

I climbed the six-foot wall of the gully and looked back to Miguel's house. I remembered from Mallory's affidavit that one of Miguel's nicknames was El Comeniños. It stood to reason that the caller labeled E.C. was Miguel. Headlights illuminated the backyard area. I heard excited voices across the field speaking Spanish. These weren't farmers or cops.

The Cutlass had bent the wheat across this field in a direct line to the crash site.

I stuffed the boy's phone back in my pocket and popped the trunk to see if there might be anything in it to help me find my sister. Nothing. I crammed random shit from the glove box into my pack and then scanned the back seat. I'd almost forgot the duffel bag.

It was overturned on the back floorboard with a blue Tupperware container protruding from its opening. When I flipped the bag right side up on the back seat, I found it was filled with these containers. I cracked open the lid to one and saw little glacier-white rocks—crystal meth. I stuffed it back into the bag and zipped it shut. I figured I had to take this duffel bag full of meth with me. Hopefully those men behind me were operating on the notion that I was a Trevino man and any Trevino man worth his salt would jack a hundred-thousand dollars' worth of crank if he got the chance.

I kicked the man in the ribs but he was unresponsive. I might've come close to ending this thing if I'd been able to subdue him without shooting him and without him calling for backup. I heard engines in the distance, coming through the wheat. His crew was headed this way.

I aimed my Glock at the man's forehead, then it struck me that the key to finding my sister might be on that phone in my pocket. I took it out and tried to open it but it was password protected so I knelt and pressed the man's thumb on the home button. That got me in, for now, but I would need access later. I unsheathed my knife. Half the length of the six-inch blade was serrated. I took off his thumb, pulling and twisting on it as I sawed into the web-like base, then snapping it like I might a rotisserie chicken leg. He moaned and his arm twitched as blood pulsed into the grass and I sheathed the knife and pocketed the phone and dropped the bloody digit into the duffel bag full of meth.

I got to my feet, feeling like a stranger to myself, and pointed the Glock at the man's forehead. I put three rounds in it. He'd seen my face. I had to make sure he kept that to himself.

11

Ben

I RAN INTO a tree line overlooking a creek about fifty yards from the Cutlass, the groan of engines behind me in the distance. I took two steps down the creek's embankment, turned, and peered through the trees as two pickup trucks broke through the wheat in trail formation, their headlights bobbing across the uneven prairie toward the gully. The second truck slowed and fell further behind while the lead truck sped on until its driver locked up the brakes, rocking the front end down and sending the truck into a skid, stopping short of the drop-off and kicking up a flurry of debris glinting in the shafts of light beaming over the gully. The second truck rolled up next to the first one and stopped, further illuminating the tall cottonwoods above me guarding this creek. I sank further down the embankment and watched three men leap from the bed of the second truck and scramble down the gully's ledge to get to the dead body. Two of them had long guns, but I was too far away in this light to see anything more.

Two more men dropped into the gully as I replaced the magazine in my pistol and holstered it. After I shut off the GPS on the man's phone, I called Keri. The men were moving in and out of the shadows, faceless voices in Spanish, speaking fast, upset and confused. I heard someone wailing for "Juan." I would know the dead man's full name soon enough when I looked through his wallet, if I lived that long.

"What's up?" said Keri.

"Miguel's men are here—probably even Miguel himself—and they're chasing me. But they haven't spotted me."

"Do they know it's you?"

"No . . . I don't think so. It's a long story. I need to keep moving. Stay where you're at. I'll come to you."

I ended the call, sloshed through the ankle-deep water in three strides, climbed the embankment on the other side, and sprinted into a treeless prairie with the duffel bag full of meth. It would take them some time to find a spot to cross the creek in those trucks, and if they crossed on foot, odds were, they'd never see me. I hadn't played centerfield in thirteen years, but I still had some speed. If I was wrong about it taking some time to get those trucks across the creek, however, I might be a dead man because there was no cover.

Engines kicked into gear behind me, and I turned to see which direction they were headed. The light illuminating the cottonwoods between us moved, wiping the darkness from right to left with a strobe-like flicker. Then the tree line went dark. But I could still see their lights moving south on the other side so I altered my course from east to northeast, looking for the next wheat field, knowing I might need to call Keri from there to change the rendezvous point.

I'd been running for five minutes when a crescendo of metallic jolts echoed in the dark, each one closer and louder than the next, until the sound faded away. It was the sound of an engineer stretching 'em out—taking up the slack in the couplings connecting the cars of a sitting freight train.

I ran up the slope toward the train until I saw a procession of freight cars lurching eastward toward Worthington. I looked back and saw lights flashing in the distant prairie behind me. The trucks had already made their way across the creek. I pulled out my burner phone and speed dialed Keri as I ran.

"Benny?"

"Change of plans. Meet me in Worthington Park, Slate Creek—by the dam."

"How are you . . ."

"Hitching a ride on a freight train."

The train was already moving faster than I'd hoped. When I got within fifteen feet, I stopped and inspected the darkness behind me. The two pickups were moving across the prairie, scanning it with their headlights two hundred yards behind me. Their lights hadn't flashed in my direction yet, but that could change any moment. I had to jump this train now—it was gaining speed with each passing car.

I focused on the ladder of an approaching tanker car moving through the night and stepped toward the train, gauging the ladder's pace with each step until I planted my foot in the ballast and jumped, slipping in the crushed rock as I did—which sent my arms flailing for control as I flew through the air. The ladder sledge-hammered my chest and the force of the blow knocked the wind out of me and I managed to grab hold and was jerked down the track.

I hung there on the ladder, somehow, gasping for breath, one strap of the duffel bag looped around my forearm. All I could do was bear-hug the ladder, enduring each moment, marked by the steady clip-clop of train wheel on track.

When I started breathing normally, I noticed the clip-clops had blurred together, and I estimated that the train was doing forty-five miles per hour. I climbed the ladder to the top of the tanker and lay belly down on the walkway watching fields disappear behind me along with the men in pickups. I watched until their headlights disappeared.

Like all the trains on this line, this one came from Amarillo and was on its way to Kansas City. They often stopped in Worthington to switch crews, and we were about twenty-two miles from there. U.S. 160 ran parallel to the tracks over my left shoulder about a half-mile off. If the cops were coming in bunches, lights and sirens blazing, it would probably be westward up this highway. I considered calling 911 to get the ball rolling. Cause problems for the men in the field. Maybe there was more meth in that old truck on cinderblocks, and I assumed there was still a dead body in the field.

But the noise of the train was deafening. Maybe the sound of my screaming voice could slip through to the dispatcher in increments, but the idea of doing that when I knew the call would be recorded was a deal breaker—what with the blood on my clothes and the five pounds of meth and the gun I was toting that had been used to kill the man who belonged to that thumb in the duffel bag I carried.

The train slowed on the outskirts of Worthington. I couldn't see the highway anymore, but off in the distance I saw the flicker of police lights. I hoped the cops would catch those men in the field, knowing the odds were against it. Their head start amidst an intricate network of country roads gave them a huge advantage. But if the men I'd seen behind me *were* detained for questioning, I would have another option to consider. I could tell the cops about the kidnapping and they would try to interrogate them. That could work out, but the more I considered it, the more I doubted it. Between the cartel lawyers' likely descent upon the sheriff's station, the ever-present threat of death for snitching on a viscous international drug cartel, and the Fifth Amendment's right to remain silent, there was little hope of getting useful information out of anyone before Ashley was dead and gone. Maybe the arrest or detention of these men was a complication I didn't need.

My tanker crept across a trestle over the river on the west end of town. I dropped the Glock I used to kill Juan into the river along with my bloody gloves. I knew I should probably jettison the meth too, but I didn't. I figured anything that valuable could be useful to a man in my position, even if it carried the risk of twenty years in a federal prison.

When the tanker cleared the river we were barely moving. I climbed down the ladder and jumped off onto a steep incline, which sent me tumbling through crushed rock fifty feet or so before I came to rest in some brush relatively unscathed. I gathered up the duffel bag, got off railroad property, and called Keri.

"I made it," I said. "I'm in Worthington Park."

"I'll be there in ten minutes. Three sheriff cruisers just blew by me going the other way. That have anything to do with you?"

"I'm sure that has everything to do with me."

12

Ben

I JOGGED ALONG the river bank until I reached the weir dam which was fifteen yards from a park road. Seeing no sign of Keri, I climbed down an embankment to the base of the waterfall. I pulled both phones out of my pocket and unholstered my Glock and set them in the wispy knee-high grass of the bank along with the duffel bag and the backpack. Then I stepped into the water to wash the blood off my clothes.

When I was done, I plopped down in the grass and tried to warm up. While I waited on Keri, I had a moment alone with the big sky—clouds floating in front of the moon, the sound of water cascading over the weir dam into Donut Bay. The wind picked up and my bones ached from the chill.

I lay back and filled my lungs with cool night air and my eyes with the light of the universe trying to feel like a second in time or a grain of sand on a beach, but there was no lightening my load.

Juan's cell phone vibrated again. I sat up in the grass and looked at it. The caller wasn't labeled "E.C." this time—just a number with no caller information. I was curious. By now, this could be the cops, but I doubted it. No matter who it was, I didn't need to tip my location—the rush of a waterfall was rare in this county.

Another call, this one from Keri, came in on my burner phone a minute later.

"I'm at the dam," she said. "Where you at?"

I looked up the embankment and saw a glow.

"I'll be right up."

I holstered my pistol, grabbed my things, and climbed up to the road. When I opened the passenger door to the Silverado, Keri's eyebrows drew together at the sight of me.

"You okay?" she said.

"Yeah."

She nodded, her eyes projecting skepticism. Then she pointed at the duffel bag. "What's that?"

"At least $100,000 worth of crank . . . and a thu—"

"What are you gonna do with it?"

"Damned if I know."

She'd find out about the thumb soon enough. I set the backpack and the duffel bag on the floorboard behind the seat and climbed in. Keri put the truck in gear and started down the road.

She glanced at me as we drove under a train trestle and I realized she'd been talking but I'd tuned her out, lost in thought.

"What happened out there, Benny?"

She looked at me again and our eyes met this time, but she broke it off to watch the road. We were alone on the street, winding between softball fields and a golf course.

"Give me a second," I said.

She nodded, slipped her hand across the seat to touch mine and asked, "Are we still headed to Wichita? Getting a room?"

I shook my head. "No, things have changed. I have to go home now."

We crossed U.S. 160, drove between a grocery store and a convenience store, entering the only high-end residential neighborhood in Worthington.

"I thought it was too dangerous to stay at your house, at least until you got a security system installed?"

"I'll explain in a second, Keri, just let me think."

I closed my eyes, trying to picture Detective Mallory's duty car in my head. All I remembered was that it was bland and black. It was one of those models that didn't leave much of an impression—the perfect car for a plain-clothes detective trying to blend in. Pops had tools that would get me access to the files I knew he kept in there.

When I opened my eyes, we were stopped at a stop sign in front of Oil Field Road. Keri put the truck in park and squared up to me in her seat. We were at the western edge of Worthington at the end of a street lined on both sides with big homes and manicured fescue lawns. Directly before us on the other side of Oil Field Road was the countryside's first wheat field. To get to my house in the country, we needed to turn right.

I looked at Keri and the expression on her face told me she wasn't going another block without hearing the story.

"I killed another one—the one from the van that did all the talking last night."

Keri pressed her spine against the backrest and stared out the windshield, audibly exhaling. "These men that were chasing you . . . any chance they knew it was you?"

"No," I said. Then I thought about it more. "At least I don't think so. The one I killed—Juan I think's his name—somehow got it in his head I was a hitman from a rival cartel."

"A hitman?"

"Yeah, I was in a ski mask, so, I dunno—"

"And why are we changing plans and going to your house now?"

"Detective Mallory will probably be calling me any minute for a search warrant. He'll be at the house later tonight. We need to let Diablo out anyway."

Keri reached across the cab and opened the glove compartment, pulled out the iPhone she bought me for my birthday a month ago, powered it up, and turned the GPS back on. She had put it in the truck earlier so we wouldn't forget to take it with us to Wichita in case law enforcement needed to reach me for a search warrant overnight. I'd put one of the other judges in the district on search warrant duty, but the cops had a habit of calling me anyway and I wanted to be available if they needed a search warrant in the Rummell case.

Keri handed me the phone and said, "Looks like Mallory already called."

I saw he'd called only five minutes earlier. "You don't happen to know what kind of car Mallory drives do you?"

"A black Chevy Impala—2014 . . . maybe '15. Why?"

"How the hell do you know that?"

Keri shrugged. "I see him driving it all the time."

"That's not what I mean. You don't seem like a car person to me."

"I'm not, it's just that my foster mom drives an Impala that looks like the one Mallory drives. Guess it stuck in my head. Why do you want to know what Mallory drives all of the sudden?"

"Turn around, let's swing by Pops' house," I said. "I have an idea."

Keri turned right on Oil Field Road, zipped up a quarter mile to Sixteenth Street, turned right and headed toward downtown Worthington.

I returned Mallory's call.

"Hello, Judge?"

I recognized Mallory's voice.

"I saw you called. What's up?"

"Where you at?"

"Almost home."

"We'd like to swing by your house for a search warrant later. Just a heads-up."

Mallory spoke loudly over background noise on his end— an engine, wind, a police radio. My guess was that he was heading west on U.S. 160. I hoped he was in his Impala.

"Right now?" I asked.

"It'll be a little later."

"Okay."

"If that's okay?"

"Sure, when do you think you'll be ready to see me?"

"Hard to say. Just makin' sure I could find a judge for a search warrant and I really didn't want to drive all the way to the east side of the county to see the duty judge if you were available."

"Yeah, okay. I'll be home all night. Let me know when you're headed my way. I'm gonna catch some Z's and might need a little time to wake up."

"Will do. Thanks, Judge. Sorry to bother you on your Saturday night."

I ended the call and laid my head back in the seat to relieve the tension between my shoulder blades. I cracked my eyes open and watched Keri tend to her driving. When her ponytail was high on her head and pulled tight like it was, she almost looked like a different girl—all bright eyes and high cheekbones with not one stray hair dangling in front of her face. It made her look older and more businesslike.

"Don't you think now's a good time to get out of those wet clothes? If the cartel has someone watching Pops' house, or your house, it's best they don't see you in that boogey-man outfit. They might jump to the conclusion that you killed this . . . Juan."

"Yeah you're right."

I turned around and reached for the suitcase in the back seat, unzipping it and plucking out a golf shirt, khaki shorts, boxer-briefs, and a pair of flip-flops.

When I plunked back down in the seat and began untying my hiking boots, Keri said, "So, I guess you want me to break into Mallory's Impala with Pops' tools while you're reviewing his search warrant? As if I know how," she added.

"If you don't mind," I said, pulling the wet camouflage top over my head and dumping it behind the seat. Then I unfastened the strap holding the sheath with the knife and put it in the glove compartment.

As I ducked my head into the golf shirt Keri said, "Man, this is getting . . . crazy."

"Yeah? Well, I've killed five members of the Mendez-Rodriguez Cartel in the last twenty-four hours, so all my chips are pretty much on the table here. Crazy's about the only play left after something like that goes down."

"You'll have to show me how to work the rods."

"All's you do is slip a wedge tool between the glass and the weather strip, insert the air jack, pump it up, and you'll have a rod specifically designed for popping the door lock on Mallory's Impala in your hands. Simple."

"I don't know—"

"You don't have to do it. It was just an idea."

I whipped off the wet pants, and before I could slip into the dry boxer-briefs, Keri snuck a peek and made her eyebrows dance up and down.

"Eyes on the road please," I said.

She made the green light above the crossing on Main Street, went two more blocks, and turned right onto B Street. "What do you expect me to find in Mallory's car?" said Keri.

"The joke is he's got a mobile office, like in his back seat where he keeps a sea of accordion folders full of reports and other sensitive information on his pet cases. I hear his trunk is full of case materials too. He's been told to clean it up because the fear is that if somebody breaks into his car, lots of sensitive information will be on the streets—peoples' social security numbers, reports from the National Crime Information Center—stuff that's not meant for public consumption. But his files somehow always end up in his car. I figure we can take a few folders worth of relevant files and he won't miss them until later as long as you don't clean out his entire back seat or something like that. If he goes to looking for something later and can't find it, it'll be just another day in the life of a slob."

"You want to know what he knows about the cartel."

"You got it."

"So, you want me to steal police reports?"

"We aren't stealing. I'll replace them later, so let's call it what it is—borrowing."

"Let's not delude ourselves," said Keri.

"Deluding ourselves, that's good. I can do that."

She took a right onto Eighth Street, drove half a block, turned left into Pops' alley, and parked underneath the cottonwood by his garage. Her last statement bothered me.

I slipped my feet into the flip-flops, then sat back in my seat and blew out a big breath of air. "Do you think we're doing the right thing here—trying to find Ashley ourselves?"

Keri's eyes were unfocused—lost in an inward gaze. "What choice do we have?"

I shrugged. "I don't know . . . call the cops . . . sit back and hope."

The answer was simple. The truth was hard.

"That sounds like giving up."

I nodded. "That's what I think. And so you know, I'm probably going to have to delude myself to get through this."

My stomach lurched as the gravity of the situation seemed to grab hold of me in a whole new way. We were going to have to break a lot of laws. Keri's eyes locked onto mine. We'd never be the same.

She reached over and pushed her fingers into my hair. "Teach me how to pop the lock on Mallory's Impala and I'll borrow the shit out of his reports."

13

Ben

TWENTY MINUTES LATER Keri set the backpack on my kitchen table as I breezed by her and Diablo on my way to the bedroom where I unlocked the gun safe, pulled out a shotgun, and loaded it.

I walked into the kitchen with the shotgun and let Diablo out the side door.

Keri held up a driver's license and said, "Is this the guy you killed tonight?"

The wallet I'd pulled from Juan's pocket was on the table, along with the digital camera and the papers from the glove compartment. I took a close look at the photo on a Mexican driver's license.

"That's him."

She took the DL from me, looked it over, and said, "Full name is Juan Mendez-Mendoza, born January 8, 1997."

I knew the Mexican naming conventions—the first surname was from the father and the second from the mother. Juan's resemblance to Miguel Mendez-Mendoza was undeniable. I hadn't noticed when he was shooting at me, when I was nose to nose with him as he was dying, when I was shooting him in the forehead by the light of the moon. But now, in the comfort of my kitchen I saw it. "He has to be kin to Miguel—probably brothers."

Keri pursed her lips. "I wonder where his funeral will be? And when?"

We could track Miguel from the funeral. That thought had barely formed in my mind before reality set in—there was no way he'd be there. Things were too hot for him now. But someone with connections to Miguel might be there, which could lead us to him—and that could lead us to Ashley.

"We'll find out," I finally answered.

Keri grabbed Juan's phone, tapped the screen and shook her head. "Damn. Password protected."

"That reminds me."

I laid the shotgun on the kitchen counter, opened the duffel bag and took out Juan's thumb.

Keri stared wide-eyed at it. "Jesus, is that a . . . thumb? Who are you?"

"Hey, the guy was dead. Mostly. I think. It's not like he needed—"

"—his thumb anymore." She arched her eyebrows.

"No ma'am he didn't. And *we* do."

"We're deluding ourselves again."

"Excellent." I wiped the thumb with a damp sponge.

Keri set the phone on the table and I pressed Juan's thumb on the home button. The phone unlocked.

Keri smiled. "Can't believe that worked."

I put the thumb in a Ziploc and hid it in the freezer beneath the T-Bones while Keri sat down at the table and went to work. While I washed my hands at the sink, I looked out the kitchen window at the driveway. With any luck, Detective Mallory's Impala would be parked there later tonight.

Keri looked up from the phone. "Need a notepad and a pen."

I opened a drawer, grabbed both, and set them before her.

She jotted down numbers from Juan's phone onto the notepad and I picked up the digital camera and scrolled through the shots I'd taken of the photos inside Miguel's house. The third one I came to caught my eye. It was Miguel, Juan, and a pretty blonde girl—all on horses. The girl had a birthmark on her neck that crawled up her chin—or maybe it was an old burn scar. She appeared in many photos with Juan: kissing on a beach, having drinks with him and Miguel at a bar, and on boats—lots of boats—ski boats, pontoon boats, even a yacht.

The back side of a romantic beach photo read: APRIL AND JUAN, JULY OF 2016.

"Anyone named April ever call on that phone?" I asked.

Keri stopped writing and looked up. "April pretty much dominates Juan's call logs, both incoming and outgoing."

"Makes sense," I said, showing her the photos of April with Juan.

"Yeah, so she's the girlfriend, or whatever. There's not a lot of calls on here. Hers was the only number with a 316 area code."

316 was a local area code, along with 620.

"What are the other area codes on the call logs?"

Keri looked at her notepad, "Let me see, there's 915—"

"That's El Paso," I said.

Keri looked at me quizzically.

"I have several area codes memorized from my days prosecuting traffickers at the U.S. Attorney's Office."

Keri looked back at the phone's call log. "There's 505—"

"Albuquerque."

"602."

"Arizona."

"And some number that starts with a 2 instead of a 1."

"2 is the country code for Mexico. I'd bet my house that all these numbers are for thirty-dollar burner phones that have already been broken into pieces and thrown by now." I thought about that for a moment. "Except for maybe 316-April."

My house phone rang.

I looked at the caller ID. "It's Mallory."

Keri put the digital camera, the papers from Juan's glove box, and her notepad into the backpack as I answered the call and spoke with Mallory.

When I ended the call a moment later I said, "He thinks he'll be here in about forty-five minutes." I nodded at the door to my three-car garage. "Time for your crash course in popping locks."

Keri nodded and took in a deep breath. We had Pops' Silverado, Keri's Honda Civic, and Ashley's Lincoln Navigator as models. Not ideal, but we had the rods for those vehicles as well as the Impala. Keri would catch on. I'd parked my Ford F350 outside behind the shed to make room for the other vehicles.

"Babe," I said, "you know you don't have to do this for me. You really don't. Maybe there's nothing in his Impala that helps us anyway."

"And maybe there is." Keri set her jaw and gave me a curt nod. "I got this. Show me how to work the tools. And for Christ's sake, when you're reviewing Mallory's affidavit, read slow."

"I'll read until you call. That'll be the signal you're done."

*   *   *

I was eating a turkey sandwich and watching out the window above the kitchen sink when Mallory's Impala crept down the drive almost an hour after he'd called. It was one-thirty in the morning. When the Impala's door opened the dome light kicked on and I saw Agent Gordon in the passenger seat. I closed the blinds.

The knock on the front door was a delicate triple tap designed not to wake my kids.

When I opened the door, Agent Gordon and Detective Mallory gave me middle-of-the-night apologetic smiles—the ones cops used on judges when one had to be rousted from the rack in the wee hours of the morning.

"Come on in," I said, stepping aside. "Have a seat there on the couch if you want."

Caroline sauntered over to the couch, followed by Mallory. Both carried matching manila folders and wore jeans and windbreakers bearing the badge and name of their respective agencies.

Mallory spoke in a hushed tone. "I knocked lightly, so as not to wake the kids."

"Okay," I said, smiling.

They both sat down on a couch shaped like an L—Pops' wedding gift to me and Natalie ten years ago. I sat on the part of the couch that put the closed-curtained window to the driveway at my back. I had them right where I wanted.

Mallory opened the folder he was holding. "You coaching any baseball this summer, Judge?"

Great, small talk. Delay was good, but a question about coaching baseball would lead to questions about my kids that I didn't want to answer.

"No not this summer. Too much on my plate with the trial and all."

And all!

When I said this, Mallory was already looking over his paperwork, counting copies. Caroline watched him shuffle the papers before slumping back into the couch and closing her eyes. I wasn't sure he'd heard me until he jabbed a handful of papers across the table at me and said, "Oh yeah yeah, I think I already knew that."

When I took the search warrant and affidavit, it didn't feel like there was much to them. There didn't have to be. Besides describing the two properties involved and how law enforcement got called to the scene, all his affidavit really needed to say was *there's a dead man in a field with multiple gunshot wounds and can we please search for evidence of murder?*

How the hell was I supposed to drag *that* out?

Mallory leaned back and threw one of his arms over the back of the couch. "I bet Leo's fired up about playing ball this summer."

One of his boys was Leo's age and their teams were scheduled to play against each other the first week in June, so of course this was a natural subject for small talk between us. Still, it felt like he was forcing the conversation in a certain direction, like usual really, so I hoped I was just feeling the paranoia that came with the strain of the situation. By now, Caroline and Mallory must've watched, rewound, and studied the part of the surveillance video when I burst through Miguel's front door in the ski mask. Some people have a certain way of moving, an unusual gait, or a tic of some kind and I hoped I wasn't one of them. I felt sweat trickle down my side.

I said, "Leo and Lindy both love to play ball . . . Caroline, you seem exhausted. Either of you want coffee? I could fire up a pot real quick. It's no trouble."

Mallory rubbed his belly, looking to Caroline who was still reclined, eyes closed, "Oh, well sure—"

Caroline's eyes blinked open and she sat up. "No thanks. We've got six dead bodies in a field behind Miguel's property, one of them headless. So, it's going to be a long night. We need to get going here."

When I realized my mouth had fallen open, I shut it.

Mallory laughed at this and said, "We got four cold bodies and two warm ones. Try and make sense out of that, would ya? And the headless one, is one of the warm bodies . . ." Mallory held out his hand, palm down, working it like a teeter-totter. "Kind of warm. Lost a lot of heat in a hurry through the neck hole I imagine. And his fingertips. Those were lopped off as well."

I said, "Headless?" But I was also wondering where all the bodies came from. When I left there was just Juan. An icy chill walked up my spine to the base of my skull and made camp.

I sorted through the affidavit wishing they'd included photos so I could see if the four cold bodies were the men I'd killed Friday night in the vans. I zipped through the first paragraph and saw that someone had called 911 about seeing trucks in a field. The paragraph was too well written and concise to have been penned by Mallory. I'd assumed he and Caroline would be consulting with Gwendolyn Sweeney—the lead prosecutor assigned to the Rummell case by the state's attorney general— but now, having read only a paragraph, I guessed this affidavit was more or less the work of the prosecutor.

"Did you catch these . . . people with trucks in the field?"

"No," said Caroline, "but deputies are still looking."

Mallory smirked. "Hell, they're long gone by now."

Caroline leaned forward, looking at me. "Do you recall what Rummell's defense attorney told the jury in his opening statement about Kramer Carter?"

On Friday morning, less than forty-eight hours earlier, Glenn McMaster, one of the defense attorneys, gave the opening statement for the defense. It was simple and shaky, like opening statements made with shitty facts are prone to be. McMaster insinuated that someone could have planted Rummell's DNA on the rebar. He said that the evidence would show that his client was too high on meth to know what he was saying when he confessed. And he pointed out that his client wasn't the only white male in the world with clown tattoos on his right arm, referencing Rummell's bandmate, Kramer Carter, as a prime example. McMaster told the jury that the evidence would show that Chainsaw's lead guitarist had the "exact same sleeve of clown tattoos on his right arm as Rummell." He made a big deal out of the fact that no one had seen or heard from Kramer Carter since the night of the Dandurand murders.

"I remember," I said. "McMaster claimed that his client and Kramer Carter had matching tattoos."

On Friday morning, I thought I knew what McMaster was trying to do—same thing all defense attorneys tried to do with opening statement—plant the seed of reasonable doubt in the minds of the jurors. *Maybe the tattoos fourteen-year-old Haley saw on the killer that night belonged to Kramer Carter. Maybe he was the killer.* Now I thought it likely this seed he'd planted—a seed he'd no doubt attempt to nourish throughout the trial—wasn't as much meant for the jury's consideration as it was mine. McMaster probably felt obliged to do his best to give me something to work with when the time came for ruling on his motion for judgment of acquittal after the close of state's evidence.

Caroline nodded. "The headless DB in the field has the exact same sleeve of tattoos on his right arm as Rummell. We think we finally found Kramer Carter."

"Most of him, anyway," said Mallory, smiling.

Caroline shook her head. "Stay classy, Bucky."

Mallory leaned forward, opened his file and pulled out some eight-by-eleven-inch photos that had been printed on paper and splayed them out on my coffee table: Juan dead in the prairie grass next to the wrecked Cutlass; the headless torso of the man presumed to be Kramer Carter; the fat-headed man I'd shot through the back of a van seat; and the three other men from the vans I'd killed. It sure looked like them anyway. How could this be? Maybe the men in the trucks were transporting the bodies when Juan's emergency call came their way, and when they found Juan they panicked and dumped the bodies, or maybe they just improvised, knowing cops could be swarming the area like bees any minute.

I gazed at the carnage, trying not to react.

"You usually attach photos like these to your affidavits," I finally said.

Mallory shrugged, "Yeah, well Ms. Sweeney doesn't think it's necessary so . . . her call. Unless you want them attached?"

"No, it's fine," I said, thinking I was probably right about who'd authored the affidavit. "Let me read this thing over now."

I hadn't read a word when another question hit me.

"So, Ms. Sweeney obviously knows you think this might be Kramer Carter in the field?"

They both nodded, and Mallory said, "Yeah."

"Did she say anything to you about how this might affect the trial Tuesday?"

Caroline nodded. "She told us she would need to tell McMaster about it first thing in the morning. Said the trial would probably have to be continued because he would surely ask for time to investigate this new evidence."

Prosecutors are ethically obligated to disclose exculpatory evidence—evidence helpful to the defense. Ms. Sweeney was playing it straight. Kramer Carter was McMaster's scapegoat, or he was a killer. Either way, odds were, he was the headless man in back of a property owned by a cartel-connected drug dealer.

I looked at both of them. "I assume Ms. Sweeney thinks there might be exculpatory evidence here?" I tapped the photos.

"Yeah, that's what she called it," said Mallory. "Except she had a weasel word in there, something to give her some wiggle room." Mallory laughed and looked to Caroline who pursed her lips and looked at her nails. "She kept saying it was '*potentially* exculpatory'."

Caroline's phone rang and she pulled it from the pocket of her windbreaker. After looking at the screen she chuckled and said, "This is Sweeney now." She put the phone to her ear. "Yes ma'am."

Mallory and I watched as Caroline listened, her blue eyes dancing around as she did.

"We're at Judge Joel's house now. Yeah, I'm looking at him as we speak." She handed me the phone. "Ms. Sweeney wants to talk to you."

Gwendolyn Sweeney was the lead prosecutor in the case for the attorney general, but more famously, she was the state's solicitor-general, the AG's leading appellate attorney who had become, at least in local conservative circles, a hero for those in favor of the death penalty. Since 1995 when the death penalty was signed into law by the governor, the Kansas Supreme Court had overturned all five death sentences handed down by juries. And it was Ms. Sweeney, an African-American woman in her mid-fifties, who'd authored and argued all five of the briefs responsible for convincing the U.S. Supreme Court to reverse those decisions.

Her presence at the trial court level was somewhat political, I suspected. With two of the seven justices on the state's supreme court facing contentious retention elections in November, the AG seemed eager to pour kerosene on the campaign to remove the liberal members of the court, telling the *Topeka Capital-Journal* last year he was assigning Ms. Sweeney lead trial counsel on all the AG's capital cases in an effort to end up with "'nothing for the justices to use as an excuse to overturn the death penalty but their own political beliefs against the measure.'"

I knew Gwendolyn. We shared a nodding acquaintance. As a young prosecutor I had tried one of the cases she had taken all the way to the U.S. Supreme Court. She looked out of place in a water-stained courtroom in southern Kansas standing in front of a middle-class jury trying to talk without uttering one of her ten-dollar words. This foray away from her milieu—appellate courts with their marble columns, learned justices with law degrees from Harvard and Yale—was off the rails. And she didn't even know it.

I put the phone to my ear and mindlessly wished Ms. Sweeney a good morning.

"No offense, but I've had better, Your Honor. Have you seen enough of the affidavit to know what's going on here?"

"Yes. I'm aware."

"Okay, well I feel like I need to call Mr. McMaster in the morning and let him know what's going on. I think all this could be viewed as potentially exculpatory. I'm sure McMaster will want to have his investigator check into this. We'll be doing the same thing, quite frankly. Just so you know, I doubt either of us will be ready to continue the trial Tuesday."

Under normal circumstances, of course, Ms. Sweeney would be right. Under these circumstances, I had no idea what to expect. McMaster might not want a continuance at all.

"I understand. Let me know if you and McMaster need to speak to me when the sun comes up, or even on Memorial Day sometime."

"Will do. Take care, Judge."

I handed Caroline her phone and read the affidavit as slow as I credibly could. There was a short blurb in the third paragraph about the arrival of the Cutlass, a man in a ski mask coming out the front door of the house and running to the back, and later, two pickup trucks blowing through the driveway on their way to the fields behind the property. I now knew for sure they'd watched their surveillance video. I cut my eyes to them talking quietly between themselves, dividing the workload for when they got back to the scene to gather the evidence. When I reached the end of the affidavit, I re-read it. This was definitely Sweeney's writing. She was the best legal writer I knew.

My home phone rang. I made a face, like I wasn't expecting a call and picked it up on the second ring. The number showing on the caller ID was the one from Keri's burner phone.

"Hello," I said.

"Thumbs-up," said Keri.

I looked at Caroline and Mallory and rolled my eyes for them. Then I told Keri, "You've got the wrong number, ma'am."

I ended the call and turned to Mallory. "You want to raise your right hand?"

Mallory did. I gave him the oath and he signed the affidavits in triplicate. I signed the search warrant in triplicate, and handed Mallory his stack of paper.

At the door, he stopped and looked back. "Hey, congratulations. I heard you got engaged to that paralegal who sits in the hallway at the courthouse."

"Thanks."

Mallory tapped his fist lightly on his leg and looked off into space. "What was her name again?"

"You know her name."

"What makes you say that?"

"Same way I know bird dogs don't ask me where the pheasants are."

Detective Mallory's laugh shot out of him as he opened the front door. Caroline was shaking her head as she walked briskly through the doorway, across the front porch, and out into the yard.

Mallory stopped on the porch and turned back to me as I was about the shut the door. "Keri Chalmers!" he said, pointing at nothing in particular. "There it is, you lucky dog."

I heard Mallory laugh again on his way to the Impala as I shut the door.

As I entered the kitchen, the door to the attached garage swung open. Keri stood in the doorway, smiling, holding two overstuffed accordion file folders.

She dropped the folders on the kitchen table and we pored through reports for twenty minutes when my field of vision began shrinking, going blurry in the periphery. Large chunks of the report I was trying to read disappeared from my sight and light flashed in the corners of my eyes. The aura was setting in, the first sign of a freight-train migraine heading my way. Or maybe this was a complication from the blow to my head Friday night but it felt like the migraines I'd experienced eight or ten times before. As in the past, there was no pain, yet, but I literally couldn't see enough to read, so I popped 800 milligrams of Ibuprofen and two Tylenols and went to bed like the doctor had told me to do when this happened. The drugs would blunt the pain when it would come, usually about forty-five minutes after the return of my eyesight. I planned to sleep through it, figuring to wake up a little tired and depleted, but functional. I thought I had enough time before the pain hit to take a quick shower.

* * *

Except for the light spilling into my bedroom from the open French doors to the master bath—still steamy from our shower together—it was dark. We nixed the idea of getting a hotel room in Wichita. The aura left me, restoring my vision, but I couldn't stomach the idea of riding in the car another mile even though the pain of the migraine hadn't yet set in. Besides, if they came for us now it would be without the element of surprise. I figured we could hold our own this time. Diablo was in the corner of the room sleeping on an old blanket. A loaded shotgun was propped against the wall and the nightstand four feet from my head. The gun safe was cracked open—all hands on deck. Every one of my three shotguns, my five pistols, my two rifles, loaded, ready for a fight.

My still damp back was flat on the bed and Keri was on top of me, her full breasts slick with sweat on my chest, thrusting her snug, wet warmth down on me—a deep soulful grind. Her hot breath was loud in my ear, catching and fitful.

I gripped her backside, feeling her glutes contract, each thrust harder than the one before until she held her breath and pinned me deep inside her. She lifted her breasts off me and slung her wet locks to her back and bucked, a soundless convulsion at first, then moans escaped from her straining red face and she dropped limp, panting on top of me.

I reached under her arms and gripped her dead weight against me and flipped us over. On her back now, she wrapped her legs around me in surrender, accepting me still, in her exhaustion, as I thrusted myself into her until I went taut, unloading everything I had.

When I woke it was dark and I was somehow still on top of her. The pain I was expecting from the migraine had never set in. Or I'd slept through it somehow. Keri was moving her hips again, stroking me, as best she could pinned on bottom as she was. We were alive as ever.

*   *   *

On Sunday morning the eggs were frying over easy in a cast iron skillet with a shotgun next to me on the counter and Diablo outside stalking the grounds in the bright sun. I watched through the kitchen window, sipping coffee, trying to jump-start my system. The bacon was in the oven on a tinfoil-lined cookie sheet and there was a bowl of cantaloupe chunks on the table. Keri sat behind me at the table in her panties, hair mussed, wearing one of my shirts and sorting through Detective Mallory's files.

I was surprisingly relaxed, but spent. I'd already talked to Pops and my children. Leo and Lindy were doing okay—even seemed energized by the excitement. Children are resilient. And Pops had good news. The Kid said he'd be here on Thursday and I could call and talk to him later today if I wished. I told Pops to tell him to expect my call.

My landline rang. I didn't recognize the number.

"Hello," I said.

"Judge, this is Gwen Sweeney. I've got Glen McMaster on conference call."

The Rummells had surprised everyone by enlisting not one, but two attorneys—the attorneys told the media they were taking this case pro bono—free of charge. Glenn McMaster and Ellen Thompson had fifty-two years of combined experience in defending capital murder cases in Texas, Illinois, and Kansas. The Rummells also hired a few forensic experts and even hired a retired detective from Laredo, Texas named Buster Reynolds as their investigator. All this fueled speculation by the cops that the Mendez-Rodriguez Cartel was funding the defense, of course, but there was little anyone could do beyond speculate. Vaughn Rummell had a constitutional right to hire the attorney of his choice and his defense team appeared to be doing a fine job under the circumstances, which I increasingly suspected included working outside the legal bounds of the justice system.

Keri stood and came closer to listen in.

"Hi Judge," said McMaster, working through a smoker's morning phlegm. "Sorry to bother you so early on a Sunday morning. Heard you had a long night last night."

I looked at the clock. It was after nine—hardly early.

"That's okay," I said. "I told Ms. Sweeney to call if I was needed. I assume she apprised you of the developments last night."

"As far as I know, she has, Your Honor, and, if I may get right to the point, I am not asking for you to continue the trial. The state has rushed to judgment here, and now that they finally realize that maybe they've made a terrible mistake, they seem to assume I'm going to want to take them off the hook by asking for a continuance so they can get their ducks back in order. Thanks, but no thanks."

Since I didn't know what to expect, this didn't surprise me. "What say you, Ms. Sweeney? Is the state asking for a continuance?"

After a long silence, Ms. Sweeney said, "No."

I said, "Well then I'll see you both Tuesday morning. Anything else I can do for you?"

"Ms. Sweeney's been real good about getting me all the discovery materials, so no, Your Honor, not right now. My experts are going to need DNA samples of the bodies as soon as possible. We'll want to compare it to the DNA planted at the Dandurand scene and in my client's Mustang."

Sweeney snickered at the cheap shot. "Fine, see you both Tuesday morning."

"Tuesday morning then," I said.

I ended the call and took Keri into my arms, feeling a clutch in my gut. The relaxed glow she had put on me a few hours ago was long gone.

14

Ben

THE ROOM'S SHAG carpet had been smashed flat and smooth in a trail that led to the receptionist's desk. My friend, Tony Cornejo, used to sell waffles in this place, but now his ads say he sells freedom for a fee. He's now a bail bondsman in Wichita working weekends and holidays when the madness of the world shifts into overdrive. His place smelled of dirty bodies and bad habits. Ah, the smell of freedom. I preferred the smell of waffles at nine o'clock in the morning.

An elderly lady with a dowager's hump sat across from us and told us of her woes while we waited. Despite my efforts at discouraging conversation, I gathered she got stuck with the one-year-old at her feet when her son got arrested. Keri was in the middle of trying to figure out if the woman had any clean diapers for the baby when the receptionist told us we could go on back.

Tony's chair squeaked in relief when he stood from behind his desk to shake my hand. His fingers were fat and wet and he smelled like sweaty fat men do when they're trying not to smell like sweaty fat men—too much cologne and it made my nose itch. He wheezed when he spoke but he moved well for a big man when he came out from behind his desk to shut his office door behind us. After he shut the door, he congratulated us on our recent engagement and gave us hugs.

When he sat down behind his desk, he frowned, taking in the looks on our faces. He looked to me and asked, "What's going on?"

"We need a favor," I said.

"I'd do anything for you. Whatta you need?"

Tony's voice didn't fit well with his big body. It belonged to one of my kid's cartoon characters—gentle and forgiving. Beads of sweat multiplied on my friend's broad brown forehead.

"Keri and I need to borrow one of your GPS trackers, if you don't mind. Wouldn't mind having more than one, if you can spare them."

Tony's head flinched back a little. "You can order however many you need on the Internet. That's where I got all mine."

Keri said, "Yeah, well we kind of need them right now."

"What for?"

The plan was to be straight with Tony but the answer to his question—*I killed a member of a major drug cartel, and now I'd like to track some of the folks attending the funeral*—was a bad place to start.

If I had a best friend growing up, Tony was it. We needed more than his trackers. We needed his time—his loyalty. He could speak Spanish. What little Spanish I knew I learned from him. In college we had fun with this, going to bars in Stillwater, Oklahoma, and speaking broken English to girls. We'd tell them we were brothers, which was a credible story in a bar full of strangers because I had one of those faces that could pass for white or Mexican. I suspected my biological father was Hispanic and Tony and I both grew up in Worthington, so for all I knew we were somehow related. I needed Tony to be all-in, but I lost confidence in him when I saw how off he was in the eyes. I wondered if it had to do with his wife divorcing him last fall and taking the kids when she moved to South Carolina a few months later.

"What for?—you ask." I massaged the ropy muscles on the back of my neck, trying to untie the knots. "Let me start from the beginning. Ashley's been abducted."

"Excuse me," said Tony, rocking back in a chair which seemed to moan from the strain.

Keri said, "We've got places in Wichita we need to check out and pictures of people that may be involved. If we can see what they're driving, and get these trackers under their vehicles, the hope is it will lead us to where they are keeping Ashley."

Tony said Ashley's name in a way I didn't want to hear at the moment. His voice was filled with pain and he said "Oh, my God," twice, his eyes now flush with tears. He was a gentle soul, and it reminded me that I hadn't cried over this. I loved my sister and I was scared to death for her. And maybe if I'd cry these knots in my neck would loosen up, but I didn't have it in me. Not yet, anyway.

Tony stood and came around the desk and embraced me again and when he pulled back he reached for Keri. When he was done with her, he sat on the edge of the desk and asked to hear the whole story.

As Keri gave him chapter and verse, I walked over to the window and watched a group of twenty-somethings filling coolers full of beer outside a liquor store on Wichita's South Broadway. They had a grimy old ski boat flying the rebel flag hitched to a jacked-up pickup. The driver had that South Broadway trailer-park strut that invites a debacle wherever it goes. It was their day in the hot sun and I admired their ability to enjoy it. Perhaps they lived in the present in a style that made them ill-suited to prosper, as I defined it. But what did I know anymore? I'd probably be disbarred when this was all over, unemployed, and in the same boat as this rabble. Maybe I should join them now to see what it's like—get ripped and turn my shirtless back lobster-red in their boat on the lake and fistfight with one of them over their horseshit flag.

Tony left us for the back room. When he emerged, he was carrying three GPS trackers—little magnetic rectangular devices that fit into the palm of his hand. He came around to our side of the desk and sat on the edge of it again.

Tony's eyes volleyed from me to Keri. "I was tellin' Ben here a while back, that whenever I have a big bond on a guy I suspect is going to jump, I make a late night visit to his driveway and stick one of these babies underneath the car. My customer has his freedom, and I my peace of mind. You need to download the app on whatever phones you want to use to track these little guys." He held the trackers out to me and I took them. "You need them more than I do. They're yours. How else can I help?"

"Rummell's trial starts again tomorrow morning," I said. "So our plate is full. We're going to run by some businesses the cops suspect the cartel uses to launder its money. Maybe we get lucky and get one of these things under a vehicle today."

"Sure," said Tony. Then he blew out a gust of air and shook his head. "Trial starts again in the morning, huh?"

I nodded. "Can you come with us now?"

"Of course. I'll help whatever way I can."

"We'll take all the help we can get," I said.

Tony clamped his big paw onto my shoulder for a moment, then left the office for the reception room where he told the elderly lady he couldn't help her.

*　*　*

Our first stop in Tony's Ford Taurus was a bar called The Porte in Wichita—Miguel's bar. It was closed on Mondays, so there wasn't much to see except an empty parking lot so we cruised to the next address on the list, this one a strip club called Club Nine on Maize Road in west Wichita. The Internet said it opened for business at 11:00 a.m. so we showed Tony the photos from Miguel's farmhouse along with photos from Mallory's reports. After snapping shots of the photos with his phone, he went in. We watched from the parking lot of a Village Inn across the street. Tony was to call us if he saw a familiar face, but after an hour he called and said there wasn't anybody from the photos in the club at the moment.

Next, we ran Tony all over Wichita and watched him walk into three laundromats, two restaurants and a car wash. He didn't see anyone from the photos.

Around six o'clock, our last stop was a small cinderblock bar called Uncle Sam's in the country south of Wichita on

Highway 81. This was the one place not on Mallory's or the DEA's radar, if the reports we'd been through were an accurate reflection of what they suspected about the cartel's money-laundering operation. I'd found a photograph of Uncle Sam's Bar in Miguel's farmhouse. In the photo, three men were standing in front of the bar I recognized from a lifetime of travel on Highway 81. Judging by the cars in the parking lot and the clothing and hairstyles worn by the men, the photograph was taken circa early '90's.

As we approached Uncle Sam's with Keri driving and Tony in the passenger seat, we saw Baltozar Rummell coming toward us in his Jeep Cherokee, slowing down with his right blinker on, poised to turn into the parking lot at Uncle Sam's.

Before I could say anything, Tony said, "Is that who I think it is?"

"Yep," I said, from the back seat with my baseball hat pulled down tight. "Keep going. Don't turn in."

Keri cruised by the bar at full highway speed as the jeep parked by the bar's front door. There were only two other cars in the lot.

"That wouldn't have been good," Tony said. "I've talked to that guy before. He's been in my place."

There was a good chance that Baltozar would recognize Tony because we were all from Worthington. Plausibly, he'd know we were good friends. It would've been too much of a coincidence—Tony showing up in this little hovel of a bar for the first time two days after the kidnapping.

Tony took us back to his office and Keri and I left for Worthington.

At home, Diablo met us at the door to the kitchen. I scratched him behind his ears and took him out to the edge of the wheat at sunset and threw a stick into it and watched him go. He zipped around in the wheat for a good fifteen minutes until he popped out of it and jumped into a baby pool Keri'd pulled out of the shed and filled with water for him. He plopped his belly down in it and played and drank.

After eating the Schlotzsky's sandwiches we'd grabbed on the way home, Keri and I went to bed at nine o'clock, behind locked doors, next to an open gun safe full of loaded weapons and a champagne-colored pit bull who snored like a bear.

* * *

I reached out for Keri, still half asleep, but she wasn't there. The door to my bedroom was open and I heard voices coming from the living room. Men's voices—a tense conversation. Might be Rod—Ashley's husband. He'd left messages on my answering machine asking me to call him about Ashley. He wanted to know if I knew where she was. I hadn't bothered to call him back. I listened to the voices still coming from the living room. No—this wasn't Rod. The digital clock next to the Glock on the nightstand read 5:23 A.M., and Diablo was gone. I reached down and grabbed my T-shirt off the floor, sat up, and put it on. I went to my dresser for a pair of gym shorts, slipped them over my boxer-briefs, grabbed the pistol, and left for the living room.

Keri and Diablo were sitting on the section of the L couch that faced the TV. Keri's elbows were on her knees, her eyes glued to the screen like they might be if she were watching live news coverage of astronauts walking on Mars. But this was Detective Mallory on the TV screen, his hands entwined behind his head, talking to a white man wearing a fedora and a rumpled button-up shirt, that familiar table I'd seen in all the videos taken at the sheriff's main interview room between them.

"Find anything interesting," I said, plopping down next to her, mimicking her sitting position, except she was holding a remote control in her hand while a pistol dangled between my thighs. Diablo looked around Keri at me like he resented my intrusion, like three was a crowd.

Keri glanced at the pistol. "Ah honey, I'm sorry, I didn't mean to freak you out." She paused the video. "I didn't want to wake you. Thought you needed the sleep."

"I do." I set the gun on the coffee table next to Detective Mallory's files and nodded at the TV screen. "Who's Mallory interviewing here?"

"Randy Harris. Ring any bells?"

"Yeah—kind of—but they're not clangin' very loud right now."

Keri pulled a paper from one of the files and handed it to me. It was a copy of a bench warrant for Randy Harris that bore my signature. He was accused of one count of distributing an $80 bag of crystal meth in February of 2018, not exactly the crime of the century. Seems he'd missed court on March 22, 2018. I looked at the TV, lower right hand corner. The time stamp on the sheriff's video read: MARCH 15, 2018, 3:16 A.M.

"I've watched this interview through to the end already," said Keri. "It ends when Mallory arrests him. Apparently, Harris bonded right out and failed to appear for court a week later. You issued that bench warrant you're holding. This was a week before the Dandurands were murdered."

"So, what's the connection?"

Keri smiled, but there was tightness in her lips. She fast-forwarded through parts of the interview, saying repeatedly, "You're not gonna like this." When she hit play, Randy Harris's fedora was sitting on the table and Mallory was pointing a finger at him.

Detective Mallory said, "I know you get your crystal directly from Miguel. I know Miguel works for his father, Jorge. I know you're a mid-level dealer everyone calls Rabbit. You like to sell your crank in quantities of no less than half a pound to whiteys in the Wichita and Kansas City areas. I also know Jorge and Miguel had a shipment of crystal stolen, and I even know who they think stole it. And maybe Miguel and Jorge are right about that, and if they are, guess what? *Guess* what? Oh yeah—you're pleading the Fifth now so you're a fucking clam. I'll answer for you then. When a small town momma's boy like Eddie Dandurand has nowhere else to turn, he turns to the cops."

Mallory snatched the man's fedora off the table, sniffed at it, made a face, and set it down. Randy Harris flipped Mallory the bird.

Keri paused the video and looked at me, her nostrils flaring. "Seems to me, Detective Mallory got the Dandurands killed."

"Um, I don't know, maybe. If Eddie Dandurand really stole the cartel's crystal, them thinking he was also a snitch woulda just been fuel to the fire."

Keri looked back to the TV, Randy's defiant middle finger frozen on the screen. "Would the prosecutors know about this?"

I shook my head. "I doubt it. Mallory kept all that information out of his failed search warrant affidavit for Miguel's house right after the murders. If he hadn't shared the substance of this interview with any cops or prosecutors prior to the murders, he damn sure wasn't gonna tell anyone about it after the murders. Not after what went down. He'd be crucified."

"Yeah, well maybe he should be crucified. It doesn't seem right."

"Chase a rat through a sewer . . . you end up smellin' like a sewer rat. It's part of the deal."

Keri slumped back into the couch. "I still say it's wrong."

"You're probably right." I looked at the files on the table. "So, did Eddie Dandurand tell Mallory about stealing the cartel's meth or what?"

"Don't know yet. We basically have an entire accordion folder of stuff yet to read . . . DVD's to watch. Some of the DVD's, like the one we just watched, aren't labeled."

I picked up the accordion folder and thumbed through the reports. "So, no clue how Mallory knew all that stuff about the cartel's crystal being stolen?"

"No, but I'm quitting my job today so I can work on that while you're in trial."

"Are you sure you wanna quit your job," I said, hoping she was. I needed the help.

Keri put her hand on my arm and said, "I've never been so sure of anything in my life. Hated that damn job anyway, and besides, I'm about to be a judge's wife, right?"

"Thank you."

"I don't want you to thank me, I want you to marry me."

"Already promised to do that—"

"Promises, promises."

"Set a date, then. I'll be there."

Keri drew her eyes to slits, "You sure?"

I put my hand on her muscular thigh and squeezed. "Never been so sure of anything in my life."

15

Ben

WHEN I ENTERED the People's courtroom on Tuesday morning, they stood, not for me, but out of respect for the rule of law and the Constitution. They stood against the tyranny of men, with respect in their eyes, not knowing I'd crossed the line. I felt their reverence—now more than ever—for the American flag, the law, fellow citizens deceased and living. Looking out across them, I knew this proceeding was an obscenity—an obscenity that was eating me in secret from within.

* * *

I didn't figure fourteen-year-old Haley Dandurand to be the first witness called by the state on Tuesday morning, yet here she was in a courtroom packed with curious locals, news media, and an accused murderer flanked by his attorneys, one at each arm. Rummell's parents, Baltozar and Maria, sat directly behind him in the gallery. The only family member here to support Haley was her uncle, but I was told the state had three bodyguards here in the courthouse to protect her. I'd heard they'd been with her day and night since the hiring of McMaster, when it dawned on Ms. Sweeney that Rummell's defense was probably being funded by the kind of people used to winning by any means necessary. In this light, calling Haley to testify first made sense.

Sweeney was locking down Haley's testimony before anything could happen to her, while weakening any motive to kill her.

Haley held her hand above the pink bow that covered the wound on her head, swearing to tell the whole truth. Before she took the witness chair, she looked up at me with a weak smile. Pangs of guilt complicated the smile I returned to her.

Haley answered a series of questions about her family, the sleeping arrangements in her house that night, and the approximate time she went to bed. When Ms. Sweeney breathed in deeply and exhaled, Haley gripped the cloth on her pink-flowered dress. I knew she had answered her last easy question.

"After you went to bed that night, Haley," said Ms. Sweeney, "tell the court how you were awakened."

"I heard loud noises. Gunshots."

Rummell looked particularly clean-cut today in his long-sleeve white linen shirt and black slacks, like he'd been out selling Bibles door to door. Fourteen months in custody away from his meth had done him good. Gone were the alien tics and twitches. His face and frame had filled out and his smooth cheeks held a pink hue. Rummell stared at Haley with polite indifference, his thick black hair still damp, like he'd recently stepped out of the shower. When she glanced in his direction, her dazed expression seemed to indicate she'd forgotten where she was for the moment. Ms. Sweeney reestablished eye contact with Haley.

The prosecutor was wearing another one of her dark, conservatively cut outfits. She probably had a closetful of suits like this one because it's all I'd ever seen her wear. She looked uncomfortable, seemingly more out of her natural element than she had been in voir dire or during her opening statement. When she clutched the top sheet of her yellow legal pad and held it up to peek at the next page, it quivered, betraying the tremble in her hand.

"The gunshots were coming from where?" asked Ms. Sweeney.

"Mom and Dad's room. There were so many of them. It wouldn't stop."

Haley's voice cracked on the word "stop." The court reporter's fingers zipped from her stenotype to the tissue box. Haley took it from her and balled it up in her fist as tears dropped from her cheeks. She was staring at Ms. Sweeney, waiting for the next question.

The prosecutor swallowed hard. "Did you hear anything besides . . . uh . . . gunshots?"

"I heard Daddy's voice for a second, I thought. During the shots. And there was a loud thud against my wall. It shook the wall."

I let my eyes wander to the defense table. I tried to read their faces—a senseless exercise. McMaster sipped water from a Styrofoam cup, his eyes fixed on Haley. He appeared to be pushing seventy, his skin looking like it had been soaked too long in a brine of alcohol before being slow-smoked to yellow leather. Ms. Thompson, a woman with short grey hair in a grey pant suit, sat catty-corner to the table, taking notes. Rummell's stare was unremarkable for a man with a black-robed ace in the hole.

"What happened then?" asked Ms. Sweeney.

"I got under my bed."

"Okay . . . could you hear what was going on?"

"I heard them walking around. I heard the floor creaking. I heard a door open, and for some reason I thought it was my parents coming to check on me. I know that doesn't make sense."

"Makes perfect sense, Haley."

"Then why was I hiding under my bed?"

Ms. Sweeney looked down at the list of questions on her notepad, tendons shifting under the skin of her hand as she worked the pearls. She finally asked the question most asked by prosecutors everywhere: "What happened next?"

"I got out from under my bed to help Mom and Dad."

"What did you see when you got to their room?"

"Two men with guns."

"What kind of guns?"

"Short ones."

"Like handguns?"

"Yeah."

"Could you see the faces of the men?"

"No."

"Was it dark in the room?"

"No. The light was on. They were wearing masks."

"What kind of masks?"

"Like a ski mask you pull over your face."

"Can you describe the build of these men?"

"Both skinny."

"Were the men wearing long-sleeve shirts?"

"No. Short sleeves."

"Can you describe the arms of these men?"

"The skinny white one had tattoos on one of his arms."

My eyes wandered over to Rummell again. The long sleeves of his white linen shirt weren't quite long enough to hide the green ink on his right arm at his wrist. That would hurt anyone selling innocence in these parts.

"Can you describe the tattoos?" asked Ms. Sweeney.

"Looked like a bunch of clowns on one of his arms."

"What happened after you got to the room?"

"They saw me and before I could run, the Hispanic one grabbed me by my arm."

"What makes you say he was Hispanic?"

"The men were both talking, yelling back and forth at each other. The one that had me sounded Hispanic."

"Were they speaking Spanish?"

"No. It was English. Just the one had an accent."

"Did anything else make you think the one that grabbed you was Hispanic?"

"His skin was like, you know, browner."

"So the Hispanic one grabbed you, held you back . . ."

Ms. Sweeney paused. Haley melted in the witness chair.

Rummell, McMaster, and Ms. Thompson looked on in stone-faced silence. Baltozar and Maria did the same. The reporters in the gallery bore pained expressions on their faces, as did Haley's uncle. It seemed as if no one in the room was even breathing.

"Tell the court what happened then, Haley," said Ms. Sweeney.

Haley ignored the tissue box the court reporter set beside her and began talking in a low whisper no one could understand while tears spilled from her eyes, dripped down her cheeks.

"Haley, do you need a break?" I asked.

She glanced at me and shook her head. "I saw my mom in bloody sheets on the bed and I saw blood on the wall. I couldn't see my dad but I know now he was on the floor on the other side of the bed."

Haley bowed her head and covered her face with her hands.

"Let's take a recess," I said.

"No. I want to finish," Haley whispered, raising her wet face to gaze directly at Rummell through the pools in her eyes.

He looked away. She had caught him off guard. She had broken his emotionless trance. When he was done looking at the wall to his left, he glanced up to the bench and our eyes met. His eyes were asking: *When the time comes, are you going to be able to do this?*

"Sure," I said. "We can continue."

I glanced at Ms. Sweeney to give her the go-ahead.

"What happened next, Haley?"

"The one holding me shot me in the head. I saw a bunch of white light flashes. Then everything went dark."

"What happened when you came to?"

"I heard voices."

"What were they saying?"

"I couldn't make out what they were saying at first. It was like I was in a dream."

"Did you ever make out what the voices were saying?"

"Yes, but it didn't make any sense. It was like a bad dream where nothing makes sense and you can't move. So I played dead. I remember thinking I was dreaming and that I was playing dead in my dream."

"What were the voices saying that didn't make sense?"

"They were talking about what to do with Eddie."

"Your older brother?"

"Yes. They were talking about roasting him like a pig—or something like that."

Ms. Sweeney walked Haley through her escape out of the upstairs window and to the neighbor's house a mile down the road. She showed Haley a damaged metal hairclip, and Haley identified it as the one she'd worn that night. It had deflected the bullet and saved her life. Then Ms. Sweeney showed her the ski mask Mallory found in Rummell's flipped-over Mustang a mile from the Dandurand house. She said it looked like the ones she'd seen on the men in the house.

"Your Honor," said Ms. Sweeney. "I would request that the defendant bare his right arm so the witness can see it. I have a few questions about the tattoos."

McMaster rose from his chair and said, "So the witness can say those were the tattoos she saw that night, Your Honor? That's leading, and unduly suggestive, and we object."

"Overruled," I said.

McMaster nodded to his client, who stood and unbuttoned the right cuff of his shirt and began working the sleeve up his arm.

"Push it up further, Mr. Rummell," I said. "That's not even halfway up to your elbow."

"It won't go any further," said Rummell.

"Then we'll take a recess and find you a short sleeve shirt," I said.

Rummell shook his head, undid the top button of his shirt.

"Mr. Rummell," I said, "what do you think you're doing?"

But Rummell's shirt was already open, his rib cage and sunken stomach visible. He whipped his shirt off like he was amped for a fistfight and it hit the carpet as deputies approached from either side.

"Hold on fellas" I said to the deputies. "Let the record reflect that Mr. Rummell has taken his shirt off in the courtroom."

"If I may, Your Honor?" said McMaster, looking at me, then his client, his arms spread apart, his fingers splayed out. He gave his client that look—calm the fuck down.

The intensity on McMaster's face vanished when he stopped glaring at Rummell and cut his eyes back to me. For me,

McMaster wore the sympathetic face of a therapist. "I think this is my client's way of trying to cooperate. He obviously isn't trying to hide anything. Maybe we take advantage of the moment and have the witness view the tattoos right now."

Ms. Sweeney nodded and said, "No objection."

"Very well," I said. "Deputies, bring Mr. Rummell into the well here, closer to the witness."

A deputy gripped Rummell's boney left arm and escorted him toward Haley.

"Close enough," I said.

Rummell's right arm was entirely inked in clowns.

Ms. Sweeney broke the silence. "Do you recognize any of the tattoos on the defendant?"

"That's the arm. Those are the clowns I saw that night."

Ms. Sweeney flipped her notepad closed and said, "No further questions."

*   *   *

McMaster stood and dangled his client's shirt from his finger as the deputy returned the defendant to the counsel table. He kept his eyes glued on a yellow legal pad he was holding in his other hand, never looking up. Rummell retrieved his shirt from McMaster like he was taking a coat off a rack.

While Rummell dove back into his shirt, McMaster dropped the legal pad on the table and snatched up a photo Ms. Thompson had produced from her briefcase. He showed it to Ms. Sweeney to comply with the court procedure for admitting exhibits into evidence. The back of it had a defendant's exhibit sticker. Ms. Sweeney shrugged and showed the photo to her second chair from the AG's office, Mr. Davidson, who shrugged in turn. The prosecutor then handed it back to McMaster, who turned to me.

"May I approach the witness?" asked McMaster.

"You may," I said.

McMaster walked over to Haley and handed her the photo and she immediately began inspecting it. I caught a glimpse of the exhibit and knew it was a photo of a person, but I didn't have a good angle and Haley held it against her dress after she'd looked at it.

"I've handed you defendant's exhibit A," said McMaster. "Do you recognize the person in that photo?"

"Yes."

"Where did you see him?"

"In the barn."

"Your barn?"

"Yeah."

"When was this?"

"A couple of months before my family was murdered."

"How many times did you see him?"

"A couple of times in the barn with Eddie."

"Do you know his name?"

"No—I don't think so."

"Does the name Juan Mendez-Mendoza ring a bell?"

I felt a jolt shoot through me. I knew I had visibly twitched. I balled up my fists behind the high bench that shielded me and looked down at my lap before peering out across the room. McMaster's eyes were on Haley and hers were on him—and every other eye in the courtroom was on the two of them.

"No," said Haley. "I didn't ever know his name."

McMaster nodded like he didn't care about her last answer before asking, "Did Detective Mallory, or any other law enforcement officer, ever ask you about this Juan Mendez-Mendoza?"

"No. Someone else. They asked me about someone else."

"They show you a picture of this someone else?"

"Yeah."

McMaster showed another photo to Ms. Sweeney before handing it to Haley.

"Take a look at defendant's exhibit B for me, Haley. Do you recognize the person in that photo?"

"No. This guy looks older. The guy I saw was younger."

Haley placed the photo that was state's exhibit B on the counter and I saw it was a photo of Miguel.

"Did the police ever show you this photo of the older Hispanic guy?"

"Yeah. I told them I didn't think this was the guy I'd seen in the barn. But I wasn't sure. I told them the Hispanic guy in the barn looked Eddie's age."

"And Eddie was twenty-one?"

"Yes."

"Did the police ever ask you about a man named Miguel Mendez-Mendoza?"

"I think I remember them asking. I don't know anybody by that name."

A sheen of sweat had formed on Ms. Sweeney's forehead and she appeared to be holding her breath, watching her star witness, a child, in the throes of cross-examination. From where I sat, Sweeney had it easy. At least she hadn't killed the man depicted in defendant's exhibit A two days earlier. Visions of Juan's head bleeding out in that field flashed through me.

"You ever see my client before?" McMaster asked Haley, while pointing to Rummell.

"Well, that night I saw—"

"I'm not asking about the clown tattoos you saw on someone's arm. I'm asking if you ever saw my client with Eddie in the barn."

"No."

"Did you ever see my client anywhere with Eddie?"

"No."

"Did Eddie ever talk about anyone named Vaughn?"

"No."

"What would you say is the race of the man in the photograph, defendant's exhibit A?"

Haley picked up the photo of Juan and said, "Mexican. Hispanic."

"Same as the one who held you back—shot you?"

"Yes."

I felt the first ripples in the calm waters of an assumption I'd held cutting loose and it didn't feel good. I felt my mind trying to close the door on it. *If I had already killed the only other murderer in that field, perhaps the cartel no longer cared what happened to Vaughn Rummell—and where did that leave Ashley?* I gripped the arms of my chair to steady myself.

"That Mexican-Hispanic guy in the photo there you are holding, the young one—you ever see him drive anything?"

"An old green car. I don't know cars."

"I understand. Can you give me a shade of green?"

"Like the color of Kermit the frog."

McMaster smiled, baring his receding gums. He walked to his counsel table and took a photo from a smug-faced Ms. Thompson and showed it to Ms. Sweeney and she gave a nod.

"Haley, I'm handing you defendant's exhibit C," said McMaster, as he approached the witness box while getting the visual okay from me to do so. "Do you recognize this?"

"That's the younger one's car," said Haley. "But it wasn't wrecked like that."

"Did you see him drive this car?"

"No, but it was always at the barn when he was."

"Did you see this green car anywhere around your property when you escaped out through the second-story window of your house that night?"

"No. I didn't see it."

When McMaster handed Haley the photo of Juan again, she placed the one of his green Cutlass Supreme on the counter in front of the court reporter where I could see it. The Cutlass was shown wrecked in the field where I'd left it.

Haley studied the photo of Juan.

As McMaster strolled back to his podium, his back to Haley, he seemed to be looking at Baltozar, whose face looked more red and bloated than usual—the color of a steak that leaves pools of blood on a plate. He looked like I felt—a pent-up bundle of stress and high blood pressure. This was all too personal. Maria was looking down at her lap, eyes closed. She touched the wooden cross hanging from her necklace, still looking down. I think she was praying.

I could join her—we could pray for the same thing—we could pray that Juan wasn't the lone accomplice. Because if he was, the Mendez-Mendoza family might have lost their incentive to leverage my judgment of acquittal, and the state no longer had any need for information from Rummell. He would have nothing to trade the state for his life, and I would have nothing to trade the kidnappers for the life of my sister. The idea my kid sister was dead seemed to materialize inside me—felt like snakes writhing in my gut. One of them seemed to be trying to work its way up my throat.

At the podium, McMaster turned to face Haley. "How would you describe the build of this Mexican guy in the photo you're looking at?"

"Skinny."

"A skinny Mexican," said McMaster rhetorically. "A skinny Hispanic—driving a Kermit-the-frog-green, Cutlass Supreme. What were Juan and Eddie up to out there in the barn, Haley? You know?"

"I don't really know. Eddie kept me away. He kicked me out."

"You don't really know," said McMaster. "But Haley, don't you kind of know?"

Haley looked as if she didn't understand the question.

McMaster retooled it for her. "Was Eddie a drug dealer?"

Ms. Sweeney stood. "Objection. Foundation. Calls for speculation."

I sustained the objection.

McMaster took his seat and said, "No further questions."

Ms. Sweeney stood and said, "No redirect, Your Honor."

I announced a recess, left the bench, and strode down the back hallway to my chambers. My head was splitting in half, and I didn't know what else to do except take 800 milligrams of Ibuprofen. But I had a much bigger problem—one that four little red pills wouldn't solve. Killing Juan may have sealed Ashley's fate.

16

Ben

I WENT TO the restroom on the first floor and splashed cold water over my face and head. Then I did it again. I tried to pray, but I couldn't quiet my mind. My thoughts ran where they would. Faith was so easy in the pew on Sunday, in between well-groomed folks chanting the Lord's Prayer, willing themselves to fear no evil before heading out the door for some fried chicken. But sitting on the bench, watching the case march on felt like being alone in a pit full of vipers—no rest, no relief, and you couldn't fight your way out because they were all over you, exercising their dominion and crawling where they would. Something told me the snakes will have their way—a hissing whisper on a loop in my head. But I would never give up, not because I didn't have a choice, but because I was too stubborn and crazy to cave in.

When I reconvened court, the state called Detective Raymond Mallory to the stand. Ms. Sweeney elicited his testimony, bit by bit. The evidence was damning. Rummell had been found on a dirt road a mile from the scene of the murders, pinned to the ground by his vehicle, lying next to a Hi-Point 9mm pistol. Sweeney had told the jury in her opening statement that the firearms examiner would testify that this pistol had fired the bullets the coroner pulled from the dead bodies of the parents, Steven and Edith Dandurand.

But the most damning piece of evidence may have been state's exhibit 1—the video of Rummell's confession. I admitted it into evidence over McMaster's continuing objection.

In an effort to keep the jury from ever hearing Rummell's incriminating statements, McMaster had unsuccessfully argued in a motion to suppress six months earlier that the confession was involuntary, and that Rummell hadn't understood his Miranda rights when he waived them. Despite having raised the issue earlier, McMaster was required to object to the evidence again at trial so appellate defenders could take up the issue in appellate court when the trial was over—standard operating procedure. He could've asked me to reconsider my ruling outside the presence of the jury, now that the cartel had me bent over a barrel, but that wasn't the smart play. The grounds for suppression were weak. McMaster probably figured any ruling in his favor only delayed matters because Sweeney would certainly exercise the state's right to file an interlocutory appeal, a type of appeal available only to the state that would postpone the trial until an appellate court checked my work. If I suppressed the confession, the Kansas Supreme Court would probably overturn that ruling anyway, putting the confession back in front of the jury. McMaster was laying back, playing it cool. No need to tip his hand or get cute. They had me. The hay was in the barn.

I granted Sweeney permission to play the videotaped confession in open court. McMaster had scored points early with the jury—for what it was worth—but Sweeney was hitting back hard with this devastating one-two combination.

The court reporter killed the lights and hit the switch that lowered the screen from a slit in the drop ceiling. We all watched the screen—an emaciated meth-addicted Vaughn Rummell sitting alone in an interview room—blades of grass from the ditch still in his hair and on his clothes, which were soiled and rumpled.

When Mallory was seen entering the room, Rummell spoke first. "I'll tell you what happened, but I'm not answering a bunch of bullshit questions."

"Sure. I'm like Burger King . . . have it your way," said Mallory, who then proceeded to recite him his Miranda rights.

Rummell waived them without any objection whatsoever and gave his confession, which contradicted Haley's version in one important way. He claimed he acted alone. He said he had come through an unlocked door in the mudroom and lay behind a desk in the unoccupied den. He said he was learning the sounds of the house—toilets flushing, the drip of a faucet somewhere. He told Mallory he lay there a couple of hours, waiting for the family to stop moving around. Then he left the den.

"When I got to the living room I saw Eddie," Rummell told Mallory. "I was going to shoot him, but he wasn't moving there on the couch so I stood there watching him sleep until I realized I could do anything I wanted to do to him so I took out my knife and jammed it into his neck. He kind of rose up, hands around his own throat, sucking for air until he dropped and twitched on the floor while I kept hacking at him. It wasn't easy. I was breathing so hard when I was done I thought I was having a heart attack. The adrenaline, you know. I had to get me some more of that, so I said fuck it and went upstairs and shot the rest of 'em all to hell."

Through the semi-darkness I saw Maria in the gallery, wiping tears from her eyes as she listened to her son's confession. She didn't look up to watch him on the screen.

The rest of the video consisted of Rummell not answering any questions about why he did what he did. Mallory asked him five different times if Miguel was with him in the house, and he denied each time that he had an accomplice. Rummell stuck to his story—no one was with him.

At one point during the interrogation, Mallory began referring to Miguel as "El Guapo." I knew from my days as a prosecutor that this was part of a common interview technique detectives taught each other at conferences. It was intended to make Mallory appear all-knowing in the eyes of the suspect, so he would eventually come to see lying as a futile exercise. Mallory even added details, explaining how the nickname derived from one of Miguel's father's fighting cocks—"a wine-red sweater rooster with white legs"—and that "El Guapo" means "the handsome one."

In response, Rummell only said, "Look, you know I've heard of the man. Most people call him 'El Comeniños' behind his back. I don't know if we're talking about the same guy, but nobody was with me so it don't matter."

"Okay," Mallory said, closing his notepad and moving to within a foot of Rummell's nose while trying to make eye contact. "Maybe you can help me with something—then I'm going to wrap this up."

"Shoot."

"Why did you do that to Eddie? Why'd you go back downstairs and set all that up with the rebar—the whole scene there in the living room?"

"You know how there's a Holy Ghost?"

"I've heard of that."

"I had a little touch of something like that. Felt movement—something greater than me . . . moving in me."

"You sure that wasn't the crystal?"

"Fuck you."

The interview ended just like that, so Ms. Sweeney shut off the video and the court reporter flicked on the lights. Maria covered her eyes with a hand that held what was left of a tissue as Ms. Sweeney announced she had no further questions for Detective Mallory.

We'd gone deep into the noon hour watching the videotaped confession. I ordered the noon recess.

17

Ben

KERI WAS SITTING in my executive's chair, a plate of pork ribs on the desk in front of her, my old suitcase-sized briefcase on rollers at her feet. She dropped a bone on her plate and smiled, still chewing. She wore a navy blue top, white shorts, and deck shoes.

I hung my robe on the coat rack and pointed at the briefcase she brought from my house. I assumed it was full of Mallory's reports. "Working lunch?"

Keri nodded at the door behind me.

I closed it, hit the lock, and took in the spread. Burnt ends, ribs, coleslaw, pig beans, and a tipped-over sack of napkins and plasticware, all from Joe's Barbecue. With the exception of Pops' barbecue, and maybe Gates in Kansas City, it was my favorite.

The smoky smell made my dry mouth water and I realized how depleted I'd become. I dropped into one of the chairs in front of my desk, screwed the cap off a sweaty bottle of water and chugged the whole thing.

Keri's mouth parted a little. "You're not going to burp now are you?"

"I'm hoping this helps finish off my headache."

A steady rush of wind made a howling noise in the windows and the tops of the elm trees on the courthouse lawn danced in the sun. I clicked on the box fan Nancy had brought up from the basement and it immediately sounded like a small prop plane was in the room preparing for takeoff. I pulled the plug on the fan, loosened my blue-striped tie, undid the top button of my shirt, and rolled up my sleeves. Sweat rolled down my neck as I stabbed a burnt end with a plastic fork and rolled it in barbecue sauce.

Keri unsnapped my briefcase and pulled out a stack of papers. "These are the records of one of Mallory's informants, CI 2016-5. He went by the name of Arturo Gallegos, an undocumented alien. It looks to me like all the information Mallory had on Miguel, Jorge, and Randy Harris came from CI 2016-5, not Eddie Dandurand."

I picked up a rib and the caramelized meat practically fell off the bone. "Maybe Mallory got the information from Eddie too."

Keri shook her head. "Huh-uh, I don't think so." She reached into my case, pulled out a disc, and held it up. "Here's the interview Mallory did with Eddie D two days before he interviewed Randy Harris. Eddie took the Fifth. Didn't say a single word. Just held up four fingers and a thumb the whole time Mallory was talking. Mallory told the kid he was making the biggest mistake of his life and Eddie laughed in his face. Pissed Mallory off something royal."

Keri tapped a blue nail on my desk. "I think Mallory retaliated by suggesting to Randy Harris that Eddie Dandurand was a snitch."

"Retaliated? Maybe. Or maybe he was giving cover to his informant. Cops are loyal to their CI's in my experience . . . will do anything to protect them. Everyone else can go fuck themselves."

"Eddie Dandurand was just a kid."

"Eddie Dandurand was a young man who made some bad choices."

Keri pursed her lips and shook her head.

"Look," I said, "I'm not saying what Mallory did was right, I'm trying to tell you how it is."

"Even if Mallory did this to give cover to his informant, if he knew the whole story he wouldn't have felt obliged to do so."

Keri pulled a report from the rest of the stack and set it in front of me on the table. I read, my elbows on the desk, my hands holding either side of a rib.

But Keri gave it to me in a nutshell. "Three days after the Randy Harris interview, Mallory learned from the DEA about his CI's association with the Angel Trevino Cartel—so maybe he didn't need much protecting. The DEA thinks Arturo Gallegos's real name is Geronimo Baylon-Fontana, only Mallory probably didn't know that until after his interview with Randy Harris."

Keri put a burnt end in her mouth and picked at her coleslaw with a fork. I skimmed through Mallory's report and saw that Geronimo was supposedly from Matamoros, Tamaulipas, directly across from Brownsville, Texas, on the border, seventeen miles from the Gulf of Mexico. This was considered Trevino Cartel turf. According to the report, the DEA seemed to think Geronimo's half-uncle was Angel Trevino himself. Everything in the report was a conclusion that came straight from the DEA. Their sources were not revealed.

I dropped a rib on my plate and grabbed another. "Is there some explanation as to why Geronimo was talking to a cop, any cop, let alone a small-timer like Detective Mallory?"

Keri wiped her mouth with a napkin and shook her head, "Huh-uh, but I haven't got all the way through the files yet either."

"Because in my experience, that's not normal behavior for anyone connected to any cartel."

Keri slapped another report in front of me. "When Mallory found out from the DEA that his informant wasn't who he said he was, he unsuccessfully tried to make contact with him for an explanation, but Geronimo was long gone. At least that's what this typewritten report indicates. But . . . look at this."

She pulled a small spiral notepad out of the briefcase and flipped it open to some handwritten notes. Cops called these field notes. "Not the easiest writing in the world to read, but look at that right there." She set the notepad on the desk before me and put her finger on the scribbled words on the first line. "What's that say to you?"

It read GERONIMO B. FONT. PH. CALL MAR 29 '18. CALLED FROM PH #405-943-9205, UNDISCLOS LOCATION.

"March twenty-ninth of last year," I said. "That's the day of the Dandurand murders. Geronimo called from an undisclosed location?"

Keri nodded. I tried to make out the rest of the note. It read JGE MEN-ROD. ORDRED MIG MEN-MNDZA TO CARRY OUT . . . WORD AT UNC. SAM'S.

I wiped my hands with a napkin and opened a second bottle of water. "Uncle Sam's? Did Geronimo say they laundered money there or what?"

"Yeah," said Keri. "That's what Geronimo told Detective Mallory, back when he was pretending to be Arturo Gallegos."

She produced another typewritten report and set it on top of the notepad. "So, check this out. Geronimo hung out at Uncle Sam's quite a bit leading up to the Dandurand murders, doing work for the Mendez-Rodriguez Cartel—small time stuff like providing security at the bar, ringing up drink orders that never happened—"

"Laundering money."

Keri licked her lips and said, "Yeah, and he was passing on things he claimed to learn to Detective Mallory for some reason." Keri pointed to the report. "Do you recognize anybody on that list of people he knew from Uncle Sam's Bar?"

I scanned the report. "Baltozar Rummell."

Keri nodded. "Yep, Vaughn Rummell's daddy. Geronimo told Mallory that Baltozar was just a bartender as far as he knew. Said Balto probably sold drinks to ghosts when legitimate business got slow in the bar, but he wasn't sure about that."

I nodded at the reports. "So what exactly does Geronimo know about the Mendez-Rodriguez Cartel's operation and how does he know it? Mallory would need specifics, and how would any of this pertain to his jurisdiction anyway?"

"No answers for you on the jurisdiction question and Geronimo's sources are sketchy. Doesn't seem like he'd infiltrated too deep. He seemed to be at a stage where he kind of hung around the hangers-on, but he heard things . . . or claimed to anyway. That's what I gleaned from what I've read so far. The story he told Mallory is basically this: Vaughn Rummell worked as a deejay at The Porte, a business Jorge and Miguel probably used to launder some of their drug money. Juan, may he rest in peace, took a liking to Rummell's gig, and the two of them kind of put together a little act—started hanging out together a lot—deejaying at clubs, weddings, drug parties, whatever. This too, Geronimo guessed, was part of the overall money-laundering operation. Anyway, Juan was brought in on some of Miguel's trafficking activities and had information about a dead drop location and slipped up and told Vaughn Rummell about it, who in turn bragged to buddies of his—band members of a frequent act at The Porte that goes by the name Chainsaw. These guys couldn't help themselves and boosted twenty pounds of cartel crystal."

"Vaughn Rummell did gigs in Miguel's bar, The Porte, and his father bartended at Uncle Sam's. What's the connection?"

"Haven't found anything yet, but there're pages of these handwritten notes I haven't had time to decipher. Cryptic and hard to read. Could be a coincidence, right?"

"No. I don't believe in coincidences like that. Maybe Baltozar got in good with the Mendez-Rodriguez Cartel and got his boy the gig."

Keri popped a burnt end into her mouth. "Father of the year."

"Little cheese dips had the time of their lives for a while I'm guessing, 'til they realized it was a death sentence. And now . . . this shit-show lands on Ashley. Lands in my courtroom."

It was all coming out of me now. Death penalty cases suck the life out of the participants, but this was ten times worse than anything I'd ever experienced. It felt like I was running out of time and we'd just begun. "I need to find a way to demand proof of life. Somehow. Shit. Goddammit. Poor Ashley."

Keri leaned back in her chair. There was nothing to say. She seemed to sense I needed a moment.

I finished off three ribs and a carton of slaw, ruminating about whether or not to fake an illness and take the afternoon to study Mallory's files. Keri was a smart paralegal, the kind that—with time, money, desire, and confidence—could get through law school and put ninety percent of the lawyer population to shame. But the fact was, I was the one with the training and experience. I was the one whose job it was to solve this puzzle. I decided it had to wait, though. I didn't want to raise any flags with the Mendez-Rodriguez Cartel this early in the game. I'd have to lean on Keri, and somehow find the time to review the reports evenings and nights.

Keri dumped her plate in the trash can behind her and said, "Anyway, the number Geronimo called from on March twenty-ninth of last year isn't currently in use, but 405 is Oklahoma City's area code."

"That doesn't necessarily mean anything. With burner phones, you have the option to create your own telephone number—can choose any ol' area code you want."

"Yeah, I know that, but listen to me." She waved at my briefcase and said, "These reports reference folks in Oklahoma City with suspected ties to the Trevino Cartel. The kind of folks who've come into too much real estate and too many high dollar racehorses too quick. Maybe Geronimo went down there."

"Or, if he's smart, back to Mexico."

Keri pursed her lips and looked out the window. "Let me ask you this. Could Mallory have used that information he got from Geronimo in the search warrant for Miguel's house back in 2018?"

"From what I know it probably did him more harm than good. An informant who lies about his identity to the cops isn't reliable, especially one who's connected to a rival cartel and has a big-time agenda—one that, maybe even Detective Mallory didn't fully comprehend. And like you said, his informant hadn't made his way far enough into the cartel to know anything yet. At a minimum, Detective Mallory would've looked like an idiot if he'd flown that kite."

"Maybe so, but I think he still has visions of meeting up with Geronimo again."

"What makes you say that?"

"The Oklahoma City Dodgers have a three-game stand against the El Paso Chihuahuas coming up—June fourth, fifth, and sixth. Mallory has tickets to all three games. Right behind the visitors' dugout."

She tossed three tickets on the desk before me. "Found those in his files paper-clipped together behind the Geronimo reports."

I glanced at them, then at Keri. "Mallory enjoys Triple-A ball. So what?"

"So, I looked up the rosters for both teams. The Chihuahuas have a left fielder named Manuel Baylon-Fontana, from Matamoros, Tamaulipas—same town as Geronimo. I printed Manuel's photo off the Chihuahuas' website. Here's Geronimo and Manuel side by side."

I looked at the photos and saw a striking resemblance. It looked to me like we were dealing with another set of brothers, one of them in the Trevino Cartel, the other, one step away from playing for the Padres in the major leagues. "You think Mallory hopes to run into Geronimo at the ballpark watching his brother?"

"Yeah, what else could he be thinking?"

I looked at the tickets. I'd played a lot of baseball in the Chickasaw Bricktown Ballpark, called the Southwestern Bell Bricktown Ballpark when I was in college. It was the site of the Big 12 tournament all four years I'd played. It was also where we'd played our games against the Sooners every year. I hadn't been to the park in years, despite the short drive of two and a half hours.

Keri said, "Presumably, Mallory will be busy with Rummell's trial all three days until at least five, so with the games starting at six o'clock, he'll miss a good chunk of all three games. And Mallory only has one ticket for each day. Why would he drive that far to watch part of three Triple-A ball games by himself three days in a row?"

"Interesting, but I'm not sure what we can do with this information."

"Do you think Mallory's a dirty cop?"

"Dirty as in cuts corners? Oh yeah, for sure."

"No, I mean dirty, as in evil."

I wiped my mouth and slouched in my chair. "I don't know, this all strikes me as one of those road to hell things."

"Meaning?"

"Meaning—and I'm giving the guy the benefit of the doubt here—most cops' intentions are basically good, but it's true what they say, I think, about the road to hell being paved with good intentions."

I cut my eyes from Keri to a copy of the Constitution I swore to uphold that was sitting on my desk. Whatever I was doing, when this was over and the truth was out, I will have undermined the public's confidence in the rule of law. "I'm not judging him. You asked my opinion so I gave it to you. After what's happened over the last three and a half days . . . I feel like I've laid pavement on that path to hell myself."

18

Ben

IT WAS ALMOST two o' clock in the afternoon when McMaster began his cross-examination of Detective Mallory from his seat at the counsel table. For about twenty minutes, he picked on Detective Mallory for getting a confession from a meth addict, who may or may not have had any meth in his system at the time. Judging by the looks jurors cast at Rummell—jutted chins, furrowed brows—McMaster's contention that the confession was unreliable was going over like bacon on a vegan's pizza. McMaster poured himself a cup of water, wet his dry, cracked lips, and moved on.

"On the night of the Dandurand murders, you submitted a search warrant affidavit to the Honorable Benjamin Joel, correct?"

"Yes, I submitted several to him that night."

"Did Judge Joel grant all of them?"

"No, there was one he did not grant."

"Which one was that?"

"The one for Miguel Mendez-Mendoza's property on Eden Road."

McMaster was up now, strolling to the podium.

"You thought there was evidence on that property connected to the murders, correct?

"Yes."

"Are you still interested in searching Miguel Mendez-Mendoza's property on Eden Road for evidence of the Dandurand murders?"

"No. You know I'm not."

"How would I know that, Detective?"

"Because we searched his property and the fields behind it this weekend—late Saturday night, and well into late Sunday afternoon. I was there when Ms. Sweeney told you all about this on Sunday morning."

"Fair enough. What did you find?"

"Well, we found six dead bodies in the field, for starters."

Everyone in the courtroom seemed to stir as one. The gruesome discovery was already known to the public, but now a connection to the Dandurand murders had been confirmed. I noted in particular the excited faces of the TV reporters who managed to contain their glee while I took a sip of water to wet my drying mouth.

"Any idea how long they'd been there?" asked McMaster.

"Not real sure, but two of the bodies were warm when we got there. Four of them weren't."

"These bodies—men? Women? Children?"

"All adult men."

"Tell the court the race of these men."

"Five Hispanic. One white."

"Would you describe the build of any of these men you found dead in the field as skinny?"

"Skinny?"

"Yeah," said McMaster. "Skinny, or lanky, like the killers described by Haley."

Detective Mallory smiled. "Yes. Two of the men found dead in the field were skinny."

"So, these two bodies—the skinny ones—were they warm or cold?"

Mallory glanced at me, then back to McMaster. "The two skinny bodies were warm."

"Now, Detective, I have some of your photos—obtained from Ms. Sweeney—that I'm going to hand to you."

McMaster returned to the counsel table momentarily to collect the photos from Ms. Thompson. Before bringing them to Mallory, he tried showing them to Ms. Sweeney, but she waved him off. Finally, he handed them to Detective Mallory, who shuffled through them quickly and then looked up.

"Do you recognize the photos marked defendant's exhibit D and E?"

"I was there when they were taken," said Mallory.

"All fair and accurate depictions of the skinny dead men you found in the field two days ago?"

"Yes sir."

"I would move to admit defendant's exhibits D and E, Your Honor."

Ms. Sweeney stood and said, "No objection."

I admitted the exhibits into evidence. McMaster walked back to the podium and looked through the notes on his legal pad for a moment.

"What's the name of the dead Hispanic man pictured in exhibit D?"

"We are not sure," said Mallory.

"You are not sure? How can that be?"

"He did not have an ID on him. And there were no documents in the car."

I could help them with this. I had Juan's Mexican DL and the contents of the glove box at my house.

"What about the car's tag?" asked McMaster.

"The tag comes back to a different car—a grey on blue Cutlass Supreme owned by the manager of the McDonald's on South Broadway in Wichita. The owner had no idea his tag had been stolen—swapped out for an expired tag of another car, a junkyard Mitsubishi."

"The skinny dead Hispanic in the field pictured in exhibit D—was his body warm?"

"Yes."

"Had you ever seen him before you found him dead in the field?"

"No."

"Ever investigate him?"

"Nope."

McMaster made his way over to the court reporter and snapped up the photo of the living Juan Mendez-Mendoza. He held it up for Mallory to see side by side with the photo of Juan's dead body in the field.

"The dead man in the photo there in the field in defendant's exhibit D," said McMaster. "Is that the same man pictured alive in defendant's exhibit A?"

Mallory looked them over. "Hard to say—maybe."

McMaster peeked over the photos he continued to hold up in front of Mallory and said, "Hmm. I see what you mean. This one's face has been through a lot," pointing at Juan's face and head. "Those gunshot wounds?"

"Yes sir."

"Did you run the deceased man's—the skinny Hispanic one—did you run his fingerprints through your database?"

"Yes, we ran his prints through AFIS." Mallory turned to the jury. "That's the Automated Fingerprint Identification System. There were no matches."

"What's that mean to you, Detective?"

"Basically it means he has never been arrested here in America."

"Here in America? You think this man is from another country?"

"We're working on that."

"Let's move on to the other warm body. The skinny white male. Take a look at defendant's exhibit E for me, Detective. Have you determined the identity of that man?"

"Not definitively. No."

"It's my understanding you found no identification on him either, correct?"

"Correct."

"What other difficulties have you encountered in determining the identity of this man?"

"He's missing his head."

At that bit of testimony, a barely suppressed squeal slipped out of one of the reporters, sending a ripple through the rest of the gallery. I saw excitement on one reporter's face. He'd be selling darkness on the television tonight and ratings would soar.

McMaster let the gallery compose themselves before asking, "And what's the problem with running this man's fingerprints through your database?"

"The tips of his fingers were cut off."

A collective gasp filled the courtroom, but the young lady on the front row from Channel Three was louder than the rest. She locked eyes with me and was already mouthing the words "I'm sorry."

"Ladies and gentlemen," I said. "If you can't contain yourselves, I'll have you removed from the courtroom."

McMaster turned all the way around and took stock of the gallery. When he looked back at me and saw I was done with them, he turned toward Detective Mallory to resume his cross-examination.

"You've neither located the man's fingertips, nor his head?"

"It wasn't for lack of trying."

"Are there any identifying marks on this body you're looking into, to help you identify the body?"

"Yes."

"What kind of marks?"

"He has the tattoos you see there in the photo."

"A picture says a thousand words, doesn't it?"

Detective Mallory looked at McMaster and didn't even pretend to think about answering.

McMaster continued, "Haley Dandurand told one of the sheriff's investigators that the white killer had a sleeve of clown tattoos on his right arm, correct?"

"Yes."

"That's a pretty good description of the tattoos on my client, is it not?"

"It is."

"And it's also a pretty good description of the tattoos on what's left of this guy you found in the field, is it not?"

"It is."

"Right arm of a white guy and everything, right?"

"Yes."

McMaster walked over to his client and told him to roll his sleeves back. Rummell did, only getting the shirt half-way up his arm again. McMaster clasped the skinny inked-up arm, held it up, and said, "In fact, would it be fair to say that the sleeve of tattoos on the headless man's right arm is exactly the same as this one on my client's right arm?"

Detective Mallory nodded. "I'd agree with that."

McMaster strolled back to the podium, asking a question as he did. "Do you think any of these men were executed in the field?"

"We're still working through everything, but yeah, that's one of the things we're sorting out."

"I mean, I assume the one guy didn't cut his own head off," said McMaster.

Ms. Sweeney didn't flinch. She was letting McMaster's improper statement ride.

"Listen," said Mallory, "I'm not disagreeing with you necessarily, there's a lot of evidence to sort through. It's very early."

"So early that you've made no arrests."

"True."

"Did you, or any of the deputies, find anyone alive in the field when you got there?"

"No, we did not."

"Were any vehicles stopped on the surrounding roads?"

"No, they had too much of a head start, I guess. This is a big county with a lot of back roads. Our closest deputy was fifteen miles away when we got a call about some trucks in a field."

McMaster stepped to the counsel table again and stood behind Rummell.

"On the night of the Dandurand murders you thought this place on Eden Road—Miguel Mendez-Mendoza's place—you thought this place held evidence of the Dandurand murders, correct?"

"Yes, but Miguel is not listed on the deed—"

"Yeah, yeah, you think there's a straw owner listed on the deed," said McMaster, seemingly annoyed at Mallory's injection of this information. It was common for drug dealers to hide assets with straw owners.

"Yes, I do think there's a straw owner here—"

"But you think the real owner, despite what it says at the register of deeds office, is Miguel Mendez-Mendoza?"

"Yes."

"And you believe that the real owner, this . . . Miguel, is an accomplice to the Dandurand murders, correct?"

"Yes, he is a suspect."

"And Judge Joel wouldn't let you search the place on Eden Road on the night of the Dandurand murders, would he?"

"No sir, I told you that."

"But you had a hunch there was evidence in that house?"

"Thought I had more than a hunch, but yeah, that's part of it."

"Every detective I know claims to follow their instinct. You do that?"

"Of course. Common sense."

"No. It's an instinct, isn't it? If you could plot it out in commonsense terms you could've spelled out probable cause in that application for a warrant, right?"

"Okay."

Before I could stop myself I said, "Get to the point, Mr. McMaster."

McMaster stepped away from Rummell and back to the podium where he rebooted his cross-examination.

"Here's my question, Detective Mallory. You catch this awful murder case—a gruesome, evil, unthinkable, triple homicide, and a dangerous accomplice is at large, you think. More people could die, you think. And you have this God-given instinct—this strong hunch, whatever you want to call it—where evidence of the second killer is located, and you do not assign any deputies to surveil the place?"

"I watched the place myself, and assigned deputies to watch the place for months, but it wasn't leading to anything and we weren't seeing any action at the house, so, as I know you know, Mr. McMaster, I opted to put video surveillance on the place."

"A surveillance camera with night vision capability, right?"

"Correct."

"Please describe the footage your camera captured late last Saturday night to the jury."

Mallory described how his camera had captured the arrival of the green Cutlass Supreme and the sheriff's cruisers and everything it recorded in between, including the unexplained presence of a man in a ski mask who burst through the front door of the farmhouse during the altercation.

I bent up several paperclips in my lap as I stewed over the clarity of the video's resolution. I hoped it wasn't good.

Following McMaster's lead and over Ms. Sweeney's objection, Detective Mallory testified about the scene inside Miguel's house—the bullet holes and the decomposing roosters and the shrine to the Santa Muerte, which according to Mallory, used to be more than just a shrine. The state's medical examiner determined that the skeleton in robes hanging on the railroad spikes was indeed a real human skeleton, yet to be identified. And the skull on the floor was a real human skull, yet to be identified. There were no drugs found on the property or in the Cutlass, but the sheriff's drug dog hit on several areas of the property, including the junked pickup in the backyard. The dog hit on the Cutlass in the field as well, but again there were no drugs found. Mallory explained that the dog's nose was keen enough to pick up the scent of illegal drugs in a space long after the drugs were gone.

McMaster circled Detective Mallory back to the arrival of the Cutlass and the confrontation between the two figures captured on video.

"Were there any signs of forced entry into the house?"

"Yes. The glass was broken on the second-story window in the back."

The shirt underneath my robe was soaked with sweat and the snakes were crawling around in my stomach again.

I glanced at Ms. Sweeney. She was focused on McMaster, her lips rigid, drawn tight against her teeth.

"You think someone broke in through the upstairs bedroom window?" asked McMaster.

"Yes sir."

"And you think that person was still in the house when the person in the Cutlass arrived?"

"Yes sir."

"Do you know why a burglar would choose to break into a second-story window in the back, way up high, when there are three perfectly good windows for him to break into on the first floor?"

Detective Mallory shrugged and shook his head. "I dunno. That's a good question."

"It is a good question, isn't it?" McMaster looked at the jury and strayed away from the podium toward his client, stopping before he got there, folding his arms across his chest and clamping his thumb and forefinger on his chin.

"Think about this with me for a moment, Detective."

A transparent bit of theater. Good attorneys do their best thinking before trial and McMaster was a good lawyer, albeit probably a dirty one. McMaster had thought this through. Even Detective Mallory seemed to know this. He adjusted himself in his seat like he was bracing for a jolt. I felt myself doing the same thing.

McMaster took his hand off his chin and squinted, his eyes now slits—the air of a man contemplating a vision in his head. "Where are the other three windows on the first floor?"

"The living room window faces Eden Road, the dining room window faces the driveway, and I think there's a window in the first floor bedroom next to the kitchen."

"And if the burglar went through any of those windows, your camera would've captured him breaking and entering, is that correct?"

Detective Mallory pursed his lips, nodding. "Yeah, I guess it would've."

"You guess?"

"It definitely would've."

McMaster smiled at the concession. "So, the burglar passes on these easy low-level entry points for this high, pain-in-the-ass, second-story window. It's like this burglar knew all about your surveillance, isn't it?"

Ms. Sweeney stood. "Objection, relevance. And it calls for speculation."

McMaster retorted. "How that man in the ski mask knew to break in through the second-story window in back to stay off camera is the key to this case, Your Honor. Our theory is that there has to be a dirty cop involved."

Sweeney broke in. "The man in the mask ran right out the front door in full view of the camera—"

"What choice did he have, what with bullets pouring through the kitchen door?" McMaster smiled, and glanced at Sweeney, whose lips were tight on her teeth again.

I cleared my throat and entered the fray. "The objection as to relevance is overruled. However, the question does call for speculation, so that objection is sustained."

McMaster licked his lips and looked at his notepad while Sweeney sat down. He'd already made his points in response to her objection, probably more effectively than he ever would have through questioning Detective Mallory. Defense attorneys called this tactic bootlegging, and if I'd been on my game I would've shut McMaster down two words into his first sentence. But I was the ringleader of a sham trial with other things on my mind.

McMaster drew in a breath, looked at the wide-eyed jury, and asked Mallory, "How many folks knew you had surveillance on Miguel Mendez-Mendoza's house?"

Detective Mallory, following McMaster's cue, turned to the jury and said, "Probably the entire sheriff's office, along with KBI Agent Caroline Gordon and the prosecutors."

"So, if any of these deputies, or Agent Gordon, were inclined to break into this house, they would know they had to go through the second-story window at the back of the house to stay off your surveillance video?"

Sweeney stood, "Objection, relevance. And it calls for speculation."

"Overruled," I said.

"Yeah, they'd know that was the way to go. Sure. But why?"

"Why?" said McMaster, laughing. Witnesses didn't get to ask questions, but McMaster wasn't about to ask the court for help reigning in Detective Mallory.

McMaster looked at his notepad and rocked his head back and forth before looking up. "The surveillance camera has the Cutlass arriving at 9:34 p.m., correct?"

"Yes sir."

"Where were you at that time?"

Mallory looked to Sweeney, who stared forward—her poker face. She seemed to be catching on. Tangling with McMaster was like wrestling with a greased pig—no matter what, you were going to end up looking stupid.

Detective Mallory finally unlocked his glare on the prosecutor's table and faced McMaster. "I was at my apartment."

"Anyone with you on a Saturday night?"

"No."

"You have three minor children, correct?"

"Yes."

"You mean to tell this jury that none of them were home with you last Saturday night?"

"I was alone. I'm divorced. My exes have custody of my children."

McMaster walked over to Ms. Thompson and leaned over, talking into her ear as she handed him a DVD. Detective Mallory's face was flaming red and he took the opportunity to glare at Sweeney and Davidson some more. From Mallory's point of view, McMaster had basically been allowed to publicly insinuate that Mallory was a dirty cop while Sweeney and Davidson were sitting on their hands. Some cops could laugh this kind of courtroom gamesmanship off. Others, like Mallory, couldn't, and expected prosecutors to launch into a tirade of objections laced with righteous indignation. The juror closest to the witness stand—a middle-aged woman who sold insurance in town—seemed particularly enamored with the drama. Her head moved from Detective Mallory to the prosecutors' table, back and forth, taking in the conflict boiling in silence, off the record.

I wiped perspiration from my forehead with a tissue and sipped on water.

Ms. Sweeney stood. "I see Mr. McMaster has the surveillance video out, Your Honor. If he wants to introduce that as an exhibit and show it to the jury, we have no objection. We will stipulate to foundation."

I took it that Ms. Sweeney wanted to show the jury she had nothing to hide.

McMaster's response to her stipulation to the admissibility of the video was, "That'll work."

I managed to nod my assent, frozen in sweat, waiting for the hammer to drop—worried someone would see something in this video that would expose me.

I stammered a bit in formulating the words to admit it into evidence. The state's technician cued up the relevant portion of the video as the court reporter flicked off the lights. Miguel's house was clearly pictured on the screen, albeit in the green tint that came with night vision technology.

My chest felt heavy and I told myself to breathe as I watched. There goes the Cutlass into the backyard. A figure—Juan—enters the kitchen door, then returns a minute later. When he unloaded that machine pistol into the door, muzzle fire flashed on the screen in silence and people in the courtroom stirred and murmured.

When the man in the ski mask—me—bolted through the front door and into the yard, McMaster froze the screen with the remote. I wasn't as shadowy a figure on the screen as Juan had been because I was closer to the camera here, but still, the picture quality was poor. And on pause it was worse. I tried to tell myself I had nothing to worry about. I'd already burned the camo pullover, the cargo pants—everything I wore that night. But you never know what might be your undoing.

McMaster hit play. I ran to the front corner of the house, then to the back of the house, before disappearing. McMaster replayed this five times.

"Any idea who this man is?" asked McMaster.

"Not a clue," said Mallory.

A sense of relief failed to manifest itself in my hands, which began to shake. I locked them together below the bench and the quake traveled to my triceps. It felt like a lot of movement to me, but no one seemed to notice.

"This man in the mask," said McMaster, "any chance he ended up among those found dead in the field?"

"No, I don't think so."

"Because of the clothes on the man here?" McMaster's laser pointer was out now. A red dot danced on the screen, circling my pants, then my camo pullover.

"Yeah, the clothes don't match any found on the dead bodies in the field, that's part of it."

"What else?"

"The runner here is lean for sure, and he's athletic. He's not emaciated like the tattooed man in the field. I don't picture the skinny white guy in the field moving like that when he was alive. Same thing with the skinny Hispanic, I mean, they are clearly different body types. And the rest of the DB's were huskier than our masked man."

"You think the masked man survived whatever happened out in that field?"

Detective Mallory nodded. "He survived and got away as far as we know."

Yeah, but it wasn't over. Not by a long shot.

McMaster fast-forwarded to the trucks blasting through the driveway into the backyard and out of sight.

"That's it," said Detective Mallory. "Next thing you'll see is all of us cops arriving quite a bit later."

McMaster shut off the video and the court reporter hit the lights.

"Your Honor," said McMaster. "If I could have a moment with Ms. Thompson?"

I nodded my assent, not yet confident that my voice would work properly.

Although I couldn't make out the words, McMaster and Ms. Thompson clearly had a spirited disagreement about something.

"You need a recess, Mr. McMaster?" I finally asked. I sure the hell did.

McMaster glanced at Baltozar and Maria.

"No. I—I think I'll wrap up with a few more questions."

McMaster strolled to the podium while Ms. Thompson unsuccessfully tried to hide her disapproval.

"Detective. What information do you have as to the motive behind the murder of the Dandurand family?"

"It's unclear."

"I've already assumed it's unclear, since you didn't touch on it with Ms. Sweeney in your direct examination, and since you didn't include any clue as to motive in your first affidavit to search Miguel's house. My question is whether you have any information that might shed light on the motive?"

"Besides rumors, no."

He was lying and fucking with McMaster and doing a good job of both.

McMaster made a face like he'd stepped in dog shit on a hot day. Lawyers didn't like answers like that—answers that begged for follow-up questions the attorney might not know the answer to. And judging from McMaster's reaction, he wasn't sure what might be waiting for him behind door number one. Rumors were inadmissible hearsay anyway, but the suggestion there was information out there—somewhere—regarding motive would linger in the minds of the jurors the way bits of dog excrement stayed stuck in the tread of a tennis shoe. Assuming McMaster knew I was compromised, none of that should've mattered to him in this situation, but when the competitive juices flow, old habits are hard to break.

McMaster took too long turning the page on his legal pad, a distant look in his eye—a moment equivalent to a kid in the park dragging his fouled shoe across the grass.

"Okay, Detective," said McMaster. Maybe he just wanted to end the silence in the courtroom because he paused like he didn't know what he was going to ask next. But then there was a renewed intensity in his voice that seemed to suggest the gloves were off. "Did you ever tell anyone that Eddie Dandurand was a snitch?"

"No."

"You never told anyone that 'Eddie D' had turned state's witness—wore a wire?"

"No sir."

"Ever insinuate to anyone that he was cooperating with you in any way?"

"No."

McMaster closed his eyes, then opened them slowly and held still as a sniper. "Ever tell anyone that young Eddie Dandurand was scared, had nowhere else to turn, and was talking to the cops?"

Movement from the prosecutor's table caught my eye. Ms. Sweeney's bottom was off the chair an inch or two when she froze, shook her head, and sat down. She could have at least objected to the compound question. God only knows why she didn't.

Detective Mallory had noticed too. When he saw no objection was coming, he looked McMaster in the eye and said. "Nope. I never told anyone that Eddie was scared, had nowhere else to turn, and was talking to us."

McMaster closed one eye and regarded Detective Mallory with the other. "Ever insinuate anything like that to anybody?"

"No. I didn't."

If Detective Mallory hadn't yet missed the files we stole from his Impala, I figured he'd go looking for them when court was over. He'd want to destroy the video of his interview with Randy Harris because it was now ironclad proof that he'd committed perjury.

McMaster flipped a yellow page over the top of his legal pad. "Alright, let's switch gears here. Do you know a person by the name of Randy Harris?"

"Yes."

"You arrested him for selling an eighty-dollar baggie of meth to his ex, correct?"

"Correct."

"But he's run off, skipped bail, correct?"

"Yes sir."

"Right after you arrested him, did you tell Randy Harris that Eddie D had worn a wire in his dealing with my client, Mr. Vaughn Rummell?"

"No."

"Did you ever tell Randy Harris that you were moving up the chain through Eddie D to Vaughn Rummell, all the way up to El Comeniños and eventually the Chicken Man?"

"No sir, I did not."

McMaster looked over to Ms. Thompson and gave her a brief I-told-you-so grin as she tried to quash the smile contorting her face.

"'Cause if you had," said McMaster, "and Randy Harris had passed this on to folks you regard as ruthless drug dealers, that might make them angry."

"Okay," said Mallory, like it was no biggie.

"Turnin' state's witness is the kind of thing that gets a man killed in the drug trade, right?"

"Sure."

"That would give my client a plausible motive."

"Yes."

"And it would give Miguel Mendez-Mendoza and Jorge Mendez-Rodriguez a plausible reason to want Eddie D dead, right?"

"Sure."

"If Eddie D was cooperating with you in any way against Rummell, Miguel, or Jorge, you would've put that in the search warrant affidavit you swore out on the night of the Dandurand murders, right?"

"I guess . . . yes."

"You guess? Adding a motive like that to your search warrant application—that might well have put you over the top on that search warrant for Miguel's house fourteen months ago. Gotten you inside, right?"

"Maybe so."

"But it's not true. Eddie D wasn't a snitch for you, was he?"

"No, he wasn't."

"And you wouldn't make up something like that and tell somebody that, particularly if it wasn't true, would you?"

"I wouldn't."

"Because that might get people killed, wouldn't it?"

Detective Mallory nodded.

"Can you answer out loud for me?"

"It could get people killed. Yes."

Ms. Sweeney's poker face had morphed into consternation. I imagined everyone in the courtroom wanted to ask this guy named Randy Harris the same two questions: *What did Detective Mallory say to you? And who did you tell?*

I had the answer to the first question at home on a DVD. Given who had probably hired McMaster and Thompson, they likely had the answer to both questions.

Regardless of what anyone believed, McMaster had tethered the state to a position—one that, perhaps not coincidentally, served members of the cartel more than it helped Rummell. There was still a confession and more than enough physical evidence out there to justify a guilty verdict and a shot from a needle full of liquid death for Rummell. Sure, Sweeney would love to have a motive—the proverbial cherry on top—but she didn't need it. Meth monsters like Rummell were irrational. It was one of their defining characteristics. I'd seen a case where an addict sodomized an infant and put her in a microwave before hanging himself in a closet and people asked why but they knew there could never be an answer. Not a real one, anyway. It's not that meth addicts didn't have motives. It's that people had grown used to not understanding them. Meth addicts had their own breed of insanity and everyone knew it. But that didn't take the shine off what McMaster had just accomplished. He had gambled and won. He figured Detective Mallory would lie to protect himself from the consequences of being perceived to have lit the match of motive that killed the Dandurand family. And he'd been right.

McMaster had accomplished something else. His last batch of questions had ignited Haley's uncle, who all of a sudden couldn't sit still. With each question, McMaster had effectively accused Detective Mallory of getting the Dandurands killed. He'd turned up the heat, pitting the victims and the powers of the state against each other.

McMaster returned to his counsel table and put his hand on Rummell's shoulder. Things weren't so cut and dried anymore. They conferred, seemingly over something as trivial as lunch.

McMaster rose from the polite conversation to refocus on the beleaguered detective. With a hand still on his client's shoulder, he asked, "Since you're at a complete loss, as far as a motive, Detective, this case could have been very difficult, correct?"

Mallory shrugged.

McMaster said, "You caught a lucky break the night of the Dandurand murders, didn't you?"

Mallory shrugged again.

McMaster smiled at his reticence. "Well I mean, my goodness, my client is pinned in the ditch a mile down the road from the murder scene. He's a sitting duck—just lying there for the cops to find him. Naturally, you find him, and lo and behold, he confesses. That's lucky, right?"

Ms. Sweeney stood and said, "Objection. Argumentative, and it's irrelevant whether Detective Mallory regards it as lucky."

She was right.

"Overruled. Answer the question," I said. It was the patsy defense. Juan called Rummell a patsy the night of the kidnapping.

Ms. Sweeney wrinkled her forehead at me and sat down.

I wanted to hear this. I wanted Rummell to be innocent, unlikely as that seemed. I wanted to believe it gave me options. If I couldn't find Ashley, I could grant the judgment of acquittal when the time came and at least be on the side of the angels. Maybe that would spring my sister—a deal's a deal. And I wanted to believe the odds that Ashley would make it through this alive improved if Rummell was innocent. I liked the simple logic of it—people that would go this far to keep the state from killing an innocent person wouldn't kill my innocent sister. But I knew, deep down, Rummell wasn't entirely innocent and cartels didn't give a damn about innocence anyway.

"Do I consider it lucky," said Mallory, appearing to mull over the clearly irrelevant question. He held up his hand in compromise with McMaster and said, "It's a nice break."

"This man is in this dangerous rollover accident, where he's flipped out of the Mustang, but he's not hurt at all. He's pinned down in a ditch so he can't get away, next to a pistol that your expert claims is one of the murder weapons—and next to a ski mask. I mean, come on! It's a little too nice a break, isn't it?"

Ms. Sweeney stood and said, "Objection, argumentative."

This time I sustained the objection. This line of questioning wasn't leading anywhere anyway.

McMaster moved on without delay. "You found two ski masks when you executed the search warrant late last Saturday night, early Sunday morning, didn't you?"

"Yes sir."

"Tell the court where you found them?"

"Underneath the passenger seat of the Cutlass."

"The Cutlass found in the field next to the dead body of a white man with a sleeve of clown tattoos on his right arm identical to the tattoos on the right arm of my client?"

Detective Mallory closed his eyes and nodded. "Yes."

McMaster announced he had no further questions and sat next to his client. Ms. Sweeney declined to ask any further questions of Mallory on redirect examination. Nice move. Never ask a question of a witness you don't know the answer to. By now, Ms. Sweeney was full of questions she didn't know the answer to.

It was almost five o'clock, so I recessed the case for the day.

* * *

I went down the back hallway to my office past two attorneys who wanted to see me about an emergency child-custody matter in one of my divorce cases. It wouldn't take a minute, they said.

It took thirty-five.

After they left, I locked myself in chambers and lay on the floor listening to a vent rattle—so much noise for so little cool air. I managed to lie there unmoving through a ringing phone.

Then someone knocked on the door. I called out that I was busy. It was the custodian wanting to know if I had any trash. "There's nothing in my trash can," I yelled from the floor. That's when he fired up the sweeper on the other side of the door and began singing, probably with headphones on as was his habit.

I needed to clear my head. The noise from the sweeper didn't bother me. The hard dirty floor didn't bother me. Neither did my sweaty face. The image of my baby sister appeared when I closed my eyes. I found myself imagining what Ashley might be doing at the moment. At least that was the hope—that she was doing something. I tried to think of something brilliant to bring this safely to an end. I asked God for wisdom, for Him to say something. All I heard was the custodian, singing something about how there ain't no easy way out.

When I woke up twenty minutes later the noise was gone. I climbed into my chair, called Keri, and told her I was staying late to research judgments of acquittal. She told me that Vanguard Security had been to the house today and installed the best security system my money could buy, then planted their sign in the ditch by the road to deter break-ins. She was looking at the monitors now and could see the entire yard out to the farm ground and the roadway. She'd have a briefing for me regarding what she'd found in Detective Mallory's reports when I got home.

I started my research project by reviewing the Kansas case law. There were only a few cases in which the Kansas appellate courts had addressed judgments of acquittal, and the law laid down in those cases was short and simple—any trial court's judgment of acquittal is absolute. Because the U.S. Constitution prohibits placing a defendant in jeopardy for the same crime twice, there was no going back, no matter how wrong the trial court had been when it acquitted him. A judge's acquittal had the same effect as a jury's acquittal—the case was absolutely over.

But there had never been a documented case of a judgment of acquittal gained through intimidation in Kansas, so to find something on point I expanded my search to all fifty states and the federal courts. The closest thing I found was a Chicago mob case—*Illinois v. Baleman*—where the prosecutor proved the judge took a $10,000 bribe to grant the defendant an acquittal. The Illinois Supreme Court ruled that a second trial would not violate the U.S. Constitution's prohibition against double jeopardy because the defendant was never actually in jeopardy in the first place—the fix was baked in the fraudulent cake. The holding in the Chicago mob case would certainly be persuasive authority—a legal theory a Kansas court might use to undo the finality of a judgment of acquittal.

If the kidnappers were getting expert—albeit unethical— legal advice about the permanency of any judgment of acquittal granted under duress, they would know a smart prosecutor like Gwen Sweeney might be successful at getting a second trial, providing she could produce compelling witnesses, like a former judge and his family, to show the facts underpinning her theory. That would put the target on our backs. When my fiancée and my family were nothing more to the kidnappers than the means of proving the ruling was gained through intimidation, we would be killed.

I had to find where they were keeping Ashley before the state presented all its evidence at the jury trial—before the defense made its motion for a judgment of acquittal. I would have to do what McMaster used to do for all his death penalty clients in Texas, Kansas, and Illinois: Choose the path that delayed D-Day for as long as possible, fight like hell, and pray for a break.

When I finally got to my truck, it was sunset. I sat and watched the TV reporters on the courthouse lawn. As they talked to their cameras, their backdrop was the courthouse—a washed-out 1950s cold war structure sitting on what was once prairie land. I couldn't tell you the exact color of the building the viewers would see on their screens that night—lackluster rust or faded peach maybe; but beyond that, the horizon was ablaze, the sun making art of the sky before the earth twisted away.

* * *

I was about to climb into bed when there was a knock at my front door. I looked at the monitor in my bedroom and saw Ashley's husband, Rod, standing there in his green auto-parts-store uniform. Keri was sitting on the bed looking up at me, leaning back on the headboard with one of Mallory's reports on her lap.

"Follow me into the living room, but stay back," I said. "And shut Diablo in here. We're not gonna need him on this one."

Wearing gym shorts and a T-shirt, I marched through the living room, opened the door and glared directly into my brother-in-law's eyes. His skin was dotted with fiery red splotches and the blood vessels on his nose looked like a network of bloody creeks. He stood there barrel-chested and rigid, staring up at me with a frown.

He lifted his chin and said, "I gotta drive all the way from Omaha because you can't return my calls?" His voice was shaky, and I heard Keri walk up somewhere behind me. He peeked around me, but I couldn't tell if he'd seen her or not.

"Even if I knew where Ashley was, I wouldn't tell you. Not in a million years."

He nodded, bit his lip, and squinted off into the darkness. I think he wanted to hit me, but I was a judge on my home turf. Even Rod was smart enough to know he'd end up chum in the water if he got squirrely. Plus, he knew I was the kind of guy that might be looking for a reason to whip his ass, like I did three years earlier when I went to his house to get some of Ashley's things after he'd roughed her up. He'd met me at the back door and drunkenly stepped aside to let me into his kitchen before asking me what my "cunt sister" had said happened. When I whipped around to face him he took a swing and I grabbed his arm and used his own momentum to slam him face down in a kitty litter box. The next day, I confessed to Father Garrahy for this—told him I'd held my brother-in-law's face in cat shit a lot longer than necessary. I heard what I suspected was a muted chuckle from behind the latticed opening before being told the penitence was two "Our Fathers."

"What'd she tell you happened this time?"

I stared through him like he wasn't there.

"Well, whatever it was Ashley told you, it ain't true."

"She told me nothing happened."

"Oh, well—"

"Which is bullshit."

Rod gritted his teeth and looked down at his black work boots. "So it pretty much doesn't matter to you what anyone has to say about what happened, does it?"

"Time to leave, Rotten Rodney."

"I need to know if she's okay. She here?"

"She's not here. I know that much."

"You don't look concerned she's missing. You must know where she's at."

"You're reading it all wrong, bud."

"Care if I . . . take a look in your garage. See if her Navigator's in there. If you do that, I won't bother you anymore."

"You're not going to bother me anyway. I've got you on surveillance right now. It's all being recorded. You haven't done anything wrong, yet. But when you come back, you'll be committing criminal trespass because I'm telling you now to leave and not to come back onto my property. The video will be runnin' twenty-four-seven. I'm gonna make a record of this and tell the sheriff I don't want you out here again. Understand?"

"Yeah, I understand, but you don't." He pointed a finger at me. "Your sister's not who you think she is."

"You're probably right about that, but I'm guessin' I'm not who you think I am either. The truth is, when I kneel down to pray tonight, I'm gonna pray your ass wanders back out here . . . drunk . . . and with a weapon. I'd like nothing more than to put you down."

"You're as fuckin' crazy as your sister. I always heard it was just her got cornholed by your momma's boyfriends but maybe it was you too."

I balled my fist.

"Go on Judge, take a swing." He smiled and I saw the Copenhagen stuck between his yellow teeth. "It'll all be on video I guess."

I shut the door on him and looked back at Keri.

She said, "I would've punched him."

* * *

Later that night I felt Keri moving around in bed. She nuzzled into me and her breath was warm on my neck. I opened my eyes and watched the ceiling fan spin in the darkness.

"You awake?" she said.

"Yep."

"I need to tell you something."

"Okay."

"And then I want to ask you something and I want you to tell me the truth."

"Deal."

"Don't be an asshole, I'm serious."

"I'm not trying to be an asshole."

"So, it just comes natural to you then?"

"Apparently."

I closed my eyes and took a deep breath before I realized how that might've sounded to her. Like I was annoyed. And maybe I was. Then I said, "Please tell me."

I felt a tickle of something wet on my chest. A tear. I sat up in bed.

"Hey, hey, what is it?" I said.

The back of her head plopped into the pillow on her side of the bed. It was her turn to watch the fan spin. I touched her cheek, moist with the trail of a tear.

"Before I was taken from my mother," she said, "I was molested. In the same way as Ashley."

"Honey, I'm so sorry."

"You need to know that. You need to know what you're getting into with me. I carry that weight around with me sometimes."

"I know how hard . . . that must be."

"You know how hard that must be," she repeated, mockingly. "Now, here's my question for you. Do you know how hard that must be, or do you know in fact how hard it is?"

"I took a beating once at the hands of a grown man when I was eight, but no one touched me sexually if that's what you're asking me."

Keri shook her head.

"Rod's full of shit," I said. "What makes you think he's on to something? What makes you think I was . . . "

" . . . molested? Jesus, you can't even say it."

"Molested," I said quickly, proving her wrong about my fear of the word while at the same time confirming her conclusion that I could, on occasion, be an asshole.

Without any pauses or hesitation this time, I repeated my question. "What makes you think I was molested?"

"I thought I saw something in your face when Rod said that to you tonight. After you shut the door and turned around."

"You saw anger."

"I saw fear. Shame."

"You're mistaken."

"If you say so, Ben."

"You're projecting what you feel onto me."

"Oh, so you're a psychiatrist now. Yes or no, were you touched inappropriately as a child?"

"Not sexually. Not that I remember."

Keri sat up, moving closer. "What the hell does that mean? Don't lie to me about this. Get it out. You have to get it out."

Before I knew what was happening, *before I knew what I was doing*, I was standing beside the bed yelling, "I am telling you the truth! I don't fuckin' know the truth!"

I shook off the moment, trying to replay the glitch in time I couldn't remember, when I must've stood from the bed and lost my shit on the woman I loved. Keri was up, coming closer, reaching for me. I let her wrap her arms around me.

I broke free from her and sat on the bed and put my head in my hands and said, "I've had a few dreams on the subject. Nightmares about Clive Hunsucker. It's just my imagination. My mother's last boyfriend coming for me. Having his way."

Keri sat next to me. "How long have you had these dreams?"

"Only had three of them. All in the week after Natalie died. Then, just like that, they went away. I don't have them anymore."

I pulled my face from my hands and looked at Keri. "You're not the first person to think I might've been molested. Pops sent me to a therapist when I was eight years old because I wasn't acting like myself and they knew what had happened to Ash. The therapist always felt like I was holding something back or repressing some horrible memory. In four years, she could never get that out of her head."

"Were you . . . holding something back?"

"Yeah. But it wasn't what she thought."

"What were you keeping from her? What are you keeping from me?"

"After Ash told me what Hunsucker did, I went to Mom, told her what he'd done. She didn't believe me but she must've said something to ol' Clive about it because he came to my room and beat the shit out of me. Hammered down on my back with a wooden TV tray until one of the legs broke. He tossed it in the corner and I saw him pick up a metal dog leash and wrap one end of it around his hand and make a fist."

"Jesus. But you don't—that didn't leave any scars?"

I shook my head. "Right then, we heard my mommy coming through the front door. Hunsucker put his finger to his lips, grinned, and told me we'd pick up where we left off if I didn't keep my fuckin' mouth shut."

"Why wouldn't you tell the therapist these things?"

"I did."

"I don't understand."

"That's the night Hunsucker died of a heroin overdose."

"The night police put you and Ash in protective custody," said Keri, remembering the bits of my life I'd let her in on. "That's the night they put you with Pops. I still don't understand."

"I killed Clive Hunsucker that night."

Silence.

Finally, Keri said, "Then how did the cops come to the conclusion he died of a heroin overdose?"

"Because he did."

"I'm not tracking, Benny."

"Earlier that day, I'd stolen one of my mom's needles when it was full of juice. In my eight-year-old brain, I thought I was helping her. She was a fuckin' zombie on that shit. I hated it more than you could ever know. She tossed the house, yelling and screaming at Clive and accusing him of stealing her fix. She looked everywhere but under my mattress before giving up and going wherever it was she went to get heroin. When Mom got home and Clive dropped the dog chain at my feet and left for the living room, I just lay there on the floor and listened. For hours. I listened until I knew they'd both be more or less comatose from the heroin. I pulled the needle I'd hidden from Mom out from under my bed and went to the living room and jammed it in ol' Clive's arm and pushed down on the plunger. He didn't even flinch. I watched him until his chest stopped moving up and down. I sat on the floor in the dark watching him on the couch until the sun came up, worried he'd wake up. I finally got up enough nerve to touch his neck. He was cold and I knew he was dead. I went to my room and waited until my mother woke up and eventually began screaming and crying. I went to the living room and watched her shake and pull at her hair and skin and try to gather all the dope and the needles and put them in a trash bag. She left me and Ash alone with the dead man before coming back and calling for an ambulance."

"Does Pops know what you did?"

"I didn't tell him."

"Why didn't you tell the therapist?"

"I thought they'd take me from Pops if I did that. I figured I'd be labeled some kind of psycho."

"You were eight."

"I was an eight-year-old murderer who didn't feel a bit of remorse for killing that motherfucker. I'd do it again today, given the same situation."

"But you said you weren't yourself. Pops knew something was wrong. So, it was . . . it still bothers you, Benny."

"Yeah okay, I see your point, but let's put it this way. I don't regret killing Clive Hunsucker. I'd feel worse if I hadn't done something. I'm glad he died."

"Besides Natalie, have you told anyone about this?"

"I never told Nat."

My eyes had adjusted to the dark now and I could see on Keri's face that she was perplexed that I'd kept this secret from my wife.

"I don't like to talk about it," I said.

"No shit."

I laughed.

"Did you tell Ash?"

"Na. Only person I told was Father Garrahy."

"Wow, I bet he was shocked—a confession like that from a kid."

"It wasn't a confession. It got back to Father I'd been telling other kids at school there was no God. When he called me to his office to ask me why I was saying such things, I ended up giving him my answer, which I didn't know I had in me until it came out. I basically told him the God he believed in couldn't exist, because a God like that wouldn't push his dirty work off on an eight-year-old. When he asked what I meant by that, I swore him to secrecy before spilling the beans. I told him what I did to Hunsucker and why."

"What'd he say to that?"

"He asked me if what Hunsucker did to Ash was wrong. I told him it was. He said, 'If there is no God, who's to say what Hunsucker did was wrong?' I said, 'The police.' Father got this little smile on his face and said, 'And what if the police, in their opinion, didn't think it was wrong?' I told Father that if the cops thought that, they could just die too for all I cared."

I reached for a Yeti full of water on the nightstand and took a drink.

"What was Father's answer to that one?" asked Keri.

I swallowed, then said, "He told me I was basically right. That right and wrong ultimately wasn't up for a vote and that I had a strong sense of that in my heart. He said it was normal for me to question God, given what I'd been through. He said it was a process and he'd help me through it. Then he told me I'd probably done bad things in my life and would repeat them, but that killing Hunsucker, given the circumstances, wasn't one of them."

I stood and walked toward the bathroom. When I got to the door, Keri said, "Benny, I know you. Seems like you always get the last word. What did you say to that?"

"I asked Father if that was his opinion, or God's."

19

Jorge

JORGE PRESSED THE rewind button on the remote control. Then he took a hit from the blunt wedged between his middle and ring fingers, slumping in his chair and closing his eyes and holding pot smoke in his lungs before letting it leak from his nostrils. He was behind the desk in his office on the first floor of his cabin in the foothills of the Kiamichi Mountains. On the big-screen TV sitting in the alcove between cabinets of polished mahogany, a figure ran backwards through a yard and into the door of a farmhouse before popping back out. Jorge watched this portion of the video two more times before clicking it off and grinding his fingers into the corners of his eyes. He felt the vessels in them pulsing, raging across the dry whites. The door to the office clicked open and Buster poked his head in. "Jay Dee's here. You ready for us?"

Jorge nodded and Buster opened the door all the way and Jim "Jay Dee" Daniels stepped into the room, followed by Buster. Jay Dee was Jorge's attorney and consultant of twenty-five years.

He made eye contact with Jorge and stepped tentatively over a sleeping St. Bernard on his way to the corner where he stood with his hands crossed at the wrist the way a chauffeur might stand by the open door of a limousine. He was a fifty-four-year-old fat man with a flat, asymmetrical nose that sometimes whistled when he was nervous or out of breath. In law school at the University of New Mexico someone dubbed him Whistling Jim, and it stuck, until a few years later when the nickname evolved to Whispering Jim because criminal cases against his cartel-connected clients were being dismissed at an alarming rate, often not based on his acumen as an attorney, but for reasons that left people whispering about what had happened. Witnesses seemed to change their stories, refuse to testify, disappear, or die when Jim "Jay Dee" Daniels was on the case. Eventually, when he entered his appearance for a client, as far as the government attorneys and witnesses were concerned, it was like the grim reaper himself had shown up for court dressed in a ten-thousand dollar pin-striped Brioni suit. Now, he wasn't wearing a coat and tie, but his slacks were freshly pressed and his blue button-up shirt was starched and his silver cuff-links were shaped like the scales of justice and shiny as his bald head.

Miguel's long, slender frame darkened the doorway, popping the top on a can of Tecate. He tipped the beer to his lips and drank, his Adam's apple exercising in his sinewy throat, his copper-colored eyes fixed on the hired help. When he pulled the can of beer from his mouth he looked at his father behind the desk. They'd all been together in this war room of mahogany and leather before.

Jorge nodded at Miguel. "Show them."

Miguel reached for the small of his back and snagged the envelope tucked inside the waistline of his jeans and flicked it at Buster who caught it against his stomach and looked at Jorge.

"Go on," said Jorge. "Open it."

Buster slipped a photo out of the envelope and winced at what he saw. "Got-dammit."

Jorge said, "Show Jay Dee what Trevino does to lawyers." He cut his eyes to Jay Dee and said, "It's your butt buddy from law school."

"Diego?" whispered Jay Dee. "Please Jorge, if it's Diego I don't wanna see it."

Buster held the photo out for Jay Dee but he wouldn't take it or look at it. He stared forward as air audibly whistled through the flattened vent on his face.

Miguel said, "It came in today's mail at the club in Wichita, along with a video. I'll guaran-fuckin'-tee you don't wanna see that."

Jay Dee finally looked down at the photo of Diego—his law school classmate, ex-lover, and Jorge's youngest brother. Diego had earned a law degree from the University of New Mexico in 1985 before telling his older brothers, Jorge and Alejandro, that he wouldn't work for them. Instead, Diego moved to Mexico City to marry the mother of his children and make an honest living selling Mexican auto insurance while Jay Dee filled the void for the cartel and found his niche. In the photo, Diego lay flat on his back in a pen full of hogs, his head sitting on his own crotch, his severed penis hanging out of his mouth.

Jorge watched Jay Dee grimace, then felt himself slip further into the darkness where the video he watched an hour earlier replayed in his mind. Hogs grunted and jockeyed for position, eventually forming a circle around Diego and knocking his severed head into the slop and manure where it was trampled in the mad scramble to devour his bowels. One hog jerked and pulled at a string of entrails which dragged the body a considerable distance through the mire and set the rest of the bloody-snouted hogs off to snort and snuff and scramble anew for a share of the feast.

"His wife?" said Jay Dee.

Jorge shook his head. "Disappeared."

Jay Dee scratched his nose with a knuckle. "His children? Grandchildren?"

"Gone," said Jorge. "They got every last one of 'em." He opened the big bottom drawer in his desk and pulled out a bottle of Don Julio tequila, nodding at Miguel who pulled four shot glasses from the liquor cabinet.

Jorge said, "I told him his family was in danger. That he needed to be careful. But he was too stubborn to accept my help. Said the Lord was his protector, not some drug dealer like me. I told him maybe the Lord sent me to save him and he laughed at that . . . like it wasn't possible, so Luciana got the idea to find some shit in the Bible to convince him to play it smart—be practical. She found what she was looking for in the words of

Jesus himself in the Book of Matthew, '*Behold, I send you forth as sheep in the midst of wolves: be ye therefore wise as serpents, and harmless as doves.*' There was a long silence on the line after I laid that quote on my little brother. I thought maybe, for a moment, I'd convinced him to let me protect him and his family. Then he said, '*An evil soul producing holy witness is like a villain with a smiling cheek, a goodly apple rotten at the heart.*' When I got off the phone I told Luciana that Diego refused my help and what he'd said . . . what I remembered of it anyway. I recalled enough of it that she recognized it as Shakespeare and now I can't forget it."

Jorge picked up the bottle of Don Julio and filled one of the shot glasses to the brim. "Isn't it strange? I quote the Bible to my brother the Holy Roller and he hits me with fucking Shakespeare."

Jay Dee turned over the photo and read the note on the back to himself. It read: DEAR CHICKEN MAN, COME OUT COME OUT WHEREVER YOU ARE. Jay Dee cleared his throat and said, "I'm sorry, Jorge. Diego was a . . . principled man."

Miguel's lip curled. "All tastes the same to a hog."

Jorge shot his son a look and filled the other three glasses full of tequila and nodded at the men to take them. When they did, Jorge raised his glass and said, "To Diego."

The other men repeated "To Diego" as they raised their shots and tossed them back. A jarring emptiness seized hold of Jorge. Maybe it was the inadequacy of the clichéd ceremony, or the pot or the tequila or the sudden estrangement of his wife upstairs, passed out on sleeping pills since being told by Jorge they wouldn't be attending their son's funeral because they'd be sitting ducks for the Trevino Cartel.

Scenes from the past had been flashing through Jorge in fits and starts since the deaths of Juan and Diego—Juan as a toddler watching cartoons, wrapped in his beloved green blanket; Diego playing soccer as a child in the back yard and his jars of fireflies on the back porch; and later, when Diego was a teenager, Jorge and Alejandro rising from the bed of a pickup in a liquor store parking lot in Culiacán, Mexico with sawed-off shotguns, black bandanas over their faces, fire pouring out of their muzzles, buckshot ripping the faces off two teenage boys who had beaten Diego almost to death for being gay.

Jorge stood with the bottle, walked around the desk, and said, "Now, gentlemen, we drink to my youngest son, Juan, who I know, all of us in this room agree got what he had comin'. I hope that in the end, the same cannot be said of me, but if it happens that way and I end up with my balls on my chin, then, as they used to say at the bars on the border in Laredo, 'fuck all ya'll.'" He patted his attorney's cheek with an open palm, noting the shock in his eyes. "What's the matter? You look pale, even for a gringo who doesn't get enough sun."

Jay Dee stared into Jorge's eyes, then glanced at Miguel and Buster and said, "We've all got a lot of money . . . more than we could ever spend. It's time to walk away while we can."

Miguel held a dip of chew above an open can of Skoal and tucked it inside his lower lip, brushing the granular bits still stuck to his thumb and finger off on his jeans. "You're suggesting we cut and run?"

"Walk away from it," said Jay Dee. "There's no percentage in fighting Angel Trevino now. You've had a good run. You've all got a hell of a lot of seed money. Concentrate on legitimate businesses and investments like you all have talked about for years."

Miguel smiled, his lower lip fat with tobacco. He snatched the tequila from his father and drank straight from the bottle— a sloppy hit that left his lower lip glistening. "Jay Dee, you know as well as anyone that this game we play only ends one way. We finish this on our terms, or we die. No one gets out alive. Not Juan or Diego. Not you. No one. That's how it is and always will be. There's never been a percentage in it."

Jay Dee turned to Jorge. "That what you want? To hit back. Play out your hand?"

Muscles flared along Jorge's jaw line and he cupped the back of his attorney's shaved head and drew him closer, bowing his back and leaning in so that their foreheads almost touched. "Play out my hand? Na—fuck that! I want Trevino's head on my desk so I can skull fuck it at my leisure. Then I want some strange pussy and a nice steak and shots of tequila that cost $400 a piece. When this is over . . . then we can talk about our investments like Yale fraternity fags if you want."

A fleshy nose-whistle escaped from Jay Dee as Jorge released him and took the tequila back from Miguel. He took a hit straight out of the bottle, then filled the shot glasses and they all drank to Juan.

Miguel walked behind his father's desk and picked up the remote control and clicked the TV to life. Muzzle flashes from Juan's MAC-10 flashed and Miguel paused the video. "Juan called me right before he was killed. I figure it was sometime right after he shot these rounds into the kitchen door here."

Miguel hit the play button and said, "He seemed to think the guy you're about to watch run through the front door on the screen was a man he knew from Uncle Sam's that went by the name of Arturo Gallegos. About a year and a half ago, we decided we could use him. So, we had Buster run the usual background check on the guy. Buster got hold of his fingerprints and had a cop buddy of his in Laredo run 'em in their system. Turns out the guy's real name is Geronimo Baylon-Fontana, a *sicario* for the Trevino Cartel. He may be Angel Trevino's half nephew. Juan knew all this when he encountered this guy in my house Saturday night."

Jay Dee said, "Someone tell me how this guy got away from us a year and a half ago."

"Ol' boy knew his cover was blown and was gone with the big south wind 'fore we could get to him . . . obviously," said Buster.

"What's the rest of the story?" said Jay Dee. "What'd he just up and lose his nerve all the sudden, after finally breaking in with us? We need to know if someone tipped him off. How, specifically, do you think he knew his cover was blown?" He made eye contact with Buster. "You know how important details are to me."

Buster rolled his eyes and said, "He was providin' security at Uncle Sam's—more or less a legit job. We decided to approach him 'bout doin' some real work for us. I sat down with him myself over a beer . . . asked him the usual. Where he hails from, family, why he's up here in Middle America fiddle-fuckin' 'round in a cinderblock bar like he was, and on and on like that. He did real well answerin' the questions. No red flags. Came across like a rollin' stone that rolled over the border . . . then back and forth like they do . . . a rudderless man of average intelligence inclined toward shortcuts—more balls than patience. Seemed like the perfect man for the job we had in mind—collecting cash from some of our lower volume distributers. Start him off slow and go from there. I wasn't hinked up 'bout him in the least, but I did my due diligence and snagged his beer mug anyways. Only thing is, I think now I underestimated the man. I think he did *his* due diligence and watched the security camera after I was done with him. My guess is he saw me put his beer mug in a bag and leave with it. Since he'd been arrested in the states and deported, he knew his prints were in the system and that his real name would pop right out of it. So he up and disappeared. By the time we figured out who he was, he was long gone."

Jay Dee watched the replay of the man running through the yard in a ski mask. "How sure are we that this is Geronimo Baylon-Fontana?"

Buster said, "Shit, Jay Dee, you know we ain't sure in the sense you're talkin', but Juan sure thought it was him. And it makes sense for him to be in there rootin' around lookin' for somethin' that leads to Jorge or Miguel."

"Is Geronimo built like that man on the video?" said Jay Dee.

"Tall, athletic," said Buster. "Yeah, that could be Geronimo near as I can tell, but I only met him the one time. Has a brother in the Padres' farm system by the way so it runs in the family."

Jay Dee set his shot glass on the desk and plopped down in a chair in a way that suggested his legs were weak and tired. "I saw on the news that McMaster suggested in court today that this unidentified man in the ski mask might actually be Detective Raymond Mallory."

Miguel snickered and Buster smiled.

Jorge brushed by Miguel and sat in his executive's chair and crossed his feet on the desk and closed his eyes. His body buzzed with warmth and a little smile crept onto his face as the adrenaline of the fight opened his imagination and a spirit spoke a bold, clear plan to him in a whisper only he was blessed enough to hear.

Jay Dee's eyes watched Miguel, then shot to Buster. "Dirty cops pull shit like this sometimes. Why's it so farfetched to think this might be Detective Mallory?"

"Listen podna," said Buster. "And this is straight from the horse's mouth now. I asked McMaster if he actually thought that might be the detective runnin' 'round out there in a ski mask and he laughed real fuckin' hard at that one. McMaster's fuckin' with that detective. Pure sport. There's nothin' more to it."

Jay Dee threw up his hands. "Why couldn't it have been the detective in that house, looking for some way to nail Miguel for the Dandurand murders?"

"I would agree with you," said Miguel. "But Juan—"

"What exactly did Juan say to you on that last cell call anyway?" said Jay Dee. "Exact words if you can remember. It's very important."

Miguel squinted until his eyes closed. "He said, 'I think I just found Geronimo inside your fucking house.'"

Jay Dee's eyes crossed and he seemed to be amused. "And we all think now—or at least we strongly suspect—that Juan was hiding the crystal that he stole from the organization behind your house."

"That's my theory," said Buster. "The drug dog hit on the old truck in the backyard and on the Cutlass in the field . . . and yet, no crystal. The dog's not wrong, he's hittin' on residue of course. I think the ski mask got away with a little bonus for his trouble."

Miguel nodded. "My guess—it was Juan's share of the crystal he helped Dandurand, Rummell, and Carter steal fifteen months ago. The little fucker had his own game, may he rest in peace."

Jay Dee leaned toward Miguel and said, "When Juan called and told you Geronimo was inside your house, I'm guessing you were wondering what Juan was doing there in the first place."

Miguel palmed the top of his head and closed his eyes again. "It was a confusing call because Juan was supposed to be ahead of us on the highway, warning us about cops he saw on the road, speed traps, DUI checkpoints . . . whatever. We needed him to keep an eye out—keep us from runnin' into shit we didn't need to run into while hauling those bodies to the spot. When I answered the call he was whispering . . . talking real fast in a panic. I thought he was talking about my place in Wichita at first, where I lived, but that didn't make any sense because he was supposed to be ahead of us on Highway 160. When I finally realized he was talking about the farmhouse it made some sense at least because we were in the area . . . but we weren't heading to the farmhouse on Eden Road. I asked him what the fuck he was doing there."

"So," said Jay Dee, "is it fair to say that there was a lot going on in that last conversation you had with your brother?"

"It's fair, but what's your point?"

"My point is that we shouldn't rely on Juan in death any more than we did when he was alive. We should dive deeper. Consider other people who might have motive to be inside your farmhouse that night."

"Other people with motive," said Miguel, rubbing the back of his head. "Holy shit, you're right. Could've been some other cop, or some other Trevino hitman. Brilliant. Problem solved. Papa, whatever you're paying this guy, it isn't enough."

"I think I know what Jay Dee's drivin' at," said Buster. "He's thinkin' it may've been the judge."

Jay Dee shook his head. "All I'm saying is that we put him on the list because he's got motive, that's all."

"Put him on the list all you want," said Miguel, "but—"

"But what?" said Jorge, opening his eyes and glaring at Miguel. A vessel in his left eye had broken and blood pooled in the corner of it. "You don't think the judge could've pulled something like this, after what he showed you he's capable of Saturday night?"

"I'm sorry, Papa, but I'm with Buster on this—we think Juan stashed some of the crystal he stole in my old truck behind the farmhouse. But it wasn't there, and I don't see the judge running off with the crystal like that. What the fuck's he gonna do with it? This faggot lawyer of yours is making things more complicated than they need to be."

Jorge pinched the bridge of his nose and squinted. "Buster's of the opinion that the sheriff's drug dog hit on a *residual* odor of crystal in that old truck in the back. You're telling me that you've never stashed crystal in that truck?"

Miguel shook his head and said, "Fuck no, never. I think Juan had the crystal he stole hid there for a long time and finally got desperate enough to go get it, no matter the risk."

Jorge shrugged. "Or maybe the sheriff's dog ain't worth a shit and there was never any crystal in that truck to begin with?"

"Bullshit," said Miguel.

"Yep, that's bullshit. I'm with Miguel on that one," said Buster. "The dog's top notch, I checked it out. Was trained by Barton's group in Colorado Springs. Cost the sheriff's office upwards a twenty-five thou I bet."

Miguel set his jaw. "Whoever killed Juan stole the crystal like Buster said and I don't see no judge running off with it."

"It doesn't seem so farfetched to me that the judge would take all that poison and chuck it in a river somewhere," said Jay Dee. "But while we're on the subject of the Honorable Benjamin Joel, there's something you all need to understand about how I think things are likely to play out from here. Jorge, we've discussed this—"

"Hang on," said Jorge. "Buster, who killed my boy?"

"Whelp, the way I see it, smart money's still on some kind of Trevino connection. But I will say this about the judge, what I learned from talkin' to locals. Got a reputation as a true believer . . . God, the law, baseball, Apple pie . . . the kind of ol' boy folks looked up to before the sixties. Had a tough upbringin' I hear but came out the other side like you see him now, with a bit of a mean streak. In my experience, those are the kind with the fortitude you'd just a-soon not square up on if you can help it."

Buster sat in the chair next to Jay Dee and leaned toward Jorge. "Here's the problem I see we got with this guy. I don't think he's capable of ever doin' what we've asked of him.

Seems to me he's one of those guys that has this vision of himself he won't shut off for anybody. If he didn't turn it off last Saturday, he's not gonna turn it off now, or in two weeks, whenever the state's done presentin' evidence. Ya'll saw what he did in that van. That look like a man with an off button to you? I wouldn't entertain any illusions of him givin' up and followin' through like he said he would. Vaughn Rummell's not gettin' his judgment of acquittal, in my humble opinion. He'll be safe and sound in the El Dorado pen, lookin' to deal—lookin' to talk about all of us. Anything he can to keep the needle out of his arm."

Jay Dee nodded, looking back and forth between Buster and Jorge. "I agree with everything Buster said. Plus, there are solid strategic reasons Judge Joel may do everything he can to avoid granting the judgment of acquittal. Remember, Jorge, we talked about that?"

Jorge's feet were still propped on the desk. He peeked around them at his attorney. "Of course I remember."

"So," said Jay Dee, "you remember me telling you about the mafia case, *Illinois v. Baleman*?"

"Sure. Not the name of the case, but the takeaway."

"Forgive me," said Jay Dee. "But you've been drinking . . . smoking weed. It's my job to make sure you understand what I'm telling you . . . *what I've told you*, about the stark reality of the situation this judge should realize he's in right now, if he's competent at all, and I think that he is. It's important that—"

Jorge held up his hand, "Enough! God knows I love you, but you're such a hand-wringing little bitch." Jorge peeked around his shoes again at Jay Dee. "Makes me nervous."

"Forgive me. I'll . . . cease being a little bitch if you'll show me you grasp the situation as a lawyer would see it. As this judge will probably see it."

The two men stared across the desk at each other.

A wry smile crept across Jorge's face and he said, "Here's the situation. Any attorney in the world worth two shits is gonna know . . . that after the judgment of acquittal is granted we will have to wipe out the judge and his family to keep the state from proving in court that Vaughn was never actually in jeopardy in the first place . . . because we'd fixed the case."

Jay Dee looked at Buster, who shrugged.

Miguel said, "Is that right, Jay Dee?"

Jay Dee adjusted his round body in the seat. "Yeah, that's . . . good enough. My guess is that the judge has researched this issue and knows by now that we can't risk letting him and his family live after he grants the acquittal . . . so why would he do it? The incentives aren't right and he'll see that. He's going along with it now because he can't tell the cops and he knows we can't kill his sister until we don't need her anymore to prove to him she's still alive. So, Jorge. Enlighten us. What're you gonna do about that problem?"

Jorge dropped his feet from the desk to the floor, stood with the bottle of tequila, and raised it to his lips, talking into it while poised to take a hit. "It's pretty simple really. I guess I'll have to give him some other reason to grant the acquittal." He tipped the bottle to his lips.

Jay Dee pinched the bridge of his nose. "I'm sure in your head, with the weed and the tequila on board, that that sounds like a plan, but it's not."

"No? Let me guess, you want specifics?" said Jorge, wiping his lips with his forearm.

"Lay 'em on me if you got 'em. Please."

"I will," said Jorge. "Soon as I take a piss and get something to eat. Let's finish this in the kitchen."

Jorge set the bottle on the desk and walked past them toward the door.

Buster said, "Jorge, come on! What's the plan, man?"

Jorge stopped and looked at Jay Dee and said, "What's the penalty for killing a cop in Kansas?"

"It's punishable by death, why?" said Jay Dee. "What's that have to do with anything?"

"That has everything to do with anything," said Jorge. He nodded to himself, satisfied, and said, "Buster, I need you to find out what the judge is thinking if you can."

Buster said, "I'll tap whatever phone I can get to, but I know the courthouse has surveillance, so that's out."

"Do what you can. I'd like to know exactly where we stand. Oh, and something else. Juan's visitation has been set this Friday evening at the Long Family Funeral Home in Darby. The services will be there at ten the next morning. I want that put in the papers and on the Internet."

Buster said, "Do you want me there to see if I can spot and track Trevino's men?"

Jorge nodded. "I'll have men close on standby to help you track 'em. You lead them boys to the scent and let 'em take it from there."

"I 'spect there'll be cops there too . . . hoping to see you or Miguel."

Jay Dee said, "As Vaughn Rummell's investigator, it would be completely appropriate for you to have an interest in the folks attending the visitation, given that McMaster has painted Juan and Kramer Carter as the killers in court. I wouldn't worry about the cops spotting you."

Buster regarded Jay Dee with a furrowed brow, then looked back to Jorge. But he was already out the door. The St. Bernard stood, unhurried, and yawned before walking after his master, the overgrown nails on his paws clicking on the wood floor.

Jorge hit the head upstairs, then checked on Luciana. She was curled up on her side sleeping in her clothes on top of the comforter. Jorge put a blanket over her and pulled strands of hair from her face and checked underneath her nose to make sure she was still breathing.

20

Ben

AT TWO IN the morning a deputy called to tell me that the other judge in the county had suffered a stroke and was taken to the hospital by ambulance. When morning light came, I got a call from young Tommy Gerard, the local prosecutor. He said he hated to bother me at home, but wanted to know what my plan was for the child-in-need case that Judge Russell was supposed to hear at nine o'clock this morning. Last week, police had taken three children into protective custody and they were up against an unmovable deadline. A judicial determination granting the removal of the children from the home had to be made today, or they'd have to be returned to their mother. I told the prosecutor that would be the first problem I'd tackle when I got to the courthouse.

When I arrived at eight o'clock, Nancy hit me with the scheduling problem I already knew about, then told me that one of the jurors had just called in sick. She handed me a sheet with the phone numbers for the Office of Judicial Administration in Topeka and the other five judges in the district. I could ask OJA to send me a senior judge to handle the child-in-need case, but with the time constraint this wasn't a realistic option. Since I was the chief judge, my best option for getting court coverage on short notice was to order a judge from one of the other counties in the district to drop everything and head this way. On the bottom of the sheet Nancy gave me were the schedules of the other five judges. Two of them were in jury trials on life-sentence child-molestation cases, two had full dockets, and one was in Belize on vacation.

I poured a cup of coffee, went into my chambers, and shut the door. I threw my feet on the desk and gazed out the window. Sunlight glittered off the elms in the stillness of the morning. I'd been given a plausible reason to delay the case for twenty-four hours and I was going to take it. When I finished my coffee I called the local prosecutor and told him I'd be hearing the child-in-need case myself. Then I got Nancy on the intercom and told her to call OJA to see if they could get a senior judge down here tomorrow and in the foreseeable future to cover Judge Russell's cases, along with the cases he was slated to cover for me while I was in trial.

At 8:45 a.m. I called McMaster and Sweeney into chambers and gave them the news that I was sending all the jurors home for the day on account of the complications. If an absent juror had been the only problem, I said, maybe I would've been inclined to simply substitute one of the alternates and keep rolling, but Judge Russell's stroke had really put the court in a bind. Both attorneys said they understood, but McMaster seemed to be evaluating my manner, his arms crossed and pressed tight to his chest. I could've moved heaven and Earth to keep this trial moving and he knew it. Now that the kidnappers had felt their fish wiggle on the line, it occurred to me that they might jerk it taut to sink the hook deeper. I'd made the right call, but a sick feeling passed through me as I wondered what the ramifications for Ashley might be.

* * *

The child-in-need hearing went into the noon hour, but it was a no-brainer. Some live-in boyfriend to a mother of three was on the sex offender list. This was not the primary concern of the day. The boyfriend had defecated on the children's mother in front of her five-year-old boy. The mother was passed out from heroin when this happened. I put her children in foster care, temporarily. The law was set up to give her every chance to straighten up—get the kids back under her roof, such as it was. The mother seemed to think this was an unreasonable outcome, and made a bunch of noise about it.

Detective Mallory entered the courtroom and stood at the double doors, arms crossed, looking serious as he watched the show—a woman spewing her conspiracy theories to no one in particular, her version of speaking truth to power, as attorneys stood quietly and packed files into their briefcases. When I stood to leave she yelled, "Today the wolf is at my door. What will any of you lawyers do come tomorrow, when it's at yours?" If the past five days was any guide, the answer for me was simple. I'd shoot it. She was too mentally unstable to hold in contempt so I did us both a favor and spared her my sermon about her choices and her dicey courtroom decorum. I left the bench without another word.

I found Mallory pouring himself a cup of coffee in Nancy's office.

"You got a minute for me?" he asked.

I nodded and we stepped into my chambers. I was guessing this had something to do with my brother-in-law's visit to my house last night. The fact that Mallory was here alone was a good sign. If a connection had been made between Ashley's absence from her home in Omaha and this trial, I'd be looking at Gwen Sweeney and God knows who else about now. I hung my robe on the coat rack and went behind my desk and remained standing, my attempt at signaling this needed to be a short meeting. There was a note in Keri's handwriting on my chair and I wondered if it had anything to do with why Mallory wanted to meet with me. I picked it up and slipped it into my pocket as Mallory positioned himself behind the chairs in front of the desk.

"Your brother-in-law's at the sheriff's office right now. Says he wants to file a missing person's report on your sister."

"Yeah, he was at my house last night. I meant to call the sheriff's office about that first thing this morning, but, with all that's gone down today, I forgot."

"He told me about that. Said you told him to stay off your property. He seems to think you might be hiding your sister out there."

"Well, I'm not. I told him that last night."

Mallory nodded. "Okay, so what's the story here, Judge, if you don't mind?"

"Rod's a violent man and Ashley's scared of him. Same ol' song and dance."

"Alright—good enough for me. Sorry to bother you. The sheriff asked me to check with you—make sure your sister wasn't really missing."

"Sure, I understand."

Mallory stepped toward the door and paused—an oh-by-the-way look on his face. "My boy's got a game against Leo's team next week. Well, the team Leo played on last year anyways. I talked to Coach Hatfield yesterday. He said your boy wasn't playing for any of the Worthington teams."

"That's right," I said, recalling what I'd told Coach Hatfield. "Pops wanted to take Leo and Lindy on a . . . retreat, for lack of a better word. 'Fore he gets on up in years."

Mallory nodded. "That's what I heard . . . it's what Coach Hatfield told me. How nice. Where'd your grandfather take 'em?"

"All over," I said. "It's one of *them* trips." I smiled, trying to sell the answer, using the unwritten rules of polite interaction as cover, hoping Mallory wouldn't breach them and ask me what the hell I meant.

Mallory bit his lip. "One of them trips, huh? Okay, well I know Hatfield sure misses his shortstop. Maybe we'll have a chance to beat you guys this year."

"Maybe so," I said.

Mallory nodded, told me to take care, and left.

I ran my fingers through my hair and pulled Keri's note out of my pocket. She saw on the news that Rummell's trial had been postponed and wanted to know if that fact had freed up any time to meet with her and Father Garrahy. Prior to the kidnapping, Keri and I had finished our six-month Pre-Cana course—consultation for couples preparing to be married in a

Catholic Church—and needed to find a time to meet with Father to finalize the program. Apparently, he had time for us over the noon hour today, and since he'd noticed our absence from church last Sunday, the note said, he offered to make himself available for confession too. Keri ended the note with a smiley face.

I looked at my watch. It was 12:28 p.m. Judge Russell's delinquent-child-support docket was scheduled to start in forty-five minutes. I needed to cover all of his cases today to keep up appearances, but the truth was that I didn't feel like consulting with a priest, and even though I'd killed five men in the last five days, I couldn't think of anything I felt like confessing either. I'd rather grab a quick bite and come back to the courthouse for the deadbeat-dad docket. I figured I'd throw some of them in jail for not paying their child support. It wouldn't cleanse my soul, but it wouldn't feel bad.

My cell phone rang. It was Keri. She'd run into Nancy on the way out of the office and already knew the meeting with Father wasn't in the cards today. She was calling because her Internet research revealed that Juan's funeral was scheduled for ten in the morning this Saturday at the Long Family Funeral home in Darby, Kansas, a twenty-five minute drive from Worthington. There'd be a visitation Friday night from six to eight.

Keri had more news. She'd just got off the phone with Pops. Apparently, the Kid would be here tonight around ten o'clock. She asked me what the Kid was like. I told her what I knew about him.

His real name was Richard Beck and I guessed him to be in his mid-fifties now. I'd met him a few times, the last time being ten years ago when he came with his father to visit Pops. Back then, he had a fish-tail beard and wild unkempt hair. I remembered thinking that he had spent too much time alone in the mountains because of his abrupt manner and wild eyes. He reminded me of an artist's rendition of John the Baptist that I'd seen, minus the camel-hair jacket and the leather belt, but he still somehow looked like a man perfectly willing to live off locusts and wild honey. Pops told me his wife of five years had rounded off some of those rough edges, but that his beliefs hadn't changed. He'd still never filed a tax return or used a bank or a credit card. He didn't have a driver's license, and had never tagged a vehicle. He had little use for stores in general, though, when he did, he bought his goods with cash he'd earned from odd jobs.

Beck continued to live in a cabin devoid of any modern utilities on an expansive piece of property owned by a well-healed libertarian survivalist who'd bought up a bunch of property in Idaho and migrated from the east coast and made his property available to like-minded conservative Christians, Messianic Jews, or Orthodox Jews, in preparation for society's inevitable collapse. Beck had told me ten years ago, that when the banks fail and the missiles land in the cities, there'd be no more law enforcement, and the extent of society's moral depravity would finally be known. It was best, he said, to choose your neighbors wisely.

"How's this guy gonna be able to help us, Benny? Check that, how's he even gonna get here without a tagged vehicle or a driver's license?"

"I'm kind of interested to see that myself."

21

Friday Evening, May 31, 2019

Ben

ON THURSDAY, THE juror that had been ill returned and the senior judge sent by OJA was in my office at 8:30 a.m. for her briefing about the cases she'd be covering in the county over the next couple of weeks.

When I finally resumed the Rummell case at 9:30 a.m. that Thursday, Sweeney called the pathologist who performed the Dandurand autopsies to the stand. Her testimony took the entire day, and all the jury learned from the good doctor was that the Dandurands had died from their wounds. I suppose if the state hadn't put on this elaborate analysis of the evidence, the jury might be inclined to think the Dandurands died of high cholesterol.

Today, Friday, Sweeney and Davidson did more prosecutorial grunt work, introducing physical evidence found at the Dandurand premises on the night of the murders, including shell casings and the rebar extracted from Eddie Dandurand. They introduced a video of the crime scene taken on the night of the murders along with a plethora of photos, going into great detail about how evidence was gathered and the crime scene preserved. On cross-examination, McMaster put the cops through their paces, scoring only minor points.

I adjourned the case for the weekend at 4:55 p.m. and headed home where I changed into baggy sweatpants, an Aerosmith concert T-shirt, and tennis shoes. I slipped on a pair of dark-rimmed sunglasses, pulled a baseball hat down tight over my brow, and headed to Darby, Kansas. I stopped at the dirt road intersection of South 47th Street East and East 103rd Street South between Worthington and Darby and retrieved a key card for a room at the Pear Tree Inn out from under a basketball-sized rock in the ditch. Tony's bounty hunter booked the room in his name and stashed the keys for retrieval by us as needed. Tony, Keri, and Richard Beck had been there since noon, watching the funeral home from the hotel window.

When I got to Darby, I parked in a residential area six blocks from the Long Family Funeral home and walked to the Pear Tree Inn, arriving around five-thirty. Richard Beck was sprawled out on the bed and watching a fly walk on the ceiling. His old Browning pistol was on the nightstand and he wore a pearl-snap shirt with the arms ripped off and pieces of thread entangled with the hair on his shoulders. His beard was grey now, still fish-tailed, hanging to the middle of his chest and his brown Carolina work boots were on the floor beside the bed.

Tony was reclined on a small couch, his feet propped on the coffee table. His eyes fluttered open and he looked my way when I walked into the room and stood by the TV. Apparently, it was Keri's turn to stare out the second-story window at the front entrance and green metal roof of the Long Family Funeral Home. Several of the digital photos I took at Miguel's house and that we'd printed at home were spread out along the window sill.

The sound of Keri's voice broke the quiet in the room. "That's the fourth time I've seen that blue Pontiac drive by."

Tony struggled to stand up and looked out the window. "That's the second time I've seen it."

By the time I got to the window the Pontiac had passed, but I saw a man entering the funeral home carrying a giant stuffed animal—apparently a St. Bernard dog. I made a note of it on the hotel's notepad and slipped it into my pocket. I learned long ago from my detective friends that important facts can brush by unnoticed when you don't know what to look for.

Tony lifted his own notepad from the little desk against the wall and inspected his scribbling. "There was a blue Pontiac parked at the bookstore down the street when I got here. Looked like a black male, mid-thirties, was slipping a key into the driver's side door when I drove by."

"The guy driving this car I keep seeing is not black," said Keri.

Tony looked at me, then at my empty hands. "Where's the food?"

"Forgot it. Saw some Kentucky Fried down the street. Who's up for chicken?"

Everyone nodded while Keri handed me a sticky note with the tag number of the blue Pontiac.

Beck stood from the bed and got my attention with his eyes on his way to the bathroom. "Come in here. Let's fix you up."

When I got to the bathroom door, I saw four brushes and three silver-dollar-sized containers of makeup on the counter. "So, this is the makeup kit you told me about?"

Beck nodded and pointed a rough, dry finger at the various items splayed out on the counter. "Got your basic flat brushes— two small flats and two wide flats, highlighter, shadow, and your basic-brown eye liner. That's all we'll need. Now, have a seat here next to the sink."

I took off my hat and sat on the counter. It was a strange moment, staring up at this mountain man while he sized up the lines of my face. "So I guess you weren't puttin' me on. You really are some kind of backwoods make-up artist."

He shrugged. "Call it what you will."

"What kind of survivalist are you, anyway?"

"We don't have televisions in the mountains, Ben, but I have a community of friends. And sometimes . . . we like to entertain ourselves by putting on plays. I'm the make-up man."

I nodded.

"You believe that, do ya?" he said.

"Sure, why not?"

"You're about a gullible sonofabitch."

"Yeah, well I don't get out much."

Beck grabbed a brush and dabbed it in one of the containers. "The wife tells me I got a great sense of humor but I think she's the only one thinks what I say is funny. By the way, I was joshin' ya a second ago 'bout the plays and you didn't even come close to smiling."

"I was laughin' on the inside."

"I get it, man. You got a lot on your mind. Now, raise your eyebrows and wrinkle up your forehead for me. Let me show you how this is done."

"How is it that you have this particular . . . skill set? I mean, why?"

"So I can go to the store. Buy clothes. Groceries. Whatnot."

"And you go in a . . . disguise?"

"If I'm gonna be millin' around in a store I do. Can't be too careful. I haven't filed an income tax return in over twenty years."

"You really think they're lookin' for you—the feds?"

"Not in the sense these guys you're dealing with are gonna be lookin' for you when this is over. I'm here to help you in whatever way I can, but you're gonna need someone to help you get outta here and stay off the grid when this is over. That's really why I'm here—the way I see it anyways. Your Pops has already got a batting cage built for the kids up there. Hits 'em grounders every day. Maybe next year we can dummy up some birth certificates for the kids—I know a guy can do that for us— get 'em in a league in Boise or some small town up there. But you're lookin' at homeschoolin' them kids for the foreseeable future."

I noticed Keri standing in the bathroom doorway. She'd heard what Beck said, but she didn't look surprised or shocked. We'd talked about this. I made eye contact with her and said, "We know they won't ever stop coming for us. Show us your magic, big guy."

The whole process took less than twenty minutes. When he was done with me, my eyes appeared sunken in, my nose wider, nostrils bigger, and my lips thinner. Add to that the crescent-moon bags under my eyes and the new wrinkles on my cheeks and forehead and I was unrecognizable to myself.

Keri handed Beck his camera and he had me stand in front of a sky-blue background he'd tacked on the bathroom wall.

Beck said, "Alright, look all pissy like you've been at the DMV for three hours." After snapping the photo, he looked at the digital image on the screen and said, "Nailed it. I'll get this to my guy and we'll have a fake driver's license for you in two days."

I knew from earlier discussions that his "guy" was his driver, who we didn't get to meet, and apparently weren't going to get to meet. Beck's friend agreed to drive him to Kansas and help on the condition of anonymity. I'd asked Beck if his anonymous driver was Pops and he assured me it wasn't. When I called Pops yesterday he promised me he was still in the Sawtooth Mountains with the children, then put them on the phone.

Beck set the camera on the counter and looked at Keri. "You're next."

I threw on the ball cap, the shades, and walked three blocks to the KFC. When I got there I saw a blue Pontiac pull into the bookstore parking lot across the street, but I couldn't see the tag. After parking his car, the driver sat and stared out at the road between us as I came down the sidewalk. I saw he wasn't black, and if he'd noticed me, that's probably all he could tell about me from this distance—the color of my skin.

I entered the KFC and ordered some extra-crispy—a single order. I sat where I could look out between the K and the F painted on the window. All I saw was the outline of a man's head in the Pontiac.

I spotted a black man with a cane walking down the street in front of the KFC, heading toward the funeral home. He limped to protect one leg, then the other, glancing in the direction of the Pontiac and smiling. His face was familiar to me, even from this distance—even if I couldn't place his name right away. I recognized his shoes because I had a pair in the exact same style—Adidas something or other—they were black and white with no frills.

Then it suddenly came to me. He was a KBI agent named Washington. I'd noticed his shoes when he was in my house with Caroline Gordon on the night of the Dandurand murders. They'd come to my house at two in the morning and obtained a search warrant for the Dandurand premises.

I finished up the extra-crispy, and put orders in for Keri, Tony, and Beck. While I waited, I went back to the window to peek through Colonel Sanders' painted-on head. The Pontiac was gone. I decided on the scenic route back to the hotel to avoid the cops. Behind the KFC, there was a wooden footbridge over a creek that led to a running path through some woods.

I grabbed my bag of chicken and stepped outside into the parking lot, or more accurately, into the path of the drive-through. I was ten or fifteen feet from a man in a Suburban reaching for a sack from the window. The driver's profile was unmistakable—big nose, small chin—an anemic man with predatory teeth, big ears and limp strands of oily black string for hair. This was Vaughn Rummell's investigator, a retired detective from Laredo named Harold "Buster" Reynolds. He'd been in and out of the courtroom on Tuesday and Thursday, conferring with McMaster and Thompson. But today he was absent, which I found odd, since as a former detective he'd be uniquely qualified to point out any irregularities in the gathering of the evidence from the crime scene.

Rummell's investigator was careful not to spill his sack of food, and I was careful to walk fast enough to get past him before he looked up. When I got to the footbridge, I glanced back as the Suburban slipped slowly onto the roadway in the direction of the Long Family Funeral Home. We were all circling Juan's corpse like hungry turkey buzzards.

* * *

When I got back to the room, Keri and Tony were standing in front of the TV, their eyes riveted to the screen. Beck was watching the funeral home through the window and I saw that he had done Keri's makeup while I was out. She looked like a thirty-year smoker who'd spent all night playing slots at the nearby casino. I set the sack of food on the bed and watched the TV.

One of the media people I'd seen in the courtroom was interviewing a woman for the six o'clock news. On the screen was a still photo of Vaughn Rummell and another guy on a makeshift stage in some scrubby place—maybe a dive bar. Rummell had his shirt off and looked like he might be trying to swallow a microphone in front of a small audience. The interviewer explained that Rummell was the lead singer of a local rap metal band called Chainsaw. The shirtless guy with him was on the guitar. The focus of this story was the guitarist, as the camera zoomed in dramatically to draw attention to his clown tattoos.

"We will miss you, Kramer," the interviewee said in a voiceover as a close-up of Kramer Carter in mid-angst over a guitar riff covered the screen. Then that image gave way to the teary-eyed face of a pale young woman with dyed black hair who said, "He's been missing for over a year and now that we know he's been murdered, Vaughn's defense attorneys are taking advantage of the situation and trying to convince people that Kramer was the one that killed those people. It isn't right . . . and it hurts. Kramer wasn't a violent person. If anybody knows anything about this, please come forward."

The reporter signed off from the pale young woman's couch while the two newscasters on camera back at Channel Ten's studio shook their heads in dismay. One pronounced it a "sad deal," and the other added somberly, "there are a lot of questions." They let that linger for all of two seconds before a chair swivel and a switch in camera angle took viewers off that subject and into the controversy about whether Wichita's city fathers should vote in favor of treating the drinking water with fluoride.

After Tony turned off the TV, I walked over to the window and said, "Getting a tracker on a car in that lot is going to be as tough as we thought."

"What makes you say that?" asked Keri.

I pointed at the black man with the cane crossing the street below. "That's one reason," I said. "Man with the cane is a KBI agent."

We watched Agent Washington limp through the rock garden, past some plastic trees, under the canopy, and through the front door. The blue Pontiac cruised by again, and from the other direction, a minivan pulled into the funeral home parking lot. Four Hispanic women and two teenage boys emerged and entered the building. I watched them through my binoculars, but I couldn't see the tag number because of the angles. One of the women resembled someone in one of the photos I took from Miguel's house, but between the poor quality of the image and my distance from the woman, it was hard to determine if they were the same person.

"You think the cops tailed that van?" asked Keri.

"Maybe," I said. "And maybe Agent Washington's timing is no accident either."

Tony tore through the bags of food on the bed and handed Keri a box of chicken.

"McMaster's investigator is here too. I saw him in the drive-through. He's the one from Laredo I told you about."

"Did he see you?" Keri asked.

"No. But he might be holed up right next door to us for all we know."

I described Buster's appearance for them.

I tossed my ball cap on the bed and rubbed my head. When I looked up, an obviously pregnant white girl with dishwater blond hair was climbing out of the driver's seat of a beat-up Honda Civic in the parking lot. Studying her through my binoculars I saw she was the girl we'd been watching for. She had a birthmark or an old burn scar that started on her neck and crawled up her chin. This was Juan's girl. I looked at the photos on the sill of her. In one of them, she was standing between Juan and Miguel on the deck of a yacht, drink in her hand, topless. So I knew she had met Miguel. I had photographic evidence of it.

I believed her name was April. I had a number for an "April" in the contacts list on Juan's burner phone. Hers was the only number with the local 316 area code. Others included 915 for El Paso, 505 for Albuquerque, or 602 for Arizona, and some started with a "2" country code: Mexico. I figured all the other numbers were for burner phones that had long since been destroyed. But I held out hope for 316-April. It dominated Juan's call logs, both incoming and outgoing. We were about to see if April still had her same number.

I handed the binoculars to Keri. "Check out the blonde in the parking lot."

Keri raised the binoculars and after looking through them for a few seconds, set the binoculars on the sill and said, "That girl looks like she was due yesterday." Then Keri reached into her purse and pulled out a brand new burner phone. "Sure looks like our girl. Let's make sure."

Keri dialed April's number. We all watched as the girl stopped about twenty feet from the canopy and dug around in her purse until she retrieved her cell.

Keri held her phone so we could all listen.

"Hello?" I heard her say, sounding surprised.

"Hello, who is this?" asked Keri.

"Who is this?" asked April.

"Sorry, wrong number," Keri said before ending the call.

* * *

Two hours later, Tony was down the street a few blocks from the funeral home, waiting for April. If she turned left instead of right, we would let him know. When she finally ambled out to her car at eight-thirty with the clan from the van, she climbed into her Honda Civic and turned right, in Tony's direction. I hit redial for Tony and told him April was coming his way, alone. Then we watched as a funeral home employee locked the front door.

Beck, Keri, and I kept an eye on the place for a while on the off chance there'd be an after-hours visit from Miguel or Jorge. Agent Washington apparently had the same idea and Buster Reynolds was lurking around too. Washington was sitting at the bus stop and Buster parked his Suburban in a bank parking lot down the street. When the nine o'clock news came on, I watched myself talking to Vaughn Rummell in court, the part I'd missed earlier. Then came the footage of the pale black-haired girl pleading for someone to come forward again, followed by the still photo of Rummell and Kramer Carter living the dream on stage. The talking heads back at the studio shook their heads ruefully again when the story was over.

Tony called just after ten o'clock. He saw April entering #137 of the Silver Springs apartment complex on Tyler Road in West Wichita—it was probably her home. He called again half an hour later. The GPS tracker was installed without incident, so he was on his way to bail some clients out of jail.

Once we realized Tony wouldn't be offering to bring us any food, and that the Pear Tree Inn didn't have a restaurant or provide room service, Keri and I slipped out of the hotel and into the night. Beck stayed back to take a shower and catch up on sleep. We left on foot because Agent Washington and Buster Reynolds were still lingering and we didn't want either one of them spotting Keri's Honda Civic or my Ford F350. We were far more recognizable in our cars at the moment than we were on foot, owing to our makeovers. We walked to Denny's where we ate omelets and drank coffee.

* * *

We were on the sidewalk heading back to our hotel when I spotted Buster Reynolds' Suburban heading in the opposite direction. We stopped and watched it unseen from our cover, a thicket of trees that shielded us from the road. He went through a stoplight and into a gas station. We walked in his direction, watching him pump gas. When he was through, we stood in a narrow alleyway across the street, invisible in the dark. We watched him drive the Suburban down the same road south, away from the funeral home. We stood there until all we saw were his taillights turning right.

"What do you think he's doing down that way?" Keri asked.

"If he hooks a left on K-15, he'll have his pick of fast-food joints for about a half mile. Oh, and there's a strip club down that way I hear."

Keri smirked. "Little late for a taco run isn't it?"

"Lonely man in a strange land," I said.

"Yeah, we should check the bitch house."

That's what the locals called their strip club—the bitch house. The real name was Jezebel's Beach House.

I took out my phone and called for an Uber. Our driver frowned a little when Keri told him to drop us off at the bitch house. I guess our money was still good though.

The strip club had a gravel drive-through to the front steps, which were fashioned out of about thirty ascending railroad ties plugged into a slope. Neglected flowerbeds flanked the stairs. A rickety wood fence surrounded the place and hid most of the cars from view of the highway. The smashed-grass parking lot ran to the back of the building on the north side. Buster's Suburban was parked furthest from the highway at the rear of the lot next to a little tin shed in the corner where the fence ran from east to south. We walked toward it.

The place was packed and noise spilled into the night. Neon palm trees and blinking flamingos lit our faces. When we got to Buster's Suburban I stuck the tracker on the undercarriage below the front passenger's seat as music from the club became louder and less muffled as if a door had opened up somewhere. We slipped into a thicket of weeds and head-high volunteer trees between the tin shed and the fence.

Peeking out from behind the shed between the trees, I saw Buster Reynolds turn the corner and walk toward his vehicle, and us, alone. He was already close enough to notice any movement in the trees so I looked at Keri and whispered, "Don't move."

He walked between the front of the Suburban and the fence while reaching for his waistband. As I balled my fist, he stopped and faced the fence, a web of young tree limbs between us. We were within seven feet of him—close enough that I could smell the smoke coming off his clothes. I heard a zipper, then piss hitting the fence as the old cop moaned. I was as relieved as he was.

22

Ben

FROM MY VANTAGE in a car on the south side of the Wichita Hyatt Hotel parking lot, I watched a duck stalk a toddler carrying bread on the lawn near the hotel's main entrance. I was waiting for Buster to emerge. When all you want to do is fast-forward through time, this is what you get to see while you wait. Some geese were racing from the bank of the Arkansas River, but the little boy hadn't noticed yet. He was having fun keeping ahead of his benign little stalker. But when he finally noticed the gaggle of more aggressive birds coming at him, he dropped the bread and ran to his mother. The duck got a nibble before a big white goose hissed, scaring off the competition and getting the bread.

It was ten a.m. and Juan's funeral had started. Keri and Beck were watching from our hotel room. I had spent much of the night sitting in a car borrowed from Tony's bounty hunter, keeping tabs on April and Buster Reynolds via the GPS app I'd downloaded onto my burner phone.

My phone trilled. It was Keri.

"No Miguel. No Jorge," she said. "And I saw April enter the building alone."

All the coffee I'd drank through the night left me jittery and the sun was hot and bright and irritating. The sunglasses took the edge off the glare, but the trucker hat with the built-in ponytail was itchy on my neck and the old jeans I had on were cramping my balls. The shirt I wore—prison blue and reeking of grease and gasoline—was too tight on my shoulders, and something on the back side of the patch that said *Nate* was stabbing my nipple. Tony had borrowed the outfit for me from a private-investigator friend.

"What kind of man skips his own son's funeral?" Keri asked.

"A hardened one," I said. This thought tightened my belly, adding to my overall sense of discomfort. The kidnappers lived in a world of alternative conventions, and it reminded me how little I had in common with my enemy. I wondered if they were sophisticated enough to understand that I knew granting a judgment of acquittal was ultimately a death sentence for me and my family. If they were, they must have something else in store for me. But what?

"Any sign of Buster Reynolds?"

"Not yet. Just sitting here stewing in the sun," I said. Buster's Suburban had come directly from the strip club to where it was parked now. I was surprised it was still here this late in the morning. We were expecting Buster would stalk the funeral—maybe follow the procession to the cemetery.

"Maybe Buster has a second car," I said. "Or maybe he hitched a ride. He might be right there in Darby at the hotel with you."

"Haven't seen him."

"Hang on now. Finally," I said.

Buster emerged from under the shade of the Hyatt's canopy, stopping to set his suitcase on the ground and tossing what looked to be the remains of a sandwich at the geese that had congregated on the lawn. Then he closed his eyes and tilted his face toward the sun.

"What is it?"

"Buster's here," I told her.

"What's he doing?"

"Feeding geese, soaking up the sun."

I ended the call and watched as Buster got into his Suburban. I decided not to follow him close even though it might mean missing a quick rendezvous on the way to his next destination.

I felt it was prudent to mitigate the risk of being detected by staying well back and letting the tracker do the work.

Tony, who was also monitoring the movement of the trackers, called me fifteen minutes later, excited that Buster was finally up and moving, heading south on the turnpike toward Worthington. If Buster stayed south on I-35, he'd reach Laredo on the Mexican border in another twelve hours, give or take. Laredo marked the starting point for the I-35 Narco-Corridor, where illegal drugs are mainlined into Middle America, up through Wichita and Kansas City, eventually ending in Duluth, Minnesota, about 150 miles from Canada.

He got off the turnpike and went west on U.S. 160 toward Worthington. I tailed behind out of sight and got in line at a car wash once I got to Worthington because Buster had stopped at a convenience store up the road. I stayed on the phone with Tony the whole time.

After ten minutes of small talk, Tony told me what I could've seen on my phone if I wasn't talking to him on it. "Alright, he's headed west on one-sixty again."

Listening to Tony's directions and staying well back, I followed him through town across the train tracks and onto Sixteenth Street.

"He turned north on Oil Field Road. Any clue where he might be going?" asked Tony.

Buster was now northwest of Worthington on a paved road in the country.

I said, "If he turns left on Seventieth Avenue, we got problems."

"Why would he cruise by your house?"

"Not sure, but it can't be good."

I had just reached the intersection of Sixteenth Street and Oil Field Road when Tony said, "Ah shit, he's heading toward your house."

My head ached from the rush of blood and I had a death grip on the wheel—the constant pressure was wearing me out and I felt lethargic, but I turned onto Oil Field Road and gunned it anyway.

After a couple minutes of driving I asked, "Did he stop?"

"No. He's past your house now headed toward Tyler Road. Maybe he's on to us and now he's screwing with you."

"Maybe."

"Let's forget this guy. Miguel and Jorge are the guys we're really after. Maybe they show up at the cemetery tonight—to pay their final respects. Maybe we get lucky."

I don't know exactly how long I drove in silence thinking about that before I said, "Tell me where he's going. I'm following."

"He's turning south on Tyler Road as we speak."

After flying by my house, I looked to the south and saw a trail of white rock dust hovering over Tyler Road and floating over the wheat. The line went silent again for several moments. Then he said, "I got a bad feeling about this."

"Just one?"

When I turned left on Tyler, his dust still lingered in the air. It was a beautiful summer day for a drive. A beautiful day to grovel for a break with your heart in your throat. A beautiful day for the kind of longing for the way things used to be that sucked your soul dry and left your eyelids leaden. The brilliance of the day taunted my listless mind with visual whispers—the pumpjacks were pumping for oil and the cows were swatting flies with their tails by the man-made prairie ponds—and the beat goes on. When I got to U.S. 160, I followed him east for two and a half miles to U.S. 81 in Worthington, before heading south out of town again. This was a familiar road.

"Any clue where he's going now?" asked Tony.

"Yes."

"Where?"

"Keri's house. I think he saw the security company's sign in my front yard and decided to move on, find an easier target."

The silence on Tony's end lasted long enough to make me think I'd lost the connection.

"Tony, you still there?"

"Yeah, just thinking."

"Call Keri and Beck and tell them what's goin' down. I'll call back in five minutes." I ended the call before Tony responded. Then I slammed the accelerator to the floor.

I flew past the gravel road I would've normally turned on to get to Keri's house. Instead, I went a mile further south where I hit the brakes, fishtailing in the gravel through a right turn.

I called Tony, who answered halfway through the first ring and told me what I already knew from the GPS app on my phone. "He's heading toward Keri's house like you said."

"Did you get hold of Beck and Keri?"

"Yeah."

"Good. I'll check in when I need to."

I ended the call and kept the pedal down as much as I dared for two miles where I parked the car on a trail that ran along the field side of the shelterbelt.

I ditched the hat, holstered my pistol, grabbed my binoculars, and ran into the wheat field toward Keri's rental home, a single-story house with a lean-to carport big enough for one vehicle. When I saw the roof, I ducked down and kept moving through the wheat, checking the map on my phone— Buster beat me there. By the time I reached the edge of the field, I was on my belly near an old windmill.

He was sitting in his Suburban in the driveway with the windows down, smoking a cigarette. I used the binos to see him up close. His tokes were deliberate and he let the smoke out through his nostrils. He seemed to be in a daze.

When his trance broke, he stepped out of his vehicle, donned a shoulder holster and a western-style suit jacket, and headed for the front door. He rapped on the door and when no one answered, he took a look around before pulling out rubber gloves and slipping them on. He tried the knob, but the door was locked. He checked under a potted plant and a doormat. I knew Keri's spare key was actually closer to me, beneath a cinderblock near the windmill.

Buster gave up the search and walked back to his Suburban and pulled out a black bag that looked like something a doctor in an old movie might use to make house calls. He went over to the side of the house to the phone utility box, prying it open with a flathead screwdriver. Then he fumbled for a moment with alligator clips. After that, he worked with the steady confidence of a service technician, finishing in minutes. When he got to his Suburban he tossed the black bag on the seat, unzipped his fly and took a piss right there in the driveway with his gloves on.

23

Ben

I WANDERED THE rows of the dead by the light of the moon looking for a fresh mound of dirt. Sheet lightening flashed and thunder rumbled above me. Where the hell are you, Juan? Can I call you Juan? Or do you prefer Mr. Mendez? Perhaps I should call you Mr. Mendoza—maybe your mom likes to hear it that way, in her family's name. Was she here today at noon for your burial—somewhere by the mausoleum next to the statues of Jesus and the Virgin Mary? I don't see evidence of you anywhere now in this darkness, Juan. This is where Keri said you'd be—she was looking for your brother or your father but neither one showed. She was way over there, watching your burial from afar, looking like a haggard chain-smoking mourner standing before a random grave. But you couldn't care less—you're dead.

I made my way to a secluded spot between two hedges near the statue of an angel.

Buster hadn't gone back to the Hyatt. He now had a room at a rundown roadside motel less than three miles from Keri's house—damn near in Oklahoma, something Tony confirmed visually. We figured this was where Buster would listen to the calls he intercepted from her landline. Beck's driver, who I now called "the Voice" since I was able to talk to her on a cell phone, was somewhere in Wichita surveilling April in case she was meeting up with any of Juan's relatives. Keri was in her rental, armed with a shotgun, waiting for me to call her at 9:55 p.m. on her tapped landline. Beck was set up in the field next to her house with a high-powered rifle.

Noting that it was about time to phone Keri, I made my way through the tombstones to the fence that surrounded the cemetery and climbed over, seating myself on an old stump amidst some trees. I pulled Tony's last tracker out of my pocket to get to the script Keri and I'd put together for the call I was about to make. I planned on sticking around another hour or two, looking for an opportunity get a tracker on a cartel vehicle.

The script we'd developed was meant to protect my sister by sending the message that I'd grant the judgment of acquittal— but only if I knew my sister was still alive. I needed proof of life. If Ashley was already dead, this charade was over anyway. It'd be time to tell the authorities.

The time on my phone read 9:55 p.m., so I pulled out my script and a penlight, and made the call. She picked up on the third ring.

"How you holding up?" I said in a hoarse whisper.

"Fine. You?"

"Not too good. You know that thing we've been talking about."

"Yeah."

"About somehow signaling to McMaster to file a motion for bond. I could grant it, so his client could . . . bond out and disappear."

"Right, have you figured out how to do that?"

"No, that's just it. How would I know Ashley would actually be released, I mean, I don't even know if she's still alive. So I'm thinking now . . . that if I don't get any proof she's alive by Tuesday, I'm going to blow the top off this thing."

Keri hit the scripted long pause and said, "So . . . what do you mean? You goin' to the cops?"

I paused like I was putting the words together on the fly. "I'm going to mull this over for a couple days . . . it's not set in stone . . . but I'm thinking . . . without proof of life, you know, without that . . . I should come clean with what's going on. Get the search started. You know, get things out in the open and put the pressure on them . . . and off me."

"Okay. I understand."

"As awful as it is, what I have to do, if I knew I would get her back I wouldn't hesitate. I'd do it."

"Right, I get it."

"But what assurance do I have that she'd be released?"

"None," said Keri, her first ad lib. "I've been thinking about what you said, about when this is all over, what we'd have to do. Where we'll have to live."

"And?"

Keri sniffled. "I still want to marry you and I'll go wherever you go. We can vanish with the kids together." This wasn't in the script and if it had been I would've cut it—too much. But it sounded perfect coming from her.

I needed whoever was listening to think I planned to go all the way on this thing, if only they would hold up their end of their deal. They needed to know I would get the kids to a place away from inquisitive locals. They needed to know I would make it my mission to keep them quiet.

"You know we'll be vanishing together even if Ash is already dead—which she probably is—you know that, don't you?" My voice cracked a little. I was saying my line, word for word, but I wasn't acting.

Keri was silent on the other end. Then I heard a muffled cry. This wasn't in the script either. She finally said, sniffling, "If she's already gone, I know we're next, but you can't think that way."

Whoever was listening now was hearing a real conversation. It occurred to me that I really was going to shut this deal down if proof of life did not come by Tuesday—if they mailed it on Monday, it would probably be in my box on Tuesday. The deadline I'd just set for myself made the possibility of Ashley's death more imminent in my mind. I also knew that if they'd already killed her and couldn't get me the proof I needed, the cartel would be coming at us full bore in a hurry. "Maybe you're right. I need some sleep now. Get my head on straight before I do anything rash."

*　*　*

Ten minutes later headlights shone through the cemetery gate.
I tucked the tracker into my pocket, hopped the fence, and made
my way to the mausoleum which I used as cover. The SUV
stopped with its headlights illuminating the fresh pile of dirt
Keri had pinpointed as Juan's final resting place.

Two men exited the black Suburban—driver and front
passenger—both wielding what looked like assault rifles. Both
men looked around as two back-seat passengers stepped out.
The men with the rifles stayed in the dark but the back
passengers walked toward the grave and into the light—a man
and a woman holding on to each other. As they got closer to the
grave and to me, I saw they were both Hispanic, at least sixty
years old. The woman wore a black dress with a black jacket
over her shoulders. The man was slightly overweight, shorter
than his wife, and had a full head of thick black hair. He wore a
jacket I recognized from the photos from Miguel's house—tan
and dirty, well worn. I bet—if I got closer—I'd see that his eyes
were bloodshot like they were in every close-up photo I'd seen
of him.

This was Jorge and Luciana, whom I'd pegged as Juan and
Miguel's parents. They'd appeared in many of the photos from
Miguel's house. On the back of some of the older photos the
names "Jorge and Luciana" was scribbled. In more recent
photos, Jorge was usually pictured by himself and if there was
any writing at all on the back, it was usually "Papa." Jorge was
one of the men pictured in front of Uncle Sam's Bar from the
early '90's. The family resemblance between Jorge and his sons
was strong—the same mix of intimidating slits for eyes with
high cheekbones and smooth skin. Because of the discrepancy
in firepower—my Glock versus at least two assault rifles—
there wasn't a damn thing I could do about Jorge being here at
the moment. Keri and Beck wouldn't be here for another half
hour. Because of the hyper-vigilant way the men with the rifles
were scanning the area—something I saw them do when the sky

flickered with lightning—I couldn't even position myself to see the tag number of the Suburban.

They gazed at the headstone for a short time, then Jorge looked up and sniffed at the air. It was a warm summer night, but a breeze had kicked up, cooling the air, which all of a sudden smelled of rain. Jorge retrieved a vase of flowers from the Suburban and set it down next to the grave and the wind tipped it over and the rain came down before Jorge and Luciana climbed into the back seat of the Suburban. A driving rain pelted and cooled me as I watched them leave the cemetery.

24

Caroline

CAROLINE PARKED THE Crown Victoria behind Detective Mallory's Impala in an alley west of Main Street in downtown Worthington at 10:38 p.m. As she walked to the foot of the rusty stairway that led to Mallory's apartment and looked up, the steady murmur of voices and music from the bar next door poured into the alley. The stairs were steep, as close to straight up as any she'd ever seen. She looked left down the alley through the narrow chute formed by the backs of buildings on both sides. Lightning flickered mutely in the northern sky. The storm that had almost put the Crown Vic in a ditch twenty minutes earlier would miss Worthington, but its wake now blew cool wind on her face.

The prosecutor, Gwen Sweeney, had called Caroline a couple hours earlier and asked her to contact Mallory because, for some unknown reason, he wasn't returning her calls. After unsuccessfully trying to contact Mallory by phone herself, Caroline called Sweeney and explained she wasn't having any luck either.

Before asking Caroline to make a trip to Worthington to find him, Sweeney explained that evidence collected last Sunday from the field behind Miguel's farmhouse had been tested. She'd received reports from the KBI's DNA experts at noon, reviewed them, and forwarded the lab's complete packet of materials via e-mail to Glenn McMaster in an attempt to satisfy the state statute regarding discovery. For strategy reasons, she'd decided she wanted to recall Mallory to testify on Monday.

Sweeney explained she needed to question Mallory again because he had collected the two ski masks located underneath the seat of the Cutlass Supreme that was found wrecked in the field next to Juan's and Kramer Carter's bodies. The state's forensic scientists had now compared DNA found on the masks to DNA taken from Juan's and Kramer Carter's corpses. Not surprisingly, the DNA found on one of the masks matched the known sample taken from Juan. And the DNA on the second mask wasn't a match to the known samples from Kramer Carter, Juan, or Rummell. However, the KBI's expert was of the opinion that the DNA found on the second mask in the Cutlass belonged to a close relative of Juan Mendez-Mendoza. Without a known sample from the actual relative, that's all the expert could say—that the two were closely related.

The only good news for Vaughn Rummell—and it wasn't that good—was that the most recent testing showed that Juan's and Kramer Carter's DNA were all over Rummell's Mustang, which wasn't surprising since they were in the same band together. All it really showed, was that the whole band had been in Rummell's Mustang at some point.

Unfortunately for Rummell, the evidence against him was even more overwhelming than before, which was saying something. The state's firearms examiner had already concluded in his report that the bullets pulled from Dandurand's parents during the autopsies were fired from the Hi-Point pistol found in the ditch next to Rummell. A print matching Rummell's right thumb was pulled from the pistol's muzzle. Swabs taken from the right hand and clothes of Rummell on the night of the murders showed he had gunshot residue on them. Rummell's DNA was found on the Hi-Point's pistol grip and at the scene of the crime—in particular on the spit holding Eddie Dandurand. Finally, the black ski mask in the flipped-over Mustang tested for DNA that matched Rummell's.

The overall effect of the most recent testing—the comparisons of DNA from the ski masks found in the Cutlass to the known samples—was that any claim by McMaster that

Kramer Carter committed the Dandurand murders would be almost impossible to believe. Now, more than ever with the additional forensic evidence, it looked like Juan, and someone related to Juan, helped Rummell commit the Dandurand murders. Other than perhaps Carter's sleeve of clown tattoos, there was nothing placing him inside the Dandurand residence. And there was still zero evidence Carter had ever possessed the pistol used in the killings.

By testing the evidence found behind Miguel's farmhouse and getting the reports completed in less than a week, the KBI's lab had moved as quickly as they ever had in their entire history. And the effort had been worth it. The results helped plug a hole in the state's case that McMaster had been exploiting for four days. Now the jury could be sure that the tattoos Haley saw that night belonged to the defendant, not Kramer Carter. Gwen Sweeney was eager to get this evidence before a jury to take the shine off of McMaster's red herring. Having stripped away the most compelling piece in McMaster's defense, he'd be more or less reduced to making bald claims that someone—maybe the cops—had set Rummell up by planting this mountain of evidence against him. It was important to Sweeney that she arrange a time to meet with Detective Mallory on Sunday to prepare him for what might be coming his way during McMaster's cross-examination.

Caroline had tried to call Mallory one final time before breaking a date with her ex-boyfriend, Jack, whom she first met in college at Wichita State. Jack didn't take the news well, and accused her of having a better offer, which, sadly, was typical of Jack in the months leading up to their original breakup. He was tall, handsome, and had a nice family who lived in a rich suburb of Wichita. Caroline had fallen for him her sophomore year, and they had a good run, but in April of her senior year Jack's good manners and sense of humor had been obscured by his needy and jealous side, which was why she jettisoned the relationship when she left Wichita after college to be a cop in KCK.

Much to Caroline's surprise, in the six years since their breakup, she hadn't dated anyone she liked more than Jack. So when he called her out of the blue two weeks earlier she felt the old spark, something she hadn't felt in years. When they met for coffee, the conversation was pleasant and Caroline agreed to tonight's date. Jack called every day after that, sometimes leaving awkward, almost lovesick, messages on her iPhone. Caroline felt smothered again, somehow, just listening to the recordings. She knew she would never like Jack as much as he liked her and that was a problem because Jack needed lots of attention. He was a well-heeled trust fund kid whose world came to him on a platter and his insecurity reminded her how soft he'd always seemed to her, bereft of the sharp edges a man like her father needed to survive as a combat soldier in Vietnam. Caroline hated to admit it, but she wanted that edge. She found herself hoping, in that quiet time before she fell asleep, that something legitimate would come up on Saturday so she could ditch her date with Jack and not feel so bad for doing it.

So a night in Worthington looking for Raymond Mallory wasn't all bad.

Her fear—a fear she didn't share with Sweeney—was that Mallory was passed out drunk in his apartment, something she'd heard he was prone to do on weekends after a pressure-filled week. She resented the fact that Sweeney was putting her in this situation, and that Mallory wasn't man enough to pick up his damn phone when he'd gotten a load on. If indeed, he had.

Halfway up the stairs leading to Mallory's apartment door, Caroline looked down and to her left into the outdoor fenced-in area of the bar. Strings of lights hanging on poles crisscrossed, forming an X over several picnic tables and two round tables with Corona umbrellas above them. A bald man was sitting at one of the picnic tables with a mug of beer in front of him and a group of young woman were heading back inside the bar. Now alone, the man put a cigarette in his mouth and inhaled. His head hung over his left shoulder and only one side of his face seemed to be sucking on the cigarette. He looked at her through the strings of light, then away as he blew smoke into the night. Something about the way he did this made her nervous.

She touched the Glock on her right hip with her forearm. She wore a burgundy sleeveless tactical women's top she had for undercover work that hung just below the waist of her jeans and covered the pistol. The top looked so good on her, she had been in front of a full-length mirror toying with the idea of wearing it on her date with Jack when Sweeney first called.

When Caroline reached the landing at the top of the stairs she could smell the cigarette the man was smoking as she knocked on the door. If she were at the base of the stairs she'd have only been fifteen feet from the man, but now she was twelve feet above him too. While she listened for footfalls from behind the door, she glanced down at the man in time to see him flick his cigarette butt into the darkness over the fence onto the brick alleyway where the tip of it shattered into tiny orange balls before blinking out.

The man picked up his cell phone and made a call.

Caroline looked at the shabby backs of the buildings—a cluster of tightly packed irregularly shaped weather-broken redbrick structures caked in flaking stucco. She followed the thick black electrical lines that were at eye level to her, drooping from utility pole to utility pole along the alley, then to the buildings and back. She tapped her thigh with her fist and looked down at the man again. He was still sitting, looking off into the distance over the part of the fence between him and the alley.

She knocked on the door, harder this time, and yelled, "Raymond, open up, it's Caroline."

There was no trampling of feet coming from behind the door. Nothing. The man inside the fence was up now, turned away and walking, reaching into his pocket, maybe for another cigarette. Caroline reached for the knob. It turned—unlocked. Chicken skin dotted the back of her neck.

Something jerked in her peripheral vision from the direction of the man below and she'd barely turned when she heard the shot that brought the heat to her thigh.

She reached for her pistol, dropped flat, and fired through the railing as incoming bullets ricocheted off the landing.

Bullets tore through Mallory's door—someone was shooting from the inside—a pattern from high to low. Her only escape was straight down.

Caroline rolled—fell—down the steps, leaving a bloody trail as the ground rushed up and drilled her into a world of stunned silence where nothing seemed to matter.

She sat up anyway, adrenaline taking over.

Her tumble down the stairs had put the fence between her and the shooter in the courtyard.

Her leg was hot and wet, but the pain was less than she would've expected and she'd managed to hang on to her pistol.

She looked for movement between the slats and knotholes in the fence and saw the man run out the back exit into the alley. She pointed her Glock up the stairs at Mallory's door as she stood and limped to the alley where she peered around a dumpster at the man running away from her. She raised the pistol to take aim, but could barely see him in the darkness, and there was a city park with a playground in the line of fire beyond the man. She lowered the pistol, then heard glass breaking inside Mallory's apartment. Whoever was up there was probably escaping onto Main Street.

She hobbled down the alley after the man who had disappeared out of sight around the corner of the building at the end of the block. When she got to the corner, she felt lightheaded and went to one knee. When she felt stable enough to move, she peeked around the building, down the empty brick sidewalk. She set her pistol on the bricks and used both hands to put pressure on her thigh to stop the bleeding.

The street was quiet, and blood was flowing through her fingers. She remembered a cop she knew in KCK who'd been shot in the thigh by a gangbanger the year after she joined the force. The bullet severed his femoral artery and he was lucky to survive, but he lost his leg. She tried to vanquish the thought, but damn that was a lot of blood. She pressed on the wound as hard as she could with one hand while getting the cell out of her pocket with the other. Sirens kicked up in the distance as she called the Worthington Police Department dispatcher.

In that moment of time before the dispatcher picked up, she thought about Jack, and what he'd think of her with one leg.

25

Early Sunday Morning, June 2, 2019

Ben

IN MY LIVING room after midnight, I signed KBI Agent Eric Washington's search warrant for Detective Mallory's apartment. Two assailants had attacked Caroline Gordon on the landing to Mallory's apartment door, one shooting from inside the apartment, the other from the outdoor area of a bar called "The Dore." She sustained one gunshot wound to her thigh and was being prepped for surgery. Despite the manhunt that had been underway for over an hour, nobody had found Detective Mallory or the two shooters.

When Washington left, Keri and Diablo came out of the back room. Beck was monitoring the trackers on the computer in my basement, Tony was staked out in a stand of trees, watching the door to the room of the motel Buster was in near Keri's rental house, and the Voice was in Wichita sleeping at a hotel near April's apartment waiting to hear from Beck, poised to follow her upon notification she'd left in her car.

"I heard bits and pieces. Who got shot?" asked Keri.

I told her everything Agent Washington told me, then handed her his affidavit so she could read it herself. When I did this, I noticed she was holding a childhood photo of me and Ashley.

She set the affidavit and the photo on the coffee table and said, "Assuming this was done by the cartel, why would they try to kill Mallory and Gordon? Why not come after us?"

"The night is young," I said.

Keri positioned herself in front of me and grabbed my hands. "What's this mean for Ashley? For us? I don't see how this fits into their original plan. Maybe they've scrapped it." A thought seemed to grip her and her face darkened. "Do you think we caused this with our call?"

"I'm not gonna pretend to know the answer to any of those questions." I brushed her hair behind her ear and said, "All I know is that, right now, unless something changes, I'm waiting until Tuesday before I tell the authorities what's going on."

"Tuesday?"

"Tuesday at noon," I said. "Just after the mail comes. If they haven't provided proof of life by then, I'm convinced it's because they can't."

The gravity of what I'd said hit me like a blow to the temple and I plopped down heavily into my L couch. Keri fell in next to me, our thighs touching. We both stared up at the ceiling.

"I've got an idea for tomorrow," said Keri. We turned to each other and she bit her lip like what she was about to say might be controversial. "After Mass in the morning, we go to Kansas City."

"What for? Get married?"

"No, funny guy. To find Randy Harris."

"Randy Harris?" I nodded at the spare bedroom—Keri's war room—where Mallory's reports were spread out over three tables and a desk. "From the reports I read, Mallory spent a great deal of time not finding him."

"Mallory didn't want him found, there's a difference. My opinion—his official reports are designed to look like the trail to Harris had gone cold, but after hours of deciphering Mallory's scribblings—"

"Scribblings?"

"His notes . . . in his god-awful handwriting."

"You mean his field notes," I said. "I couldn't make heads or tails out of any of that. Looked like hieroglyphics."

"Right—field notes, hieroglyphics, whatever you want to call 'em, they were a bitch to follow. But I think I'm on to something. I might know where Harris is hiding. I think

Mallory tracked him down so he knew where to send up a flare if another cop was close to finding him. If people knew for sure about Mallory's hand in getting the Dandurands killed, his career's over."

I cleared my throat and said, "Looks like it might be over now anyway."

Keri's eyes were wide open and still, solemn, like she was imagining Mallory's end.

"Carpe diem," I said.

"What?"

"No time like the present. Let's go find Randy Harris right now."

"And do what? Break into a place he *might* be hiding? In the middle of the night?—It'll be three in the morning when we get to KC. Besides, you've been on the schedule to do the first reading at Mass tomorrow for months."

"I don't show up for Mass on the date I'm scheduled to do a reading, someone fills in. Happens all the time."

Keri wouldn't hear it. She said I needed some sleep and made the case that the information in the reports was stale enough that Randy Harris had likely moved by now anyway. She was right and I told her so.

Her eyes held mine.

"What?" I said.

Keri pointed at the coffee table and said, "That photo—Is that you and Ashley?"

I leaned forward and picked up the five-by-seven photo, dog-eared and bent. Two young kids holding hands, backs to the camera, watching a storm roll in. "What makes you think it's me and Ashley?"

Keri wrinkled her nose. "Because it was in your closet, and the photo looks too old to be a picture of Lindy and Leo."

I shrugged. "I've always liked this picture."

"I like how the two of them are up to their waists in the wheat, holding hands as those black thunderheads tower above them." Keri put her hand on my thigh. "The world is so big and they're so small."

I handed the photo to Keri and stood. "My mother took that photo of us. I remember thinking it seemed like she was going to be okay at the time. Like a veil had lifted, and she wasn't going to be sick anymore. I remember how happy she was that day."

"I'm sorry."

"She was . . . artistic. Had all the tendencies of an artist, too. No business sense, addicted to everything, like a lot of artists seem to be."

"Can't imagine how that hurt you."

"I don't really look at it that way, but I know Ashley does. All the shit that happened to us, all the shit we saw . . . is a convenient excuse for her problems, or it's the reason for them. I try hard not to pass judgment on her. One thing I know, she had it worse than me. It feels like somethin's trying awful hard to tell me it's my turn to lay down."

"But you won't."

"Na."

Tears filled Keri's eyes. "Do you still have faith we'll get her back?"

"Faith?—I don't know. I know one thing for sure. If I'm upright and walking this Earth, I'll give these people hell till it's over."

"You have to believe she's alive right now."

"The way I see it, I don't have to believe anything, as long as I keep answering the bell. I can't see what the hell's wrong with that."

Keri stood and tucked her head into my chest and I held her tight. Holding her reminded me of all the good in the world—all the things that were damn well worth fighting for.

26

Sunday, June 2, 2019

Ben

I PARKED MY Ford F350 on B Street in front of Pops' house, and Keri and I walked half a block down a red brick sidewalk to St. Anthony's Catholic Church at 7:45 a.m. Fifteen minutes earlier on our way out the door, Beck came up from the basement to tell us that Tony had watched Buster climb into his Suburban wearing sweatpants and tennis shoes and leave north up U.S. 81 at 7 a.m. He said Buster's Suburban was parked in front of the bank around the corner from the YMCA in Worthington, one block west of Main Street. Tony was able to spot Buster walking in the front door of the YMCA. Keri said she thought it was odd and I agreed. Buster didn't seem like the type for early morning workouts.

On the sidewalk in front of the church, I called Beck on my burner cell and told him to contact me about any further developments, while Keri called Tony to check in with the same message.

Upon entry into the church vestibule, we were handed pamphlets outlining the day's Mass, complete with the scripture I was scheduled to read. I nodded at a few acquaintances as we made our way through the entry to the nave where we blessed ourselves with Holy water and made the sign of the cross. We sat in the third pew from the front amongst other members I recognized. Keri got on the kneeler and prayed and I pulled out a Bible and looked over the scripture I'd be reading, Acts 1:15-

17; 20-26. According to these verses, Judas had already betrayed Jesus for thirty pieces of silver and hung himself and St. Peter was speaking to a gathering of approximately one hundred and twenty believers about finding his replacement. They cast lots, and chose Matthias to replace Judas and that was that, as they say. It struck me as a strange way to replace a traitor. Maybe when it came time to replace me, the state's Catholic governor would take note of this passage. Maybe he could place all the judicial candidates around a table and do eeny, meeny, miny, moe.

When it came time for the first reading, I made my way to the front, pulled the Lectionary from the cubby, and set it on the pulpit as I sneaked a peek at the congregation before me. There were maybe ninety people in the pews this morning, a couple of them coughing, a few clearing their throats. One man I didn't recognize was walking away, heading for the vestibule. A ribbon marked the day's passage as always and I flipped the big book open and looked down at a typewritten note wedged in the gutter between the inner margins of the Lectionary. I reached for the paper to get it out of the way but my eyes picked up on the word "sister" and I felt my face flush.

When I looked up, the door to the vestibule was closing and the man was gone. I looked down again at the note and read it in full. It read:

> IF YOU WANT TO TALK TO YOUR SISTER TODAY, GO TO THE WORTHINGTON PUBLIC LIBRARY RIGHT NOW AND LOOK UNDERNEATH THE BIRDBATH NEAR THE SOUTH ENTRANCE. COME WITH WHOEVER IS WITH YOU. AS YOU LEAVE OUT THE FRONT OF THE CHURCH, HOLD YOUR PHONES HIGH, TURN THEM OFF, AND THROW THEM INTO THE BUSHES, AND DON'T MAKE ANY DETOURS ON YOUR WAY TO THE LIBRARY. WE'RE WATCHING.

I already knew who was watching the library, which sat catty-corner from the YMCA. I figured the retired Laredo detective was walking slowly on a treadmill about now, waiting and watching for us through those tinted windows. Probably had his cell phone right there in front of him on the magazine rack, ready to take or make a call.

I folded the note, slipped it into my slacks, and found Keri's eyes. I could tell by the look on her face she knew something big had just happened and she mouthed the word "What?" People in the congregation looked on, or at each other, with polite concern on their faces.

I smiled, cleared my throat, and said, "Sorry, thought I opened to the wrong passage for a moment." I proceeded to read from the Lectionary in as normal a tone and pace as I could manage. When I finished, I left the podium, nodding at Keri as I passed her pew heading for the exit.

Outside the church, I held the note out for Keri as she came through the front doors.

She took the note from me and read.

I looked across B Street, past Roosevelt School's barren playground, at the homes lining A Street and found the one house with a sight line to the front door of the church that didn't fit in with all the others. It was a dilapidated two-story structure with no front door and weeds two feet high. If anyone needed a place to watch us leave the church, that house would work.

"Change of plans," I said.

Keri looked up from the note. "We doin' this?"

"Going three blocks to the library? Yeah, but that just sounds like step one to me. I'll let you know what I think, depending on what we find under that birdbath."

"I don't wanna give up the cell phones."

"We don't have much choice in the matter." I nodded at the ramshackle house across the playground on A Street. "When we went into the church they were probably over there watching us talk on our cells, so they know we've got them. We don't follow their rules, we don't get proof of life."

I pulled out the burner phone in my pocket, shut it off, crushed it against the steel railing along the church steps, and threw it into the bushes. I didn't need them finding it, hacking into it, and seeing that I've been tracking Buster and April. Keri followed suit, and we walked to my truck.

The Carnegie Library was closed, and we parallel parked in front of the sidewalk that led to the twenty stairs and a bronze lion that guarded the south exit. The streets were eerily quiet, like they always were this early on a Sunday morning. I pointed at the YMCA across the street.

"I'd bet almost anything Buster's right up there behind that tinted glass on the second level. He'd shit himself if I got out of this truck and marched across the street and jerked his ass off that treadmill about now."

"What would that get us?"

I shrugged, slipping my .45 caliber Glock into the holster inside my slacks, untucking my long-sleeve button-up Oxford shirt a little to hide it. "Cheap thrill."

Keri climbed out. "Let's go."

There was only one birdbath near the stairs leading up to the south exit and it was only about four feet tall and couldn't have weighed more than a hundred pounds. I tilted it over and Keri looked underneath the footing.

"See anything?" I said.

Keri nodded, reached in, and pulled out an envelope.

I set the birdbath back to level. Keri pulled out the handwritten note and unfolded it so we both could read.

> *Drive to Old Car Woods with your fiancée. Park your truck at the edge of the tree line just off the road near the ice cream truck. Find the red 1953 Buick Roadmaster Skylark with the trees growing through where the engine and hood used to be.*

We looked at each other when we were done reading.

"This might be the end for you," I said.

"Whaddayou mean? It says no one stays behind."

"Right, they don't want anyone staying back because they could go home . . . or anywhere, and call the cops." I pointed at a bench on the library lawn. "But if you sat on that bench over there so Buster Reynolds can keep an eye on you, maybe that'd satisfy 'em."

"I have to go—"

"Look, I figure it's fifty-fifty right now whether this is a proof of life operation, or an ambush. This strikes me as a good time to hedge a bet. If it's a proof of life deal, you sitting on that bench in plain view of their scout isn't much of a complication. But if this thing is meant to be an ambush, complication is good."

Keri nodded. "I understand, but this discussion is over." She marched to the truck, climbed into the passenger seat, and looked back at me.

I was still standing on the lawn between the steps and the birdbath in the morning sun, imagining the sound of Ashley's voice, feeling like a moth drawn to the proverbial flame.

27

Ben

OLD CAR WOODS was part salvage yard, part wildlife preserve. In the 1950s, a man who owned an auto salvage yard bordering the woods started storing some of the cars on the other side of his fence. If anyone noticed, no one complained—for thirty years. When the man died in the early 1980s, there were over two hundred junked classic cars so deeply embedded in the landscape that much of it would have to be cleared to get them out.

We parked the truck at the edge of the woods and stepped out. I rolled up the sleeves to my shirt, already soaked with sweat in the suffocating heat which would continue to rise with the sun—and it was still only nine-thirty in the morning.

I looked through the trees behind the rusted-out ice cream truck—on which someone had long ago spray-painted the words, RUST IN PEACE—at the default entryway into the forest. Beyond that, I saw a few of the old cars, hunkered down, headlights peeking out from under a layer of leaves and limbs and ivy, their broken grills smiling at us.

Keri blew out a breath and said, "Wish they would've hid a phone outside the library and called us, let us talk to Ashley there."

The old forest towered before us, reaching high into the clear blue sky. "This'd sure make a good place for some killin'." I gave Keri a sidelong look. "It's not too late. Let me take you outta here. She's my sister. I have to go."

Keri pulled off her sunglasses and gave me her from-under stare. "I figure they've planted a phone in the Skylark. Out here, they'll have the benefit of being able to watch us. Make sure they're still dealing with us, not some law enforcement hostage expert."

"Maybe that's it. But like you said, they could've accomplished all that at the library."

Keri's face hardened. She slipped her sunglasses back over her eyes and said, "The library's too public for a private operation like this. Don't manage me, Ben. You're not talkin' me outta here. Now let's get on with it."

She took off toward the woods. When she noticed I wasn't following she stopped and looked back. "What?"

I considered asking her to stay back again but wild horses couldn't't've dragged her out of here so I said, "I love you."

Keri smiled. "Of course you do."

* * *

There wasn't much of a trail. We stomped through a hundred yards of woods, looking for the red Skylark. We were constantly moving sideways and backwards looking for something red—we found a red Mustang, a red Corvair, some red Chevrolets and Fords. Both of us had sweated clear through our clothes, and the holstered pistol on the inside of my slacks was rubbing my hip raw. My brown cap-toed Oxford shoes wore a layer of dirt and leaves, and my slacks a smattering of cockleburs and thorns. Over a berm we saw a clearing of a hundred yards or so and the red Skylark sitting at the edge of a tree line. Its hood was missing, and a couple of trees twenty-five feet tall had grown up through where the engine used to be. The driver's side door faced the clearing and the passenger side faced back into dense foliage behind it. We stood there on the berm, scanning the scene, catching our breath.

Keri wiped the sweat from her face and rubbed it on her jeans. "Where do you figure they're at?"

"They could be hunkered down a lot of places out here and still see that Skylark. I suppose that's the whole idea."

We took off across the clearing toward the Skylark in a trot. When I reached the car, a phone trilled through its windowless shell. Keri trotted up behind me and we looked at each other. I ripped open the Skylark's rotting door, dove onto the seat and saw the phone sitting in the open glove compartment. I grabbed it midway through its fourth ring.

"Yeah," I said.

"Benny, it's Ash."

Tears formed in my eyes at hearing her voice. I climbed out of the Skylark and stood, as Keri gripped my shoulder and moved her cheek closer to mine so she could hear.

"Sis', are you okay?"

"I'm fine, all things considered."

"Are they . . . hurting you?"

"They haven't raped me or anything like that and they feed me well, but I'm not supposed to say more than that."

I said, "I'm working on getting you home," as I looked around for the spotter responsible for the perfectly timed call. Then I realized Ashley wasn't responding to me. "Ash? Ashley, are you still there?"

"Look under the leaves where the engine would be," said a digitally altered voice.

I reached down into the hollow Skylark at the foot of the trees and swatted at the leaves until I found a sizeable stack of hundred dollar bills.

"You see?" asked the digital voice.

"Yes."

"That's a ten-thousand-dollar down payment toward the cost of the judgment of acquittal."

"Ten-thou—what? I want Ash back safe. I don't want your money."

"You'll get the rest after you grant the acquittal."

"The rest? I won't take it either."

"We need you to have it—so you can disappear properly. And we need you and your kids to disappear, one way or another. At least for several years. You can't disappear without money. So we're giving it to you—when you've fulfilled your promise. It's your play."

"Money or bullets?"

"Those are the two staples of this business, yes."

"How much you giving us to disappear?"

"A million . . . in cash of course."

"I won't take your money. This is extortion, not a bribe."

"Judging by the green laser light on Ms. Chalmer's pretty little head, I'd say that's accurate."

At first I didn't see it, because it was faint in the sunlight, but it was there, right above her left ear. Keri's eyes blinked rapidly and her nostrils flared and her lips drew in tight against her teeth. The gunman had to be close, probably within eighty yards to get the dot to appear at all in the bright light.

"Okay!" I said. "I'll take the money."

The green dot disappeared, but I figured both of us remained in riflemen's crosshairs.

The digital voice said, "Can't you see how we'd prefer this to look . . . like a bribe . . . so that you have some skin in the game when this is over. A man in a ghillie suit is headed your way. Hand him the notes in your pocket—the one from the church and the one from the library. This man isn't planning on shooting you with anything other than a camera. We know you got that pistol tucked into your pants, but I wouldn't pull it right now if I was you. I wouldn't want to see this end in the wrong kind of headshot."

I turned to reach into the Skylark's shell for the money and a man appeared from the woods looking like the forest incarnate. As he stepped to the edge of the Skylark, two other figures in ghillie suits rose from the foliage on the forest floor, both carrying camouflage assault rifles. The man closest to me by the skylark had a hook-shaped scar on his chin underneath the camouflage face paint, a pistol in his hand, and a shotgun hanging behind him on the sling over his shoulder.

I held up the one hand that wasn't holding a phone to my ear and said, "I'm reaching for the money, if that's okay."

He glanced at my midsection and nodded. "Give me the notes in your pocket. Then you can get your money."

My money. His tone assumed I couldn't wait to get my hands on $10,000, a meager sum in exchange for the end of my legal career. I wondered how believable they thought that was, but then again, that was the amount of cash the Chicago judge took in *Illinois v. Baleman* as a bribe, so I guess there was precedent. Still, I couldn't imagine how a video of me holding the stack of cash strengthened their position much because it would clearly look staged, but this was their railroad and they'd run it as they saw fit.

I dug into my pocket and handed over the notes as the men in ghillie suits behind him stepped through the brush toward us. After I picked up the stack of bills held together with rubber bands, the ghillie suit with the hook scar was still inspecting the notes. He stuffed them into his pocket and walked around us into the clearing. He didn't get out his phone or a camera and didn't seem interested in recording me holding the money at all. The back of my neck turned hot with premonition.

Right then, an engine kicked up in the distance behind me. When I turned to face the clearing, I didn't see anything at first, but eventually a John Deere Gator appeared from the trees headed our direction, driven by a tall, gangly man in an olive-green ski mask. In the bed behind the driver was another man, this one fat, also in a green ski mask. When they reached us, I saw the hog-tied arms and legs of a third person over the top of the Gator's side rails. My mouth went dry and I felt a little dizzy and I realized I had taken the phone down from my ear. Keri was holding her stomach as we both watched the fat ski mask in khaki pants jam his knee into the captive's back while grunting like a powerlifter over the rev of the engine.

When the Gator came to a stop ten feet in front of us and the driver shut down the engine, the ski masks jerked the man to the ground, and I saw that duct tape had been repeatedly wrapped all the way around the back of his head and over his mouth. When he rolled over, Detective Mallory's bulging eyes locked onto mine and he tried to say something through what had to be ten layers of tape wrapped tight enough to turn the skin on his temples the color of the blue veins on the tops of my hands.

I dropped the cash and the phone and reached for my pistol.

A strong hand gripped my wrist, and someone lifted my shirt and slipped the Glock from the holster inside my slacks.

One of the ghillie suits snatched the phone from the ground, handed it to me, and said in an accent from south of the border, "You need to listen, *señor*."

I put it to my ear.

The digital voice said, "You're going to shoot Detective Mallory in the head and chest, and we're going to record it. If anyone in your family talks to the law about the kidnapping, or the extortion, we'll release the tape, see to it that the cops find Detective Mallory's body and the murder weapon, and you'll be wanted for murder."

And the video would still look staged, but it wouldn't matter. Compulsion wasn't a defense to this kind of murder in Kansas.

The tall ski mask took my Glock from the ghillie suit and dropped the magazine from the pistol and cleared the chambered round into his gloved hand. He held the jacketed hollow-point .45 caliber ammunition cartridge up at eye level with his thumb and forefinger. It was the same kind of round I had fired repeatedly into Juan, designed for the projectile to spread out upon impact in a star-shaped pattern inside the wound channel for maximum damage. If this guy was privy to the firearms and toolmark report that Sweeney forwarded to the court and McMaster on Friday, his wheels had to be turning. The state's firearms expert concluded that the jacketed hollow points pulled from Juan were fired from a .45 caliber Glock. Even though Glocks and JHP's were ubiquitous, and the pistol that fired the rounds into Juan was at the bottom of Slate Creek, I was more than a little nervous how things might look to them—like the truth. He put the cartridge in his jeans' pocket, reinserted the magazine, and racked the slide to chamber another round.

He stood before me and touched his index finger to my chest. Still with the phone to my ear, I glanced down at his finger and the green dot next to it on my sternum, then returned my attention to his masked face. His eyes were the color of pennies. I recognized those orbs glaring at me through the eyeholes. I'd seen them in the photos I'd taken from his farmhouse on Eden Road. This was Miguel. According to Mallory's files and the affidavits I'd read, Miguel was six feet three inches tall and one hundred seventy pounds. Standing face to face with him now, I'd say that was about right, though he seemed taller on the heels of his cowboy boots.

He said, "Suppose we have our expert check your Glock against the shell casings found in that field next to Juan?"

His eyes scanned my face, looking for a reaction.

"Like most people, I figure it was a Trevino hitman Juan walked in on out there." I could tell by the acceptance in Miguel's eyes and the tiniest of nods that he approved of my response, but what the man on the phone thought was anyone's guess because he stayed silent. "But go ahead," I said into the phone, reassuring Miguel with an earnest nod. "Have an expert look at it." The gun that left its own distinctive marks on the shell casings next to Juan was in Slate Creek below the train trestle.

"We'll do that," said Miguel.

He glanced back at Mallory, turned back to me and said, "Now, back to what brings us here. Look on the bright side. We do this so we can return your sister to you. Now you see how releasing her makes sense on our end."

He looked to the ghillie suit with the chin scar holding up a phone like a video recorder and nodded.

Miguel held my Glock by its handle before me and said, "Take it."

Several feet behind him in my line of sight, Mallory worked the ropes on his wrists and ankles, blood vessels in his forehead bulging from the effort, a condemned man fighting to free himself while the identity of his executioner was decided. Whatever happened, I vowed to myself that it wasn't going to be me.

"Take it," Miguel repeated, this time more forcefully.

I looked into Miguel's eyes and said into the phone. "I won't do that."

Miguel nodded like he'd expected me to say that. "Give me the phone."

I handed him the phone and watched as he put it to his ear and listened.

With expressionless eyes, he handed the phone back to me, and placed the Glock's muzzle on Keri's temple.

His index finger curled around the trigger.

Keri's eyes squinted shut and she groaned in expectation of the end and I yelled, "Wait!"

Miguel pulled the gun from Keri's head and stepped even closer to me. His sweaty face was so close to mine that I could smell the wintergreen Skoal on his breath.

"If you won't pull the trigger on the detective, we figure you don't have it in you to pull the trigger on the acquittal either, and I will be forced to kill him myself, right here in front of you. If you choose to go that route, I think the question you have to ask yourself is . . . what do you get for all your morality?"

Miguel turned to Keri and winked, then looked back into my eyes. "Because I think you know what happens next."

Sweat rolled into my eyes and stung them, but I didn't blink.

"We run a train on your gash. While you watch. Then we kill her. While you watch. Then, your sister. Same. We'll torture you, from head, to dick, to toe. For so long that you won't even know what you're saying anymore. Who knows, you might even tell us where your kids are . . . after you've lost your mind."

He glanced at Keri then fixed his glare on me again. "The mind goes. Did you know that? I've seen it. I'll do what I have to do."

He sneered at Keri. "Might even enjoy it."

His tongue wagged on his lower lip and his eyes took a walk all over Keri before he turned to me and said, "Say their names, *amigo*. Say the names of the women you love who will be raped and killed, so you don't have to be the one who pulls the trigger on the bag of shit detective behind me who started this whole thing. Say the names of your children . . . who will die in the name of their daddy's moral code."

I put the phone back to my ear and said to both men, "I got a better idea about how you can spend that million dollars. It's a better plan for both sides."

The digitized voice said, "I'm listening."

Detective Mallory stopped working the ropes and a glimmer of hope seemed to show in his face, but my proposal wasn't going to help him. Nothing I could say would help him now. "Gwen Sweeney is likely to ask for a continuance tomorrow morning because one of her case agents was shot over the weekend, and the other is . . ." I glanced at Detective Mallory, " . . . still missing." Mallory's eyes dropped in despair. "If the state does this, it's the perfect opening for McMaster to suggest that if the trial is delayed, the court should reconsider setting a bond? Let's say I set it at, what?—that million dollars you were going to pay me. You see that Rummell makes bond, and then disappears."

"And if the state doesn't ask for a continuance?" said the digitized voice.

"McMaster asks for one himself. Maybe he wants time to consider filing motions for mistrial and change of venue based on the shooting of Agent Gordon and the ongoing search for Detective Mallory and the media storm that's brewing. That's how this would all play out normally—McMaster would argue that Rummell can't get a fair trial under these conditions. Delay of trial is always occasion to resubmit a motion for bond to be set. And setting a million-dollar bond won't raise near the suspicion that the judgment of acquittal would."

Miguel said, "It's a nice plan, *amigo*. So good, that it was our original plan. Only problem was, Rummell said he wouldn't sign an appearance bond. Seems he was afraid of the way we'd disappear him."

The digital voice added, "He seems to think we'll come for him either way. He thinks he can last longer without the added complication of being a fugitive wanted by the government."

Miguel dangled my Glock by its grip for me to take. "Nice try."

Two of the ghillies pointed their rifles at me and Chin Scar held up his phone, ready to record the murder.

"We both know if you kill me," I said into the phone, "Rummell's gonna squeal, and then it's over for you. You'll both be on the run like you've never been on the run before."

"Rummell ain't talkin'," said Miguel. "He knows we'll smoke his parents if he does."

"Then why all this . . . fuss, over me. You see, I've asked myself that question—why wouldn't you just threaten to kill Rummell's folks? That almost always works for the cartels. I know, I used to prosecute drug mules all the time—some sad sack in a rental van stopped by a trooper with a drug-sniffing dog for failure to signal a lane change. If they'd sing or become an informant, anything to get us up the chain a bit, I'd let 'em off with a plea to something that'd get 'em five years or less, but almost all of them ate a decade or two in federal prison because they had family in the states or Mexico. They weren't talkin'. Not in a million years. So why won't this play work on Rummell?—this, drug-addled scrote-bag. I came to two possible conclusions. He either doesn't believe you'll kill his parents, or he doesn't care."

Miguel's eyes drew to slits, my pistol still dangling before my face.

I said, "You want to frame me for murdering Detective Mallory, I can't stop you. You'll have more than enough leverage to keep me quiet when this is over. But I won't pull the trigger. I won't do your dirty work for you. For me, there are worse things than dying."

The slits in Miguel's eyes drew down another notch, his lower lip drawn tight against his teeth, the skin of his chin pregnant with snuff. He put the muzzle to my forehead and said, "Not the way I'm gonna kill you, motherfucker."

My eyes snapped shut and I remember thinking, *this is it*, as the digitized voice yelled something Spanish into my ear. When I opened my eyes the muzzle was still on my forehead and Miguel's copper eyes were open wide and he was breathing heavily, listening to the loud, urgent, digitized Spanish pouring through the phone. Somehow, in what seemed like my last moment on Earth, I still had that phone to my ear.

Miguel pulled the muzzle from my forehead and said, "Give me the fuckin' phone."

He snatched it from me, put it to his ear, and stepped back, saying something in Spanish in the high-pitched tone of impassioned agitation.

After listening for a moment, he slipped the phone into his jeans and stepped to Detective Mallory, whose head and neck were fiery red and puffed out as his muffled screams bore a hole in my soul. I glanced at Keri. She was looking down and seemed to be wincing, her face contorted with anguish.

Mallory looked up at me. I mouthed the words, "I'm sorry."

The muted screams stopped and he closed his eyes.

Before I could turn away, Miguel pointed and fired three times—two in the chest, one in the head. The world grew quiet in the wake of the shots, and I watched Miguel check Mallory's back—for exit wounds I guessed—as Mallory's body twitched against the ropes. Miguel stepped back, apparently unsatisfied, and fired six more times into Mallory's head and chest.

When my hearing returned to normal seconds after the shots, I heard Keri's muffled sobs.

Miguel gathered the spent shell casings at his feet with his gloved hands and put them into a paper sack held open by the fat ski mask.

When Miguel stood, he stepped to me and said, "Open your right hand. Let me see your palms." After I did as he asked, he dropped the magazine out of the pistol and pressed my thumb on it in several places, rolling it and pressing it so as to optimize the chances of a usable print. When he finished, he pulled the bullet from his pocket and pressed my thumb onto the casing before pressing it back into the magazine and slapping it back into the pistol.

He tucked the pistol into his waistband and pulled a straight-edge tactical knife out of a sheath hooked on his jeans and said, "I was told to get your blood on the pistol. I'll need your hand again."

I held out my hand, "I've got court tomorrow morning. I don't think you want me to have to answer a bunch of questions about my hand."

He grasped my pinkie finger and hovered the edge of the knife above the tip of it. "I'll be . . . delicate. Delicate as I can."

He seemed to savor the moment, before making a small incision and letting go. He sheathed the knife, pulled the gun out, and took hold of my pinkie again, smearing the globule of blood along the pistol grip.

As he placed my pistol inside a paper sack held open by the fat man, he said, "What's the maximum penalty for killing a cop in Kansas, Your Honor?"

"Death," I said.

A firearms and toolmark expert could probably match the spent cartridges they'd leave near Mallory's body to the murder weapon that probably had my fingerprints on it. Apparently, that was too much uncertainty for them, so without the video of me committing murder, they wanted my DNA on the pistol as backup.

Two ghillie suits threw Mallory into the bed of the Gator like a dead deer as Miguel climbed into the driver's seat. "If all goes as planned, no one will ever see Mallory's body or that pistol of yours again."

Miguel started the engine as the fat man climbed into the passenger seat. We watched them ride away, same way they came, until they disappeared into the woods adjacent to us. When I turned around, the ghillie suits were receding into the woods, the sound of the Gator's engine growing faint in the distance.

* * *

We left Old Car Woods and went home. Keri went outside with Diablo, and I called Pops from an extra burner phone we kept in a kitchen drawer. I told him how I'd come to speak with Ashley and what happened after that.

I watched through the kitchen window at Diablo running through the yard as the line went silent.

Then he said, "You remember what I told you when you told me you wanted to go to law school?"

"You said I was too nice a person to be a lawyer."

"I was wrong about that. I've known that for years now, even before all of this. And I don't mean that in a bad way. You have my mean streak. It kept you and Ashley alive today. Kept Keri alive. Probably kept your children alive too, who knows?"

"For now."

"For now, Ben, that's right. What else you got but now?"

"What would you do now?"

"What you've been doin'. Keep clawin'. You're on the side of the angels, Benny. That sound alright to you?"

"Sounds like something a terrorist would say."

"Yeah, well, that's the lawyer in you talkin' right there and I'm no lawyer. I'm not the kind to wring my hands a whole lot about my mindset when defending what's left of my family. You've spent your years in the air-conditioning thinking about civilization. Great. I love you for it. Proud of you—you know that. But I think you see now how the world works in the shadows. No one gets to be John Wayne anymore. You try to come out of something like this playing by the rules, you don't stand a chance. You did what you had to do. You extended the fight. Now you have to bring the fight to them, on your terms."

Keri came through the kitchen door and I turned to her. She still had that shell-shocked look I felt hanging on my own face.

Pops said. "There's a couple someones here anxious to talk to you. That'll do you a world of good right now."

I heard Lindy and Leo fighting over whose turn it was to talk first and it made me smile and tear up at once.

* * *

We spent the rest of the day trying to reread and decipher Mallory's handwritten notes, but we were having a hard time concentrating and nothing of importance happened with the trackers. At eight in the evening, Gwen Sweeney called with Glenn McMaster on another line for a conference call. She wanted to meet with us in my chambers at eight in the morning to discuss the weekend's events and their potential effect on the trial schedule. She let us know that Agent Gordon's surgery went well, and that the earliest she'd be released from the hospital was Tuesday. McMaster didn't say much, other than to say he'd heard about the shooting and the missing detective like everybody else. We both agreed to the meeting.

By one in the morning, Keri and Beck had a plan to locate Randy Harris in Kansas City while I was in court so we all turned in for the night.

At four in the morning, Keri sat up in bed and said, "How'd you know Miguel wouldn't kill us?"

I'd been tossing and turning and my eyes were open and the whites of her eyes glowed back at me in the darkness.

"I didn't, and not to quibble, but I'm pretty sure he would've killed us. The man on the phone held him off."

"Why, I wonder?"

"Don't know, but I was talking to the man on the phone as if I was talking to Jorge Mendez-Rodriguez himself. It figured to be him. It's his empire that's on the line."

"Do you really believe that there are worse things than dying . . . the way I thought we were goin' down?"

"I'll say this. I sure as hell didn't believe it when I said it."

"Good. Because when we were standing there, and it was about to go down, I didn't believe it either."

We watched the ceiling fan spin for a while.

She said, "What possessed you to say that, then?"

I didn't have an answer, so I ignored the question, sat up on my elbow and said, "I'm going with you to Kansas City tomorrow."

"What about court?"

"Gwen Sweeney's lost both her case agents this weekend. They have to be in disarray right now, working the shooting, trying to find Mallory, and prepping the Rummell case without both lead investigators. I'd be surprised if Sweeney didn't request a continuance to at least Thursday or Friday."

"But you don't have to give Sweeney more time, right?"

"Right. Whether or not I grant a continuance is totally within my discretion, but it'll look like the right call to the public."

"The cartel won't like it. Isn't that all that matters?"

That had occurred to me, of course, but I figured I had to press the envelope. I drew in a deep breath and released it.

"What was that?" said Keri.

"The sound of me rethinking an idea I discarded an hour ago."

28

Monday Morning, June 3, 2019

Ben

THROUGH MY CHAMBERS' window I watched the neighborhood street guy dig through the stubs in the public ashtray below for his usual early morning smoke. When he saw the suit with a cigarette coming down the sidewalk, he suspended his search and waited for the man to approach him. He seemed glad to see McMaster. The bedraggled man took the cigarette McMaster offered him. I watched them light up and sweat it out in the heat. McMaster's oily hair danced in the wind. I could feel the heat of the sun radiating off the window, and felt a drop of sweat rolling down my ribs beneath my armpit. The temperature was supposed to reach a hundred degrees by one o'clock.

McMaster looked at his watch. It was 8:00 a.m., and he'd be a little late for the meeting in chambers. He ground his cigarette into the tray and blew smoke into the wind. The sound of Ms. Sweeney's voice came through my door. Nancy told her she could go on in, but she said she'd wait on McMaster.

* * *

I can gauge a room, I think. Any trial lawyer worth their salt can gauge a room. It's how trial lawyers pick juries that are open to seeing things their way. It's how you find friends that agree with you. Legal skills don't mean squat for a trial lawyer without street smarts. I was sitting across a desk from two other people-readers—and we were all gauging each other. I dropped the effort and did what a judge is supposed to do. I leaned back in my executive's chair for the ride.

McMaster's face was shiny with sweat from standing outside smoking, and his hair was uncharacteristically mussed. But with a few strokes of his comb, his shiny black hair was back in Cary Grant formation, thanks to a residual layer of greasy pomade.

"So, Ms. Sweeney," I said. "Your meeting. What's on your mind?" As if I didn't know.

"The obvious, of course," she began. "I've lost the help of my co-lead detectives over the weekend. Also, I had planned to recall Detective Mallory to the stand this morning as a precursor to calling our DNA experts. If we can't find him, I need time to talk with Agent Gordon, figure out a way to get the ski masks from Juan's Cutlass Supreme admitted into evidence. Mallory was the one who actually performed the search and can lay the foundation for admitting the two ski masks he found underneath the seat. They've now been tested. None of the DNA found on the masks matches the known sample taken from Kramer Carter. This tends to disprove the defense theory that Kramer Carter was the killer Haley saw with the clown tattoos."

"My expert hasn't had a chance to review this evidence," said McMaster. "Ms. Sweeney just faxed the reports to me on Saturday."

Without a crack in her straight-ahead stare, Ms. Sweeney said, "Another good reason for a continuance, Your Honor."

McMaster looked bemused. "You've got other witnesses you could call."

"I don't want to call other witnesses yet. Not before I pull the rug out from under your assertion that Kramer Carter could have been the other killer. And besides, don't you have mistrial and change of venue motions you need to be filing? Death penalty defense 101. Quite frankly, I think you need the continuance more than I do."

McMaster's eyebrows danced up and down as he made conspicuous eye contact with me while Sweeney was looking away from him. "With all due respect, Ms. Sweeney, I think you're all wrong about that."

There was a knock on the door as it slowly opened. Nancy poked her head in and said, "The sheriff has ordered everyone to evacuate the building immediately. Someone called in a bomb threat, and there's a suspicious suitcase in the ground floor bathroom."

I did my best to look surprised.

Ms. Sweeney turned to Nancy and said, "Oh my God, what's next? Do they really think it's a bomb?"

Nancy said, "Sweetie, I'm sure they don't know, but your KBI agent got shot over the weekend and a sheriff's detective is missing." She looked at McMaster and said, "Whoever you're tangling with isn't one for bluffing. I'm gettin' the hell outta here and I suggest you all do the same."

I stood. "Nancy, when you leave, go across the street to Falstaff & Drysdale and see if you can use their spare office to call the jurors and tell them court's been cancelled for the day. If they're already on their way, they'll find out soon enough what's going on." Then to Sweeney, I said, "Looks like you got your continuance to Thursday. We'll have to make a record of all this then."

Ms. Sweeney stood and made her way to the doorway that had already been evacuated by Nancy.

McMaster stayed seated, tilting his head to the side. "A fucking bomb threat? Are you shittin' me?"

Sweeney stopped in the doorway and looked back at us as I grabbed my wallet and keys out of the desk drawer and said, "Nothing surprises me anymore. Seems nothing is sacred to some people."

A wry smile creased McMaster's face as he stood and strolled out behind Sweeney, not the least bit worried a bomb was about to leave him crushed and suffocating in a pile of rubble.

29

Monday Evening, June 3, 2019

Ben

IT WAS FIVE o'clock at Skinny Pete's Bar in South Kansas City. My beer sat on a high round table in the corner next to a rack of warped pool cues. I hovered over the stained felt of the only pool table in the place, slid the cue between my thumb and forefinger, and took my shot.

The place smelled of sour towels and vomit. There were two other customers in the bar and one of them was an old yellow-bearded man in the corner booth whose scowl seemed directed at me. I could've been mistaken about this, of course. Perhaps, like me, he resented foul odors, though from the looks of him he would feel at home in any stink. I wasn't here to see him. The man I wanted to befriend went by the name Charlie Green, and he was in the restroom. I knew Charlie by a mug shot in Mallory's reports and the laundry list of criminal convictions stapled to it, mostly burglaries, thefts, and drug possession. We didn't have a clue as to why Charlie's stuff was in the file on the Dandurand murders until Keri found a note scrawled on a stained napkin lining the bottom of an accordion folder that read: R.H. STAYING WITH COUSIN CHARLIE GREEN?

My decision to accompany Keri and Beck to Kansas City freed Beck to case Charlie Green's neighborhood on an old bicycle dressed like a homeless man in hopes of locating Randy Harris while we pursued another angle. Beck wasn't happy about the assignment, but it beat his earlier one of leaving a suspicious suitcase in the courthouse and calling in a bomb threat. After that, we'd met back at my house where Beck gave us fake IDs and did our make-up so that we looked like the photos on them. The Voice rented a white cargo van she left sitting in a Village Inn parking lot for us before resuming her duty of monitoring April, who ended up at the Hospital around noon. We wondered if she was going into labor. Tony continued to track Buster Reynolds, who'd done nothing—as far as Tony could tell—but meet McMaster for lunch at a restaurant in Worthington.

The television behind the bar was broadcasting the story about the shooting of a KBI agent and a missing detective who were witnesses in a death penalty triple-homicide trial in Worthington. The news anchor from the Kansas City station asked a female reporter on the scene at the courthouse in Worthington about the latest development and the young woman told the viewers of the bomb scare, almost yelling into her microphone so as to be heard over the wind while deflecting with her free hand the hair that lashed at her face.

I'd become so absorbed in the broadcast that I failed to realize I had downed my entire beer so I ordered another as a prop and continued waiting for Charlie to come out of the head.

Finding Charlie Green was a story all its own. Detective Mallory's reports had Charlie's address as 9588 East Independence Avenue, but when we got there we saw a weathered man in his fifties wearing painter's pants that wasn't Charlie Green walking across the yard to an old pickup in the driveway. The front door to the residence was propped wide open and I saw that the man was carrying a putty knife. I got out of the cargo van, pointed at the house, and asked the man if Charlie Green still lived there. The man laughed the way people do when they're pissed and told me the son of a bitch was finally gone. He told me he aimed to sue his ex-tenant, so I told him I wanted to sue him too. He told me "the cocksucker" tore up all the walls in the house, and then asked me how Charlie had fucked me over. I told him it was personal. I made it sound like I might kick Charlie's ass. He liked that and gave me what his lawyer thought was Charlie's most current address.

The house the landlord hoped was Charlie's newest residence was actually among a cluster of vacant, but decent, homes in South Kansas City that backed up to the countryside. The place was a bit of an eyesore, a single-story structure with canary-yellow siding on both ends and weathered brown clapboard siding in front. The front door was framed by two giant elm trees in a steeply sloped, barren yard—the black sheep of this ghost town of a neighborhood. When we first got there, an old Grand Marquis was sitting in the driveway in front of the closed door of a single-car garage. We called Tony with the tag number, who got in touch with a cop he'd bought information from in the past, before calling back ten minutes later with the good news that the tag belonged to Charlie Green. A little after four o'clock, we saw Charlie come out of the house and back his car into the street and leave. We'd followed him to Skinny Pete's, leaving Beck scowling in the street on his bike.

After knocking the eight ball into the corner pocket on my third attempt, I put seventy-five cents in the money slot of the pool table and punched in the lever and the balls dropped and rolled through the table's innards. I was about to go to the restroom to check on Charlie when I felt my cell vibrating in my pocket. I answered the call and Keri said, "Don't look now, but that loon is out front peeking through the front window at you."

"Charlie?"

"Yep."

"Alright, I won't look. Call me back if he leaves." I ended the call.

Right then the front door jingled open and I turned in time to see him step in. So he'd left out the back and now here he was coming through the front door again. I glanced at the bartender, cleaning mugs behind the bar watching the news, seemingly oblivious to what the hell Charlie might be up to. The air conditioning unit above the front door dripped water on Charlie's head. He ducked and looked up, smiling in good humor. A self-conscious man wouldn't have dared to grin like that. Even from this distance I could see that his front teeth disappeared into gums peppered with lesions that resembled black compost. He ordered a bottle of Budweiser and set three quarters on the pool table.

"Want a game?" he said.

"Be my guest."

He pulled the triangular rack from its slot, set it on the table, and said, "Charlie."

"Jim," I said, remembering the name on my fake ID, *James N. Perry.*

Two hours later he had won two hundred and eighty dollars from me, and I had bought most of the drinks. I had a little bag of crystal to show him later—maybe, if the situation called for it. I'd taken a smidge of crystal out of Juan's Tupperware. I didn't plan on giving it to Charlie or selling it to him. I didn't want to amp him up. I wanted to wind him down. I wasn't exactly sure how I was going to use the meth, but I wanted to give myself some flexibility—a way to go if the night went in a certain direction. I thought maybe I could show the crystal to him and insist we do the bumps somewhere private—maybe his house. From the looks of him, it appeared to me it went that way most nights.

I was content to let the alcohol take its course with Charlie, since he was well on his way to incapacitating himself. On my end, I poured my drinks down the bathroom sink when I could. I would have been on the floor if I'd tried to keep up with him.

"How 'bout we hit Felicia's? I'll buy you a lap dance," said Charlie.

"Sure, you'll have to. You got all my money."

It took some convincing, but Charlie let me drive his Grand Marquis. I told him my old lady had my car for the night.

While navigating traffic on a busy interstate highway in Kansas City on our way to the strip club I said, "My old lady's gonna be pissed as hell at me losin' all that money, man. I got something maybe you'd be interested in."

I slipped the baggie of crystal from my shirt pocket and said, "You got a place we can hit this shit before we go to the club? Maybe I get some of my money back."

His eyes grew big and he reached for it. I drew the bag back, "No, man, not in the fucking car."

He pulled a wad of money—my money—out of his pocket and said, "I ain't drivin' bitch. You take a hunnerd for the whole bag?"

"Not happenin' man. I'm gonna hit it too and I'm tellin' you this shit kicks like a bull. I can't be drivin' when it comes on. Let's just go, wherever, I don't care, just not in the car on these busy-ass-motherfuckin' roads."

In my peripheral vision, I saw him scratching his neck and when I glanced at him he had a pinched expression on his face. "You're gonna want some of this," I assured him.

"There'll be no goin' to my place so you can get that out of your head."

I wanted to think he had a roommate named Randy Harris who didn't want any visitors. I fingered the keys dangling below the ignition and wondered if one of them was the key to Charlie's house. "You're gonna have to buy all the drinks then, man."

"I already said I would. I'm playin' with house money, motherfucker!" Then he flipped four twenties on my lap. "Give me the whole bag right now and . . . and! . . . I buy all the booze you can drink and we let that pussy grind on us 'til the money's all gone. Blow this motherfucker out!"

I glanced at the money on my lap and changed lanes.

"You know," he said. "I thought you was a cop earlier. At the bar."

I snorted out a laugh. "A cop?"

"Yeah. I thought you looked a little too . . . well nourished. Out of place. That's why I left out the back of the bar. Had a bad feelin'. I went around the block to the front and looked in at you from the window, did you see me?"

"No, man, I didn't see you. I wasn't payin' any attention to you, dude."

"I saw you in there playing pool by yourself. Cop wouldn't've stayed after I left and played pool by himself. Wasn't anybody in there 'cept that homeless fuck."

I didn't want Charlie revisiting my street cred so I did something most undercover cops would never do and reached into my shirt and flicked Juan's crank at him. "You're about a paranoid sonofabitch."

Charlie opened the little baggie, dropped a thumbnail hunk of crystal into the cup holder, and began crushing it up with the nose of a pair of pliers that came from who-knows-where. There was a lot of random shit lying around his car. His head darted below window level as he jammed the powder pinched between his thumb and middle finger up his nose and snorted violently. His right leg stomped the floorboard twice and he sat bolt upright and howled like a coyote.

Felicia's was on the outskirts of South Kansas City near an industrial park. I bought drinks and shots and kept them coming. Charlie was too messed up to notice I wasn't drinking.

When he grew bored with lying on his back on stage with money in his mouth, he had a couple of strippers on us in the V.I.P. room—an intimate place with a three-hundred-pound bouncer in the corner. My girl had eyes that rolled back in her head when she ground her hips into my crotch. She was too rough with this and it wasn't pleasing at all. She asked me if my friend had AIDS and I told her probably, in the hope this would disgust her enough to leave us, ending this sexual assault on my loins. But Charlie produced more cash.

When he finally passed out after midnight, I gave my girl an extra hundred dollars to convince the bouncer to let me take him out the back way. She agreed, tucking the hundred dollar bill into her thong and nodding at the bouncer who waved at me to follow him. I did, carrying Charlie out the back of the club like a newlywed husband carries his wife across the threshold.

Half an hour later, I pulled the Grand Marquis into Charlie's driveway and killed the headlights. Charlie was still passed out in the back seat. I checked his pulse. I couldn't find a remote for the garage door, so I got out of the car and tried to open it but it was locked. I went back to the car, shut off the engine, and found the key to the garage.

There was a dining room table and boxes of clothes sitting in the garage where I wanted to park the car. It took me a few minutes to clear a path. Then I drove it in, cracked the windows for Charlie, and turned off the engine. Beck stepped into the garage. Before he pulled the door shut we heard what sounded to me like fireworks coming from somewhere outside.

* * *

Flaming balls shot out of a tube held by a man sitting in a lawn chair in the backyard, cutting the night open with light, exploding in shades of orange and red above the back fence. I watched the show from inside the house, through the glass of the sliding door, but I was no more than three steps from the back of his head.

The place was hot and smelled like wet dogs. I stood there, soaked in sweat, listening for sounds of another occupant or a pet inside the house when Beck slipped into the room and nodded. The place was clear. We had this man to ourselves and he looked harmless enough. I tucked my pistol into the waistband at the small of my back, noticing a sweat-stained fedora hanging on a wooden chair in the corner as I did.

The man took a drag off a joint the way dopers do and pulled another Roman candle from a box as I slid open the glass door.

"Throw a pizza in the oven, would ya'?" he said, not looking back.

The Roman candle he held out stiff-armed at a forty-five degree angle away from his face thumped out its first fireball. By the light of it I saw a pistol underneath his chair. Not as harmless as I'd thought. Last thing I needed was another gunfight.

Thwump—the second fireball sizzled through the night. In the streak of light, I caught a glimpse of the man's sweaty bald spot as I stepped closer and took his pistol.

Thwump—the third fireball hissed into the sky.

"I'm going to need help with Charlie," I said.

The man whipped around in his chair and looked up at me.

His face went dark as the fireball flamed out, but I'd seen enough to know this was Randy Harris.

He jerked in his chair, drawing his arms in close to his body.

Thwump—the fourth fireball zipped straight up, a close shave, sparks peppering his face. He yelped and stood.

He looked at where his gun had been, then at me.

I grinned, then showed him his pistol as the last fireball thumped high into the night. In the light of the exploding firework I saw terror on his face.

"Relax," I said. "I need a little help with Charlie. He's passed out in the car."

"The fuck you think you're doin', man—walking into a man's house? And give me my fuckin' gun." His fear had turned to anger, something I needed to manage without shooting him.

"You gonna help me with Charlie?"

"No. Get the fuck off my property."

"I'm not going anywhere until I see that Charlie's in the house."

"I'll take care of it, man—just give me my gun and leave."

I leveled the pistol at Randy. "Not until I get Charlie inside."

Randy dropped the empty Roman candle tube and stepped into the house. I followed. He went through the kitchen and headed toward the front door.

"He's in the garage," I said.

Randy stopped—and turned around, looking perplexed.

I pointed at the door to the garage and said, "Car's in there, dude."

He stood, silent for several seconds, before heading over to the living room window. He peeled back a curtain and looked out toward the driveway before glancing my way again. He was baked from the weed, but he also looked to be lost in some internal debate: *Is something wrong here or am I being paranoid?*

"Car's in there, brother," I said, indicating the garage again.

Randy dropped the riddle, and finally we both entered the garage.

"There he is," I said, pointing to the car.

While Randy looked in at Charlie—who was sleeping on his back, mouth agape—I set his pistol on a storage shelf lining the wall. When Randy reached for the door handle, I grabbed his wrist and twisted his arm behind his back, slamming him face-first to the concrete where I zip-tied his wrists together while he shook off the blow to his head.

"Fuck, dude—you a cop?"

I flipped him over on his stomach and said, "Do I look like a cop?"

"Yes."

Beck stepped out of the shadows so only I could see him over the car. We made eye contact and he shrugged. We needed to work on my disguise.

* * *

"Are you a bondsman?" asked Randy Harris.

"You don't know what your bondsman looks like?" I asked.

The cargo van rumbled south down the Kansas Turnpike. Randy and I were in back. A little curtain near the cab separated us from Keri and Beck. We'd met up with Keri on a country road south of Kansas City. Randy hadn't seen her because I'd wrapped layers of duct tape around his head and over his eyes before Beck and I lifted him out of the trunk of the Grand Marquis and dragged him to the van. Now, Randy and I were facing each other—our backs against adjacent walls of the van. He was strapped down.

"Where you taking me?"

"Wichita. At first."

"At first?"

"At first."

"Are you the bondsman's bounty hunter or something?"

I let him stew.

"You're not. You wouldn't be taking me to Wichita. My warrant is out of Worthington."

I watched him wriggle against the restraints and wince. I kept mum.

"Can I talk to Miguel? I told him what the detective said about Eddie Dandurand so he could protect himself. I mean, shit, I'm not going to tell the cops that I told Miguel about Eddie bein' a snitch. I followed his fuckin' instructions, man . . . he told me to get lost. So I got lost. How could I have played it any better—been more loyal?"

"You could be dead?"

Randy Harris blubbered, wept, and begged for his life. After a few minutes of that, he aimed lower. "Can I have a cigarette?"

"No," I said.

"I have some in my back pocket."

"Second-hand smoke kills. Such an ugly habit."

"So, you *are* a cop."

"What makes you say that?"

"You're judgmental."

An occupational hazard for judges too. An astute observation.

"Well if I'm a cop, Randy, you just gave the cops Miguel's motive for killing Eddie Dandurand."

"Prove you're a cop. Show me the warrant."

"No."

Going to jail didn't scare Randy so the warrant would stay in my pocket.

"So you do have the warrant," said Randy. "You are a cop."

I picked up the audio recorder I had running at Randy's feet and stopped the recording. I hit rewind for a spurt, then hit play—"So you do have the warrant. You are a cop," went the recording.

"Cop! You're a cop. Okay, okay—" He smiled like he liked the idea I was a cop.

"I'm no cop, Randy."

"Then what's the recording for?"

"To record what you say."

"That's what fuckin' cops do."

"That's where I got the idea."

We sat with nothing more than the sound of the road for a while.

"You know I'm not a cop. You're just too fucked up to do the math. This feel like a cop's ride to you? And why would cops put duct tape over the eyes of a pussy like you? You're not exactly Pablo Escobar."

I let the sound of the road grind this into Randy's soul.

"This is of concern to us—this panic you display. You just blurted out Miguel's secret to—whoever we are. Are we cops? Are we bondsmen? Maybe we're bounty hunters. You cracked, and we never even touched you. Maybe Miguel should kill you—because you're stupid."

"I'm not going to tell the cops—"

"Maybe not on purpose."

"Not by accident either."

"Want to hear the recording? It says otherwise."

Randy fought his constraints until I put the muzzle of my pistol to his forehead. He froze.

I said, "I need the pin number to your phone."

Or maybe your thumb, I thought.

* * *

I climbed out of the van and changed my clothes at the river's edge. Because I was going to remove the duct tape from Randy's eyes, I slipped on a black ski mask. Even in the darkness of the van with my face disguised as it was, more face time with Randy was a bad idea. I wanted him to see the tools I might use on him, and if he thought I was someone other than his original kidnapper, all the better. I lit two cigarettes—one for me and one for him. I'd taken them off him before we threw him in Charlie Green's trunk. I climbed back into the van and shut the doors.

Randy shook like he was cold, but he was wet with sweat. I cut the duct tape with my blade and peeled it from his eyes. The sight of my ski mask broke him down more. I put the cigarette in his mouth. He sucked on it. It soothed him.

With his cigarette bobbing up and down on his lip he said, "Did Whispering Jim tell Miguel he needed to kill me? Is that what happened?"

I held up Randy's phone. "Why don't you ask ol' Whispering Jim yourself? You have his number on your cell, I see."

Whispering Jim Daniels was an attorney with a 505 area code—Albuquerque, New Mexico. The same number was on

Juan's phone, so I'd already researched him on Lexis. In the early eighties he was permitted to enter his appearance *pro hac vice* by a Cook County judge for a defendant on a murder case in Chicago. It meant "one time only," since he wasn't licensed to practice law in Illinois. Per the local rules, he became affiliated with an Illinois law firm for the duration of the case.

Daniels' client waived a jury trial and asked for a bench trial before the Honorable Theodore Wilson, who ultimately acquitted him of murder. A few years later, several of Whispering Jim's colleagues from the Illinois firm were investigated for fixing cases in front of several judges, including Judge Wilson. Wilson was questioned by an FBI agent at his retirement home in Sun City, Arizona. He was found dead in his backyard three days later with a single gunshot wound to the head. It was ruled a suicide but in light of what I was going through I doubted that.

"I used Whispering Jim one time," said Randy.

"When you had sex with your little neighbor girl in El Paso four years ago—the little eighth-grade girl."

"She dropped the charges. Said it never happened—but how did you know that?"

Mallory's reports told me that. I'd already learned that Randy's nickname was Rabbit on account of his promiscuity.

"Assume I know everything, except how to find Jorge and Miguel. And you're going to help me with that."

"What? But Miguel sent you."

I shook my head.

"Then who are you?"

"I'm the man who killed Juan."

"Trevino," whispered Randy. "You're with Trevino?"

I took a drag off the cigarette, letting his natural assumptions kick in.

"I'm the real reason your bosses are hiding," I said, before blowing smoke in Rabbit's face.

As if this reminded him he was burning coals too, he took a drag off the cigarette still on his lips. Muscles along his jaw flexed and he frowned, his cigarette drooping. A long ash hung in the balance.

"You gonna kill me or what?"

The ash dropped into Randy's lap.

"You wish," I said.

"Oh, God."

"What did Miguel think about you dealing for Trevino?" I asked.

"I never dealt for Trevino."

"You dealt heroin."

"I didn't *deal* it."

"You gave some to your old lady in Worthington, didn't you?"

"Yeah, I gave some to my old lady—fuckin' skank didn't tell Detective Mallory about that."

"You did a little more heroin dealing than just slippin' some to your old lady."

I didn't know this, but I stated it as fact.

"Yeah, okay," said Randy.

"Miguel and Jorge ever move any heroin?"

"No."

"Then you've been selling for Trevino, whether you knew it or not. So I can assume Miguel's in the dark about that?"

"Yes."

"Miguel and Jorge do any human trafficking?"

"No, man."

"Any kidnapping? You know anything about any kidnapping?"

"No. No kidnapping. Not my deal anyway. I get the crystal to bikers, rednecks, and college kids—some trailer trash—that's my deal."

"You wanna work for us?" I asked, poking my cigarette in an old Coke can.

"Yeah, yeah, I can give you the biker gangs—the ones that won't deal directly with Mexicans."

"First, you gotta tell me how to find Jorge and Miguel."

"I—I don't know where they are. They're hiding from you. They're pretty much hiding from the cops now too—worried Jorge's grandson will blow the top off the whole works."

"Jorge's grandson?"

"You don't know about that?"

"I'm about to, or you lose a finger."

"Jorge's grandson is the fucker that killed that family near Worthington . . . his trial's been on the news—"

"Vaughn Rummell?"

"Yeah, Vaughn Rummell is Jorge's grandson . . . illegitimate as fuck."

"Illegitimate grandson?" I had to think about that. Baltozar has a ruddy complexion, and even beyond that, there was no resemblance whatsoever between him and the photos of Jorge I'd seen. I didn't think it likely that Baltozar was the biological son of Jorge. But Maria . . . "So . . . Maria Rummell is Jorge's biological daughter?"

"Yeah, I think that's her name but I'm not sure. Jorge is losing control, man, letting that tweaker fuck with him. When shit like that happens that's the end, man . . . it's just a matter of time. You've got 'em on the run and I can you help you finish him. I'll give you the biker gangs—"

"Never mind that, pussy. We'll take whatever market we want. Tell me where to find Miguel and Jorge."

"They don't tell me shit like that, man."

He was probably telling the truth, but I was here to push it, so I picked up a pair of bolt cutters that I'd brought along for this very occasion. They were about half the height of a small woman.

Rabbit's shiver went to a shake and he said, "Here's what I know, man. Honest to God it's all I got. Dude like you can figure it out from what I know—"

"Spit it out."

I dropped the cutters to the floor and took the cigarette out of Randy's mouth.

"Jorge owns a flower shop—"

I knew this from Mallory's reports, so I let Rabbit know how on top of his shit I was.

"Fancy Flowers in Darby on 34th Street," I said. "He's never there—"

"Right, right, I know. There's a woman there named Helen. She—"

"Last name?"

"I—I don't know. You can figure it out real easy, though. Helen is this little old lady. I mean she's really fucking old, right. Works in the flower shop. On paper, she owns the farm."

"The farm?"

"The ranch—the fuckin' chicken ranch or whatever you call it—where Jorge and Miguel keep their fighting cocks. They take their best roosters to Oklahoma sometimes to, you know, cockfight and shit."

"How do you know this?"

"Uh, man . . . not sure I remember. I think I was getting some flowers with Juan one time at this Fancy Flowers shop, and I saw him steal some for a girl he liked. Well, since I thought he was stealing I started laughing and giving him shit about stealing flowers and he told me he couldn't steal the flowers because he and his family owned the place."

"That doesn't answer my question."

"Right, well . . . I think Juan just told me, you know, 'See that old lady over there? She owns the fuckin' chicken ranch.' I laughed because we called Jorge the head cock."

"Jesus, that's all you got." I grabbed the cutters. "Which finger do you use the least? We'll start there, I don't want to be an asshole about this."

"What?—man, what I just told you is golden. You can find Jorge and Miguel that way."

I stayed quiet, gazing into Randy's eyes, trying as best I could in a ski mask to look unimpressed before dropping the cutters to the floor again and slapping a length of duct tape over his eyes and wrapping it tight around his head.

"What's that mean?" he asked.

I pulled my ski mask off. "You think your information is pretty good?"

"Jorge and Miguel love those fuckin' roosters, man. Find the ranch, you find them."

"Pray I find Miguel and Jorge, because if I don't, Trevino wants me to kill you. He's willing to assume you're protecting them. Unlike Jorge, Trevino hasn't lost his nerve. He won't be satisfied until I kill your whole family."

Randy nodded. "You kill me, my mother, and my sister."

"You have a sister?"

Randy's head dropped, "Ah shit—"

"I kid—of course we know about sister Katie. She's a registered nurse with a fireman husband, two small children, and lives on Apache Road in Dodge City. Real pillar of the community. How'd you turn out to be such a fuck-up, by the way?"

With that, I left out the back of the van and filled Keri and Beck in on the details. Then she drove us to Tony's house, where we crashed for the night, after strapping Randy Harris to a steel pole in the basement.

*   *   *

Fancy Flowers opened at ten on Tuesday morning, so Keri left Tony's at nine fifteen. She wore a baseball hat and a hoodie, with wraparound sunglasses she borrowed from me. Right after she left, Tony called to tell me he was following Buster Reynolds south down I-35. They'd just crossed into Oklahoma.

Later in the morning at eleven, I was downstairs with Randy feeding him a bologna sandwich with a side of Doritos when Keri phoned me on her way back from Darby. She said, "The lady running the flower shop . . . her name is Helen Bertrand."

"How'd you get her name?"

"Easy. I watched a nice-looking elderly woman get out of her car and open up the shop, called Tony with the tag number, he got with his guy, and called back twenty minutes later with the name Helen Bertrand. She owns two properties. One, a house in Darby, which I assume is where she lives. The second one is on the eastern border of Sumner County on the Arkansas River south of Oxford about ten miles. Bet that's the rooster ranch."

"How'd—"

"Internet. Looked at a few county appraiser's websites. I'm familiar with the land in that area along the river—even talked to some of the folks who own land down there for the company's land man when he was out with gout."

"Get here, and we'll both go. We've got five hours before we leave for Oklahoma City, if the weather holds."

I still had Mallory's ticket for the Dodger Chihuahua game at Chickasaw Bricktown Ball Park at six o' clock tonight. Like Mallory, we were hoping to find Geronimo Baylon-Fontana by the visitors' dugout watching his brother. If Randy Harris was right, we had information we could use to find Jorge and Miguel. And maybe, just maybe, we had the man that could corner the Midwest's biker meth market strapped to a pole in Tony's basement. If we located Jorge and Miguel, I could always call the cops and the kidnapping would be investigated and maybe even prosecuted. Maybe I get my sister back, maybe I don't. Either way, I'd be playing footsy with these guys by bringing in the cops, which meant I'd probably have to spend the rest of my life in hiding with my family. I figured what I needed was more in line with what Trevino wanted, which is akin to saying the devil and I had something in common. We both wanted every big name associated with the Mendez-Rodriguez Cartel dead.

Keri said, "I'm listening to the weather now. It's hitting us hard in about an hour but I think it'll miss Oklahoma City to the north."

I looked at the radar on the Weather Bug app on my phone and saw Keri was right. We were in for some severe weather, but I didn't want to wait for it to pass—we had things to do.

30

Tuesday Afternoon, June 4, 2019

Ben

THE BLACK THUNDERHEADS rolled in and cut loose its rain on us in the ditch where we lay. We peered through the high grass at Helen Bertrand's old boarded-up saltbox house a quarter mile away.

Through my binoculars I saw that the first-story windows were well fortified against storms and unwanted visitors alike. I handed the binos to Keri and she gazed at the place.

"This may be a waste of time," she said.

"If I don't find any roosters inside that house, I'm calling Beck and telling him to kick the shit out of Randy until he gives us something we can use."

"What if he's told us all he knows?"

"Then it's going to be a long day for him."

I checked my burner phone—it was 1:16 p.m. The weatherman had got it right this time. I put the binos in my backpack with some burglary tools and we climbed out of the ditch and pushed through a churning wind toward the house. By the time we reached the back, the wind had shifted and the temperature had dropped—maybe fifteen degrees or so. There was no staying dry in this downpour, but we had on rain gear, which helped. Underneath our gear, we carried pistols and blades in holsters and sheaths.

I pulled off the board on a window on the lower level with a crowbar, only to find it in perfect condition and locked up tight, my view inside blocked by aluminum foil stuck on the inside. Keri and I reattached the board, so as not to arouse any suspicion. There was a window up high that wasn't boarded up. I thought I'd give that a try.

I jumped for the gutter where the roof swooped down to its lowest point, about nine and a half feet high. I caught it with both hands and swayed in the high winds, trying to calibrate my lift to the roof. Cold water spilled from the gutter down the insides of my sleeves. I felt it rushing past my armpits and over my ribs into my pants as the wind jerked me around.

"You're never going to make it," screamed Keri, though I could barely hear her through the storm.

She was right.

I dropped off the roof and we headed for a decrepit old barn to wait it out.

From there we watched the rain turn to hail—first the size of marbles, then golf balls. When they began shooting through the broken places in the roof and hitting our shoulders, we scrambled around the barn looking for cover, using flashlights because it was dark as early dawn. The roof in the northwest corner was mostly intact, and there were no hailstones next to the junked refrigerator underneath so we huddled together next to it.

The hail stopped and pounding rain kicked in again, along with higher winds, and some boards from the hayloft hit the floor somewhere with a clatter. Keri covered her head with her hands and I reached for the ground to change my position.

When I did, I noticed the dirt underneath my right hand felt uneven. I moved over and aimed the flashlight on the ground next to the old refrigerator. There was a large piece of flat particle board stuck in the dirt. Keri and I looked at each other then back to the board. She wedged her fingers under it and pulled. But it was held firm in the ground by the weight of the refrigerator. I wobbled the refrigerator away and Keri scraped off a layer of dirt with her hands, gripped the board, and jerked up. The board cracked, but held together as Keri and I pulled it clear of a cast-iron manhole cover underneath. When I removed it, we saw a hole four or five feet deep.

I climbed into the hole with my flashlight and saw that I was standing at the end of a long tunnel—as long as the beam of my flashlight anyway. It was roughly square, four feet high and wide, reinforced with wooden boarding.

Keri climbed in next to me and gazed down the tunnel.

I said, "Hope you're not claustrophobic."

Keri didn't answer.

Forty yards into the tunnel it forked, and we went the direction of the house, saving the other option for exploration later. We moved quickly, in part, by my way of thinking, for fear of being buried alive, though the tunnel seemed sound. When we reached the end, which didn't take long, we pushed away several large boards that blocked the exit, emerging into the dim light of a house creaking against the storm as birds flapped around in their confines.

It looked like we were in what used to be the dining room, now equipped with heaters, egg incubators, and mating charts. We continued through the kitchen into the pantry, where the shelves were full of antibiotics, syringes, vitamins, and steroids. The roosters and chickens were housed in the climate-controlled living room in spacious individual chicken coops with automated feeders and watering systems. The entire floor was covered in a hard rubber surface that banked to a drain in the middle of the room. I noticed a hose coiled around a spindle of sorts against one wall. All the birds appeared well fed and healthy, and their cages were relatively clean.

In what probably had been a bedroom, we found more paraphernalia—spikes, gaffs, and knives to strap to the gamecocks' legs for the fights. There was a trophy case containing several trophies. In an upstairs bedroom, there was a small mattress on the floor in the corner surrounded by food wrappers. Upstairs the house seemed louder—the noise from the storm and the birds combining into something surreal.

After ten minutes of looking around, there was nothing more to be learned. We knew someone connected to the cartel would be here eventually, so we needed to check on the other end of the tunnel and cover our tracks as best we could. We returned to the dining room and climbed back into the tunnel. After replacing the boards that covered the opening, we crawled as fast as we could manage straight past the turn that led to the dilapidated barn. It seemed like we crawled a long way this time. We had no clue, really, how far we'd gone into the darkness of the tunnel, but I would've guessed close to half a mile. I figured we were on the other side of the hill located north of the rooster house.

When we paused to give our knees a rest, I went down flat on my stomach. I flashed my light ahead and saw a glint off something shiny in the distance.

"What's that?" said Keri.

"I don't know, but let's keep moving."

When we got closer my flashlight revealed what was before us—several leather bags with shiny silver buckles that were reflecting the light. When we got to the bags, we saw the end of the tunnel, or maybe it was the beginning. I counted seven bags, all filled with stacks of hundred dollar bills, amounting to hundreds of thousands of dollars. We made our way through the bags and the last ten yards of tunnel to the entrance. I stood and pushed up another manhole cover.

We emerged in a clump of trees being boxed by the storm. A limb snapped as loud as a gunshot somewhere and a flurry of snapping limbs that seemed way too close followed.

We climbed back into the hole and placed the manhole cover above us.

"We could find a place out there to hide and wait for them ourselves," said Keri. "Then call the cops if they show up."

"Yeah, if we saw Ashley, that'd be a good play."

"But . . ."

"But with no Ash, whoever the cops manage to arrest would promptly be read their Miranda rights and they'd lawyer up—these are cartel people. By the time the cartel attorneys got in the mix it would be Monday before the negotiations for information about my sister could even begin."

My phone burred in my pocket, and I realized I'd felt the vibration moments before when we'd stepped out of the tunnel into the storm. I now recognized the alert as an incoming text. Since Keri was going after the phone in her pocket, I figured we'd both gotten the same text. When we got to our phones, we saw we had two texts. A text from Beck's anonymous friend told us April was home from the hospital. With child. Another text, this one from Tony, told us he was driving through Tulsa, following Buster Reynolds in the direction of southeast Oklahoma.

That was all potentially promising information, but what we'd found in this tunnel was a bird in hand and we weren't letting go.

"However we decide to play it," said Keri, "we can learn a lot, just by sitting near a hole full of money in the woods."

"You're right," I said. "That'll be Beck's job. Let's cover our tracks and get out of here. I've got an idea."

On our way back through the tunnel, I slipped ten thousand dollars out of one of the bags. Maybe I'd be back for the rest. Maybe I wouldn't.

31

Ben

AT SIX O'CLOCK Keri and I sat in our seats two rows behind the visitors' dugout at Chickasaw Bricktown Ballpark in downtown Oklahoma City holding Dodger Dogs and wearing plastic fifty-cent ponchos. The sky had dropped close—a blanket of strange yellow cloud cover shaped like a series of saggy pouches that gave the nine-thousand-seat park an ominous glow as a light rain fell on the field. The game was delayed thirty minutes so we took turns looking through binoculars trying to spot Geronimo amongst the few fans still in their seats. We had the photo of him from Mallory's files with us.

When Geronimo's brother finally came to the plate in the first inning the rain had passed, the stadium was half full, and there were two outs. While Keri scanned the crowd with the binoculars, I couldn't help but feel we were wasting precious time. I found myself watching the batter. Like me, Manuel Baylon-Fontana batted left and threw right. He put a charge into the second pitch he saw, hooking it into the right field seats just foul. As he walked back to the batter's box Keri said, "Got him. Think I found Geronimo."

"Where?"

Keri handed me the binoculars and pointed to the seats in left field. "The Budweiser Deck. Lower tier. Third table to the right of the foul pole."

I checked out the Budweiser Deck's lower tier, a patio with a single row of four-topper tables and chairs spaced apart from the foul pole to the bullpen in center field. When I honed in on the third table, I saw Geronimo sitting with two other men drinking beer. The crack of the bat on the ball pulled my eyes away from the binos in time to see a line drive land in left-center field. Geronimo's brother rounded first and held. I raised the binos to my eyes again in time to watch Geronimo high-five the other two men at his table.

"Let's go," I said.

By the time we got to the Budweiser Deck, the Chihuahua's had made their third out. Keri and I looked on as an usher stood watch at the entrance to the deck, checking tickets of fans coming in and nodding at those filing out.

"How we gettin' in there?" said Keri.

"I'll buy a ticket if I have to, assuming I still can."

Just then a man in his mid-twenties who had left the deck strolled past us and into a nearby restroom. I followed.

While we were washing our hands next to each other at a row of sinks I said, "I saw you come out of the Budweiser Deck. How much those tickets run you?"

"Twenty bucks. But I'm here with my fraternity and we got a group rate."

"Listen, I think I saw an old friend of mine in there. I'll give you a hundred dollars for your ticket."

He looked at me like I'd made some kind of indecent proposal and moved quickly to the paper towels but was held up by a man already at the dispenser.

I wiped my wet hands on my jeans, pulled a hundred-dollar bill out of my pocket, and held it up.

"For real," he said.

"Can I have the ticket?"

He slipped it out of his back pocket and we made the exchange.

* * *

I flashed the ticket at the usher as I walked by and he nodded. Geronimo was standing in front of his table, leaning over the railing and yelling something in Spanish to his brother warming up in left field. The other men I'd seen sitting at the table with him were gone, so I sat in one of the seats and waited for him to turn around.

When he did, he wrinkled his forehead and said, "This table's taken, friend." His plastic smile seemed designed to show me the four silver crowns on his upper incisors. I knew from the files he was thirty-five and it looked like he'd spent some time in the gym, but looking at his face, I would've guessed he was at least forty.

I smiled back at him and said, "I don't have a lot of time, Mr. Fontana, so I'll cut to it. I can give you the people you've been looking for."

His head pulled back and he glanced around the park uneasily.

There wasn't anyone within earshot at the moment so I kept talking. "Jorge Mendez-Rodriguez and Miguel Mendez-Mendoza."

His face turned intense and he locked eyes with me.

I didn't blink. "I can find them for you. But I need something in return."

Geronimo shrugged, "No idea who those men are. And who-the-fuck-'re you?"

"My name is Benjamin Joel. Judge Benjamin Joel."

His head drew back, further than before, but he maintained eye contact. "Judge?"

"Yeah, I'm the judge on Vaughn Rummell's death penalty case."

His eyes studied my face, so I took my baseball hat off. He pulled his smartphone out of his pocket and began popping the screen with his finger. His two friends returned with beers and said something in Spanish to him while glancing at me. Geronimo showed them what I saw was a photo of me in my robe on the state's judicial website. They shrugged and Geronimo said something in Spanish to them and the only thing I understood was him repeating the name, Vaughn Rummell.

I said to Geronimo, "Do you want to find Jorge and Miguel or not?"

"I told you I don't know those men." He looked at the beer his friend held out for him. Instead of taking it, he said, "I need to take a piss." He nodded at me to follow him so I did. His two henchmen fell in behind me and we marched past the usher in single file.

I followed Geronimo into a family bathroom while the two men stood watch outside. Once alone inside, he turned around and said, "Arms up."

I put my arms up and he frisked me, then asked for my hat. He looked that over, then slapped it back on my head and said, "What is it you want from me?"

"I want to show you where you can find these men you've been looking for and then . . . well, nature will take its course I'm sure. All I ask is that I be allowed to go along, and that we take steps to rescue my sister . . . whatever that entails." I handed him a photo of Ashley. "Presuming she's still alive, of course."

He looked at the photo. "They kidnapped your sister?" He spoke in a tone that made me think he didn't believe me.

I nodded.

"You're telling me that the Mendez-Rodriguez Cartel kidnapped your sister—an American judge's sister?"

"That's what I'm telling you because that's what's happened. I'm supposed to cut Vaughn Rummell loose at the trial in a few days."

Geronimo put his tongue on his upper lip, his eyes dancing as he thought. "Fuckin' idiots. You know they'll eventually kill you, your sister, whatever family you got—after they get what they need from you?"

"That's the way I see it too. That's why I'm here."

"Why *are* you here?—looking for me?"

"Because the enemy of my enemy is my friend."

"Yeah I get that. I mean, how do you even know who I am?"

"Because I have access to Detective Mallory's files and I know all about you. I can tell you what the DEA knows about you too."

"Wait—so because you're a judge you have access to this information?"

"Forget about how I know the information. Just know I have it and that's how I found you. From what I learned in the files, I had a hunch you'd be here."

"Detective Mallory's missing. I saw that on the news. What's going on here?"

"Mallory's dead."

"You know this how?"

"I watched Miguel pump nine rounds into his head and chest from point-blank range. Miguel shot him with my gun. They got his body. They got my gun and the shell casings from the spent rounds. They got my prints and my DNA on the gun."

Geronimo smiled big—not the plastic one from before but a real big I'm-enjoying-the-shit-out-of-this smile. But it was short-lived. Maybe he noticed the tension I felt in the muscles of my face. "They framed you for murder. That's supposed to make you think that they'll feel comfortable trusting you after you get your sister back. They thought you needed more incentive to follow through. Since you're here, you must not be satisfied with the arrangement."

"You'd be right about that. I'm not in the habit of cutting deals with a cartel, but yet, here I am with you."

"Whoa, whoa, now Judge, for the record, I'm not a member of any cartel." Geronimo brushed imaginary lint off my shoulders and clasped them with his vice-grip hands and said, "I'm just a concerned person who wants to help you get your sister back home safely, and that's it. Understand?"

"Of course I understand. And I need you to understand that I don't want this made public any more than you do."

Geronimo grinned and said, "You came to the right place, *amigo*. You know the number-one rule in this business?"

"What business?"

"Ha! You learn quickly. I already like you very much."

Oddly, even though I figured he had to be a ruthless killer, I couldn't help but like him right back. I noted the feeling and reminded myself I was charming a snake, or he was charming me. Either way, my eyes needed to be open and my moves careful. Here in this ballpark he was presumably without a weapon, having walked through metal detectors. And we were surrounded by hundreds of potential witnesses. In another setting, I assumed he wouldn't be so congenial.

"The number-one rule in any business then," he said, "is this: You don't kill the goose that lays the golden egg."

"You don't want to invite backlash—put the American market at risk."

Geronimo nodded and squinted his eyes. "Kidnap a Mexican judge's wife or daughter. Sure, why not? But never in America."

"Help me find my sister, and I'll help you take these guys out."

"And if they've already killed your sister?"

"Then they'll come for me and the rest of my family next. It's the same deal any way you slice it."

"How do I know I can trust you?"

"I've got a man chained to a pole in the basement of a house in Wichita. He sells the Mendez-Rodriguez Cartel's meth to all the biker gangs from Wichita to Kansas City. He's how I found the cartel's favorite stash house—the place where Jorge and Miguel keep their gamecocks and hundreds of thousands of dollars in cash at the moment. He's willing to buy the product he sells to the bikers from Trevino. You can have him—do whatever you want with him. I'd rather you not kill him, but I don't have the time or the resources to keep him alive. I assume you can put him to good use."

"I find it strange that you talked to him about working for Trevino."

"The subject came up quite naturally because I let him think I worked for Trevino. He brought up the idea of selling for you guys when he was begging for his life, and I went with it."

He beamed at me. "You've got Randy Harris."

"That I do. Want him?"

"That I do." He was still beaming at me, seeming to admire me. "Clarity is good, *amigo*. Men with clarity under pressure are a rarity these days. Alright, let's get the fuck out of this bathroom before we get accused of being a couple of fags."

On our way back to the Budweiser Deck Geronimo told one of his toadies to bring me a beer. This time, Geronimo chose the empty table closest to the foul pole because it was next to another empty table that he ordered his other associate to occupy to give us space to talk freely. Over beers we watched the game and talked over specifics, like the need to take prisoners if we couldn't determine the actual location of Ashley. In the sixth inning, Geronimo made it clear he would handle the questioning of anyone captured.

"Wouldn't have it any other way," I said.

Suddenly my phone chimed. It was Tony and I accepted the call.

"I have eyes on Jorge as we speak," he whispered. "He's talking to Buster Reynolds in the foothills of the Kiamichi Mountains down here in southeast Oklahoma."

I glanced at Geronimo who took a sip of beer and watched as the Dodgers' shortstop fielded a grounder and threw a laser to first base.

I said, "Any sign of Ash?"

Geronimo's eyebrows went up and he looked at me.

Tony's electric whisper came through the receiver between his gasps for air. "No, and I don't think they'd keep her here. This looks like the big guy's home to me. Nice . . . high-dollar cabin. He's got a St. Bernard following him around."

"St. Bernard?"

I was trying to remember why I cared about the dog when Tony filled in the gap before my mind could.

"Yeah, remember the big stuffed animal—the St. Bernard— we watched someone carry into the funeral home at Juan's visitation?"

"Yeah," I said. Still a useless bit of information it seemed.

When I ended the call Geronimo said, "Jorge has had a St. Bernard by his side since 1989 when he shot-gunned my father behind a bar in Laredo. He took my father's cocaine . . . and he took Suzy."

"Suzy?"

"My dad's St. Bernard—his *pregnant* St. Bernard. I was five years old at the time. I loved that dog. As the story goes, the dog

Jorge has now comes from Suzy's bloodline. All his St. Bernards have come from her bloodline. I want that dog—that's my fuckin' dog."

A bonus—this was personal for both of us.

I looked at the GPS app on my phone and clicked on recent history to see the trail that the tracker on Buster's Suburban left for us. He left I-35 to go east through Tulsa onto the Muskogee Turnpike, then I-40 and U.S. 59 through Poteau, where the Suburban abandoned the main highways for back country roads all the way to Jorge's cabin.

I smiled at the breakthrough. "The dog is yours."

He nodded, maintaining eye contact with me. "Do you know why I disappeared fourteen months ago just when I was about to be accepted into Jorge's operational circle?"

"Because Detective Mallory found out you were Trevino's half nephew, using the alias Arturo Gallegos?"

"No, he knew exactly who I was all along. He may not've known it on paper, but trust me, he knew. What happened was, after I agreed to run money for Jorge, this guy calling himself Buster Reynolds shows up and introduces himself to me at the bar where I worked—a place called Uncle Sam's."

Geronimo cocked his head and looked more directly into my eyes. I gave him a knowing nod to let him know I knew the place.

He drank from his beer and continued. "I'd been told an old white Texan did the vetting for the cartel so this was what I was expecting. He told me he wanted to have a few words with me so we sat in a booth as he nodded at the bartender. When the bartender brought us beers and referred to him as Harold I could feel the hair stand up on the back of my neck and I didn't even know why at first. Halfway through our first beer, listening to that Texas drawl it hit me. *Harold Reynolds* was the name of the first cop to arrive at the scene after my father was killed in '89—I've read the reports. I'm thinking: *this can't be a coincidence.* So after he left I was so shaken up I watched the surveillance video at Uncle Sam's because I couldn't stop thinking about the guy. Glad I did. I watched him slip my beer mug into a paper sack and leave. Now I'm thinking, who has access to a fingerprint database that works for a cartel but a former cop with law enforcement connections, right? There was nothing more I could do but disappear. I've been deported twice. My prints are in the system under my real name. I was about to be outed."

He reached across the table, his elbow bent to a ninety-degree angle, his forearm vertical. I clapped my hand into his, forming a two-handed fist.

He held on longer than I'd expected and said, "You'll be worse off than you were before if you fuck me over."

"That's a fact."

He nodded. "We will get your sister back, my friend."

32

Early Morning, Wednesday, June 5, 2019

Ben

ON THE TRIP home from Oklahoma City while Keri drove, I checked the call log on my regular iPhone—the one actually in my name—and saw that Caroline Gordon had called three times but didn't leave a message. I was both concerned and curious as to why she was calling, but in the end, decided not to return her calls. Whether it was intuition or paranoia, something kept me from calling her back.

When we got home, I'd barely had time to get to the bedroom to take off my shoes when we heard a knock at the door. Keri glanced at the surveillance monitor in the bedroom and said, "Caroline Gordon. This is no good."

A feeling that something awful beyond the kidnapping had happened to Ashley washed over me and my throat suddenly felt dry and narrow.

Diablo was up, excited at the chance to walk me to the door. When he locked eyes with me I said, "You're gonna be sittin' this one out again I'm afraid." Diablo cocked his head to the side like this perplexed him. We weren't hiding the fact that we were watching Pops' pit bull while he was gone, but we weren't advertising it either. We shut him in the bedroom.

When I swung the door open Agent Gordon looked up at me with a grave look on her face. I knew her presence on my porch signaled something momentous, given that she'd been shot and had surgery three days earlier and wasn't expected back on the job this soon. Her hair was up in a ponytail, and she wore loose-fitting jeans and a long-sleeved KBI-issued windbreaker which rumpled at her hip where her Glock was holstered.

"Sorry to bother you at home, Your Honor, but could I have a word with you?"

The humidity was stifling, and I noticed a few strands of hair had come loose from her ponytail and were stuck to the sweat on her neck and face.

"About?" I felt Keri walk up behind me. The open door blocked Caroline's view of her.

"I want to talk to you about Miguel," said Caroline. "Off the record."

"No such thing as off the record, Agent Gordon. So no, you may not have a word with me about that."

"Okay then, I have other business to tend to here."

"How's your leg? You should be home in bed. I granted the state a three-day continuance so you could rest up. Now, here you are, out here in the middle of the night, making a liar out of Ms. Sweeney."

"The leg hurts like a mother, but surgery went well and the doctor expects a full recovery. Thanks for asking."

"Glad to hear that, Caroline. Now, I'm beat—"

"Is your sister out here, Judge? Her husband keeps calling the sheriff's office. Says she's missing. Says you may know where she's at."

If Agent Gordon had breaking news about something bad happening to my sister, she would've probably led with that, which should have given me some sense of relief but it didn't, given the hour and intensity in Caroline's face. "Mallory already hit me up about that and I'll tell you the same thing I told him—"

"I read Mallory's incident report. You think she's hiding from her husband. But his report didn't say, one way or the other, whether you'd heard from her or knew where she was."

"Sounds about right."

"Well, now I'm askin'. When's the last time you heard from her?"

"Friday night. May twenty-fourth, I think. She ate dinner here."

"Have you tried to contact her since then?"

If I answered no, I'm either a no-account-asshole-brother or something's amiss. If I answer yes, Agent Gordon will know I'm a liar when she gets Ashley's cell phone records. Maybe she already had them. Lying about making calls almost proved something was amiss so I decided it was time to play the part of the no-account-asshole-brother.

"I've been pretty preoccupied, with the case and all. Have you tried to call my sister yourself? Maybe leave a message and a number for her to call?"

"Of course I've done all that. Mallory did too. She's not returning calls and we can't find anybody who's seen her for ten days. That doesn't concern you?"

"Sure, but you have to understand something about Ash. She does things like this for attention from time to time. Always has. I used to get real upset about it too. But, I've got a life to live."

Caroline's eyes narrowed. It was working. I was becoming an asshole to her.

I said, "I don't expect you to understand."

"Your kids? I don't suppose they're back from their trip with your grandfather?"

"No, they're still with Pops." I wasn't sure how Caroline knew my kids were with Pops but I wasn't about to ask. Now wasn't the time to look defensive.

"Of course they are."

"You doubt that?"

"I'm beginning to, with all due respect."

"What's going on?"

"You don't know where your sister's at, and your children are with your grandfather."

"Yes. Are you high on pills or something?" It was a mean thing to say, but she did seem off—more tired than spaced out on drugs—but I wanted to end this conversation and hoped the insult would move things along.

"Where?"

"Where what, Agent Gordon?"

"Where exactly are your children?"

I shrugged before I could stop myself.

Caroline's brow drew down over her eyes at the tell.

I said, "At the moment . . . Leo and Lindy are with Pops somewhere in the northwest, I think. It's one of those trips."

"What the hell does that mean? Jesus, I came out here to relieve my suspicions but maybe I *am* on to something."

"What is it you think you're on to?"

She looked off into the darkness beyond my porch and said, "It's going to sound crazy."

"That'll be nothing new for you tonight. May as well go all the way."

"Last night, I was in bed in the hospital talking to my folks. Channel ten was hyping college baseball—showing old highlights. They played some old footage of you running from first to home in the regionals—that time you jumped over the tag. Thought I saw something in your stride—something that reminded me of the way the man in the mask ran on Mallory's video."

My heart skipped a beat, but I managed to grunt out a laugh. "Maybe the painkillers have made you a little punchy. You probably ought to let Keri drive you home. In the state you're in, I'd hate to see you get in trouble."

She didn't pull her glare off me. "I'm taking my concerns to Sweeney. I've got a feeling the cartel has compromised you and you're doing your best to fight back, but you're overmatched. I'll show her the videos side by side, show her what I'm talking about. It won't seem that crazy. Not after I've been shot and Mallory went missing. Not after the cartel lawyers descended upon Vaughn Rummell to protect Miguel. I'm not letting these fuckers get away with this."

"What?—you think I broke into Miguel's farmhouse and killed those men in the field? Why? Why would I do that?"

"You were trying to find your family, and in self-defense . . . well, maybe you didn't kill all of those men in the field."

But I had killed all those men in the field, except Kramer Carter. The truth was stranger than she could imagine. I weaponized the almost unbelievable truth of what had happened to stoke her gathering doubt.

"Someone else did then? Is that your theory now? Listen to yourself . . . you sound nuts. We'll probably never know what really went down in that field, but I damn sure wasn't involved and if you, a cop, get people to thinkin' I *was* involved, then that puts me and my family directly in the cartel's crosshairs. I'll have your ass for that, believe me."

Caroline looked down for the first time, her face flushed. This was hard for her. The girl had guts and somehow knew she was on to something—boy was she on to something—but I saw doubt creeping into her eyes. I felt guilty deceiving her, especially after all she'd been through. Part of me wanted to break down and tell her the truth, see if she'd keep the truth from Sweeney long enough for me to get Ashley back. She could no doubt be a big help to me, but I couldn't risk it. I raked the tips of my fingers back and forth across my cheeks and jaw thinking about all the things I had to take care of that I didn't want Agent Gordon to know about. I had to play dirty the way Gordon never would.

Caroline finally broke her silence. She wasn't quite ready to give up. "The casings found in Miguel's backyard and in the field next to Juan came from a Glock and you shoot a Glock."

"I shoot lots of guns, and Glocks are everywhere. So what?"

"Yeah, but you have the same stride as the man in the video, you shoot the same gun, and—maybe—your whole family's missing. And I don't think that man's actions in the video are consistent with a cartel *sicario*. If that was a cartel hitman, Juan would've never made it out of that farmhouse alive."

"Would it help if you could talk to Pops and my children, on the phone, right now?"

"If you don't want me going to Sweeney with this, yeah."

"If I didn't like you so much I'd let you do that and ruin your career. But I'd hate to see that happen and I need to protect my family. I don't need any rumors swirling around about how I went all cowboy on the cartel out there in that field. This may take a minute. It's twelve-thirty in the morning. Sane people are sleeping."

Agent Gordon took her gaze from mine and gingerly took a seat in the cushioned chair on my porch.

I said, "Okay then, I'll be right back so you can go home and get some rest, so we can both forget this Lortab-induced fever dream you're having."

I shut the door on her. When I got to the bedroom I found Keri already on the phone. She looked up and said, "Pops is waking up the kids right now."

Apparently, she'd slipped out of the living room without me noticing when she could tell where the conversation with Agent Gordon was headed. Smart girl. Keri said, "Here's Ben," into the phone and handed it to me.

Assuming it was Pops on the other end, I grabbed the phone and said, "Did Keri tell you what's going on?"

"How sure is this KBI gal that there was a kidnapping?" said Pops.

"Sure enough to come all the way out here after being shot to give the chief judge in this district the third degree. I'm not sure what all she knows but she told me she thinks I'm the mysterious running man on the video. Says she saw a highlight of that play at the plate of me they sometimes play this time of year."

"Ah shit! Give me a minute to brief the kids on what not to say to the popo. One of life's lessons I guess, one that'll surely get me nominated for great-grandfather of the year."

"Hope it doesn't get you arrested. Caroline Gordon is smart. And she's not messing around."

"Okay, give me a second."

I heard him talking to the kids, explaining what they could say and what they couldn't say to the nice police woman. The kidnapping was off limits. So was their current location. Given the recent violence against the authorities over this case, it seemed reasonable for me to want to keep that information a secret, even from the cops. If that bothered Agent Gordon, then so be it.

"Okay, Benny, we're ready," said Pops. "I'll talk to Agent Gordon first and set the parameters. Given that she's been shot and Detective Mallory's missing, we're not telling a soul where these children are until this trial is over. Seems reasonable to me."

"Exactly what I was thinking."

I walked the phone out to the porch and handed it to Agent Gordon before she stood. She put the phone to her ear and said, "With whom am I speaking?"

She nodded and after a moment of listening said, "Can I speak with Leo and Lindy?" She bit her lip and listened again until her face brightened. "Hi, my name is Caroline Gordon. I'm an agent with the Kansas Bureau of Investigation. Your dad is right here with me, so I'm going to put you on speaker phone so he can hear too, okay?"

She put the phone on speaker mode, held it away from her, and said, "I have a few questions for you Leo. Is that okay?"

"Yeah, that's okay."

The sound of his voice put a smile on my face.

"Are you having a fun time with your grandpa?"

"He's my great-grandpa."

"Oh, he's your great-grandpa, that's right. Well, what are you guys doing for fun?"

"Fishing, lots of fishing. Hitting balls in the batting cage we built. Shooting guns. That's about it."

"Sounds like you and your sister are having a great time." Caroline looked up at me and took in a deep breath. "Can I ask you kind of a weird question?"

"How weird?"

Caroline chuckled. "It's pretty weird. Did anything scary happen to you before you left Worthington with Pops?"

"Like what?"

Caroline looked up at me and wrinkled her nose. "What do I mean? Hmm. Were you or your sister kidnapped?"

"No."

Caroline nodded and pursed her lips at the flat denial that came a bit too quick, like he expected the question. Hearing my boy lie to a cop—I almost cringed. One of the casualties of this whole affair was the innocence of my children.

"Okay Leo," said Caroline. "Let me ask you this. Do you know what happened to your Aunt Ashley?"

"Something happened to Auntie Ash?"

Agent Gordon's shoulders slumped. "Well—"

Lindy's voice came through the phone next. "Is Ash okay? Oh my God!"

"Listen, kids," said Caroline. "I don't know . . . I'm sure your aunt is fine." She looked up and seemed to direct the next question to me with her eyes. "No one's talked to you about your aunt?"

I shook my head slowly for her, giving her the now-you've-upset-the-kids look.

Pops' voice came through the phone. "I think I've had about all I can take of this, Ms. Gordon. I hope you can find my granddaughter, but trust me, this isn't the first time we've been through this. I'll let you know when I hear from her. Goodnight."

The call ended on that note—well-tuned righteous indignation.

Caroline handed me the phone and stood. "Sorry about all this, Judge. I'm headed home to get some sleep. I apologize."

She limped down the steps to the sidewalk, stopped, and looked back at me. "You think I'm crazy now, don't you?"

"I think you've been through a lot. I'm glad you're okay." I looked out into the darkness, wondering if someone from the Mendez-Rodriguez Cartel was watching and what they'd think of all this. Hell, by now, maybe the Trevino Cartel was watching too. Suddenly, I was concerned for Caroline's safety. "Are you worried whoever shot you will try to finish the job?"

"Yeah, I am. You worried they'll come for you?"

"Sure I am. My kids aren't even in the state, remember?"

Caroline smiled. "I'm sorry I bothered you."

"Get some rest. You're a damn good cop. This episode tonight will be our little secret."

Caroline nodded. I watched her limp to her Crown Vic and drive away. I felt tears well up in my eyes as Keri sidled up next to me and slipped her hand inside my arm. We watched Caroline's lights move east down Seventieth Avenue the same way we'd watched Ashley's ten days earlier.

33

Wednesday Night, June 5, 2019
9:18 p.m.

Ben

I WAS HOLDING a stuffed-animal version of a St. Bernard in a headlock as I walked along the lantern-lined sidewalk that meandered through April's apartment complex in northwest Wichita. Even in the darkness, April couldn't help but notice me since we were heading directly toward each other. Her arms were full and she was hugging her newborn to her chest on one side and a bag of groceries on the other.

Her face brightened as we got closer. "I bet I know who that's from," she said.

"Do you recognize me?" I asked.

"Yes," she said. But she didn't. Pops would've had trouble picking me out of a lineup with my face disguised the way Beck had taught me.

"I recognize you from the bar," I said. The photos from Miguel's house had established she'd partied at The Porte on several occasions.

A blank look. She was thinking.

"The Porte," I said. "I work there. In the back mostly, so it's fine if you don't rec—"

"No, but I *do* remember you!"

"I'll walk you to your door. Looks like you've got your hands full."

Once inside her front door, April set her baby on the floor with the groceries. She turned and said, pointing, "You can put the dog down there, on the couch."

When I remained outside on the porch, as if uncertain about entering, she waved her hand and said, "Come on in."

"Jorge wants to see his grandson," I said as I stepped inside.

"Where is he? I thought Papa wasn't coming back here for a while."

"No, of course he's not *here*. I'm supposed to take you to see him." I handed her the St. Bernard. "I'm supposed to tell you to check the barrel."

"The what?"

"The . . . barrel. Around his neck—on the dog's collar."

"Oh. Okay."

April set the dog on the couch and unfastened the barrel. Three rolls of cash shot out onto the floor, rolling by her green-hued toenails.

Drug money from the tunnel.

"Oh, my God!" April exclaimed.

"That's $10,000. You're supposed to count it."

"I trust you."

"Jorge wanted me to make sure you count it."

"If he asks, I'll tell him I counted it."

"You can tell him in person in about an hour or so if you want."

April smiled, showing off her handsome square-jawed face and fluorescent white smile. Up close I still couldn't tell if the red stain on her neck was a birthmark or a burn scar.

Once we were in the parking lot next to the Dodge Grand Caravan—another rental by the Voice—I showed her to the back seat where I had a car seat base hooked up, ready to go.

"Is that a Chicco base?" she asked, the handle of the car seat resting on her forearm.

"I think. I don't know. Will it work?"

She hoisted the seat onto the base and snapped it in. A perfect fit. She was thrilled.

I shrugged. This, of course, was no accident. We knew a lot about April. She sat in the back seat with the baby.

Before I got onto I-235 and headed south, I tossed an eye mask behind me—the kind people wear to block out light when they sleep.

"What's this?"

"Precaution—you understand."

I looked in the rearview mirror. Geronimo was behind me, driving his black, armored Cadillac Escalade with Keri sitting next to him in the passenger seat. If my trick hadn't worked, April would be in the back of that Escalade on the floor with duct tape around her mouth and eyes.

"Ah, shit!" I said.

"What?"

"I forgot to ask for your phone."

"Why do you need my phone?" She sounded perturbed.

"So I can turn off the GPS. We have our rules."

"Oh, sure. I get it. No worries. I'll turn it off."

"I still need it. I'll give it back when we're through. I promise."

This time she handed it over—dropping her pink-sequined phone onto the passenger seat—then slipping the mask on over her eyes.

"Pin number?" I said.

"Oh yeah. Eight six eight six."

No fuss, no muss this time. I smiled at the small cooler containing Juan's thumb on the passenger floorboard.

I turned on the radio—local news. They were talking about the Dandurand trial. I used the pin number she gave me to get into her phone, turn off the GPS, and power it down.

"You following the trial?" I asked, looking at her reflection in the mirror.

"I don't watch news."

I turned on my left turn signal for a few seconds but didn't change lanes. Geronimo got the signal we'd worked out ahead of time and passed me on the left. I gave Keri a thumbs-up as they went by. We were on our way to an abandoned farmstead less than a mile from the Arkansas River and one mile upstream from Jorge's chicken ranch. Keri knew all about the place because of her job researching properties for the oil company.

The owners were a couple in their sixties who lived in New York and hadn't been to Kansas in years and for whatever reason had declined to lease the farm ground to any farmers. They jumped all over the oil money though.

About ten minutes after putting on the mask April said, "Wow, I think I dozed off."

"Sleep when the baby does. What my old lady used to say."

When we arrived at the farmstead, I parked in front of a detached garage that stood fifteen yards from the screened-in back porch of the ramshackle house. I held April's hand and led her through a path we'd cleared through waist-high grass and weeds to a storm shelter on the opposite side of the garage as the house. I carried the baby in his car seat with my free hand.

The storm shelter door was flipped open and Keri and Geronimo were watching us from the bottom of the stairs. It was a crude, brick-lined hole in the ground big enough for maybe five adults—something the owner's ancestors no doubt used to protect themselves from tornados and high winds back in the day.

"Watch your step here," I said. "Got about eight or nine steps down."

"It smells like we're in a cave," April said.

"Pretty much," I said, handing the baby to Keri.

"Can I take this mask off now?"

"Almost there," I said. Then I cuffed one of April's wrists and then the other around a rusty old support pole, fast and gentle, hands behind her back.

"What the fuck!" she screamed.

"Jorge will be here later," I said. At least that was the plan.

"Let me go, goddammit! I have to feed my baby, you asshole."

"Carmen here will take care of that for you, ma'am. She's all set with formula and all of the—"

"I fuckin' breast feed."

"Not tonight you don't. Carmen's got it all under control. Even the diapers."

"Fuck this—I'm telling Papa you ripped me off, motherfucker. I'll say you only gave me five grand."

That caught me off guard—that she didn't get the gravity of her situation. "I'm guessin' that'll be the least of his worries." I started up the stairs, but stopped, curious about something. "What's the baby's name?"

"What?" she yelled. "It's Juan-Jorge you fuckin' 'tard."

Lovely lady—she still didn't get it. From the look on Geronimo's face he wasn't going to put up with her talking to us this way for long, so I needed to make her understand she wasn't in the hands of friendlies. "That's right ma'am," I said. "How could I forget? Oh yeah, maybe it's 'cause I don't really work for Jorge."

Keri was already at the top of the stairs with little Juan-Jorge. A smile creased Geronimo's face before he turned and jogged up the stairs. I followed as April switched gears and begged for us not to hurt her baby. It was a loud wailing in the night until Geronimo muted it by slamming the shelter door shut—a cold move that reminded me where I didn't want this to go. Geronimo had promised me April and the baby wouldn't be harmed, and now that we were at the point in the operation where he was more in control of how this would go down than I was, I was on alert for any deviation from our agreement. For what good it would do, I still had a couple aces left to play. Beck and the Voice were hovering around somewhere out there with night scopes and high-powered sniper rifles in case this went south. With all the high weeds and grass surrounding this house, however, this plan of action was far from ideal. Geronimo's men would have a lot of cover the second bullets started to fly. As a last resort, I gave Beck Caroline Gordon's cell phone number.

Keri pointed in the direction of the farmhouse and said, "I'll be in there with the baby. The mosquitos are awful out here."

Geronimo walked behind the garage, I assumed to relieve himself. I stepped to the van, climbed into the driver's seat, and powered up April's phone to check her call log, leaving the GPS disabled.

Two days ago at 8:54 in the evening, she received a call from "G-Papa" and talked for twenty minutes. I smiled when I recalled that the Voice had tracked April to the hospital that day.

"G-Papa" was no doubt excited about the birth of little Juan-Jorge.

We still had no idea how to find Miguel. But the call log on April's phone revealed that a caller labeled "E.C." had phoned her two days ago at 9:36, forty-two minutes after the "G-Papa" call. I still figured E.C. was short for El Comeniños—one of Miguel's nicknames—and I knew a contact labeled E.C. on Juan's phone had called Juan right after I had killed him.

Geronimo walked up to the still-open door of the van and looked at the phone's call log.

"E.C.," he said, unable to stifle a smile. "Looks like we got the number we're looking for. By the way, El Comeniños means 'the child eater.' Did you know that?"

"No, Geronimo, I didn't. Why do they call him that?"

"What else would you call someone who does what he does with women and children?"

"The child eater—I hope to God that's a metaphor."

Geronimo chuckled. "For kidnapping and trafficking—human trafficking. Even sells the livers and other organs of some of his victims on the black market."

Of course that sent my concern for Ashley into another orbit. And it got me to wondering what all Geronimo was into. It seemed to me that all these guys subscribed to the same basic business model.

As if he sensed what I was thinking, he said, "It's alright to ask me if I've done that—human trafficking."

"Have you?" I asked.

"No."

"Would you tell me the truth if you had?"

His smile spread wide, the crowns on his teeth looking gunmetal blue in the dark. "We both know the answer to that."

34

Wednesday Night, June 5, 2019
10:21 p.m.

Ben

GERONIMO AND I watched the box truck trundle down the dirt road that dead-ended right in front of the farmhouse. Beyond where the road ended I saw the woods stretching high in silhouette against the night sky. Less than a mile beyond the woods was the Arkansas River.

When the truck pulled into the driveway and parked behind the Dodge Caravan, Geronimo and I stepped to the back of the truck and swung open the doors. Men carrying assault rifles and wearing jeans and ballistics vests piled out. Geronimo had told me some of them were ex-members of the Mexican military. I counted ten of them. Besides a case of bottled water, the only thing left in the back of the truck was the dark figure lying in a heap that I knew was Randy Harris.

Geronimo popped on his phone's flashlight and pointed it at Randy. "Wakey wakey eggs and bakey, motherfucker. I'm your new business partner."

Randy lifted his head slowly and I saw new bruises on his cheeks and his lower lip was now fat. When I spoke with Randy this morning, I thought he understood that the men coming for him weren't going to kill him. Maybe he didn't believe that, but I doubted Randy could put up much of a fight even if he wasn't tied up, so the gratuitous beating concerned and angered me. His hands were still tied behind his back and the duct tape I'd wrapped around his head two days ago still covered his eyes, but it looked like the men had added a fresh layer of tape to make sure he stayed completely in the dark.

I looked at April's phone. It was 10:28 p.m. I was due back in court in ten and a half hours. Before that happened, this would be over. At least that was the plan, which was, by design, about to go one of two ways. I was either going to ride in the back of this truck with members of the Trevino Cartel on our way to the foothills of the Kiamichi Mountains to join two *sicarios* already near Jorge's property, or Jorge was coming to us. Either way, Geronimo thought he'd have enough men to neutralize Jorge's protection and kill him. Whoever was taken alive would be interrogated about the location of Ashley and given a chance to live, except Jorge and Miguel, of course. They'd be offered a quick, relatively painless death in exchange for my sister. April, her baby, and Jorge's wife were, by the agreement I'd made with Geronimo, off limits, except as a bluff—bargaining chips. First things first, though—we needed to find Miguel if we could.

I said to Geronimo, "Do you need to talk to Randy before we make the calls or do you want to play it by ear?"

"Let's ask *guero* what he thinks."

Tony used to call me *guero* in college. It meant whitey.

"Hey Rabbit," said Geronimo. "I need you to talk to El Comeniños for me."

Randy lifted his head and opened his mouth to talk but the only thing that came out was a globule of spittle.

I climbed into the bed of the truck and sat Randy up, positioning him where he could use the truck's side as a backrest. Once he was propped up I ripped a bottle of water from a case of them, unscrewed the cap, and tipped water into Randy's mouth. He drank until it was running down his chin and into his lap. Geronimo stood watching from outside the truck, a couple of feet from us.

"If you want to live," said Geronimo, "you need to get your shit together."

Randy cleared his throat. "You want me to talk to Miguel?"

"That's what I said."

"What do you want me to say?"

"Tell him the truth," said Geronimo. "Tell him Trevino has you. Tell him that he and the Chicken Man need to close up shop. All he can do now is continue to hide like the faggot he is. Tell him you work for us now."

"Okay, but I don't understand," said Randy.

"What's there to understand?"

Randy shrugged, "I don't understand what you hope to accomplish. I know you know he'll never give up. You'll have to kill them. All of them. If you don't get them all, they'll come after me. I'll be a dead man."

Geronimo looked at me and seemed to be measuring his words carefully. "It's my understanding from the discussion you had with my friend this morning that Miguel was made aware a long time ago that you knew how to find the rooster house."

"Yeah. He knows that I know it's owned by a woman named Helen that works at the flower shop. I made the mistake of joking with him about that once. He jumped my ass and made me tell him how I knew about it so I told him it was Juan that told me. He told me never to talk about the rooster house again."

"Well, the way I see it, as long as Miguel knows it's you that's talkin', it doesn't much matter what you say. It's what we can beat out of you that will concern him. But make sure to call him a fag for me, okay. That's real important to me."

I sat with my legs hanging off the edge of the truck bed and pressed Juan's thumb to the home button on the phone I took off him the night I killed him. Geronimo seemed to be admiring me as I placed the thumb in a Ziploc bag and handed him Juan's unlocked phone. Then I pulled up the most current number we had for Miguel/E.C. on April's phone and showed it to Geronimo. He punched the numbers into Juan's phone and handed it back to me without sending the call. I then hit the send button on April's phone—*calling E.C.* I put the phone on speaker and sat it on the edge of the truck bed. Geronimo would do the talking. We wanted to feed Miguel's assumption that Geronimo killed Juan and walked away with his phone. We wanted him to know that Randy Harris was in the hands of the

Trevino Cartel, along with April and little Juan-Jorge. The hope
was that Miguel would conclude that with Randy captured it
would only be a matter of time until Trevino's men would be
scurrying around the rooster house like ants on a hill. Truth was,
four of his men were already there, lying in wait.

The first call went unanswered. I tried again. The call was
picked up.

"What's going on, April?"

I recognized the voice. It was Miguel and he sounded
annoyed.

Geronimo said something in Spanish. I didn't know what it
meant, but it sounded hateful.

"Who is this?" said Miguel.

"Who am I?—Here's a hint. I've had Juan's phone, and the
thumb that unlocks it, for quite some time, and now, because
I've got April and her phone, I've got your current number. And
I've got your brand new nephew."

"Fuck you! You ain't got shit!"

Geronimo ended the call and chuckled. "Seems like
Miguel's got about as much use for Juan's baby-mama as I do."

"Okay, we knew that was a possibility. Let's see what
Miguel thinks about this?" I sent the call from Juan's phone.
Again, I put the call on speaker.

There was an answer on the third ring. Silence.

Miguel finally said, "Tell Angel Trevino I will find him."

"Yet, you are the one hiding like your friend we caught
slinging your nasty gack to the Kansas City biker gangs."
Geronimo reached out and prodded Randy in the thigh with his
fist. "Anything you want to say to your old boss?"

"I'm sorry, Miguel, they're going to kill me, they're going
to kill me oh my God I don't want to die—"

Pfft!

Geronimo struck as fast as a copperhead snake—straight-
jabbed Randy in the nose.

The back of Randy's head rebounded off the side of the box
truck with a clang. He slumped over, unable to use the hands
tied behind his back for balance. A stream of blood emerged
from his nostrils and dripped onto the steel floor until gravity

planted his cheek into the expanding puddle. Some kind of guttural scream flowed out of Randy. If Geronimo wanted to make it sound like Randy was being tortured, he'd succeeded as far as I was concerned.

Miguel said, "I'm going to kill you."

Geronimo laughed. "So you do know who I am?"

"I know who you are, Geronimo. And I'm going to kill you."

Miguel ended the call.

Geronimo had a smirk on his face. "Fucker got the last word . . . and you, Rabbit . . . you forgot to call him a faggot. I give you one thing to do and you fuck it up. Let's call him back."

"I think we got it," I said. I looked at Randy, still struggling. He was breathing hard in fits through his mouth, spraying blood as he did. "You get the effect you were after with that jab to his face?"

"Effect? I just couldn't take his blubbering anymore. If he's going to be a Trevino man, he's gotta grow a sack. Hey Rabbit—you understand don't you? It's not personal."

Randy, still face down, coughed into the pool of blood and tried to speak but misfired. On his second try, he eked out a meager, "Yes."

"Good," said Geronimo. "That's very good. I'll get the jumper cables and hook them to your balls then. See what your newfound cojones are made of." He laughed and looked my way but I wasn't laughing.

"I like to kid," he said. "*Guero* is a good find. I won't hurt him."

Randy struggled to sit up, weak as a newborn colt.

"He's served his purpose tonight," I said. "I'm going inside to get him something out of my provisions to eat. I think he's earned it, don't you?"

Geronimo nodded. "Hey Rabbit—you know I had to do that, right?—all part of the plan?"

"Yeah," said Randy.

"See," said Geronimo. "We're good."

I left Geronimo to check on Keri and the baby, looking out into the darkness hoping to hell Beck and this woman I called the Voice were ready to start picking these guys off if things went to shit.

*   *   *

Tony called me twenty minutes later. I took the call sitting next to Keri and Geronimo on the edge of the box truck. The baby was asleep in his detachable car seat behind us and his mother was quiet in the tornado shelter a few feet away. I'd assured her we wouldn't hurt her or her baby—told her everything would be fine like I knew it was a sure thing. Randy Harris was on the screened-in porch with most of the men avoiding the mosquitos but there were a couple of them hovering around the box truck with their AR's at the ready and one of the men was a half mile up the road in a shelterbelt watching for traffic, ready to warn us of any vehicles headed our way on this dead-end road.

Tony was still watching Jorge's cabin in Oklahoma. All he told me at first was that lights had come on. I stayed on the phone with him, as he walked me through everything he was seeing. About thirty minutes into the call he told me that four men left through the front door of the cabin, including Jorge and Buster Reynolds, followed by the sound of engines revving in the large shed on the other side of the cabin. The sounds grew loud enough for me to hear through the phone at one point. I knew Tony was watching them through a night scope I'd given him. As he watched, he described them disappearing past the threshold of the trail down the slope in ATV's.

In the end, he counted seven men, not knowing where the other three had come from. He didn't even know they existed until he saw them heading down the hill. He wasn't sure of the total number of men, but he was sure of the only thing that really mattered to me. He didn't see Ashley. But I had good news for Geronimo before I got off the phone. Jorge was on the last ATV to head down the slope and his St. Bernard was with him.

Two Trevino *sicarios* were imbedded in the trees on the slope adjacent to the gate in front of Jorge's property on the roadway. In ten minutes, one of them called Geronimo with a report of what sort of weapons they saw the men carrying—

assault rifles and machine pistols. This came as no surprise. The *sicarios* watched five of the men climb into a black Suburban, while Buster climbed into the driver's seat of his white Suburban with Jorge in the passenger's seat. With the GPS still in place under Buster's vehicle, we'd have the luxury of tracking them from a comfortable distance, with no fear of tipping our hand.

I ended the call with Tony. He was supposed to call back when one of the *sicarios* took the cabin and kidnapped Jorge's wife. This wasn't supposed to happen until sometime after we captured or killed Jorge, unless something didn't go as planned.

I hopped off the edge of the box truck, shook the knapsack off my back, and put on my Kevlar vest in preparation for whatever was to come. I was dressed head to toe in black, and carried a black ski mask in my pocket. It would take Jorge's men four or five hours to get here, assuming that's where they were headed, but Miguel or one of his scouts might already be in the area as far as we knew. When Jorge and his men got close, I'd climb into the armored Escalade with Geronimo and three of his men. The other seven men would pile into the Dodge Grand Caravan. We'd all leave for the back roads while monitoring the tracker on our phones and looking for an opportunity to stop them on the roads coming in before they had a chance to spread out.

Geronimo and his men had over a hundred *estrellas*, or tire poppers, in each vehicle. Each individual device was slightly larger than a woman's softball and was made up of four spikes shaped like a tetrahedron so that one of the spikes always pointed upward from a stable base. When I asked if this was how he planned to stop Jorge's vehicles Geronimo said probably not, explaining he preferred to throw these *estrellas* out his windows in bunches to flatten the tires of pursuing police cruisers, or for that matter, any pursuing vehicle. He liked to think of *estrellas* as defensive tools useful in retreat. He had seven other tire deflating devices for offense, each one the same—a string attached to a nylon sleeve which fit snugly over three triangular sticks, each stick about three feet long and three inches wide that was designed to be thrown across the length of a narrow road. The triangular sticks in the sleeve always landed with hollow spikes pointing upward. Geronimo was looking to plant a man in a ditch to throw the sticks out in front of the vehicles at the last second before the driver could do anything about it.

My phone vibrated. It was Tony.

I answered the call. "What is it?"

"There's a woman on the upper deck of the cabin now with a gun . . . shotgun maybe."

"What's she doing?"

"I don't know but there's a man in the doorway . . . looks like he's trying to calm her down. I think this lady's gonna kill herself—Oh shit!"

"What?"

"Oh, man."

"What?"

"She did it, man. Oh my God."

I realized Keri and Geronimo were watching me.

Keri said, "What happened?"

"A woman at the cabin just killed herself," I said.

Geronimo added, "Probably Luciana—Jorge's wife."

It was a cold thought, but it popped into my head nonetheless—one bargaining chip off the table. Even worse, the guy standing over the woman's body would certainly call his boss with the bad news. Maybe Jorge doubles back—probably does, assuming it's his wife. Keri had the same thought. She was already looking at the GPS app on her phone.

I said, "What's happening now, Tony?"

"He's checking her . . . okay now he's cussing, loudly, in Spanish."

"I assume he'll be making a call."

"You'd think . . . yep, he's got the phone out."

"Alright, sit tight. My guess is, Jorge and Buster double back."

"Shit," said Tony. "I was hoping the ball was in your court."

"Me too."

With so many moving parts to our plan, of course I'd thought through several scenarios—the obvious ones—and visualized how I needed to react, but the woman's suicide caught me off guard. I ended the call with Tony and opened the GPS app on my phone, watching the little red dot, waiting for it to backtrack.

35

Jorge

JORGE ENDED THE call and looked out the window at trees passing in the darkness. "Luciana killed herself."

Buster pulled his eyes from the road to glance at Jorge who was still looking away. The St. Bernard was sleeping in the back seat.

Buster left the cruise control at sixty-five.

After a long minute of silence, Buster said, "We should turn around."

"No."

This time, five minutes of silence passed.

"I'm taking you back to the cabin."

"She's gone. There's nothing for me back there."

"No?" Buster looked at Jorge, then back at the road. He'd been trying to convince Jorge not to leave for Kansas ever since the call from Miguel forty-five minutes earlier. "You should be the one to tell Miguel what happened. Both of you need to be at the cabin tonight, together, dealing with the loss."

Another minute of silence passed before Buster was back at it. "This whole thing with April and Randy Harris and the rooster house—I'd let it go, podna, I really would. Especially now. Losin' that money in the tunnel hurts, but we can make do and I damn sure don't wanna die over them fuckin' chickens, no offense. At a minimum, I'd say we oughta lay back, and when I say lay back I don't mean within a mile or two like we sometimes've done in the past . . . I mean waaaay back . . . as in Tulsa. I got a place we can land there. No one'll find us. Not for a while anyways."

Jorge finally glanced at the ex-deputy but didn't say a word.

Buster splayed his fingers wide, his palms still on the steering wheel, nodding at the black Suburban on the highway in front of him. "Let those boys in front of us handle this unsupervised. And if I was you, I'd tell Miguel to stay clear of that place. My guess is there's ever' chance some of them are of a mind to kill us themselves and run off with the money before the nights up, providin' Trevino's men don't show up and kill them all first."

Jorge was used to this—Buster the survivor lobbying to keep himself well clear of a fight. But he knew Buster was right about the threat of defection from within and a Trevino ambush at the rooster house. Jorge knew the Rabbit didn't stand a chance of keeping mum for long with the silver or lead proposition Geronimo had no doubt laid on the table. Jorge admitted to himself that his enemy would find the rooster house but clung to hope it wouldn't be tonight.

"I gotta tell ya'," said Buster, "this feels like a trap if I ever saw one. There's no shame in being scarce at a time like this."

"You're a goddamn coward. Always were."

"I'd kill for you, my friend, but I won't die for you. If that makes me a coward, then so be it. I mean, Jesus, I hope I'm wrong, but I just as soon be wrong in Tulsa than anywhere near that fuckin' chicken ranch . . ."

Jorge slipped into something of a trance—felt like he was seeing the world through Luciana's eyes. Dark. Meaningless. Empty. But there was background static in this earthly version of hell—the slow-talking Texan was still making his case.

"Buster!"

"What?"

"Shut up and drive."

"Yeah okay, but tell me this ain't about them birds. I don't wanna die over poultry. I got a nice lady waitin' for me in Tulsa if I ever get there again. She's got friends—"

"To hell with the birds."

"What?"

"This ain't about them birds."

"Well that's good. So . . . is it . . . what? The money?"

"If it looks like we can grab it, we will."

Buster cleared his throat. "Wouldn't be much of a trap if the money didn't look safe to grab. You send those men in there tonight, it's liable to end up lookin' like a turkey shoot." He cracked a window, lit a cigarette, and spoke loud over the wind. "So, I gotta say, if it's not about your roosters or the money, then maybe you got a death wish. Whatever you're thinkin', I'm tellin' ya', seems to me like you're in the midst of makin' one helluva piss-poor decision."

Jorge watched Buster take a drag. "How would you prefer to die?"

"Splittin' gash, then a heart attack from the exertion I guess—clogged artery from all the red meat."

Jorge laughed. When he realized he'd laughed, thoughts of Luciana rushed in and crushed the mirth that had broached the darkness. What he took for a moment of clarity washed over him, ending the amusement for good. *She'd wasted herself—the selfish bitch!* Luciana found her way out, and now Jorge saw his—a vision that brought sweet relief like a cramped muscle relaxing. "I'm calling Geronimo to make a trade. Me, for April and her baby."

Buster looked at him. Incredulous. "What?"

"You heard me."

"Okay—I'll play along. When'd you decide that?"

"Just now. You're right about the death wish. Might as well make it count for something. I don't want to be here anymore."

Buster frowned and took another drag, deep and long, like he was smoking up as much life as he could while he had the chance. "I'll be damned if that don't go against ever'thing I ever heard come out of your mouth. You'll die a slow, miserable death. You always said that was your nightmare—said you'd rather die in the fight so that you didn't pay the dyin' part so much mind."

Jorge pulled out his phone and called April's number. "That last part sounds like something I might've said when I was high."

The call was answered on the second ring. "Thought you'd never call. In case you were wondering, this is Geronimo Baylon-Fontanna speaking."

"Don't give a fuck who you are. I need to speak with April."

"You're Jorge?"

"Yep."

"Why would I do that, Jorge? What's in it for me?"

"Me."

"You?"

"Yeah. You give us April and her baby in exchange for me. How's that sound?"

"Sounds too good to be true."

"That's the offer."

"If that's a real offer, it's certainly one I would've taken seriously fifteen minutes ago."

The turn of phrase settled heavy in Jorge's chest. He'd thought he found a way to redeem himself—not totally . . . not even close, but at least he could reach for the light with his final act and have someone left besides Miguel to inherit what remained of his crumbling empire—account balances in offshore accounts, cash buried in holes throughout the Midwest. Someone else to revel in the spoils and keep the legend of his life alive. But the lies he held fell away leaving only truth. Luciana's darkness swam in his veins again. "Fifteen minutes ago?"

"Yeah, fifteen minutes ago. Before I put bullets in their heads. It was a sweet thought you had—giving your life for theirs—but you and I both know that's all it was . . . a thought that counts for nothing."

Geronimo ended the call, but Jorge still held the phone to his ear, frozen.

A thought that counts for nothing—those words played in Jorge's head the way last words sometimes do. Damned if he hadn't reached for God one last time and grasped air. He looked up like a fool—as if Luciana and Diego were out there somewhere in the ether. Now he knew, again, that they weren't there. They were nowhere.

A thought that counts for nothing. To Jorge, those words embodied a broader concept he'd toyed with in his younger days, mostly when he was smoking pot—the idea that nothing he thought, said, or did mattered. Ever. He always found this thought experiment of his an exhausting one, one that inevitably led to memories of his childhood in the church. The words from priests and other believers danced through his head in whispery snippets. Often, the voice he heard was Diego's, insisting there'd be a reckoning like the one outlined in Revelations. He always thought Diego was wrong about this. When he heard his brother's bones crunching in the jaws of those hogs, their faces wet with bloody entrails, he thought he knew for certain Diego had wasted his life on a fairy tale—*where is your God now?*

The idea that when he died he would cease to exist on any level was no longer exhausting. It was profoundly appealing. It meant escaping the pain—all the pain he felt, all the pain he caused—forever.

Buster poked his cigarette butt through the inch of space where the window was cracked open before closing it.

Jorge said, "Why wouldn't he make that trade?"

"Maybe he already killed them."

"That's what he said."

"You doubt him on that?"

"No, I guess not. He seemed so damned uninterested."

Jorge called Miguel to give him the news about his mother. He dialed the number before organizing his thoughts. When Miguel picked up the phone, Jorge said his son's name, then tried to speak Luciana's name. His voice cracked, and he bit his lip.

Nothing matters.

Diego was in his head again, whispering, *Then why are you crying my brother?*

* * *

When they reached the Kansas border at 4:21 a.m., Jorge called Miguel again. He'd decided to go onto the Bertrand property with Miguel and the men in the black Suburban. The thought of fighting again stoked the adrenaline he felt rushing through him. Killing was a joy he'd kept at arm's length for so many years now, watching his roosters, occasionally sucking the blood out of the beak of a mortally wounded champion before sending it back into the pit. Sure, there was money on the line, but Jorge knew now his gambling on the roosters was his way of satisfying the bloodlust burning within him. There was nothing like being in the fight. There was nothing like the real thing. He thought about the last time he'd personally killed a man. Behind that tin-roofed bar in Laredo in 1988. Or was it '89?

Miguel answered the call.

Jorge said, "We just crossed the state line. Where do you want to meet up exactly?"

"I'm at the cabin with JV. We can meet up here."

JV was Javier—the man assigned to keep watch of the judge's sister at the moment. She was being held in a hunting cabin in the woods along the Arkansas River, two miles upstream from the chicken ranch.

"How's the cat?" said Jorge.

"Sleeping."

Buster glanced at Jorge. They all knew to talk in code about the judge's sister on the phone—standard practice, like tossing phones every few days. The cabin was a real pain in the ass to get to by vehicle because the only path to the place led through a low-lying meadow that stayed wet with standing water much of the year and only dried completely in a drought.

"You and JV meet us at the church. The cowboy tells me his four-wheel drive has been acting up. You two hop in with me. The cowboy can watch the cat."

"Stay back, Papa, I got it."

"I can still handle myself."

"I don't doubt that, but you should stay back with the cowboy."

"Meet us at the church in thirty-five minutes."

"You want us to leave the cat alone?"

"Make sure it's secure, then both of you come."

"JV and I will go to the church early. Scout it—make sure we're alone. Which way you comin' in?"

"We'll be comin' in from the north on the asphalt."

"Okay, have the rest of the men go on to the spot underneath the bridge we talked about earlier. I have a man posted there now to make sure it's safe. I don't want all of us sittin' in one place out in the open lookin' like a caravan."

When the call ended, Jorge stared straight ahead and said, "Take the dog with you to the cabin."

Buster took in a deep breath and closed his eyes slowly for a beat, then opened them as he exhaled and tended to his driving. "What about court in the mornin'?"

"What about it?" Jorge undid his seat belt, reached behind his seat, and pulled a ballistics vest out from under an AK-47 lying on the floor.

"McMaster and Thompson like to have me there. Doesn't look right if I'm not at least there lookin' like a dedicated part of the defense team."

"Don't it look like I got bigger problems at the moment?"

"Nonetheless, your lesser problems ain't goin' anywhere. What're your plans for the judge's sister?"

"If things go bad for us, Buster, you may be disposing of a body by morning light. It's best you have Javier's Tahoe for that anyway. You don't want her body in here—in a vehicle registered to you. When the sun comes up, you might be all that's left of this cartel."

* * *

The church came into view as Buster's white Suburban rolled south down the asphalt of Oxford Road between fields of wheat on either side. The black Suburban ahead of him sped past the church—the chicken ranch was further south and so was the meeting spot below the bridge on Deer Creek Road. Buster tapped the brake, disabling the cruise control, and the Suburban began losing momentum down the gradual slope. He used a switch and buzzed the window down. Lit a cigarette—took a drag.

Jorge had his cell to his ear. "We're here."

"Still clear," came the reply from Miguel.

Jorge ended the call and set the phone in a cup holder.

Slate Valley Baptist Church was painted pristine white with a humble steeple, and sat on the southwest corner at the intersection of Oxford Road and Eightieth Street, which was a gravel road. There was about twenty-five feet between the glass front doors of the church and the asphalt and nothing but a small slab of concrete and gravel in between. No curbs or ditches. The area directly in front of the church looked more like an extension of the gravel road than it did church ground, the only visible demarcation between them being two large cottonwoods and a few stubborn weeds poking through the hardpan surrounding the stop sign. A stand of trees as high as the church's steeple, maybe twenty yards in the air, flanked the back end of the church and fields of ripening yellow wheat stretched out in the distance in all directions.

Jorge said, "I gotta piss like a race horse."

"At your age, podna, I rather doubt that."

"The less time you spend thinking about my dick the better."

"Hey, I'm impressed you held it this long. I'd-a-pissed myself if we hadn't stopped in Braman."

Buster turned right onto the gravel road and the Suburban's headlights swept over the Chevy Tahoe which sat parked facing the stop sign ten yards in front of it. Javier stepped out carrying a machine pistol, his bald head canted well over his left shoulder. Miguel stepped out of the passenger seat with a similar pistol and both were wearing ballistics vests.

Buster said, "I been meanin' to ask you, what's the deal with Javy's head, all slung over to one side like that?"

"His old man hit him upside the head with an ax handle when he was fifteen."

Buster passed him standing in the road, made a U-turn, and put the Suburban in park behind the Tahoe next to the two large cottonwoods. "Kinda wished I hadn't asked you that. Anyone hits their own child deserves the death penalty in my book." He killed the lights, but left the vehicle running.

Jorge put his hand on the door handle, looking fatter and older than ever in his ballistics vest. "Javy sees it like you do. Unlike you, though, he's not all talk. Walked out of the Mexican hospital the same day they got him to his feet. Poor sonofabitch walked all the way home looking like his head was glued to his shoulder—same way he is now more or less. When he got home he found his dad passed out drunk on the kitchen floor. Grabbed a long kitchen knife out of a drawer and sank it right into his father's Adam's apple, running it length-wise up through the throat and into the skull."

Jorge's phone jingled and he accepted the call and put it to his ear.

Buster sat transfixed, apparently thinking about Javier's story. "Je-sus." He grabbed his revolver and had barely stepped out of the vehicle before being met by Javier, who handed him a little silver key and explained in broken English that it went to the cuffs holding the judge's sister to the pole in the cabin.

Buster got the St. Bernard out of the back and it followed him while Javier climbed into the driver's seat of the Suburban and shut the door. When Buster reached the back of the Tahoe he heard a vehicle door shut behind him and looked back. Miguel had climbed into the back seat of the Suburban and Jorge, a step or two from the front passenger door, was facing the trunk of one of the cottonwoods, head down, working his belt, looking desperate to relieve himself.

Buster yelled, "Ever'thing comin' out okay?"

Jorge looked over his shoulder. "I told you to stop thinking about my dick. And get some new jokes."

"Oldest joke in the world's right in your hand."

"Get out of here before I decide to take you with me."

"Heard that," Buster said to himself as he opened the rear door of the Tahoe for the dog. It jumped heavily onto the back floorboard, climbed onto the seat, and sat looking at Buster.

"Looks like it's you and me now, buddy. How'd you like to live on Tulsa time?"

Buster turned the Tahoe left and headed north up the asphalt.

Jorge didn't know if it was the sound of the engine in the distance or his own silent reflection in the cool breeze of night, but he seemed to know Buster was done. Buster wasn't going to the cabin to keep watch of the judge's sister at all. Jorge tried to shake this feeling but couldn't. He'd never questioned the ex-deputy's loyalty. His courage, yes. Never his loyalty. But things had never been this bad.

Jorge fastened his belt and turned to get into the Suburban when an SUV heading south veered off Oxford Road in a half-turn. Its headlights kicked on and washed over the Suburban, over Javier, Miguel, and Jorge.

Javier snatched up the machine pistol and flung open the door. *Bailing out*—too late.

The driver punched the accelerator. Jammed the door on Javier—crushed it around his shattering fibula. His torso shot through the window, momentum folding him in half, slamming his face into the SUV's hood.

Javier lay motionless, his chest resting on the machine pistol between him and the hood. He coughed out teeth in a bloody spray, which seemed to jolt him to consciousness.

Behind him, Jorge was pinned too—between the Suburban and the cottonwood—with a view of Javier's ass through the passenger window. He'd felt his ribs snap when the Suburban jumped into him.

Miguel groped in the back seat for his MAC-10 in the dark.

Jorge pushed to free himself but pain tore through his core and he was weak and breathless and blood already coated his teeth and was so thick at the back of his throat that he felt like he was drowning.

Javier lifted himself from the hood, looking like a bloody-faced predator at a carcass except for the confusion in his eyes which vanished when he saw the machine pistol. He fired a stream of bullets into the windshield, at the man behind it. One and a half seconds of devastation. He collapsed, his face smacking the hood as shell casings were still clinking off it.

Miguel appeared beside Jorge, hunkered down behind the Suburban's right front tire. They made eye contact, then Miguel moved his MAC-10 around the headlight and made for the SUV in a crouch. When he looked inside, he lowered the pistol and stood straight.

A dark SUV crept across the asphalt road with its headlights off. When its wheels crunched in the gravel Miguel turned to see it rolling toward him. Jorge seemed to understand before Miguel that the SUV inching toward them in the darkness wasn't their black Suburban.

"Run, Miguel!"

Miguel stood his ground as the Escalade slowed and stopped ten yards in front of him.

The driver dropped the gearshift into park.

Miguel leveled the machine pistol and spewed bullets into the Escalade's windshield.

One and a half seconds later there were thirty-two more spent casings at his feet. There was damage to the windshield, but something was wrong.

"It's an armored vehicle," screamed Jorge. "Get another mag in. Save your ammo and keep them inside until our men come back for us."

Gunfire erupted in the distance from the south.

36

Ben

THEY'D DROPPED ME off a hundred yards east of the intersection on Eightieth Street. I'd crossed south of the church, using the wheat and the trees behind the church as cover to get to the back of the Suburban, arriving in time to see Miguel firing at the windshield of Geronimo's Escalade.

Now I heard the automatic gunfire to the south. Jorge's crew in the black Suburban would have their hands full with Trevino's men—at least that was my hope. Miguel and Jorge could no longer count on their help.

Miguel took a couple of slow steps backward toward Jorge. His eyes were glued to the Escalade as he dropped the empty magazine out of his MAC-10 and grabbed another in a pouch on his ballistics vest.

I moved toward Miguel from behind with the assault rifle I was carrying before breaking past the tree where Jorge was pinned, a few feet from Miguel, aiming the rifle at the back of Miguel's head.

Jorge screamed "Miguel!" and tried to swat at my rifle but I was a step beyond his reach.

Miguel's head snapped my way, a fresh magazine to the machine pistol in his left hand. He hadn't heard me at all, and looked startled to be staring down the barrel of the rifle.

"Tell me where my sister is and I'll make this quick."

"What?" He looked down the rifle—at my face this time. When we locked eyes, I had his full attention as his MAC-10 remained toothless and pointed in the general direction of the Escalade.

The doors to the Escalade clicked open but neither of us bothered to look. As the men got closer Miguel's eyes wandered from me to the men walking up on us.

"What? I don't . . . how?" Miguel stopped himself and looked back at me with confusion in his eyes. "You're the judge?"

Geronimo put the muzzle of his pistol on Miguel's temple and said, "And I'm the executioner. Answer his question, *pendejo*. Where's his sister?"

Miguel said, "I'll take you to her, but you have to let us go. Otherwise, your sister dies."

I felt my eyes narrow. "Geronimo and I already have an agreement on what our deal with you two will be and I expect he'll hold me to it. You and your father give us my sister, and we set April and her baby free. What you get in return is a quick, relatively humane death. Mr. Fontana—does that pretty well sum up our agreement?"

"Yeah," said Geronimo.

"Whaddaya think of his counter offer?" I said.

"Don't like it."

"Nor do I."

"Then you'll go to prison for Mallory's murder," said Jorge from behind us. "Either one of us dies, my wife's been instructed to send an anonymous letter to the cops telling them you killed Mallory and where to find the body, the gun, the casings—"

"Bullshit," said Geronimo. "We watched your wife blow her head off in Oklahoma four and a half hours ago."

Miguel's lip twitched.

"Easy does it, Miguel," I said.

His eyes found mine. "It's like you said last time we talked. There are worse things than dyin'."

I remembered that conversation. Anyone in the drug trade knew what came next. "Like being tortured for so long you don't even know your own name?"

"Something like that." Miguel was edging the magazine closer to the pistol, daring us to kill him and save him from hours of abuse.

I nodded toward Jorge. "What about your father? You gonna take the easy way out and leave him behind?"

I jumped at the explosion before I knew what it was—a shot fired by Geronimo. Somehow I'd managed to not let a round of my own fly at the jolt. When Miguel hit the ground Geronimo fired into his head until the pistol's slide locked back.

Geronimo looked up at Jorge and walked toward him. The old man reflexively turned away, his chest rising and falling like a piston as Geronimo got close and whispered into Jorge's ear. "Where's that cop taking my St. Bernard?" Geronimo gripped Jorge's bloody chin and turned his face so that they were nose to nose. "You killed my father with a shotgun behind that bar in Laredo in '89. This night has been a long time comin'."

Jorge's eyes grew wide.

Geronimo let go of Jorge's chin and withdrew. "But we'll have plenty of time to talk about that later." Shots were still popping to the south. "We need to get the hell outta here."

Jorge looked at me and said, "I'll take you to your sister right now. You and me, alone, with April and the baby." He coughed and more blood oozed over his lip.

Geronimo said, "You ain't gettin' out of this."

Jorge raked the back of his hand over his chin and wiped the blood off on his ballistics vest. "You sure about that? I'm seeing three of you at the moment and this isn't mom's salsa I'm spittin' up. Besides, the judge here can shoot me dead after he has his sister. I trust he won't kill April and the baby." His eyes steered blearily to Geronimo. "I don't trust you. The judge can leave my body behind for you so that you know I'm dead."

Geronimo's eyes found mine and we nodded in unison.

I said, "Okay, but you tell me right now where to find Detective Mallory's body, my Glock, and the shell casings."

"Mallory's in a freezer in the basement of a house in Wichita. Eight twenty-one South Greenway. No one lives there. Place is owned by a straw man named James McAdoo. Your Glock and the shell casings are in the glove box of the Suburban right here. I thought we might need them to finish setting you up by night's end . . .you know, in case we had to kill your sister."

To get to the glove box I went through the back hatch which was already open and climbed over two sets of seats. Jorge watched through the glass as I pulled out a paper bag, opened it, and saw the Glock. I popped on the light to my cell phone and checked the serial number. It was my gun. I counted nine shell casings—one for each round Miguel had fired into Detective Mallory. That's as good as I was going to do tonight. Needless to say, I was feeling the need to get the hell out of here more than ever.

When I got back to the front of the Suburban Geronimo said, "We good?"

I reached underneath the Suburban next to Jorge's feet, grabbed the tracker with both hands and jerked it free from the undercarriage. I stood, showing Jorge the little black box. "We're good." Jorge's eyes dropped. Buster Reynolds had gotten sloppy and gotten them all killed. Unforgiveable—but neither condemnation nor forgiveness belonged to Jorge anymore.

Geronimo focused on Jorge. "One other thing. I want the dog tonight. Where's that old cop headed?"

"My guess," said Jorge. "Tulsa. Put one in his head for me would ya?" Old habits die hard.

One of Geronimo's men had his phone out. While looking at a text, he said, "Rafael and the judge's man are still following that guy, Buster. As of five minutes ago, he was headed west on one-sixty."

Rafael was the other *sicario* who had trailed Buster and Jorge from Oklahoma. My man was Tony Cornejo, and I knew the two of them were trailing Buster in separate vehicles. Tony, at least, was following in hopes that it might lead him to Ashley. Without the benefit of the tracker, tailing Buster would be a dicey operation because they'd have to keep him in sight without getting so close as to alert him, a tricky thing to do to an experienced detective who was spooked and probably on the lookout for a tail. But then again, maybe Buster wasn't as sharp as he used to be.

Geronimo looked to the south and said, "You hear that?"

The gunfire had ceased.

One of his men said, "I don't hear nothin'."

"Exactly," said Geronimo. "One of you call and find out what the hell is going on while the rest of us load up and get outta here."

37

5:25 a.m.

Ben

THE DODGE GRAND Caravan crawled through the muck. At some point during the night the base for the car seat had been jettisoned to make room for Trevino's men so April was now holding her baby in a third-row seat with duct tape wrapped around her head covering her eyes. The baby was screaming bloody murder. I was sitting in a blood-smeared second-row seat to Jorge's right, one hand clenched around the soft inside of the drug kingpin's upper arm. He was on his knees on the floorboard between the two front seats looking out the web of fractured glass so that he could provide directions, hands still tied behind his back.

Keri stomped on the gas pedal and the engine revved and the tires were slipping but we still moved forward, riding momentum through this wet meadow. We'd gone about as far as this van full of bullet holes could take us, but I'd thought that for the last fifty yards.

I was told that two of Trevino's men had been left for dead in the roadway and two had been shot before climbing back into this van. But according to the report we got from Trevino's men, Jorge's men got it worse, all five of them killed or bleeding out in the black Suburban or the ditch in which it had come to rest with four flattened tires and a driver dead at the wheel with a gunshot wound to his head.

Jorge spoke loud over the engine, wincing in pain as he did. "You know Geronimo is out there somewhere, following us. You know that don't you? He's not going to leave it to you to kill me. And he's going to kill April and her baby too. You're not still carrying that tracker are you?"

I gave Jorge's arm a squeeze. He looked at me and I shook my head and nodded at April behind me. Letting April in on snippets of conversation that shed light on my relationship with the Trevino Cartel could hurt me later, provided Jorge wasn't right about Geronimo's intentions to kill her.

But he was right about Geronimo wanting to be sure Jorge was dead when I was through with him. Fifteen minutes earlier at the abandoned farmstead, after all but one of his men were rolling away from us in the box truck, Geronimo made sure I understood he was leaving nothing to chance when it came to Jorge's execution. I didn't argue because it would've been a waste of time. Besides, after I got Ashley back, as far as I was concerned, my business with Jorge was over. If Geronimo wanted to kill Jorge personally, I couldn't stop it. I didn't want to. Hell, I was helping him kill Jorge by carrying the tracker and giving him the directions—as I understood them—to the cabin. I told myself it was a necessary evil. I didn't believe Jorge when he told me Ashley had been left in the cabin unguarded, tethered to a pole by a pair of handcuffs. Geronimo didn't buy this either when I passed the information on to him.

So, damn right I'd left the tracker on. It was still in my knapsack working like a champ. I was concerned Jorge had one more surprise for me, and since I didn't know when it might come or how many men might be coming at us, I liked the idea of having more than just Beck and the Voice hiding in the woods as snipers for backup.

At this point I thought there was good reason to believe Jorge was wrong about Geronimo double-crossing me and killing April and the baby. The way I saw this unfolding, it was starting to look like Geronimo might be one of those people that kept their word even when it put him at risk he could otherwise avoid. If he'd wanted, he could've killed us all already and left with his men before every cop within twenty miles descended upon the area surrounding us.

"We told you," I said to Jorge. "April and the baby will be fine." I looked him over. "Speaking of fine, I noticed you're not coughing up blood anymore."

He winked at me and said, "I'm makin' a comeback."

Keri slammed the gas pedal all the way to the floor this time and the engine whined as the tires spun in place. When she finally took her foot off the gas and shut down the engine the cab fell silent and we could hear the far-off sound of sirens wailing from the west through our blown-out windows.

I slid my door open and tugged on Jorge's arm. "A comeback, huh? That's what I'm afraid of. Come on. Time to hoof it."

The watery muck was higher than ankle-deep and poured over the tops of my hiking boots. When both Jorge's feet were in the soup, I nodded at the woods eighty yards away. "How much further to the cabin?"

"Maybe half a mile."

I called Tony. Keri had called him twenty minutes earlier and told him to peel off Buster's tail and come back for us. We knew the moment we saw the Dodge Caravan back at the abandoned farmhouse that there was no way with all the cops that would be swarming the area we could put this bullet-riddled bloodmobile back on a regular road. Now that it was stuck it wasn't an option anyway. Keri had also told him we had the tracker from the Suburban with us. If he could find his way to the red dot on the GPS app, he'd find us.

When Tony answered, I said, "Where you at?"

"I was about to call you. Just hit the city limits of Oxford, so . . . looking at the GPS, I'm about nine miles northwest of you. And I see you're not on a road anymore. How's it going?"

Keri came up next to me with the baby in her arms, holding a bottle to his mouth. His beautiful shiny brown eyes glistened in the dark as he worked on the nipple.

"The van's stuck and we're on foot. We're a half mile away from her." Jorge and I exchanged a look. "Maybe."

I pulled the ski mask out of my back pocket and showed it to Keri while listening to Tony's idea for a rendezvous point, which involved him turning south on an asphalt road rife with dead bodies and cops. I slipped the ski mask over my head and watched Keri hand the baby to April who was still sitting in the van with duct tape covering her eyes.

"Hold up," I said to Tony, stepping away from the van so April couldn't hear me. "I don't think that'll work. Now listen. The cops gotta be all over the place on this side of the river so I wouldn't turn south on Oxford Road at all. Stay east on one-sixty and cross the bridge. Find a good spot on the other side of the river and call us. I'm thinking after we get Ashley, we'll get across the river and you can guide us in or come to us."

"The river's way up with all the rain? How you gonna get across? What about the baby?"

"Beck's bug-out route involves crossing the river, so he has two rafts with life jackets on the bank somewhere. It's how he and the Voice got here in the first place. Their vehicle is on the other side of the river where I want you to be."

I ended the call. Keri pulled a ski mask over her head before removing the duct tape from April's eyes so she could walk and carry her baby.

Jorge hacked up blood and dropped to his knees.

When the coughing subsided, he looked up at me. "If I die before we get there, find the only spot you can see up there in the woods that looks anything like a path and follow it. You'll find the cabin."

I nodded.

"Promise me something," he said.

"I won't let anything happen to your grandson . . . or April."

"I know you'll do your best with that. It's something else. When the time comes, put me down quick. Don't leave me to Geronimo."

"If you live that long, I'll shoot you dead and leave you for the coyotes. Now stand up and enjoy the walk."

38

Caroline

AT FIVE-THIRTY in the morning, Caroline Gordon flicked on her flashlight and took a good long look at the Hispanic man pinned between his door and the body of an SUV by a battering ram in the form of a Toyota Sequoia. The man was face down on the hood of the Sequoia, head pitched to the left. Maybe his neck was broken. Or maybe this was the sonofabitch with the head that hung over his left shoulder who had shot her four and a half days ago. Looked like the same bald head, the same build, and by the looks of that machine pistol resting on the hood of the shot-up Sequoia with a dead man behind the wheel, the same violent lifestyle as the man who'd tried to take her out.

She heard someone walk up behind her and looked to see the old sheriff standing there with an unlit cigar in his mouth. There were cops and police cruisers from four different law enforcement agencies milling about and blocking roadways all around them.

She nodded at the sheriff and said, "Has someone photographed this guy yet?"

"Think so. Why?"

"I'm pretty sure this is the man who shot me."

"Really?" The sheriff adjusted the cigar in his mouth with his tongue. "So we got Miguel Mendez-Whatever's body right over there and now maybe we got your shooter too. Take a look at his face if you want."

Caroline pulled a pair of latex gloves out of her windbreaker, put them on, and lifted the man's head from the hood of the car and turned his face toward her as the sheriff illuminated it with his flashlight.

"That's him," she said, careful to place the man's head back on the hood as she had found it. "He been IDed yet?"

"No. Unfortunately he wasn't carrying his DL on him like a good boy."

She ran her light over the Suburban, illuminating the Texas tag. "I know this Suburban—belongs to Vaughn Rummell's investigator."

"Yep. Good call. We determined that a few minutes ago."

Caroline walked to the front passenger door, noting its close proximity to the tree and the dent in it before pointing the light into the window, looking down at the open glove box. She noticed an odor and pointed the flashlight at the trunk of the tree near the ground. "What the hell?—smells like piss right here."

She flicked off her flashlight, stepped away from the vehicle and nodded to the south. "What's up the road?"

"A goddamn mess of dead Mexicans—seven of 'em. All laying around and inside a shot-up SUV with four flat tires."

"No Harold Reynolds?"

"Nope."

"Survivors?"

"Not a one."

Caroline scratched at the area around the wound on her leg. It'd started to itch this morning. She was told by the doctor this might happen. "We need to call Gwen Sweeney."

"Already did."

"Good. What'd she say?"

"Her exact words were, 'Ah, shit.' After that, she didn't say a whole lot worth repeating."

Caroline's lip wrinkled—almost a lopsided smile but she was too tired to smile and her leg was beginning to throb. "Any hope of finding who walked away from this fight?"

The sheriff shrugged. "We're all over the roads with everything we got in the area. But I'm starting to think whoever did this had a little head start before the 911 came in. Still, you'd think if there's a vehicle outside our perimeter with some serious bullet holes in it, someone would take notice."

Caroline walked by Miguel's body toward Oxford Road with the sheriff in tow. When she got to the middle of the asphalt road, she looked out across the wheat to the east toward the river. "Maybe they're still here?"

The sheriff pulled the cigar out of his mouth and mimicked Caroline's gaze across the fields. "Why would they stay?"

Caroline looked at the sheriff. "Why were they here in the first place?"

The sheriff lit his cigar. "We're trying to get some dogs down from Wichita right now to help us comb the fields best we can. Any man out there now would see us way before we saw him. I'm not sending my men into those fields or the woods down by the river until daylight. Hell, may not send them in then." He looked at the watch on his wrist. "So, when daylight comes in another forty minutes I'll think about it."

"If there's a bad guy still out there, Sheriff, he'll have had enough time to tunnel outta here by the time you get your shit together."

"Just as well."

Caroline shot him a look.

"What?—not what you wanted to hear? What if we did corner a group of 'em?"

"I get it. It's too dangerous right now with all the automatic weapons in play."

"Not sure what we get out of it."

Caroline shrugged. "Is that why you do this? To get something out of it? It's your job."

He regarded her with a sidelong look. "You wanna walk out there with your nine-millimeter and your shot-up leg you go right ahead. I'm takin' the position we ain't winnin' the war on drugs tonight."

Caroline shook her head, closing her eyes as she did.

The sheriff noticed. "This ain't something I'd say to the Kiwanis Club, but I don't want my deputies runnin' into whatever hell pigs may be roamin' around out there at the moment. My main goal right now, after seeing this shit-show again, now for the third time in a year and a half, is to get my deputies home safe to their families each night. Already got a detective missing and you've been shot. And what for? So if the drug dealers are out there somewhere squaring off in the dark then I say let 'em have at it. Maybe we oughta stay out of it as much as we can."

Caroline shook her head. "Let 'em all kill each other—Is that it?"

"I was told you haven't been cleared yet for anything but court. Maybe you should go home and get some rest."

Caroline turned and walked away from the sheriff. Behind her, she heard him yell out, "Maybe I'm too old for this shit. You think you can do better, run for sheriff."

Caroline kept walking and never turned around. "I'm not sure I like this place enough to do that."

She walked past the two sheriff's cruisers blocking traffic from the north, their red and blue flashers blinking in the night. When she got to her Crown Vic she pulled out her phone and speed dialed Judge Joel even though she knew he wasn't the duty judge for the night. The judge who was on duty actually lived close by and since Caroline wasn't cleared for duty herself, the only flimsy excuse she had for calling Judge Joel was to tell him how Harold Reynold's Suburban was found at this scene.

When she heard the voicemail message she ended the call and put the phone in her pocket. It bothered her that he wouldn't answer.

39

Ben

WHEN WE GOT to the tree line my regular iPhone vibrated in the pocket of my cargo pants. I looked at the caller ID.—Caroline Gordon.

I looked behind me. April was struggling to take a step with the baby cradled in her arms and Keri was holding her upper arm to steady her. To the southwest beyond the meadow we'd just left was the church. As the crow flies, it was maybe three and a half miles away.

I showed Keri the screen of my phone so only she could see. She shook her head which I took to mean: *Don't take the call*.

I didn't. But my burner phone was going off now too. It was Beck.

I took that call. "What's going on?"

"The Voice found the cabin, but Geronimo beat her to it and he just left with Ashley. He's headed your direction down the trail with her, alone. The guy he was with took off the other way toward the river. We're guessing he's scouting for a way out of here. I suggest we do the same."

"How close are you to us?"

"Less than fifty yards. Keep walking and I'll come to you."

I ended the call, made eye contact with Keri, and said to the group, "Got a friendly coming here to get you all out of here safely. Everyone except me and Jorge, so no freaking out. What's about to happen is a good thing, okay. I promise."

April nodded her head and so did Jorge.

The trail here was rutted and wide enough for a vehicle. After trudging twenty yards into the woods with the aid of my phone's flashlight, Jorge went down on his knees again, I thought for good this time. More blood than before shot out between his lips and ran down his chin. He was panting like a dog in the hot summer sun when Beck stepped out of the darkness with a ski mask and his rifle.

April jumped back and started to fall with the baby in her arms, but Keri caught her.

I held up my hands. "It's a good thing, remember?"

April looked like she might be holding her breath and her eyes were wide and unblinking. Keri put a hand on her shoulder. "It's alright, sweetie. We're gonna get you out of here so we can take you home."

Beck said, "Follow me," leaving the trail and receding into the woods with Keri, April, and her baby following.

Jorge nodded what I assumed was his approval of my decision to disconnect April and the baby from the GPS tracker. "You're right not to trust Geronimo."

Now that April was gone, I pulled off the ski mask. The morning air felt cool on my sweaty head. "Just hedging my bet." I gripped him by his arm and helped him to his feet.

The trail narrowed and we passed Geronimo's Escalade.

Jorge said, "You gave him the directions didn't you?"

I didn't answer.

Five minutes later he said, "If he can't kill them tonight, he'll kill them later. And there'll be no one around to stop him."

"Is that supposed to make me feel bad?"

"I suppose that's what I was shootin' for. I admire what you've done to save your sister. You're a warrior. But don't think what you've done is righteous . . . or good."

"Let me ask you, what do you mean by good?"

We kept walking. Dawn broke and the woods turned grey and I no longer needed my light to see the ground right in front of me.

Jorge said, "Like you, I was raised Catholic. So I suppose when I say good, I mean good in the Biblical sense."

"I knew what you meant. Just wanted you to say it."

Suddenly, I heard the voice of Geronimo yell out. "It's me. Don't shoot, I have your sister with me."

"Where you at?"

Geronimo said, "Stay on the path. I'll do the same."

"Now's the time," whispered Jorge. "Kill me."

I glanced at Jorge, walking him further down the trail. "Shut up."

She appeared before me, first as a silhouette next to a larger one and as we converged I saw Ashley's face. I let go of my hold on Jorge's arm and knocked brush and limbs aside as we made our way toward each other and embraced. She cried so hard she shook. I felt someone brush past us and I assumed it was Geronimo making his way to Jorge, but my eyes were closed.

When Ashley pulled back from me, her face was wet with tears and her lips were dry. She'd lost weight but her hair looked fairly clean and so did her clothes.

"You okay, sis'?"

"I'm gonna be."

I nodded, "They really didn't hurt you?"

"Nothing physical. They fed me, gave me water, like a pet they never took for a walk."

"Well, we're going to do some walking now. Maybe even some running, okay?"

Ashley smiled a little before her eyes got big at something she saw behind me. I turned around.

Geronimo had a Bowie knife in his hand standing above Jorge who was on his back yelling, "No, no, no!" Geronimo moved in for the kill, blocking a frenzy of fearful kicks, laughing as he did.

I turned back to Ashley as she buried her face into my chest. I cupped the back of her head, listening to the struggle in the weeds behind us which ended with a sort of truncated grunt.

When I turned around, Geronimo stood holding the bloody knife and said, "Not the payoff I was lookin' for, but it'll have to do."

I said, "Maybe you built it up too much in your mind, you know, how it was going to be?"

"Yeah, I guess. Now I feel . . . empty."

"Seriously?"

"No," he said flatly. "I kid. He died like the dog he is—was. It was great." He bent over, wiped the blood off his blade on some leaves. "Speaking of dogs, Buster got away with mine. He shook my guy, you believe that?" He raised back up and looked around. "Hey, where's the rest of 'em?"

I smiled at him.

He sheathed his knife and walked up to us. "Don't blame you for hiding them, but I was going to keep my word. Remember what I said—don't kill the goose that lays golden eggs. Killin' babies in America is bad for business."

"What business?"

Geronimo laughed. "Any business?" He looked around at the gathering light. "Time to get out of here."

"Good luck," I said.

He looked down at Ashley. "Like we talked about, Ms. Ashley, you don't know me. That man behind me dead in the weeds, he won't come for you anymore. Your brother tells me you have a real piece of work for a husband. Maybe I pay him a visit sometime if you want."

"No, no, that's alright," she said, wiping tears off her cheeks with the backs of her hands. "Thanks anyway." She tried to smile.

He grinned at her, then me. His silver capped teeth looked gun metal blue again in the low light. "I'm not going to wait for you, but I suggest you all follow me as best you can to the other side of the river. My man tells me he hasn't seen a cop car over there yet." He pointed at my knapsack. "But you may want to lose that gun in the channel. I'd break it apart and throw the pieces in different spots. Do it while the river's up. Just a suggestion."

We watched him run off through the trees toward the river.

Ashley squeezed my arm. "Who'd you kill with the gun?"

"Nobody."

Ashley looked confused. "Then why would you need to break it down and throw it in the river?"

"Long story. We better get going. I don't want to be late for court."

40

Ben

I TOOK THE bench at the scheduled time.

When everyone in the courtroom retook their seats, I glanced at the empty jury box and ran my eyes across the room to Vaughn Rummell, alone at the defense table. I'd been told the cops found Jorge's body—his grandfather's body—about an hour ago. I doubted that he'd heard yet.

"Where are your attorneys, Mr. Rummell?"

He stood, still wearing that same white linen shirt he'd worn each day, his eyes glued to mine, looking at me like he thought I was up to something. "No clue, Your Honor."

Maria Rummell stood from her seat next to her husband in the first row right behind her son. "Your Honor, we've been trying to call Mr. McMaster and Ms. Thompson all morning. They're not answering their phones. That's not like them."

I nodded, wondering if they were on the run or even alive. From my discussion with Ms. Sweeney in chambers ten minutes earlier, I knew she had the same concerns. She'd been trying to call them since 8:15.

I made eye contact with the deputy sitting next to Caroline Gordon directly behind the prosecution table and said, "Better go check on them. Find out what's going on. Now, bring in the jury. We'll send them home for the day."

When I got back to chambers, Caroline was waiting for me alone in Nancy's office.

She stood like she had something important to say. "Heard anything from your sister?"

"As a matter of fact, I did. Just last night. Got her out at my place now. She's going to be staying with us for a while until she gets back on her feet. Rod will find out she's no longer missing tomorrow, when the attorney I'm hooking her up with serves him divorce papers."

"Sure, makes sense. Sounds like she's been through a lot."

"Yeah, I was going to call you, but I figured I'd tell you in person when I saw you today." I smiled. "And here you are."

She nodded curtly, shaking off the empty pleasantry. "You look tired. Looks to me like this trial is about over. Maybe another judge picks it up from here. Your kids can come back home and play some ball. Still a lot of summer left."

"How's the leg?"

"Itches. I get that scratchy feeling that won't go away. You know what I mean?"

"I've had an itch like that before. It's true what they say— you have to let it be."

"Yeah," she said. "But I just want to scratch it you know." She touched my forearm and looked up at me. "But if I do that, I know I'll make it worse."

* * *

The next day, acting on an anonymous tip phoned in by Beck on a burner phone from somewhere in northern Colorado, police found Detective Raymond Mallory's body in the basement freezer of a rental property on Greenway in Wichita.

Two days after that on Sunday morning, McMaster and Thompson were both found dead in a hole underneath a windmill on a grazing pasture north of El Dorado when someone noticed a gathering of coyotes. They'd been executed with a shotgun.

The next day, Monday morning, I appointed the death penalty defender unit to represent Rummell. Two days later I heard and granted his uncontested motions for mistrial and change of venue. During the hearing, Rummell's eyes met mine and I wondered if he'd told his new attorneys what he knew about what had gone down. Even with McMaster and Ms. Thompson murdered—something I suspect Geronimo had done for my benefit—my part in this wouldn't stay secret forever. Nothing does.

I certified the order of transfer to Kansas Supreme Court Justice Cheryl Brannon. In her capacity as the district's departmental justice, she'd decide where to transfer Rummell's case. Whatever courtroom he landed in, I wouldn't be there. I was taking myself off the case and eventually, off the bench. My term was set to expire in eighteen months and I wasn't putting my name on the ballot. I'd failed to uphold the law and my oath. And the region's largest illicit-drug supplier knew what I'd done—an easy target for blackmail if there ever was one. I hadn't played it by the book and I was compromised. Unfit for office. There was no legal defense to many of the things I'd done—things I'd do all over again under the same circumstances.

For three nights in a row now, when I closed my eyes to sleep, morbid images of Juan and Miguel and Detective Mallory flickered through my mind. Clive Hunsucker was haunting my dreams again and I killed him over and over but he wouldn't stay dead. When I opened my eyes to escape him and made my way to the bathroom to look in the mirror, I saw something equally horrific—a hypocrite clothed in righteousness. Someone whose crimes had the potential to undermine society's faith in the law, causing more damage than any run-of-the-mill criminal. There was no getting around it now. Stepping down would only mitigate the damage when the truth seeped to the surface.

I was soon to be out from under this case, at least in my official capacity as the trial judge.

Vaughn Rummell had fared far worse. Everyone he could testify against to keep the needle out of his arm was dead. On second thought, maybe that wasn't true. He was a rat at heart. In time, with Gwen Sweeney closing in, he might say anything to save his own ass. I expect he might find it useful to weave an outlandish tale of judicial corruption to suit his needs. Forever the patsy.

41

Saturday, June 29, 2019

Ben

I LIKE TO be the one who wakes my children up in the morning. I like to watch them stretch and arch their backs and curl their toes when I turn on the lights. I like to watch them look out the window at the day.

But for now, I let them sleep because they need their rest. They'll be up late tonight dancing with me and my bride and our friends at the American Legion. Pops will watch with a can of Busch Light in front of him and Ashley will spend most of the night next to him nursing a vodka tonic.

Not everything has changed.

The coffee maker beeped as I entered the kitchen. I'd already placed twelve pieces of thick-cut bacon onto the foil-covered cookie sheet sitting on the stove. I thought about turning on the oven, but decided to wait until the kids or Keri or Ashley woke up. I poured myself a cup of coffee and looked out the kitchen window. The sun was rising and I could see Seventieth Avenue again because the wheat between the house and the road had been cut some time in the night and combines were making passes in the distance.

"How 'bout I make some eggs?"

I turned around. Ashley padded through the kitchen in flannel pajamas and poured herself a cup of coffee.

I stepped to the oven and turned it on. "Or I can. It's my turn."

She took my spot at the window and leaned her back against the sink. "It's your big day, let me do it. Over easy again?"

"Yep."

"Your whole life you like your eggs scrambled. Now you want 'em over easy every time. What's up with that?"

"Right now I want things over, or easy. Little tired of the scramble. Such chaos."

Ashley chuckled. "It's eggs."

"Just decided one day over easy was the way to go. That's how it went down." I smiled. "Random, I know, like this conversation."

"Random can be good."

"Random's like scrambled and my tastes have changed. I like over easy."

"So . . . you want this conversation—"

"Over easy." I smiled at my sister. From the look on her face, I thought she might punch my arm or kiss me. I'd go for either one.

"Maybe you should make your own eggs."

"See how you are."

The monitor on the counter showed a pickup truck I didn't recognize pulling into my driveway off Seventieth. Ashley noticed too and we watched the monitor together until we saw the truck park in the driveway through the window. The head of a St. Bernard popped up and looked around and I felt a knot form in my gut.

An assless old man with oily hair matted to his head got out of the driver's seat and stood in front of the truck looking at the window in a way that made me think he'd spotted us watching him. He threw his arms out from his sides and opened his palms. He wore loose-fitting cloth shorts that could've passed for boxers, a translucent wifebeater, and flip-flops.

"What the hell?" said Ashley. "Who's that?"

"That's Harold Reynolds."

I was in gym shorts and flip-flops myself, so I stepped to the coat rack and bench between the side and garage doors and threw on a jacket so that I had a pocket for my pistol.

Ashley said, "Isn't he . . .?"

" . . .Vaughn Rummell's former investigator." I stood on the bench below the hooks and reached my hand above the cubby holes and felt for the pistol I kept hidden high behind the woodwork against the wall. "He's the one that got away."

I stepped down and slipped the pistol into my pocket. Ashley set her cup on the counter and looked out the window as I went through the side door and across the deck to the steps, noting that there was no one in the bed of the truck as I did.

"Good morning, Your Honor. As you can see, I'm unarmed." He nodded at the surveillance camera under the eaves. "I'm not lookin' to get shot."

When I stepped down from the deck and cut through the seven yards of grass separating us he took a step back and pulled his arms in close to his ribs. I stood within a foot of him, looking down my nose into his milky eyes. "You lookin' to talk to the cops? I'm guessin' they'd love to have a word with you."

"When we're done here, you're gonna have good reason to get Geronimo off my ass."

"Geronimo?—Aren't you a little old for cowboys and Indians." I glanced at his truck. "You plan on stayin' a while?"

"What makes you say that?"

"Truck's not runnin'."

"Maybe I'm concerned about global warming."

He opened his mouth to say something more, but I stepped past him to the driver's door, opened it, and popped the hood. I noticed the dog watching me from the passenger seat with steady curiosity as I reached across the steering column and turned the key to start the truck. There was a little wooden barrel no bigger than a man's wallet hanging from the dog's collar.

Buster watched me step to the grill. I shooed him back until he was a good eight yards from the front bumper. Keri walked out onto the deck carrying a shotgun. She glared at Buster, then looked to me. I nodded at her as I released the latch and raised the hood, exposing a smartphone duct taped on top of the radiator. I hit the button on the screen to end the recording and slammed the hood shut.

Buster smiled and shook his head as I walked up to him and said, "What do you want?"

"What I said. I want Geronimo off my ass."

"Why's that my problem?"

"Because I talked to April and you don't wanna go to jail for kidnapping."

"Who's April, and why would she think I kidnapped her?"

"She doesn't, yet. But the story she told me 'bout how it all went down . . ." He nodded toward Keri, "I may not know how ya'll pulled it off, but I know you two were involved in April's kidnapping because if it was left up to Geronimo she and her baby'd be dead."

"Well, you got your opinion. I got mine."

"April will say what I tell her to say, unless you get Geronimo to back off."

"You turn April on us for kidnapping, maybe Geronimo gets all nervous about it too. That what you want?—Geronimo motivated to eliminate April as a witness. I wonder what Jorge would've thought about you putting a target on his grandson's only living parent like that?"

"Jorge is dead."

"And not causing me anymore heartache at the moment. But here you are. On my wedding day."

Keri sidled up next to me and handed me a burner phone. She no longer had the shotgun, having handed it to Ashley, who was standing beside her. Like me, Pops had taught Ash how to handle a firearm.

"Who is it?" I said to Keri.

She shrugged. "Guy named Geronimo."

I put the phone to my ear. "Hello."

Geronimo said, "I've got a man in the area heading your way."

I winked at Buster. "How quick can he get here?"

A stream of urine ran down Buster's right leg onto his flip-flop.

"Thirty minutes," said Geronimo. "You okay with that?"

"Here's a suggestion," I said. "Take five-thousand dollars of the money you got out of the tunnel and have someone give it to April. Maybe they tell her how Buster Reynolds turned on Jorge and got the whole lot of 'em killed. Make sure she knows

Buster may try to contact her again in the future. It's my understanding he already has. Maybe the money keeps coming each month for a year or two, providing she calls your people when and if Buster ever tries to contact her again. Perhaps you have someone suggest you'll be watching her—for her own safety."

Geronimo said, "Okay, so . . . let him go then?"

"Yeah, he's pissing himself in my driveway. Literally. He's had enough."

Geronimo laughed. "Tell you what—I'll do it, but only if I get my dog back."

"As a matter of fact, the dog's right here."

"Fine then. My guy'll pick him up at your place in thirty minutes."

I ended the call and wagged a finger at Buster. "Time for you to go. Leave the dog."

He walked to the driver's door and opened it while making a snick-snick sound in his cheek. I was right behind him with my hand on the pistol in my pocket. The dog ambled out and stood by the open door as Buster climbed in behind the wheel.

"What's the dog's name?" I said.

"Suzy. All of Jorge's dogs were named Suzy."

* * *

We stood together in the driveway watching Buster's truck drive away on Seventieth until I said, "Kind of a sweet story really."

Keri said, "Sweet? How's that?"

I scratched Suzy behind her ears and she nuzzled her nose on my leg. "The story of a young boy and his dog—how's it get any sweeter than that?"

"Mimosas," said Ashley. "I'm in desperate need of a drink."

"Count me in," I said.

Keri didn't answer, still watching Buster's truck getting smaller in the distance. "What the hell was that?"

"The man's desperate," I said. "Not thinking clearly."

Keri said, "That was too easy. He wants us to underestimate him."

"Is that why he urinated on himself in my driveway? Mission accomplished."

Keri undid Suzy's collar and set it and the attached barrel on the driveway. She held out her hand to Ashley and asked for the shotgun. Ashley handed it to her and looked at me. I shrugged as Keri cracked the barrel open with the butt of the stock. She reached down and swatted at the splintered wood and nabbed a hunk of it from the rest and stood, flipping it over and displaying a little rectangular box still glued to the scrap.

We gazed at the tracker, our mouths making little O's.

Getting a tracker on Geronimo would've been one hell of a Trojan-horse-style coup. The stuff of legend for whoever Buster was working for now—the newest head to grow back on the immortal beast that feeds the country's addictions. Geronimo's first night with Suzy could've been his last.

I couldn't help but shake my head in appreciation of Buster's con. "The old man still has some moves."

Keri said, "Are you surprised? This'll never be over for Geronimo."

I nodded. "This may never be over for any of us."

Ashley turned away from us and walked toward the kitchen door. "Over or not, I'm having a drink. Can't drink all day if you don't start in the morning."

Keri watched Ashley cross the deck to the kitchen then turned to me with a toothy grin. "You ready for this?"

"Oh yes, I've been looking forward to Ash's mimosas all morning."

Keri tried to frown, but couldn't help smiling. She slid her hand across my neck, cupped the back of my head and kissed me. Her playful tongue found mine and she pressed against me and I could feel her heart beating and the rise and fall of her chest. My hand wandered to the small of her back and I pressed her tighter to me, lifting her off the ground. Her body was hard and light.

When she pulled back and looked into my eyes I was so lost in the moment that a mimosa might've been an African snake.

Or not—seems like I wanted a mimosa and I'm not partial to snakes.

CPSIA information can be obtained
at www.ICGtesting.com
Printed in the USA
BVHW042151091222
653910BV00004B/64

9 780578 329642